Catbird Winter

MONTÉ HILL

Dedication

To my mother,

who taught me to make my own salvation.

Contents

Introduction

I grew up in Western North Carolina, where Spring's arrival was never an assurance that Winter had relinquished its icy hold. Long after the vernal equinox had come and gone, cold spells would vie with the warming sun, creating microcosms of winter that became associated with the plants and trees blooming during those times.

There was Redbud Winter, when the redbud trees began to bud in mid-March to early April. Dogwood Winter came with the profusion of dogwood tree blooms several weeks later, often accompanied by a hard frost. And just when you thought you could squirrel away your long pants and sweaters, fence lines and trails would be shrouded in a blanket of white blackberry blossoms, heralding the onset of Blackberry Winter.

Blackberry Winter wasn't the end all, however. Catbird Winter arrived around late May or June, when the Gray Catbirds returned from their winter vacations in Mexico and Central America. Their appearance just after Blackberry Winter is timely, as blackberries are one of the Catbird's favorite foods.

These gray-and-chestnut-colored birds are related to thrashers and mockingbirds, sharing their talents of mimicry. It's their distinct call note, however, that earns them their feline moniker, crying out as they mew beneath the underbrush and brambles of mountain forests and farmlands.

It is against the backdrop of these seasons-in-miniature that the story of Annie, Trevor, and *Catbird Winter* unfolds.

The winter is past; the rains are over and gone. Flowers appear on the earth. The season of singing has come, the cooing of doves is heard in our land. The fig tree forms its early fruit. The blossoming vines spread their fragrance.

Arise, come, my darling; my beautiful one, come with me...

Song of Solomon NIV 2:11-13

Prologue

Verdun, France – February 1916

Réveillez-vous, Monsieur Middleton! Réveillez-vous! The young Senegalese's African-tinged French ricocheted inside the ambulance driver's foggy brain. Wake up! Wake up! The boy shook Trevor's aching shoulder, his neck unable to turn in either direction by more than a few degrees. Jawara bent close to his face, his dark breath reeking of onions and thyme. *Monsieur, it is urgent!*

Urgent? Weren't all things urgent in war? Trevor was having a difficult time taking such summonses seriously these days. Prior to this abrupt awakening, he had driven forty-eight straight hours for The American Ambulance Field Service through shellfire and snow, with only a few winks of sleep caught in the back of the Model-T on a blood-stained stretcher. Before that, he'd pulled several twenty-fours, three out of seven days, if he recalled correctly.

He'd not eaten much either, save for some Bovril spread atop a slice of stale, moldy bread, but sleep pulled on his sagging eyelids harder than hunger tugged at his stomach. Drunk with fatigue, Trevor stumbled towards the barracks only to be intercepted by Jawara and a bowl of *Benachin*, a traditional Senegalese dish, steaming in the frigid, winter air.

Manger, eat – Jawara had urged. The aroma of garlic, onions, thyme, and curry were like smelling salts, awakening him just long enough to devour the rice and chicken in a few gluttonous gulps. It was the best thing he'd eaten in months.

With his belly full and his body warmed, Trevor had slipped into a comatose-like sleep, causing him to miss the alarm which precipitated Jawara's urgent wakeup call. Trevor looked at his watch, realizing he'd also missed the dinner bell, too.

Digging past the lint balls and grit that had settled at the bottom of his pocket, Trevor removed a tin of crackers, eyeing it with a touch of disdain as he compared it to last night's indulgence. Maybe he'd find a loose can of sardines in the mess kitchen to squirrel away in his jacket on the way out. He could make a cup of tea – one brewed from the radiator in his flivver when he got to the next dressing station, or *poste-de-secour*, as they were called. *Delicious!*

Outside the glowing tips of scattered *Gauloises!* waxed and waned with each drag. Trevor patted his other pocket to be sure his own pack of cigarettes was on hand. Beside his ambulance, affectionately known to him as Molly Mae, his friend, Owen, was arguing with a new recruit about his ability to drive, as the young boy had more than his fair share of *pinard* - a raw, red wine. Trevor chuckled as he bent over to turn the crank on his ambulance when he heard a loud *pop* and a cry that shrieked over the sounds of rumbling engines.

"Oh, God, I think I broke my arm!" The guttural sound of retching followed.

"Goddammit, Richardson, you puked all over your uniform! Get your sorry ass to the infirmary *now!*"

Trevor straightened himself to see the young driver stumble towards the little stone cottage that housed a dozen or so ailing ambulance drivers at any given time, holding his arm and cursing every few steps.

"Hey, Coot, you need to follow your squealer there?" Trevor wasn't sure how Owen got the name, Coot, but he sensed it had to do with an ill-gotten gift from a local *prostituée française*.

"Well, well, well, Lazarus has risen. 'Bout time you joined this god-damned war."

Trevor ignored his friend's sarcastic jab. "What's up with Richardson?"

"Showed up drunk as a fiddler. Crank kicked back so his wrist is probably broken. Rookie mistake."

"Which means one less rookie driving," Trevor complained with a trailing *dammit* to emphasize his frustration. "Why didn't you wake me up?"

Coot pitched his cigarette and stomped it into the accumulating snow. "We thought we'd let you sleep this one out. Commandant wouldn't hear of it, though, so he sent Jawara to roust you up."

Trevor threw up his hands. "Commandant was right. We need drivers," he lamented as he blew a puff of nicotine into the night.

"You seem on edge tonight. More than usual. You alright?"

"I'm fine, Coot." Snowflakes whirled in the howling wind as flashes from bombs and shellfire lit up the night. Trevor hadn't seen stars in so long, he believed the Germans had blown them out of the sky along with any romantic ideals he'd ever had of becoming a war hero.

"Well, okay, but your mother just died. You didn't go home for the funeral. You've pulled more forty-eights than anyone I know. Best I can tell, you've not been laid since you got here. You should take some time off."

What the hell's my mother got to do with anything? The day of his mother's funeral was just like any other day. His mother had been tormented by devils for as long as he could remember, and if she were able to silence the voices in her head by strangling them with a rope, then so be it.

"I'm fine," Trevor repeated. "And if I haven't been laid, as you suggested with such couth and sophistication, it's really none of your business."

"Fine," Owen shrugged as he took a swig of something from a flask and extended it to his friend as if in supplication.

Trevor sniffed. "What *is* that?"

Owen grimaced as he swallowed. "Pinard?"

"Thanks, but no thanks."

"Suit yourself, but before this war is over, you'll be lowering your standards in wine *and* women."

"Maybe," Trevor laughed as he closed the hood and leaned up against Molly Mae, tossing the stub of his *gauloise* onto the ground. He stood in a momentary stupor, watching its spark fade into the melting slush. "Look, sorry I'm so ill-tempered."

"Don't apologize, man, but you should take some time off. Talk to Doc Andrew tomorrow when he inspects the section. I'm sure he'll work something out. You know, before you start training for *The Escadrille.*"

"I'm fine. Honestly. I just need some sleep."

"Wow. You really *do* have high expectations." Coot popped his friend on the arm then cranked his ambulance and sputtered off into the night.

Trevor assumed his own cranking position and gave the handle an experienced twist, smiling as the pistons fired and the engine turned over.

As soon as Trevor reached the main thoroughfare, he killed the carbides and eased Molly Mae onto the road, staying a few minutes behind Owen so as not to create an easily targeted caravan on *de Verdun route.* Charred and twisted silhouettes of beech and oaks slipped by him. Or was it soldiers waving stubby, blackened limbs - begging for a ride or even a *coup de grace?* In this snowstorm, it was impossible to tell.

What the hell had he been thinking when he volunteered for this? Less than a month of hauling *blesses, couchés,* and *assis* from the frontlines to a poste or hospital had incinerated any misguided notion of becoming a war hero. What had risen from the ashes was a suffocating sensation of helplessness, as most days passed as though he were driving a hearse rather than an ambulance.

The drone of his engine began to churn up recollections. When he had joined the AAFS, he thought he could do his bit for France – to safeguard a way of life that was as much a part of his own as the one he was born to in Charleston, South Carolina. Trevor's father and uncle owned a shipping business that ferried cotton, steel, and iron to France and other parts of Europe. Consequently, Trevor had visited France more times than he'd traveled to any of the states, save for his uncle's home in Savannah, Georgia. France had become a part of his soul, perhaps even more so than his home in Charleston.

He'd made friends and had grown fond of duck confit, bright, crisp Saisons, and pretty Parisian girls who smelled of lavender. The nonchalance of the French was especially appealing as it provided a pleasant contradiction to his now strained relationship with his father. He had ambitions of living here, permanently.

By joining the ambulance service, he'd imagined it as a logical "next step": reuniting with old acquaintances during *en repos*, savoring a cassoulet as he and his buddies tossed back glasses of beer, playing dominos and reliving old memories as they created new ones. But that thought he now counted as fantastical and naive. The only way he would be reunited with those friends now was if they presented themselves on a stretcher with their guts jiggling about like a jack-in-the-box.

On one particularly dreadful afternoon of hauling the wounded from the frontlines to an evacuation hospital, Trevor had heard the rumblings of a plane flying low overhead. As he looked up, the pilot waved. It seemed to Trevor as though it were an invitation to join the aviator in the skies. He could feel the drone of the engine and propellers thrum inside his chest. Since the day he'd seen the play, *Peter Pan, or The Boy Who Wouldn't Grow Up*, he had dreamed of flying. *Don't be so dramatic*, his mother had admonished, but he had never stopped imagining the possibilities. That moment on the ground had been a resurrection, a rapturous epiphany, calling him to take to the skies rather than spinning his wheels on the ground. He decided then and there he would become a pilot. If he could kill the Germans, he might actually help end this war instead of perpetuate it ... and perhaps have some fun in the process.

The next morning, he spoke to Doc Andrew about joining the *Escadrille Américaine*, a group of American pilots who were training to fly aerial combat missions for The French Cause. Initially, Doc had been reluctant to support Trevor's request. He'd be losing one of his most valuable drivers from field service, but Doc also knew Trevor had talent and an ambitious nature and would leave for greener pastures, or bluer skies, regardless.

The next day, Doctor Piatt Andrew gave his blessing in the form of a contact written on the back of a wine label – Victor Chapman, one of seven pilots sanctioned to fly with the *Escadrille Américaine* in late spring.

Two weeks later, Trevor and Victor met over cocktails at the Hotel Chatham in Paris to discuss his enlistment. Chapman was a soft-spoken but personable Harvard graduate who had honor running deep inside his veins. (His father had burned off his own left hand as self-punishment for assaulting a man.) Trevor also learned that Victor was a talented architect who could have had a successful career in the private sector but chose to fight in the trenches with the French Foreign Legion. He later joined the *Aéronautique Militaire*, the aeronautical arm of the French military, where he was promoted to the rank of sergeant before his recruitment to the *Escadrille Américaine*.

Victor was duly impressed by Trevor's engineering background, supported by a degree from The Citadel, and believed Trevor would be an invaluable asset to The Escadrille. Both men craved adventure and believed it a duteous honor to fight alongside their French comrades. An intense hatred of the Germans solidified their burgeoning friendship.

Trevor had been too late to be included in the roster of inaugural pilots, but with Chapman's endorsement and Doc Andrew's letter of commendation, Trevor was accepted as a candidate for the next slate of pilots and was to start his training next month. Victor would be his mentor through the entire process. If he could survive the next few weeks of ambulance detail, he could get on with living, even though that meant killing in the process.

As Trevor navigated the *Voie Sacrée*, The Sacred Route, that connected Bar-le-duc to Verdun, he was anxious to pick up speed. A low rumbling gear might draw attention from the Germans; but the wind whipped through the air like an eggbeater, swirling snow with loose debris from the trucks transporting ammunition and supplies to the lines. Visibility was reduced to nil, as was his speed. He'd never encountered such inhospitable weather.

From out of the black night, a flash of artillery fire produced an eerie photo-negative of the world around him with a deafening explosion following on its heels. Coming upon a snow and ice-covered curve, Trevor pressed his foot on the brake pedal, which yielded a similar consistency as stomping on a loaf of day-old bread. As he eased his ambulance around the curve, every alarm inside his body began firing red. Something was horribly amiss.

Trevor found himself nose to tail with another Model-T, ramming into her backside with a definitive *clank.* Flares of mechanical lightning illuminated the skies as rumbles of bombs drowned out any other discernible sounds. A blanket of snow was accumulating on the road, masking shell-holes and graves of artillery fire. As the bombardments pounded the city of Verdun, waves of anxiety broke against Trevor's typically steadfast resolve. His foot began tapping on the floorboard of his ambulance, wishing the driver would get his flivver out of the way, but the ambulance merely rocked to and fro in the whistling wind. He decided that if he and his fellow driver were to be of anyone's good use this night, he'd better get out and see what the trouble was.

As he approached the stranded ambulance, Trevor noticed blood making fresh, warm trails over the steering wheel. Opening the door, his eyes met Owen's sightless stare across the hood of the car - a jagged shell fragment planted firmly inside his neck.

"Oh, God, no. *No! OWENNNNN!*" Trevor screamed, but the wind blew his words sideways into the war-torn air. His eyes searched the surroundings for help - other drivers, soldiers, the Gendarmerie, or military police - but there seemed to be no one left on this godforsaken earth apart from him and his dead comrade.

Defeated, Trevor went to work removing the two Model T's that now posed a road hazard for the parade of war traffic. After ensuring the spark lever was in the proper position, he staggered to the front and turned the crank on Owen's ambulance. Nothing. Two turns. Three. *Shit!* Trevor sank against the ambulance and willed himself to be calm.

A couple more turns and the ambulance fired to a rumble. Trevor pushed Owen to the side, supplanting himself in the driver's seat and adjusted the spark and throttle. The ambulance's wheels spun in the slush as Trevor aimed the Model-T off the road and into the relative safety of a ditch.

Trevor ran to the passenger's side and gathered Owen's body into his arms with the intentions of placing him on the floor of his own ambulance, but the dead weight turned out to be heavier than he anticipated. At the same time, a gust of wind created a snow blind, lessening visibility to inches. Trevor fought against the frigid blast, his feet unable to gain any sort of traction in the ice and snow.

Fearing he would drop his friend with an irreverent *kerflump,* Trevor placed Owen's body across the still-warm hood of the ambulance and waited. Someone was bound to come along that could assist him. *Stay calm, Trevor. Steady as she goes. Just do your job. Do...your...job.* As he began to catch his breath, the squall broke, removing the moon's clouded mask, revealing a slaughter that belied Trevor's worst nightmares.

The bright flash of light he'd witnessed earlier had been a shell falling on a contingent of French troops and horses pulling artillery and supplies in a wagon. Before his eyes, just on the opposite side of the road, lay a grisly array of dismembered bodies, horses, and debris.

He counted at least three horses, some splayed atop human bodies. He paced the perimeter of the massacre, searching for signs of life, some fragment of sanity that he could grab hold of.

The wagon's once solid floor lay in splinters. As Trevor plucked shards of metal and wood from amongst the jumble of limbs and bodies, he caught the glint off the buttons of a *poilu's* jacket. Upon tugging it from underneath a wagon wheel, a severed arm went flying into the air. It was the embodiment of Dante's Inferno, descending through a funnel of disconnected limbs and serrated bone fragments.

By now, the *Gendarmerie* and a contingency of the First Aid Nursing Yeomanry, or FANYs, as they were known, had arrived and were getting on with clearing the scene. Were it not for their woolen skirts, one would be hard pressed to discern the difference between the women and the men. FANYs had no qualms about rolling up their sleeves - getting muddy, bloody and dirty alongside their male counterparts. He found their matter-of-fact presence to be a dichotomy of militaristic competence and maternal comfort.

With the arrival of French detachments, Trevor returned to the task of attending to Owen's body, but as he made his way towards the ambulance, he spotted another horse, panting, its yellowish teeth now covered in a pink-hue of foam and blood. *A coup de grâce* would be the kindest course of action, but ambulance drivers were forbidden to carry weapons. Trevor scoured the ground, bracing himself as the wind created another whiteout. *Dammit all to hell!* Pressing ahead, one grueling footstep at a time, he stumbled against a chunk of debris in the road. Kneeling to ascertain what the obstruction was, he discovered yet another dead soldier – this one with his pistol still tucked inside the holster. Trevor grabbed the weapon and returned to the dying horse, laying the barrel against the animal's head.

It was the hollow *click* of a misfire that was to be his last conscious memory on that dreadful night.

Redbud Winter

*He seizes the lightning with his hands
and commands it to hit the mark.
Thunder announces the approaching storm,
and the cattle know it is coming.*

Job 36:32-33 (GNT)

Chapter 1

HICKORY NUT GORGE, NORTH CAROLINA

The full moon created luminous puddles across the splintered pine floor that evaporated and reappeared as the wind spun whirlpools of clouds across the night sky.

Annie lay frozen on her feather-tick bed, flattened by mounds of quilts as frayed and ragged as her spirit. She pulled the bottommost blanket tightly around her chin, which did little to stave off the frigid air poking its fingers through the cracks in the wall.

She rolled onto her side, wishing she had something to read other than the Bible. She'd had a book, *The Woman in White*, given to her just before Christmas by her teacher as a reward for making the highest English grade in her class. She'd nearly won the math award, too, but her brother, Jacob, beat her out by just one point. It was a one-room class of twelve, but she was still proud. Her mother, Ida, speechless since the stroke, beamed a lopsided grin at her two prodigies. Annie was so happy, she cried.

Upon finding the book, her father, Lester, had forced her and Jacob to quit school, proclaiming their teacher a succubus who would, "...lead his children straight into eternal Hell and damnation". Annie declared she was already in Hell, so she didn't need directions.

Annie cried again when Lester tossed *The Woman in White* into the Rocky Broad. She screamed. She kicked and she flailed, but the book slipped through her fingers as Lester flung it into the river's icy waters. When the book sank, so did her hopes for a life outside of this hellhole she was born into.

Lester taunted her, daring her to go after it if she believed it worth the cost of her salvation. She would've done it if Jacob hadn't stopped her. He grabbed her by the arm, tight, yelling she'd die of frostbite if she dove into the river in the dead of winter. Lester laughed. Said she'd thank him one day for saving her soul from the Devil.

"The only devil I need savin' from is *YOUUUU!*" she shrieked. Lester stood on a rock beside the riverbank, hurling scripture like stones.

"And if it seems evil unto you to serve the Lord, choose ... you ... this ... day ... whom ... you ... will... SERVE!"

Annie screamed, *"I HATE YOU!"* Her screeches could be heard all the way up the mountain. Her old friend, Effie, said it made her blood curdle.

"Will you serve the God of your father or the gods of the *heathen*?" her father hollered. "What say you?! As for me and my house, Annie Grace, we will serve the LORD! You hear?"

"Serve yo'r own goddamned self!" she cried.

She'd not said more than a fistful of words to her Pa since, speaking only to him when necessary. Used to, just to make peace, she would beg and plead for him to forgive her after they'd quarreled, but she realized now there was nothing to forgive. Not on her side of things. It was her father that needed to repent, but she knew that would never come about. Keeping as much distance between herself and her father, insomuch as possible, was the only way to survive.

But what if she wasn't content to just survive? What if she could break her way out of these rock-hard prison walls and *thrive?* The idea seemed preposterous. Who had that ever worked out for? Certainly no one she knew. Well, save for her best friend Birdie's sister. Lola had met the man of her dreams at a barn dance in Rutherford County and never looked back. She'd gone from red-blooded farmgirl to blue-blood socialite faster than you could dance the *Virginia Reel* – her toe-sack dresses now replaced by fine silk – a diamond large as the moon and twice as bright, sparkling from her finger.

What Annie wouldn't give for a moment like that! For someone to pluck her from the jaws of these canyon walls and gently lay her in a bed of down feathers and room service.

Her Pa had always been volatile, but typically his aggression was passive, though he'd hit Jacob a time or two. He'd be fine for weeks, even months, but then for no reason at all, he'd stop talking. And he wasn't just quiet. He was angry-quiet. Effie'd say, "You can smell the anger boilin' off 'im." If you asked him to explain what was eating at him, he'd pretend you didn't exist and just keep on doing whatever it was he was doing at the time: studying his sermon for that Sunday; hoeing beans; milking cows. Annie had wished, more than once, one of their cows would rear back and kick her father in the head.

Since Lester's brother, Phipp, had died, however, things had gone from bad to worse. Virgil, Phipp's only child, had come to live with them after a chimney fire broke loose through a crack in the mortar and burned the house down to a cinder.

The day of Uncle Phipp's funeral, there had been a steady, freezing drizzle that clung to the bare branches of the trees, dressing them in a hoary veil. Icicles hung like frozen minnows caught in a seining net of bare twigs and hemlock boughs. Young Virgil clung to Annie's skirt as the congregants swayed back and forth to the lilt of the hymn.

Oh, the land of cloudless day,
Oh, the land of an unclouded sky,
Oh, they tell me of a home where no storm clouds rise,
Oh, they tell me of an unclouded day.

A melting icicle dripped on her bonnet and wound its way through the threadbare cloth that draped across her bony shoulders, causing a shiver that racked her entire body. She'd never forget Virgil looking up at her with his little red nose and even redder eyes that sought answers to his unrequited questions. Annie patted him on the head, knowing he'd probably never find those answers. She certainly hadn't.

Lester had insisted on preaching his brother's funeral, even though Uncle Phipp had long since left the Middlefork Church of God for the more sedate pastures of the Methodist church up the road. Her Pa believed that Phipp was bound to eternal Hell for leaving his flock, but if Lester oversaw Phipp's last rites, his endorsement might somehow override Satan's claim to his brother's soul.

She and Virgil watched clumps of mud roll down the yawning hole and splat onto the pine box, her father's voice thundering across the valley. As sure as a pot boils over a fire, Lester's entourage of mourners and admirers began to whoop and holler. Hands flew up towards the sky, impervious to the sleet that pelted them with a skin-stinging vengeance.

"My brother Phipp here, God rest his soul. He strayed."

Help him, Lord, help him.

"He strayed far from the fold. From the teachin' of his youth."

Help him, Jesus.

"Which of you, havin' a hun'erd sheep, would not leave yo'r flock to find the one who'd strayed?"

Yes, Lord. Yes.

We would go.

Hallelujah.

Praise God.

Lester choked on a tear. "I never gave up. I prayed for my brother."

Bless him, Lord.

"I visited with him. Read him scripture." Lester began to pace to and fro, shaking his tattered *King James Bible* high into the air. "Satan buffeted me. Night and day." Lester shook the accumulating rain from his brow like a dog. "Day … and night." A loud *hissssss* arose from the congregants. "Said I was a *FOOL* for believin' I could change my brother's heart."

Devil's a liar!

Preach, Lester! Preach!

"As my dyin' brother drew his last breath, I saw a shine come across his withered face." Lester once more raised his Bible high with his left hand and stabbed at the clouds with his right. "I heard him whisper, *God forgive me.*"

Annie was right there by her uncle's bed, holding on to Virgil as he said goodbye to his Pa. Uncle Phipp's face had been steel blue and the only sound she'd heard was his lungs gurgling and bubbling up black mucus.

Thank you, Jesus. Thank you.

Praise God.

Yes, yes, yesssss.

"I saw my brother's spirit rise UP!" Lester shouted with a loud thump on his fat *King James.* "And I saw Jesus, come to carry my brother away on his shoulders."

HalleLUUUUjah!

Praise God!

Come quickly, LORD Jesus!

I like that!

I see Jesus! one shouted above the passionate crowd, his eyes closed hard, his chilled finger pointing towards a crow perched in a Hickory Nut tree.

"Tell me. Who does your heart belong to, the Devil?" Another *hisssssss* seared the damp November air. "Are you ready to meet your savior?" Lester queried.

Ohhhhhh, let 'em be ready, Lord!

"My brother. He's lucky." Lester paused then chuckled. "He got one last chance, but ... *YOU!*" Lester shouted as he knifed his finger at young Virgil, or maybe he was pointing at her, Annie thought. She always seemed to end up on the wrong side of her father's religion.

"You, my son ..." Lester scanned the crowd. "My sister." Lester smiled. "My neighbor ..." Lester caught sight of Effie standing on the periphery of the multitude and glared, jabbing an accusing finger in her direction. "You might not get that chance. Are you ready? Let the Holy Spirit *IN-NNNNnnnnn-uh!*" With that, the chosen few broke into a cacophony of murmurings and whisperings, speaking words that were discernible only to an interpreter – one whose mind and tongue had been touched by The Holy Spirit.

For Annie, the line between being possessed by The Holy Spirit and being possessed by demons had always been a murky one. Both spirits appeared to cause folk to do that which they would not do otherwise in public, and frankly, she found the concept of whooping and hollering in church appalling. It angered her even more that preachers like her father preyed upon people's grief and suffering to pad the numbers in their pew, and ultimately, their purses. She'd heard her father admit once, when he was coaching one of his deacons (a word which was eerily close to demons) in the ways of circuit riding, "The more souls we save, the more people'll come to service, and the more people that come, the more we fill our coffers. Lord knows, I got a family to feed." As far as she was concerned, Lester was no different than those traveling salesmen that came through The Gorge every now and again, words as slippery as the snake oil they pedaled.

Following the lightning from her father's eyes, Annie had found Effie leant up against a proud hemlock, barely discernible from the gnarled bark and cleaving lichens. She wasn't sure why Effie had even come to Phipp's funeral, but Effie was an odd sort, and Annie had learned long ago not to question her ways.

Effie was considered a miracle worker by some, a witch by most. She'd been forced to leave the church by Lester and his trusty deacons for wearing lace on her petticoats and on a lesser charge of casting spells. Effie couldn't have cared less. She only went in the first place because her friend, Neil, wanted her to. When Effie was tossed from the Middlefork congregation, Neil walked out to join the likes of her Uncle Phipp and other members of the Methodist church who were bound to burn in Hell.

Before her excommunication, Effie would bring along a gallon of eggnog to the Christmas Eve service, subtly spiked with a jigger or two of the rye whiskey Effie and Jacob distilled deep inside Bat Cave. "O Come, All Ye Faithful!" had never sounded so festive. In recent years, since Effie had been unable to make the midnight trek to the cave, Annie thought Jacob's rendering of that time-honored recipe had suffered in the absence of Effie's expert supervision, but just like good whiskey, Effie had assured her that Jacob's skills would mature in time.

It wasn't any particular sound that brought Annie back to the present, but more the peculiar silence. *Where were Virgil and Jacob?* She'd not heard a snigger out of them since they'd locked up the cows. After supper and chores, they usually camped under the improvised tents in their room, constructed by hanging quilts over ladder-back kitchen chairs. Lord knows what they did in there. Annie knew they'd often cop a gander at the women's underwear section of the Sears and Roebuck's catalog. She'd once heard Virgil shout the word, "Boobies!" and then laugh so hard he'd peed his pants. But not tonight. The only sound she heard was her father and mother snoring a duet. Annie forced herself from beneath the warmth of her blankets to peek inside the boys' room. It was empty, and that could only mean trouble.

Finding Virgil and Jacob missing, Annie threw on a coat and ran out to the barn, calling as loud as she dared for her brother and cousin, but no one answered. The cattle gate was swinging in the wind and their prized bull, along with all their milking stock, was gone. *Shit fire and save matches! Where could they be?*

Annie's eyes scrambled across the rutted ground. Her father would pitch a conniption fit like The Gorge had never witnessed when he discovered the theft. By tomorrow evening, Lester would be off on one of his preachin' circuit rides - gone for several days, but that didn't help her now. She had to find those two boys, and their cattle, before morning.

Chapter 2

Jacob and Virgil stared at the herd from the edge of the pinewoods gazing upon an open field with their pubescent hormones pulsing, unsure of their next move. A dozen pairs of twinkling eyes hovered above the ground. Forty-eight legs, the color of burnt caramel, provided the support for the cattle, four of which Jacob and Virgil aimed to punt out from under a sleeping heifer. The herd shifted with the intrusion of the boys' unbridled energy.

"Are they sleepin', Jacob?"

Jacob rolled his dark brown eyes into the back of his head and sighed. "How the hell should I know? Eldridge says cows sleep with their eyes open, but Pa says 'that's a bunch of cow dung.'" A derisive laugh burst into the frosty air. "You know Pa. He won't say, 'shee-it.' Might send him to Hell or somethin'." Silence fell over the pasture once again as breath from the two youths formed clouds of icy vapor in the February air.

A hoot-owl glided into a nearby chestnut tree, loosening the last of its hulls. Their precipitous fall resulted in a couple of the spiny casings bouncing off the head of a sleeping bull, rousting him from his evening nap. The sire rose to paw at the velvet-lined shells.

"Shit!" Virgil screamed.

"Shut-up you big goober! You wanna start a stampede?"

"Somethin' ran across my foot, Jacob! You don't hafta be so goddamn mean."

Jacob gave a condescending grin. "Yo'r such a lily-livered coward. Prob'ly just a little ol'e mouse. Hell of a sight smaller than them cows. You sure you got the balls for this?"

"I got balls, bigger'n yo'rs!"

"Yo'r such a big horse hang-down. Just you wait. I'll tell everybody how a li'l mouse got you all chicken. They'll laugh you here to Asheville." Jacob made a fist and bent his arms, bringing his taut hands up to his armpits, stretching his elbows out as far as possible. Squatting ever so slightly, he strutted to and fro, kicking up frozen grass and sod, waving his human wings.

"Bachk, bachk, bachk!" Jacob squawked as he extended and retracted his leathery neck.

"I ain't no coward," Virgil whined. "If your Pa finds out we've snuck outta the house again, our ass's grass!" Across the valley, a bobcat scream pierced the icy air. Virgil shuddered as a few cows emitted a bellow, tucking their tails between their legs. "Besides, Pa used to say that if a cow moos after dark, someone's gonna die."

Jacob huffed as he extracted a Camel cigarette and a faded match box from his overalls. Virgil stared at his elder cousin, wild with equal parts admiration and disbelief.

"Where'd ya get those?" Jacob gazed at this young disciple, slowly extending the lit cigarette for his cousin to have a try. "You stole 'em, didn't ya?" Virgil quizzed as he accepted the Camel, not quite sure what to do next.

"Go on. Just put the end to yo'r mouth and suck. And you tell anyone, I'll kill you!"

Virgil obeyed, his lungs expelling his first drag of a cigarette with a violent cough. Jacob burst out laughing, retracting the smoldering cig from Virgil's hands before it dropped on the frost covered ground.

"Uh-uh," (*cough, cough, cough*). "You wouldn't kill (*cough cough cough*) yo'r own cousin." Virgil's tease was tinged with a bit of uncertainty.

"No, but I'll strip you naked and drag yo'r sorry ass down to them bottomless pools. Then, I'll tie you up and leave yo'r scrawny ass rollin' on the ground, just a-screamin', and when the Little People find you, they'll strap you to a chair and hang you from a tree, and then… ."

"Jacob?" Virgil's voice began to tremble. "Who's the Little People?"

"Fairies. They live all up'n down this mountain. I seen a bunch of 'em in Bat Cave. They're about knee-high. Long hair. If you steal somethin' they'll throw rocks until you give it back."

"You stole cigarettes. Did they throw rocks at you?"

Jacob thought about his mistake for a second. "Well, you see, the Little People like tobacco, so I gave 'em a couple of my cig's and they let me pass. Anyways … they'll tie you in this chair, naked as a jaybird. Then, they'll throw this rope over a limb that hangs over that deep … dark … water … and tie the other end of it to the chair."

Jacob made a twisting motion around his body with an imaginary rope, the glow of his lit smoke pulsing like a firefly. "That's when they'll pull on the rope, like you's a church bell, liftin' you high as the heavens above the water." He extended his arms, palms up, stretching them towards the stars like his Pa when he was preaching about the second coming. "When the Grand Fairy gives the command, they'll let the rope loose and *sssssPLASHHH!*"

Jacob clapped his hands in front of his cousin's wild, disbelieving eyes. "You'll fall down, down, down." His arms dropped as he continued to whisper the words, *down, down, down* until they faded into the frigid night air. The smoldering cigarette left a powdery trail in its wake.

Over by the chestnut tree, the dark-faced bull began chewing his cud, his dewlap jiggling in the broken moonlight. The sire turned sideways, his gray, crimped horns stretching far out to either side of his large, devilish head.

"Then, you'll feel the water crushin' in. Leeches'll start suckin' yo'r blood. Worms'll crawl in yo'r ears and outta yo'r mouth and asshole. Yo'r lungs'll start burnin' like Hell's fire, and just when you think yo'r about to die, they'll raise you outta the water, like Laz'rus. Then they'll dunk you again, and again, and again."

"Will I die, Jacob? Am I dead?"

Jacob laughed. "Nah. You won't die. Not at first. You'll just wish you's dead." Every drop of blood drained from Virgil's face. "When they've bored of their fun, they'll just let loose the rope and you'll fall forever into yo'r wat'ry grave."

Virgil stood with his mouth agape. "You'd save me though, right Jacob? You won't let me die?" Jacob paused, pretending to be unsure of what decision he would make when faced with such a dilemma.

"Nah. I'm just shittin' ya," Jacob laughed as he tousled his cousin's hair. "If you was dead then I'd have to do all the milkin'."

Jacob dropped to his hands and knees, crawling into the field with Virgil following close behind. Fallen thorns from the crabapple trees impaled the webbing between their fingers, making tender indentions.

"Jacob, how *did* you get those cigarettes?" Intermittent clouds blowing across the face of the moon created a ghostly play of light across Jacob's face as he sat down in the field.

"Well, it's like this. Pa goes down to Harris's to witness to Old Man Fowler. He gets right down in Fowler's droolin' face, and it's just oozin' with tobacco. He's preachin' hellfire and damnation until Fowler asks Jesus into his heart." Jacob expelled a derisive snicker. "Fowler's drunk as a coot but he just plays along to get Pa outta his face. While Pa was milkin' the old man, I filched this pack of smokes." Jacob straightened up to his full height, inserting his thumbs into the shoulder straps, raising his other eight fingers in a mocking wave as he rocked back and forth from heel to toe, the cigarette's ashy end falling like snow onto the front patch of his overalls.

"What's *filch* mean, Jacob?"

"Stolt, Virgil. I stole 'em." Virgil's eyes grew wide as milk saucers. "Virge, now don't be goin' all soft on me. God'll forgive me." Jacob winked at his cousin as he returned to a crawling position, but he could hear Virgil blubbering behind him. "Goddammit, Virge. It's fine. Don't you listen to Pa's preachin'?"

"Yeah, and yo'r goin' to *Hell!*"

Jacob sat back, expelling a sigh of exasperation. "No, I ain't."

"Are too! That's what yo'r Pa says!"

Jacob reminded Virgil that all one had to do when faced with their sins was to ask for forgiveness. He'd asked Jesus into his heart, assuring him a seat at the heavenly banquet, and *surely* Jesus wouldn't mind him havin' a little fun. After all, didn't Jesus turn the water into wine? It was obvious that Jesus enjoyed his earthly life and expected his children to do the same.

Besides, Jacob had been dragged up to the altar and made to repeat the sinner's prayer more times than he cared to remember. He wasn't sure how many times you had to say it before salvation was yours to keep, but he was pretty sure his spiritual piggy bank had a few pennies left in it.

"Okay, so here's the plan. On three, we'll charge that heifer up on the ridge. You aim for the back legs, and I'll knock 'er down on 'er fronts. Ready?" Virgil was paralyzed.

"One..." Jacob stood, helping his cousin to his feet. "Two..." he continued. "Two and a half..."

"Eat shit and die!" Virgil fired. Suddenly, a Hoot Owl folded her wings and swooped straight in front of the two youths. Startled, Jacob stumbled, dropping his foot deep in an old post hole as Virgil tumbled headfirst overtop his cousin and into a bail of neglected wire. Barb after barb dug deep into the child's soft muscle. The more Virgil flailed the more his body became entangled in the mass of metal. Tender flesh was ripped from his bones like vultures picking at a carcass.

Jacob pulled his leg from the post hole and limped towards the screaming but was stopped cold by the sound of thundering hooves. His heart raced as there was no way to move him and Virgil from the herd's path before they were trampled. He did the only thing he could and threw himself on top of the knot of barbed wire and child, praying the cattle would spare them their hooves. One by one, a dozen stampeding heifers sailed over and around the cluster of boys and wire.

An eerie quiet settled over the field. Jacob braced himself for another onslaught but hearing none, he picked himself clean of the barbs. Making certain the cows had disappeared down the hill, he jumped to his feet and began loosening Virgil from the twisted hank of wire. The dirty barbs ripped the flesh from the underside of his arms, his shirt now hanging in shreds. The throbbing pain from his wrenched ankle radiated up his shin, through his hip and into his stomach, bringing on a malicious wave of vertigo and nausea.

Virgil's screams had quieted to something akin to loud puppy whimpers. As the wind peeled back the thickened clouds, Jacob could see Virgil's minced skin. Seeping blood on tattered fabric marked cuts where the rusty spines had plowed deep furrows into his body. A barb stuck in Virgil's left eye, ripping through the white like a hot knife through butter. A stream of blood oozed down his cousin's cheek and dribbled into the corner of his mouth, coloring his teeth pink.

The return of Virgil's screams scared Jacob backwards onto the grassy field, binding up his wrenched ankle beneath him. Once more, Virgil began flailing from inside the wire.

"Juh-juh-juh-JACOB! Get me ouutttttt! Get me ouuuuttttt!"

"Goddammit, Virgil! I'm tryin' but you gotta calm down."

"He's comin'! He's cuhhhhhmmmmmmiiiiiinnnnnn!"

Jacob heard a guttural snort. The bull, about fifteen yards away, tossed back his head and pawed at the dirt. In the pale moonlight, Jacob could see steam billowing from the bull's nostrils, dust erupting from the ground with each dig of a hoof into the earth.

Jacob squared his body in front of the bull as the Jersey hurtled with the ferocity of a runaway train. Jacob waved his arms and screamed, but the bull barreled towards them, head low. With a tremendous thud and one flick of his goring horns, the beast tossed Virgil high into the air. Wire and flesh fell hard on the frozen earth as the bull whipped one-hundred and eighty degrees to make another run and go. The bull returned to full gallop, once again spearing the ball of metal twine and heaving it towards the moon. The thorny cocoon crashed to earth, coming to rest at the foot of the great bull. It looked at Virgil, his face turning side to side, sniffing with primal affection.

Virgil's screams went hauntingly silent. The bull seemed displeased, so he gave Virgil a push towards the center of the bald. If the bull continued its present course, Virgil would be driven over a precipitous rock cliff, squashing any life the child might have left. Jacob began screaming and waving his arms, summoning up his most abusive and caustic repertoire of cuss words.

"Hey! ... Hey! Look at me you ugly bastard!" The bull eyed him with an amused stare. "I'm talkin' to you, you sack of leather shit!" The bull tilted his horns as he dropped a steaming pile of excrement behind him.

The hellish beast returned his gaze to the twisted mound before him, giving Virgil another push. "You sorry peckerhead! Big ass coward! What's the matter, huh? Think I'll kick yo'r ass?" Jacob grabbed himself between his legs. "Come on, cock sucker!" The bull remained indifferent, fixated.

Jacob fell to his knees as spray from the bull's nostrils mixed with the trickling blood from Virgil's mouth. He sat, helpless, as the bull descended further into a trance, nudging Virgil's cage in between snorts. Jacob could smell the bull's sour, brassy breath and imagined that's what Hell smelled like. Just as the bull tucked his head for another toss, Jacob threw himself over the bundle of wire, somersaulting boy over boy as he and Virgil went rolling forwards, moving the bull's intended target a few more inches. Jacob cried out as the barbs dug deep, rusty holes into his bare skin.

The bull turned to have another go, exposing his broad side to show Jacob just how formidable a foe he dared do battle with.

From out of nowhere, the sound of two gunshots rang through the night. The bull raised his once steely eyes, now pitiful and bidding, towards Jacob. He pawed one last time at the ground before falling over with a heavy *thud*. The frozen ground shook.

"Damn sons-a-mighty-bitches!"

"Neil?!" Jacob squealed with a mix of fear and relief as their neighbor emerged from the dark holding his slouch hat against his head, his leather duster swishing like a trout's tail. His other hand bore a flashlight that flickered with each clomp of his leather boots on the frozen ground.

"Well it ain't Robert E. Lee, now is it, ya crazy sons-a-bitches. What the hell you two doin' out on a night like this? Cain't you see there's a storm comin'?" Jacob looked up towards where the stars once spackled the black-gray night. In the past few horrifying minutes, the clouds had thickened the sky like cornstarch. Neil banged the flashlight against the side of his leg, encouraging a surge of renewed shine.

"Get me a match, Jacob. This here flashlight ain't long for this world." Jacob reached into his overalls to retrieve his box of Diamonds, but found only twigs, pieces of dried cow patties and a tangled mat of brown grass. Jacob's arms flew up in pathetic surrender.

"Christ A'mighty. Hold this." Neil shoved the flashlight into Jacob's shredded hands. "Sons-a-mighty bitches ... fartin' around on such a night ... damn preacher's kid ... Devil's spawn ... Ah! Found 'em!" Neil lifted the match box in victory, producing a wooden jingle as he shook it up above his head. A *whick, whick, whick* on the bottom of his boot produced a *whoosh* and a flame, revealing Virgil's dire circumstances which was accentuated by the strong smell of sulfur lingering in the air.

"Sweet Jesus." Neil turned and ran back over the rock outcrop and towards his horse, returning with Sadie in tow. Fetching a pair of wire cutters from his saddle bag, Neil began clipping the barbed threads. Virgil lay silent on the frostbitten ground, his frail body covered in bull spit, urine and sweat. Sadie whinnied from the scrub brush just a few yards away.

"Get on the horse," Neil ordered, but Jacob stood, frozen. "Goddammit, Jacob, don't just stand there like a knot on a log!" Jacob shook himself free of his stupor as he hobbled to Sadie's side. His ankle throbbed with every beat of his heart, expanding into the space of his work boot, pushing his calves over its top.

"Sit back as far as you can on Sadie's haunches. I'm gonna lift Virgil up. When I do, hold onto him. Then I'll mount, and I want you to let go and wrap yo'r arms 'round me. Do you understand?" Neil made his own arms into a circle to demonstrate. "Kinda like we're the bread and he's the ham in the middle."

Neil lifted Virgil up as Jacob pulled his cousin onto the horse, nearly sliding off Sadie's hindquarters with the dead weight. Once Neil mounted Sadie, Jacob wrapped his arms around Neil's waist, creating a human splint that cradled Virgil so that his broken body would not sustain additional injuries on the precarious ride down Burnt Shirt Mountain.

"I feel like I'm gonna fall off, Neil. I'll drop 'im and he'll die for sure!"

"Hell's fire, quit yo'r whinin'. You ain't gonna fall off. Not if you do what I tell ya. Now just hold on!" Neil had a way of making you mad on purpose ... so you'd forget how scared you were.

"Where we goin'?" Jacob whimpered.

"Effie's. She'll know what to do."

Chapter 3

Effie raised herself from the cornhusk mattress, unable to sleep. A bitter wind whipped through the tops of the hemlocks, rattling loose shingles along the eaves of her home. If she and her house survived till fittin' weather came, she would have to find someone to take on repairs. Mathias Carmine, owner of the logging company, had offered her a pretty penny for her falling-down shack and property, but she'd sell to the Devil before she'd give that pasty-headed-son-of-a-bitch the satisfaction. At least with Satan as a roommate, she wouldn't freeze.

Effie walked over to gaze at the full moon through the cracked glass in her bedroom window. Its glow illuminated the floor, which was fortunate. She couldn't muster the gumption to light the oil lamp, her fingers cold and stiff with arthritis. Neil had given her a flashlight to try, but she found it equally as cumbersome and about as reliable as a wet match.

The flashlight was a Franco, made to look like a pistol, bought on the occasion of whatever-the-hell-their-relationship-was anniversary. Neil knew she wasn't the romantic, sentimental type, but he couldn't help himself when it came to marking milestones. He'd celebrate the first foal in spring by planting a rose bush in his garden, or he'd mark the day of his mother's death by writing her a letter and burying it beneath her headstone. Effie'd thought about a letter or two she'd like to write to that old witch's wart. Almira had been living proof that being hateful and cantankerous was the secret to earthly longevity. One thing was for certain. Five minutes with that venomous, back-biting canker sore was, indeed, the longest day on earth.

If Effie ever complained about Neil's mother, he'd simply shrug his shoulders and quote some lame scripture from the Bible about honoring one's father and mother. He'd then wink and pull her to him, despite her best efforts to kick and bite her way free of his brawny embrace. This scene always ended with Neil wrestling her to the ground where they would engage in amorous congress between the rows of green beans and tomatoes.

If it hadn't been for Almira, they'd have been married proper. Neil promised her that when his momma died, they'd marry. But by the time the steely bitch finally gave up the ghost, so had Effie given up such starry-eyed notions. Neil asked her to marry him - right there at his mother's deathbed - for which Effie responded with a decided *smack* across her lover's tear-stained cheek.

Truth was, in retrospect, the thought he'd asked for her hand in marriage, standin' there in front of Almira's still-warm body, did give her immense satisfaction. Effie was certain the last words the old crone heard as her spirit descended into Hell was her son's proposal to the girl she had affectionately called "That High Yeller Witch."

No-siree, she no longer pined for such silly notions as marriage. Old age had rendered her far too wise. She'd watched women of varying ages and gullibility wander dreamily into that snare, hidden by promises of protection, eternal love, and ineffable, guilt-free sex.

As for protection, she could take care of herself. She used to be able to fire a rifle or a pistol with the accuracy of a marksman. Even with her shaky, arthritic hands, she was certain no man nor beast would stick around to see if her aim was still any good.

Love? Now there was a concept. She believed her papa had loved her mother as much as any man could love a woman, but that hadn't been enough to save her. In fact, it was what killed her. She'd died giving birth to Effie. As for ineffable sex, she'd had plenty. No ceremony could improve upon that. As for guilt, that was a state of mind. "No one can make you feel bad about yo'rself … 'cept yo'rself," her Pa had told her. Love was love, and if you couldn't express it without flailing yourself over the back with a barbed whip, you'd be better suited for the convent.

A scuffling noise underneath her bed brought her back from her reminiscing. Otis, the rat, had come to abscond with her stash of roasted pumpkin seeds she kept by her bedside. She could visualize his little nose, twitching in the air, drooling as he scurried without shame or conviction towards his prize.

"You sorry sum'bitch," she lamented as she reached for the pistol that resided inside the drawer of her rickety nightstand. She knew that blowing a hole in her floor would only increase the draftiness of her house, but she'd be damned if that fool rat was going to eat her last bag of pumpkin seeds. She could stuff a quilt in a hole, but it'd be nearly a year before another crop of pumpkin seeds would be ready.

Effie pushed up the sleeves of her shift, cocked the pistol and aimed in Otis's direction. She bided her time, waiting for the precise moment when she would blow his tiny little rat brain against the wall. Her patience was rewarded when his pink nose poked into the shining moonlight, followed by a wiry whip of a tail. His paws picked at the burlap sack, prying for a weakness for which to spill some seeds. Effie locked her sights.

"You've had every chance," she whispered. "Now go straight to Hell!"

Click, and then a spray of light spread out over the floor. Otis twisted his neck to gaze into the beam of the flashlight, neither surprised by its illumination nor Effie's presence. If Otis had been wearing a hat, he'd have tipped it and kept going.

"Rat bastard!" Effie reared back and flung the flashlight. Otis darted as the fake pistol hit the wall in front of him with a *whoomph*, spraying beams of light around the pine-knotted walls.

Effie dangled her legs over the edge of her bed, her lungs heaving from her efforts. It didn't take much to wind her anymore. While she wasn't prone to quote scripture, she felt certain the thorn in Paul's flesh had been a seed-eating rodent. She'd thought about poison. A hemlock-laced pumpkin seed would do Otis a swift exit from this world. She hadn't followed through, though. Whether halted by a pang of guilt or some twisted idea that they were spiritually entwined, she couldn't say, but she'd decided to endure that miscreant until one or the other of them keeled over from old age ... or foundered on pumpkin seeds. This time however ... .

Feeling a call of nature, Effie placed her hammertoe-feet on the wooden floor and waited for the sensation of balance and clarity to return. Her claw-like toes ached from the sudden flow of blood. Frigid air poured in between the floor slats, battling with the heat from the dwindling fire in the wood stove. Effie stopped long enough to collect a few small pieces of kindling from the knee-high stack of timber sitting just inside her kitchen. She made her way towards the stove, letting out a yawn as she tossed fuel into its hungry belly.

"Like pissin' in the wind." Effie shivered as she re-latched the stove's handle and grabbed a blanket from the nearby rocking chair, snugging it around her hunched shoulders. Hobbling to the front door, she coaxed her knotty hands to turn the obstinate, dented knob. The door shrieked in protest; its rusty hinges succumbing to her insistence. Effie crossed over the threshold of the door and onto her front porch, snagging her curved toes on a bowed board, nearly pitching herself headfirst over the railing.

Effie strained to right herself against the howling northeasterly wind. She removed the blanket and held it up to the light of the moon, noting that moths had gnawed numerous holes.

"Blanket's useless as tits on a bore hog," Effie chuckled as she took in her dilapidated surroundings. *Better to laugh as to cry*, she thought.

Effie pulled the blanket around her once more, standing straight against the porch post, sniffing the night air. Winter was not letting go of its hold easily. She could smell snow coming in from the southwest. In a few hours, the full-moon's glow would be obliterated by thick, puffy clouds and the sky filled with snowflakes big as biscuits.

But there was something else. Effie couldn't put her warped finger on it. The hair on her legs stood on end as goose bumps tickled her thinning scalp and a quick, sharp pain entered her forehead just above her right eye. Her long, white hair began waving in the wind, mixing with the ominous clouds approaching from the south. They carried with them visions of lightning and the sound of distant rumbling thunder. This was not the makings of a typical storm.

Nature's call once again brought Effie back to more pragmatic tasks, urging her on towards the outhouse. Turning on her heel, she caught another vision from the corner of her eye. A Hoot Owl lit in an oak, the tips of its branches scratching against the tin roof of Effie's home. The owl let out a *who-Whooo. Who-who-who-HOOOOO.*

Effie pursed her lips to call the big bird in closer. *Pishhhhh, pishhhhhhh, pishhhhhh.* The owl flew from her perch in the upper branches and came to roost on the porch railing, just feet from Effie's outstretched hand.

"Why, hello there, Prissy!" The majestic bird preened under her right wing, lifting her feathered foot to balance herself before extending her short, round neck to give a friendly peck on top of her friend's hand.

"You hungry, Miss Priss?" The owl blinked her golden orbs. "I gotta feast for ya inside that house if you'd kill that theivin' rat."

Whoooo! Prissy cried.

"Why, Otis is his name," Effie answered, stroking the owl's soft, tawny ears. "Unless you cain't kill somethin' once you've named it. Then it's just *rat bastard.*" The owl turned her head nearly one-hundred and eighty degrees, her keen eyes detecting movement near the wood's edge. One more peck on the porch rail and the big bird flew off towards its next meal, her flight deathly silent.

Effie returned inside, shuffling over the drafty floors towards the dilapidated privy out back. She yanked hard on the back door as it was bad for sticking, but instead the door gave easily, tumbling her backwards. Now she lay sprawled on her back - her gown bunched high under her arms. Raising her head ever so slightly to ascertain the full gamut of her predicament, Effie took one look at her bare privates and chuckled. "You old fool, wonder you hadn't pissed yo'rself."

Despite her best efforts, Effie could not gain traction. Each time she tried to raise up, she fell backwards again. She imagined being found dead, days later, snow covered and naked, the only clue as to her whereabouts being her wrinkled old nipples poking through the snowdrifts that the wind would blow into her house. After taking a few more seconds to catch her breath, Effie turned onto her side. That's when she felt little beady eyes staring at her from the behind the wood stack.

"Well, don't just stand there mockin' me you old fool. Get me a chair!" Otis darted back towards the bedroom, no doubt taking advantage of Effie's predicament to devour the now unguarded sack of pumpkin seeds. "Damn carpetbagger."

Effie continued to wiggle herself onto all fours, crawling to the still-opened door that waved in the howling wind. She thrust the door shut and breathed a sigh of relief when she heard the latch catch. She then crawled to a kitchen chair where she pulled herself upright, remaining there for a few, cautious moments before attempting her journey to the outhouse once more.

"Infernal shithole. Place's fallin' down around my damned ears!" Easing back towards the door, she tugged again, only to find the door, this time, had stuck. Effie sighed in exasperation as Otis ran across the kitchen behind her, his cheeks filled to bursting with his most recent pilferage.

One more careful but generous tug on the door rendered it open without mishap. Out of habit, she pulled the door to with a swift tug, wincing as she realized she'd probably never get the door open again upon her return.

Effie sauntered towards the outhouse along the rock-lined path. Tiny pebbles clung like burrs to the crevices between her toes and warped joints. Effie thought about the toll one year had taken on her withering body. Last spring she'd hauled every one of those rocks from over by the creek, one by one, without a wheelbarrow. She'd paid severely for it the next day, but her strong sense of pride had eased much of the tenderness and stiffness from her aching muscles and angry joints. This spring, she allowed, she'd be *under* a stone if her body continued at its present rate of decline.

The privy's door swung in the gathering winds, banging hard against itself. Effie grabbed hold of its walls for balance, pulling up her gown to expose her sagging buttocks. She'd barely gotten seated on the splintered seat before her bladder let go like an aged wineskin. Effie felt herself being strangely warmed and buried her head deep inside her knotty hands, resting her sharp elbows on the tops of her thighs. Her heavy eyelids became too great to fight against as her entire body lurched forward, elbows and knees parting to make way for her slumping torso. There was no one to hear the *kerflump* that followed, and somewhere in her semi-dream state, she understood that she would freeze to death before anyone found her. Except Otis. *Damn carpetbagger.*

Chapter 4

Effie was jolted awake by her own snores, jowls flopping in the wind with each rumbling exhale. How long had she been slumped over in the privy? It was hard to tell, but probably not for long. It was a sad commentary on her bodily state that she couldn't even pee without going to sleep. Her toes and calves were numb from the cold. She better not tarry lest frost take more than a bite from her decaying, scrunched up feet. She'd heard about this man named Darwin who'd made quite a ruckus in the holier-than-thou-community about folks descending from monkeys.

Lord, Lester Conner had spit, spewed, and hollered from his Thunder Pit (as Effie liked to call the pulpit) for weeks upon end. Not that she'd gone to hear that blowhard, but she'd heard about his harangues here and there. Most didn't believe it, this evolution talk. Effie was disinclined herself, though she kept most things open to possibility. Still, she couldn't help but notice that her knuckles drug closer to the ground every day; her slumping shoulders following the weight of her wilting breasts. One look at her buckled toes and she couldn't be sure the story wasn't the other way 'round – that humans were evolving into monkeys. Seemed more likely to her.

Effie could hear the sleet pinging against the walls and roof of the out-house. She needed to hightail it back inside before she froze to death. She had no aversion to death, but if she had a choice, she preferred not to die here.

A snap of ice coated twigs deep inside the woods jerked her attention in its direction. If that bobcat took a shine to her, she had no means of protecting herself. Generally, she wasn't afraid of wildcats – they minded their business, she minded hers; but she was easy prey. It was probably a deer, even though most deer had run for other hills when the logging companies set to chewing up trees and land. Bastards. She hadn't seen the big buck in months. There was a price to pay for their reckless greed and Effie hoped she'd live to witness their just comeuppances.

"Effie!" Neil came bursting through the woods on mare's-shanks, carrying a load behind him of what looked like one …no, two boys. "Thank God yo'r up, Effie. I need yo'r help." Neil dismounted as a body began plunging sideways towards the ice-covered ground.

"*VIRGIL!*" Effie cried. Neil caught him in his arms just as he careened sideways in a full tilt towards what most assuredly would have been a broken neck, assuming it wasn't broken already. Effie could now see the other boy was Jacob Conner, Lester's son. Effie searched the woods with her cloudy eyes to see if Annie, his sister, was part of this – whatever this was – but she was nowhere around.

"I'm takin' Virgil inside." Without question, Effie followed Neil to her backdoor, leaving Jacob heaving for his breath.

"Put 'im on my bed," Effie instructed as Neil carried his load into the bedroom. "Light me that lamp over there." Effie had her hand on Virgil's neck, checking for a pulse. Effie shook her head at Virgil's weak heartbeat, but at least the child had one. Neil did as he was told, bringing the flickering lamp over Virgil's limp body.

"Sweet Robert E. Lee!" Neil cried as he stood, aghast, at Virgil's injuries. "I've seen soldiers pulled off battlefields look better!"

Rows of skin were laid bare like a freshly harrowed field with clods of blood mounded between them. Virgil's left eye was swollen the size of an apple, and as Effie lifted the lid, she could see the whites were mangled as if they had been chewed up and spit back into its socket.

"What in God's name happened, Neil? He looks like he's been run through a meat grinder!" Effie took the lamp, running it the length of Virgil's body, poking and prodding to extract any sort of reaction.

"Not sure. All I know is Virgil got tangled up in barbed wire and that damned old bull of Lester's rolled him like a ball of twine."

A blast of cold wind caused them both to look towards the door where Jacob stood, shivering, unable to move further.

"Jacob!" Neil shouted. "Shut that goddamn door! You want us all to catch pneumonia?" Jacob obeyed but returned to lean against the door jam, frozen in place with a vacant stare.

"Hope you shot the son-of-a-bitch," Effie muttered.

"The bull or Jacob?"

"The bull, you old fool," Effie snorted as she continued to probe Virgil's ribs.

"I took him down, but that devil is so mean, he'd will hisself to live just for spite." Effie thought about Neil's mother but decided against further comment.

"Well, make yo'rself useful. I got me some quilts warmin' by the stove in that rockin' chair."

As Effie removed the shreds of Virgil's shirt, she saw a puncture the size of a quarter just under his little ribcage. The wound bubbled and gurgled as blood spread over his torso and onto the cornhusk mattress.

"I'm gonna puke," Jacob announced as he fumbled with the stuck door, lurching the contents of his stomach onto the floor. Effie swore to herself she'd fix that damned thing by next nightfall if it killed her.

Neil reappeared at Virgil's bedside; a bundle of quilts piled high in his arms. Effie wrenched her head in Jacob's direction as she moved aside for Neil to spread one of the quilts across the child, tucking in the edges under Virgil's body.

"How's Jacob?" Effie quizzed.

"Hell, yo'r guess is as good as mine. Says he twisted his foot."

"How'd you find these two scallywags?"

Neil explained he'd chased that raccoon who'd been raiding his corn crib up Burnt Shirt Mountain. Just as he topped the crest, he heard the stampede and screams from the two boys.

"Ground was tore up good, but ... ah hell, it don't matter. Fact is? Things are what they are ..."

"...and what they are," Effie interrupted, "is mighty bad."

Chapter 5

Trevor Middleton listened to the pelting rain on the slate roof tiles of his uncle's Savannah home. It sounded like bacon frying, to which his stomach responded with a loud, boisterous growl. Despite his body's urge to feed, however, the thought of eating sent him spinning into a whirlpool of nausea and a disdain for all things solid.

This layover had been necessary, he supposed, but that did not diminish the tedium of it. One month ago, he'd had plans – *big* plans. His future was bright and certain. But now?

Trevor had been plucked from the ranks of the AAFS, the American Ambulance Field Service, to become one of the first pilots to fly for *The Escadrille Américaine* – an intense lot of young men who shared a penchant for danger and a passionate love for France. And if he lived through the war, he'd marry a pretty French girl and they'd have *beaucoup de'enfants*. Honor. Adventure. Purpose. His plan embodied all he'd ever wanted.

Now, his plans revolved around things like, *what pajama top should he wear today? How long could he hold his bladder before calling for assistance to use the bathroom? What would he do if he never walked normally again?* And if the answer to the aforementioned query was nothing of substance, then the ever-burning question that haunted him day and night became, *what woman would want to be with a crippled man for the rest of her life?*

The answer? *There wasn't one.* He was sure of it. Goddamn that fucking horse. If that devil was still alive, Trevor would shoot it just for spite.

On a seemingly ordinary night of carrying the wounded, or *blesses,* from the front lines, (ordinary being a relative term), Trevor had been thrust into the thick of a bloodbath unlike anything he had witnessed in his previous six months with the AAFS; not the least of those horrors being the discovery of his best friend, Owen, splayed across the steering wheel of his own ambulance – an unfortunate casualty of being at the wrong place at a most inopportune time.

It was at this point Trevor's memories became jagged pieces of a puzzle he could not quite fit into any perceptible order, though his dreams had been haunted by blinding lights of shell explosions, the wretched laments of the dead, and the damnable lack of feeling in his leg that stood to make a cripple out of him long before his young life had even begun.

From what reports he had been able to acquire, Owen had been killed by a shell fragment when a German "Jack Johnson" detonated near The Route, which left a grisly mass of dismembered soldiers, horses, and dangerous debris. Seeing there was no help for Owen, Trevor had begun to assist in the clearing of the carnage. Upon discovering a dying draught horse, he had attempted to provide it a merciful and swift exit by shooting it, but the horse unexpectedly revived.

Witnesses said that the crazed stallion shook its head, flinging loose teeth and sputum fast as machine gun fire. Despite attempts at restraint, the horse rose over and over, bringing much of its tremendous weight to bear on Trevor's right leg before the bridle snapped, the horse tearing off into the blackness and blowing snow.

His next memory was of being in *Lycée Pasteur,* the military hospital in Paris, receiving the ministrations of a lovely nurse named Hannah. Hannah had taken a special interest in his recovery, for reasons he would never understand. She had stayed by his side for an entire week and a half, insomuch as possible, encouraging him in his therapies and generally providing a distraction from the reality so poetically framed by the physician:

"Your knee is ground as mustard seeds beneath a mortar's pestle."

Above and below the joint, he had been unreactive to the doctor's scalpel prodding his potato white skin. No feeling, and just as much hope. The surgeon's recommendation was "extensive surgery", which Trevor knew was amputation. The concept was not only ludicrous, but refutable. His leg was not gangrenous - not yet at least. He'd understood from an intellectual point of view that the removal of his leg would make way for a prosthetic limb which, in theory, could allow him more normal mobility. But he feared if he caved, the damage would be irreparable and his hopes of becoming a pilot as unrealistic as finding that damnable horse.

Then there was the related matter of finding Owen, his colleague and friend, slumped over the steering wheel of his ambulance, dead. There wasn't a scalpel sharp enough to excise that painful memory.

Disregarding Trevor's insistences that he would be fine without further medical intervention, the doctor had recommended he be transported to London and admitted to Queen Mary's Hospital, which specialized in the rehabilitation of wounded soldiers, and in particular, those who had lost limbs. Trevor reminded everyone in the room that he was not an amputee, nor would he become one. His answer was an emphatic, "Hell, no."

The meeting ended with the physician throwing up his hands, stomping out of the ward, chanting expletives as freely as a monk would prayers.

The next day, Wallace Daniel Middleton, Trevor's father and the majority owner of W&L Shipping Enterprises (Trevor's uncle, Lymas, being the "L") arrived from Saint-Nazaire where his ship just happened to be docked for the week. He was accompanied by Doctor A. Piatt Andrew, director of the AAFS. If Doc Andrew was making a special appearance, things must be worse than he'd imagined.

Wallace insisted that, if Trevor was going to refute the doctor's advice, that he should return to the states to convalesce. His father would arrange for a respite in the mountains of North Carolina where Trevor's mind and body would be far away from the war-torn fields of France and a reasonable distance from his home in Charleston, where his mother had just recently passed – or to be more accurate, committed suicide.

Trevor said that he would rather have his leg sawn off than to be a prisoner in some godforsaken backwoods mountain town. He would stay in France, thank you very much.

Doc Andrew placed a kind but firm hand on Trevor's quaking shoulder and spoke in his quiet, no-nonsense tone: Trevor was of no use to the ambulance service in his current condition, and he had it on good authority that *The Escadrille Américaine* had deferred his transfer indefinitely until Trevor's situation could be fully evaluated. He must either go to Queen Mary's, as the doctor recommended, or return to the states with his father.

"Trevor," Wallace interjected. "Your Uncle Lymas has agreed to travel with us to North Carolina and oversee your recovery, if you would agree to it."

This was something Trevor had not expected. His uncle was a physician in Savannah, Georgia, and had been for the past twenty years. Last Trevor heard, Lymas was winding down his practice with his sights set on retirement. Perhaps his uncle wanted to test the waters of the North Carolina mountains as a possible location. Moreover, he and his uncle had been quite close before he shoved off to war. Something about this arrangement made this difficult pill a little easier to swallow.

Seven painful days later, Wallace and Trevor embarked on a tension-filled journey across the Atlantic to rendezvous with his uncle in Savannah. Aside from short treks to the toilet and to gaze out at the lumbering Savannah river from his window, he had been confined to the upstairs bedroom for the past week, but tomorrow, they would make their way to Hickory Nut Gorge in the mountains of Western North Carolina via his father's Cadillac and Uncle Lymas's Model-T. (Trevor strongly suspected his uncle wanted his own transport should living in close proximity with his brother prove to be more exhausting than he'd imagined.)

Wallace had secured them rooms at a quaint inn called The Esmeralda, and there they would spend the next few months – just the Middleton men – smoking cigars, sipping on bourbon, having a gay-old time. Trevor wished he could get excited about the prospect, but at this juncture, it seemed more of an attempt to distract him from the truth – that being, he might never walk normally again, much less fly an airplane.

Trevor thrust himself up on his elbows, pushing his bum leg out of the bed as it would not move by any will of its own. The heaviness of his legs was like counterweights, pulling him fully upright. A dagger of pain shot into his swollen knee, creating a spray of black dots that swirled before his eyes as yellow lava erupted in his mouth, singeing the lining of his raw esophagus to the point of a pain so violent it belied any sensation his leg had provided of late.

"Trevor!" came the alarmed voice of Ms. Duboise, Uncle Lymas's live-in housekeeper. "Are you alright? Let me get you a wet cloth."

Ms. Duboise waddled over to the washstand and wrung out a cool rag. "My sweet, sweet boy. You just lay right still now and let Momma Duboise make you all better."

"I do not wish to lie down, Ms. Duboise. I am going to be one giant bedsore if I do," he lamented as he continued to push his body upright.

"Suit yourself," she sang with a shrug of her shoulders.

Trevor often heard Ms. Duboise humming as she went about her daily rituals of maintaining Uncle Lymas's house and frequently, Uncle Lymas himself, as he was a bit absentminded when it came to the mundane, commonsense things in life. Trevor wondered if she maintained more than his housekeeping affairs. He had caught a few impious glances passing between the two and thought it silly that unmarried adults should be so secretive about their affections for one another. The visual associated with such a copulation, however, was one that nearly brought on another nauseous retch. And oddly, a tinge of jealousy.

"There you are now, Trevor." Ms. Duboise placed the cool rag upon his forehead, releasing the minty scent of lavender, which reminded him of being in France.

"Ms. Duboise," Trevor started as his stomach and mind began to calm. "How did you and Uncle meet?"

Even with her back turned, he could perceive her knowing smile. "Missing someone, are we dear?"

Trevor felt his cheeks flush, a bit embarrassed that he had been so obvious. Then again, Ms. Duboise had always possessed a rather keen sense of insight.

Ms. Duboise came to his bedside and placed her pudgy hand over the rag on his forehead before exchanging it for a fresh one. "Well, are we?"

She was a persistent one. He'd have to give her that, but Trevor simply shrugged. Perhaps it was silly to miss Hannah. He had only known her for a couple of weeks but having a pretty nurse fuss over him had been nice.

"You are avoiding *my* question, Ms. Duboise and are taking advantage of my weakened state. I cry *foul.*"

"Fair enough," she chuckled. "It really was quite ordinary on the surface of it," she began as she refreshed the cloth and placed it to Trevor's forehead. "Your uncle attended my husband, God rest his soul, when he took ill with a cancer. Several months after his passing, I was bored and feeling quite sorry for myself. I began toying with the idea of taking out an advertisement, offering my services as a housekeeper, when I saw your uncle at market. We began talking when one thing led to the other one and well, here we are!"

Trevor sighed. "And to answer *your* question, Ms. Duboise ... no. I am not *missing* someone." She smiled as she lent her hand to his back to help him try sitting up once more. "Wishing I *had* someone to miss would be more accurate. I mean, I did sort of meet *someone.* She was a nurse at the hospital. But that's as far as our relationship went. I wanted to ask her to dinner, you know, when I got out of the hospital, but there was no time for it. And besides..." Trevor sighed.

"Besides...?" Ms. Duboise echoed.

"Besides ... who would want an ol'e crippled boy like me?"

Ms. Duboise removed the cloth from his forehead "Trevor, if I may speak plainly, it is not your physical disposition that will make you unpopular with the ladies. It is this monochrome coat of pity that you wear about yourself which will send the girls running into the sea to drown themselves."

Trevor shrugged his shoulders. "Maybe."

"There is no *maybe* about it, young man. We attract that which we project. And what you are projecting is pure doom and gloom. No one wants to be around that. It's all I can do just to be in the same room with you."

Trevor glanced up, a look of hurt spreading across his face.

"Oh, sweet boy, I'm just teasing you!" she hooted as she bounced across the room to open up the curtains.

Trevor started to laugh, but his still-tender ribs reminded him that there was a long road of healing ahead of him. Instead, he clutched his sides and grinned, making his apologies.

"Aww, look at that smile. Now *that's* attractive. If I were a wee bit younger, Trevor Middleton, I'd be all over you like gravy on a biscuit."

Trevor blushed, not quite knowing how to respond. Ms. Duboise cleared her throat and continued. "So, have you written to this *someone*?"

"Well, no. Not yet. I've barely been able to hold my head up."

Ms. Duboise nodded. "If you'd like, you could dictate a missive and I could transcribe it for you."

"I appreciate the kind offer," he replied, "but I believe I should do that myself. It will be good therapy to focus on something other than my pain."

"Perfect," Ms. Duboise agreed, opening the top drawer of the rolltop desk that resided in his room and retrieving pen and paper. "I've laid your implements of affection there for you, when you feel ready."

Trevor smiled. "Thank you, Ms. Duboise. You are most kind."

As Ms. Duboise turned to leave, two noses, the size of buttons, appeared in the gap of the half-open door. Lymas's dogs, Bruce and Arabella, pushed through the crack, rendering it fully open as they scurried to greet Trevor's dangling toes. Arabella backed up several paces and wiggled her butt. A shrill *yiff* indicated her treatment session was complete and that proper respect and adulation should be bestowed in the form of the butterscotch candy Trevor kept hidden in the bedside table.

"Shhhh, Arabella. You'll let the cat out of the bag," he cautioned. "Uhm, no offense." Trevor's mischievous wink did not deter Ms. Duboise from casting a scolding glance at both criminal and accomplice. Disregarding the warning, Arabella placed her spindly front paws upon the leg of the table, whimpering as she pressed her nose against the nightstand containing the contraband.

"Trevor, I gave you that butterscotch to calm your cough. Candy doesn't grow on trees these days. These hounds are spoiled enough." A wary growl from beneath the washstand conveyed Arabella's complete disagreement.

Suddenly, Trevor jolted as a stinging pain began in his right foot, as if a yellow jacket had nailed him on his big toe.

"Ms. Duboise, go fetch Uncle! I'm getting some feeling back in my leg, or my foot at least! Arabella, you are an excellent nurse!" The dog's entire body wiggled in ecstatic canine pride.

"Shooooo, you beasties. *Shooooo!*" Ms. Duboise plucked Arabella from the floor, stuffing the little dog under her sagging arm fat while scooting Bruce outside the bedroom door with her foot. With a *plumpff* and a final warning to leave the premises, Ms. Duboise shut the bedroom door behind her as she went to retrieve Lymas and relate this guardedly good news. No more than a minute later, Lymas was at Trevor's bedside.

"I hear you have some feeling returning, Trevor. That is marvelous!" Lymas was palpating Trevor's entire leg. Trevor could feel some pressure, but other than his toes, the rest of his leg from the knee down remained devoid of any sensation at all. When Trevor expressed disappointment, Lymas was quick to counter.

"These things take time, Trevor. The fact that you already have feeling returning to your foot is remarkable," Lymas paused. "Considering the first prognosis, I should say six months in the mountains will go far in ..."

"Six months?!" Trevor was indignant and panicked. Lymas sighed.

"Yes, Trevor. Now don't fret. Your father thinks you will be there for at least six months but ..."

"At *least* six? You mean it could be *longer?*" Lymas rolled his eyes once more, visibly tiring of his family's constant bickering.

"Will you let me finish?" Trevor relaxed back onto his elbows but remained stiff in body and stern in expression. "I can only take three months away from my work here. I have arranged for a colleague to see my patients while we are away in North Carolina but cannot in good conscience abandon my practice completely." Trevor rolled his eyes and turned his head. "You and your father will be staying in Hickory Nut Gorge, until such time we deem it suitable for your return."

"Return to where? Here, or France?"

Lymas blew another frustrated sigh. "Trevor, we have been through this, ad nauseum. There is no way to tell. You simply must dig deep into your resolve and realize this is a day-by-day process." Lymas placed a calming hand on his nephew's shoulder. "You recall the alternative, I'm sure."

Trevor reluctantly nodded his head in acknowledgement of the facts. Even so, it seemed to be more than his soul could bear.

Lymas continued. "I suspect your angst lies, not just in the amount of time spent convalescing, but in the company that you will have to keep?"

"Father's presence can be suffocating," Trevor acknowledged.

"Yes. Well, I do not believe Wallace's patience will manage the entire six months. You know your father. Busy as a bee, flitting from one proposition to another. He doesn't trust anyone else to run the business. I cannot see him tearing himself away for that extended length of time, not even for the sake of ..." Lymas stopped his speech as if someone had clasped a hand over his mouth. Trevor raised himself ever so slowly to an upright position.

"Not even for the sake of his son. I know, Uncle."

Lymas's eyes held a fountain of empathy. "Listen, Trevor. Your father has been under a considerable amount of stress, losing your mother and the like. Business is suffering as a result of the war." Trevor gave his uncle a concerned glance. "I mean, he has orders, but hell, between the British and German blockades, it takes him twice as long to make port. Memories of the Lusitania are never far from anyone's mind... ." Trevor recalled several of his father's friends were lost when the Germans sank the British ship less than a year ago.

"But that is not to diminish *your* suffering, which I am sure has been excruciating, both mentally and physically. All I am saying is that if things seem awkward, it is because they are. Your father is terribly worried about you, and while he has an odd way of showing it, he wants what is best. Just remember he loves you and try to distance yourself from his psychoses ... if you can."

"Can you?" Lymas lifted his eyebrows and drew up a corner of his mouth. "Uncle, the thought of spending that broad expanse of time with him, cloistered in the mountains with nowhere to run ..." They both looked down at his leg and laughed a bit. "...seems more than I can bear. This trip is meant to be one of recovery, but I fear it may be my undoing."

"I understand. Just please, try." Lymas placed his hand on the glass doorknob, wresting another click as he turned it without fully opening the door itself. "Think of something positive. Set a course towards a goal you've always dreamed of - a beacon of light! It will pull you forward and away from the shoals that threaten to sink you – remembering you can always change course."

"I want to become a pilot, Uncle."

"Good! That's a great launching point."

"I just don't know where to even begin," Trevor admitted. "Or if I can bear the disappointment if I fail."

"Trevor, none of us have the guarantee of tomorrow, or even the next minute. Life is a roll of the dice. But forward motion is better than no motion. You can always pivot and turn, but momentum is key. And as for where to begin? I often tell my patients, *when you don't know where to start, start with what you* do *know.*

Trevor rubbed his forehead, the heavy conversation taking a toll on his limited stamina and ability to concentrate.

"Lunch is served!" Ms. Duboise's announcement from the bottom of the stairs sounded more like a recitative from an opera than a statement of preparedness.

"Trevor, are you sure you want to come downstairs? You've not done so since you made that heart-wrenching ascent the day we arrived."

It was true. The climb, or rather, *the drag,* up the grand staircase had been agonizing.

"Yes, Uncle Lymas. I would like to move to the dining room. I need to get dressed, though."

"Nonsense. We can dispense with formalities, given the circumstances. Just put on your robe and be done with it."

"I appreciate that, but I really must dress in order to feel like a man again. I've not had a decent suit of clothes on since before my ... accident. If it won't upset Ms. Duboise to wait just a bit longer?"

Lymas nodded. "I am sure she'll understand. I will be at the bottom of the steps, however. This is no time for treacherous pride." The door closed and Trevor was alone once more, save for Bruce and Arabella who had snuck back in the opened door and were now resting at the foot of his bed.

Trevor pried himself up with crutches, giving himself a few seconds before moving forward. He eyed his wheelchair that had been relegated to the corner of the room with disdain. He'd allowed himself to be rolled on and off his father's ship, but he avowed that would be the limit of his use for it.

A couple of hobbles and he was at the armoire, gazing at the wardrobe choices before him. He decided on a silk pinstripe shirt and a rather nondescript pair of black wool trousers, which he pulled off the garment hangers and tossed to the bed. This motion upset his precarious balance, causing him to stagger forward, his crutch being the only element that kept him from falling facedown to the floor. A muscle in his right lower back clamped tight in protest, sending ripples of pain up, down, and across his ribcage as if his skeletal frame were nothing more than a conduit for electricity.

"*Damn* ... ohhh damn, damn, damn." Trevor's jaw clenched so tight he feared his teeth would crack into a thousand tiny pieces.

"Trevor?" Lymas yelled up the stairs.

"I'm fine, Uncle. Please." Trevor heard a resigned sigh followed by Lymas's steps into the kitchen. He heard Lymas offer to help Ms. Duboise finish setting the table and then muddled, suppressed voices. No doubt they were discussing him and his obstinate pride.

A painstaking look at his reflection in the mirror revealed sunken eye sockets and protruding jawbones. His once strong shoulders slunk forward. A peeling scab above his left eye wagged its crusty arm. He brushed it with his left hand and watched it float to the floor and land silently on top of his bare foot. It was then he noticed his toenails needed trimming and wondered if he would ever manage such a simple task ever again. His overall form was that of grotesque emaciation which he found repulsive and frightening. He had no more substance than a scarecrow.

Donning his silk shirt and buttoning his fly were easier than expected, but his clothes, once tailored and perfectly fitted, now hung limp from his body. Still, the pride of seeing a task to its end brought a sense of accomplishment and normalcy to what had been an otherwise haphazard and abnormal existence. The only thing that remained to complete the look was shoes.

A box of Phoenix EV-R-UP silk socks stood poised at the back of the armoire. Trevor opened the box, retrieving a pair of white ones with a red and brown stripe to match his shirt. The logo inside the box read, *You're sure of yourself in Phoenix.*

"Maybe I should move to Phoenix," Trevor muttered sardonically to himself.

Bending over to slip the socks on was indeed painful – so much so that he decided to forego socks altogether and simply wear shoes without them. His left shoe slipped on easily, but he could not even force the right one over his swollen foot. He tried loosening the laces, hoping to improvise a slipper of sorts, but that mission failed as well. He did manage to clip his suspenders onto his pants without much ado.

He tucked his socks into his trouser pockets and tossed his right shoe into the armoire. Lymas could assist him in donning his socks, but his swollen foot? There was no help for that.

Suddenly, Trevor recalled the stationary Ms. Duboise had left for him. He did not want to hold up dinner any longer, so he grabbed the paper, folded it, and tucked it inside his trouser pocket. Perhaps he could pen something in Lymas's library after lunch.

With his crutches in tow, he approached the stairs, staring at the dizzying descent and wishing for all the world he could simply walk down them as a normal man.

Remembering how difficult it was to ascend the steps, he began to re-consider this bold decision to eat in the formal dining room. He envisioned himself tumbling head over heels down the curved staircase, landing in a dead, limp heap for Bruce and Arabella to sniff and contemplate, but then recalled his conversation with his uncle just moments before. *When you don't know where to start, start with what you do know.*

He knew he could not stay upstairs forever. Neither would he allow his mind to succumb to this seemingly dire set of circumstances and become a recluse like his mother. He knew if he was to regain use of his leg, even to perform the most ordinary of tasks, it would involve intentional risk and a great deal of pain. He knew he wanted to return to France as a pilot. And no matter how much everyone wanted to help, he must do this of his own accord, so he might as well get on with it. Trevor clutched the newel post with one hand then regarded his crutches, debating on how best to bring them along. *Tuck them both under his free arm? Do without?* Both of those options brought on another catastrophic vision he quickly dismissed. *Let the crutches plummet down the stairs...*

"Let me get those crutches for you," Lymas offered as he bounded up the curved staircase, two steps at a time. Okay, he might need *some* assistance – at least to start. To his relief, however, Lymas did not tarry but made his way back down to the dining room, crutches in tow, giving Trevor the mental and physical space to do that which he must.

Moving his left leg down the first step, his right leg followed, albeit a bit stiff and clumsy. *There. Only seventeen more to go.* Trevor let go of the newel post and now gripped the handrail with both hands. He hoped Ms. Duboise had not waxed it recently. *Left leg, down. Right leg,* plunk. *Left leg, down. Right leg,* plunk. Soon, he had managed to reach the bottom of the staircase without mishap, save for the aching joints in his fingers from clasping the handrail so tight.

"Why, here comes our guest of honor!" Ms. Duboise beamed from around the corner of the dining room where she had no doubt been watching the entire ordeal. He was struck by the long formal dining table set with platinum trimmed china and four candles flickering in a sterling silver candelabra. His uncle and Ms. Duboise had gone to great lengths to make this occasion, whatever it was, exceptional. Indeed, it was quite therapeutic - how the seemingly mundane act of managing the stairs filled him with pride.

"Trevor, would you like some tea?" Without waiting for a response, Lymas poured him a cup.

"Mmmm. English Breakfast." Trevor closed his eyes, inhaling the savory aroma that rose to his nose. When he opened his eyes his uncle was gone, supplanted by Ms. Duboise who stood before him - a spoon in one hand and a creamer full of milk in the other.

"Sugar? Milk?"

"Oh, yes, but I can ..."

"One spoon or two?"

"Well, one but ..."

Lymas burst into the dining room through the kitchen's swinging doors carrying two plates full of scones, flat cakes, and pan loaf bread; followed immediately by Wallace, who bore a platter full of sausages, a steaming bowl of grits, and another platter piled high with boiled shrimp. From the center of the table, four pairs of crab eyes stared at him; their salmon-red claws raised high into the air.

"Well, look who decided to join us!" Wallace chimed. A shrimp escaped from the platter as Wallace plopped the plate onto the linen covered table, leaving an oily impression of whorls on the cloth's surface. Another shrimp skittered onto the floor, upon which Bruce pounced from beneath one of the chairs. Arabella returned in kind by jumping on Bruce's back, precipitating a row of tumbling fur and savage snarls.

"Get, *GET,* you hellish hounds!" Ms. Duboise chided as she broadsided the two Cairns with a broom. Straw and bits of shrimp flew into the air as Ms. Duboise swept them out of the dining room and up the hall into Lymas's bedroom where she quickly closed the door. The terriers expressed their disapproval by clawing the door as though they had been thrown into a fiery furnace.

"Have mercy, Claudia, I'm not sure which is doing worse damage – you or the dogs!" Lymas exclaimed. Everyone turned to Ms. Duboise, now exposed to the entire world as Claudia.

"Well, yes, I suppose, well, yes. Let's eat, shall we?" Ms. Duboise glanced Lymas's shoulder with her own and Trevor could have sworn she pinched his butt-cheek as she passed. Wallace shook his head and took a place at the table to the right of Trevor. Lymas sat across from his brother, with Claudia remaining at the helm in order to provide any assistance that might be needed.

"Won't you be joining us, Ms. Duboise?" Uncle Lymas had regained some of his composure, gesturing towards Claudia that she should take her place beside him at the table.

"Don't you mean *Claudia*?" Trevor chuckled.

"Trevor!" Wallace flashed at his son's indiscretion, but Trevor thought he saw a slight smirk under his veneer. Trevor reached for the scones that were still steaming under the napkin laid on top of them.

"Damn, Claudia," Trevor exclaimed through a mouthful of biscuit. "These are the finest scones I have ever tasted! You should be a pastry chef!" A few crumbs of biscuit sprayed from his lips as he scanned his family's face for a consensus. Claudia beamed but no one else moved. "Did I say something wrong?"

"Are you drunk?" Wallace's hint of humor had dissipated.

"I don't know, Father. Am I? You should be an expert on the subject, but ..." Before Trevor could complete his sentence, Claudia interrupted.

"Oh, no offense, Mr. Middleton. Your son flatters me." She then allowed Lymas to pull out a chair for her to sit, a faint blush lingering on her cheeks. "Trevor has been through a lot. I think it's good he is, well, shall we say, a bit full of himself!"

"Full of something," Wallace muttered. "Sausage, Trevor?"

"Oh, *no!*" Trevor looked away as he shook his head, then noticed Claudia and Lymas. "No offense, mind you. I just don't believe my stomach could handle sausage right now."

"Son, you must eat something besides broth and dumplings. You are a mere *shadow* of your former self!" Wallace was staring at his son as though he was a bum invited to charity at the table.

"I'm eating scones, Father. Would you have me choke on the first solid food I've eaten in weeks?" Trevor heard his father eject another derisive *hmmmfff.*

"Would you like some marmalade?" Lymas asked, handing Trevor the butter dish as well. Wallace had returned his gaze to the table, though in mind he seemed to be someplace else.

With tensions tamed, the late morning meal was passed around with little conversation. Trevor ate the rest of his scone, and even tried a small spoonful of the grits and a few shrimps, hoarding a couple inside a napkin for Bruce and Arabella. His father said little, for which Trevor was grateful. Finally, Claudia could not withstand the silence any longer.

"So, when are you all heading to the mountains?" Claudia looked at all three men, but it was Wallace who interjected his answer.

"I, umm, I thought we might wait another week or so."

"Wait?! Why, Wallace?" Lymas was genuinely confused. "That's not what we discussed. If Trevor feels he can travel now, we should respect his wishes."

"Yes, Father. Uncle is right. I wish to leave as soon as possible. You said we would leave tomorrow." Trevor felt the panic rise in his veins. He so wanted to get on with this ordeal and be done with it.

"Trevor, you are in no condition to make such a long trip. I thought a few more days rest here in Savannah might do you some good."

"Do me *good*? I thought the mountains were supposed to *do me good!*" He heard Arabella and Bruce yap from the bedroom door.

"Son, you haven't eaten solid food in weeks. You are weak as a kitten, and frankly, your disposition leaves me not so inclined to travel just yet ..."

"*My* disposition? I was having quite a lovely day until you arrived. It would seem yours is the only disposition that I, and may I speak for the entire table, *we,* find deplorable!"

Claudia winced as she kicked Lymas in the shin in a vain attempt for him to intervene. It seemed as if Lymas thought this a battle worth having, or at least watching. Wallace slammed his fist on the table.

"Damn it, Trevor! Can't you see I am trying to help you? My God, Son. You have been a peevish ass ever since we left France. You have been rash, rude, insubordinate, and might I add *ungrateful!*"

"Ungrateful." Trevor's voice buzzed below the raucous tone of Wallace's rant. "Ungrateful? You son of a bitch."

Lymas finally weighed in. "That's enough, both of you!"

"No, Lymas. It's fine. If that is how Trevor feels, let him say it. We are men, right Trevor? Or perhaps a man would have taken the time to attend his own mother's funeral." Trevor turned his head so fast he heard the vertebrae in his neck pop.

"Are we really men, Father? Let's see. A man, at least in *my* opinion, since I have no experience on the subject, would have stayed at home with a sick wife and small child. A *man* would not have been ashamed to have brought his wife out in public for fear she might precipitate his fall from the upper echelons of society. A *man* would have ...."

The bareknuckle blow caught Trevor hard on the left side; a straight right that landed squarely beneath the socket of his eye. Claudia screamed as Lymas stood, intercepting another throw before it landed on Trevor's chin. Wallace, surprised by his brother's interference, stepped backwards as Lymas planted himself between his brother and nephew. Lymas may have been older, but he was still a force to be reckoned with.

Trevor's teeth, however, were not. He rolled a jostled tooth about in his mouth, spitting it into his hand and setting it to rest on his plate. His head moved from side to side with a shudder of disbelief, but he said nothing.

"Wallace, please leave the table!" Lymas demanded. Wallace stared at his brother as if he had asked him to fall on a sword. "I don't believe I stuttered. Excuse yourself ... at once."

Wallace sucked on the trickle of blood that had appeared on his knuckles. "Where do you want me to go, *brother*, to my room?"

"If you wish. For a walk, back to France, to Hell if the Devil will have you ... but I will not tolerate such vile behavior in my house." Wallace did not move. "I am most serious."

Wallace moved towards the front door, retrieving an umbrella from the stand, and headed into the cold afternoon drizzle.

The rest of the afternoon was mercifully quiet. Claudia escorted Trevor to the library with Bruce and Arabella padding behind, their little noses twitching in the air with the scent of shrimp wafting from Trevor's pockets. Ms. Duboise set Trevor on the couch and elevated his head and leg atop a posh collection of pillows, then treated Trevor's injured jaw with lavender compresses. When Ms. Duboise left the room, Trevor unwrapped the shrimp in his pockets and fed them to the eager hounds. He then unfurled the folded paper inside his pocket, wincing that he had been so careless as to crease it. It would have to do. Retrieving a copy of *Les Miserables* from the table beside him and a pen, Trevor pressed the stationery flat as possible upon the book's hardback and began.

Dearest Hannah,

I hope this letter finds you in good spirits. I realize my correspondence might catch you by surprise. We hardly know one another, but I find myself thinking about you ... often.

I am managing. I find that I tire quite easily, but that is to be expected, I suppose. I do have some feeling returning in my leg, so that is good news.

I wish that I were still there and could repay you in more personal ways for all of your excellent care, but such are the ways of war.

To that end, we leave for the North Carolina mountains tomorrow. Once we arrive at the inn, something called The Esmeralda, I will write to you with my address there. It seems Father has allotted six months for our lodging. No doubt, there will be tedious pauses with plenty of time to correspond. Until then, please take care.

Most gratefully yours,
Trevor

Trevor read the letter twice, then wadded it up and tossed it into the fire. Who was he trying to fool? Hannah had, no doubt, moved on to better men than him, and he couldn't blame her. Ms. Duboise was not wrong – he was feeling sorry for himself, but perhaps now was not the best time to pursue romantic relationships, especially long-distance ones.

Trevor laid his head back on the pillows and sighed. Arabella curled up in his lap as Bruce lightly snored underneath the couch. Trevor drifted off, too, unable to stave off the exhaustion brought on by the unseemly quarrel with his father.

An hour and a half later, Trevor was awakened by a knock on the door of the library, although it had remained open. Wallace filled the space, carrying a glass of brandy and some leftover scones.

"Trevor, I wish to apologize."

Trevor acknowledged his presence with a passing look, then feigned reading *Les Miserables*, which had remained on his lap during his snooze. Wallace cleared his throat. "I said, I wish to apologize." Trevor looked up from his book, his assaulted jaw aching with the effort.

"What would you like for me to do, Father, award you the Nobel Peace Prize?"

"Dammit, Trevor! This is difficult enough for me. Never mind that I am beseeching you with a plate of cold, leftover ... scones." Wallace said the word *scones* as if they were slimy slugs plucked from Lymas's rose garden.

"Trevor," he continued. "The last person I want to hurt is you. You are here for your healing, and I fear I have only caused you deeper wounds."

Trevor sighed and looked towards the hearth where a small fire crackled meant to chase away the damp sea air. "I accept your apology, but I don't need brandy." Trevor looked his father in the eye. "And I certainly don't need scones. I simply wish to be left alone."

"Understood, although according to you, my sin appears to be one of perpetual absence." Trevor shrugged his shoulders. "Well then." Wallace set the plate and brandy onto the table beside his son and turned to leave.

"Oh, Father." Wallace stopped at his son's words, without turning. "I believe we should leave for North Carolina soon, as originally planned. Tomorrow. I thought I would pack my things..."

"You need not pack at all. I will attend to your needs." Wallace now rotated his body towards his son's.

"I'm not helpless, Father. I can do some things."

"Indeed. You are not helpless, but I am hopeless, and for that there is no help. So please, allow me." His eyes were pleading.

"Alright, then. I won't be needing my wheelchair. That should save you some work." Wallace took in a breath to protest but Trevor held up his hand.

"No wheelchair, Father. That is, unless you plan to tie me in it and push me over a cliff. I will not be a burden to you. I am not my mother."

Chapter 6

The morning started off much as the previous evening had ended, time doing little to alleviate the amassed tensions from the previous day's quarrel. From the library's window, Trevor watched his father go to great pains to avoid his brother while loading up the cars, taking a circuitous route through the front door to the back where the car was parked.

Lymas skittered through his house with a pretense of nonchalance, but Trevor could hear the discomfiture in his voice as he made nervous conversation with Claudia regarding matters of housekeeping, professional emergencies, and of course, care for Arabella and Bruce. Trevor scratched his bruised chin and flinched - the dull ache reminding him of the long road before him.

Ms. Duboise leaned against the frame of the back porch door, Arabella and Bruce flanking her on either side. Her countenance was heavy and her eyes, misty, no doubt anticipating the time Lymas would be away. She was offered a place in the entourage, but she had declined, citing that Arabella and Bruce would be more comfortable in their own home. Watching the two of them say goodbye brought a pang of awareness – the sense that he had no one to miss *him* when he was gone.

"You enjoy yourselves now, you hear?" Ms. Duboise called out. The three men affirmed that they would try and then they were off.

Trevor slept most of the train ride from Savannah to Spartanburg, waking only when his father nudged him as they neared the station. The Cadillac and the Model-T were offloaded from the freight cars, and soon, they were winding their way over the foothills of South Carolina.

Three hours later, the two automobiles pulled in front of The Esmeralda Inn, just as dusk was settling deep inside Hickory Nut Gorge. Lymas rushed to open the passenger door of the Caddy, where Trevor pivoted and allowed his legs to slip outside, taking in the view of his lodging for the next several months. As his father and uncle wrestled their trunks off the back of the cars, Trevor noted a winter's chill, even though the calendar assured him it was spring. He smelled woodsmoke and felt the pull of sleep as he imagined himself sitting by a fire with a dram of Scotch in his hand. Perhaps coming here wasn't the worst idea.

The inn itself stood as an elegant contrast to the ramshackle homes they'd passed along the way, tended by overall-clad farmers who carried wet sacks of grain on slumped shoulders or swayback horses. Along the roads, he'd caught a few of their sideways glances and wondered what these mountain folk thought of people like him and their horseless carriages.

As if on cue, a gangly young man appeared at the entrance to The Esmeralda. "Looks like it could snow!"

"Hello! My name is Wallace Middleton." Wallace moved forward with an outstretched hand. "This is my son, Trevor, and my brother, Dr. Lymas Middleton. And you are ..."

"Beg pardon, beg pardon, Mr. Middleton. Name's Clavel. Clavel Lyons."

"How do you do, Mr. Lyons?" Lymas greeted as the young doorman shook his hand – with a bit more gusto than was necessary.

"Please. Call me Clavel. We're pretty informal 'round these parts."

Wallace said they were pleased to make his acquaintance. That's when the doorman noticed the trunk and jumped back.

"Well, I'll be a suck egg mule. I shoulda brought that trunk up. I'll take care'a everything. Y'all just go in and make yo'rselves at home. Mrs. Turner's expectin' you." Wallace stepped inside the inn as Lymas turned to assist his nephew.

"And I got this young feller, too. Go on now and warm yourself by the fire. Me and Trevor here? We'll be just fine." The doorman looked at Trevor and winked, precipitating a chuckle from deep inside his aching ribs.

"Yes, Uncle. We'll be just fine. Go on now. You look tired." Lymas begrudgingly turned to follow his brother into the inn.

"Name's Clavel. Clavel Lyons." Trevor gripped Clavel's hand and noted the rough callouses beneath the surface.

"Yes, I heard. Nice to meet you."

"Oh, well, beg pardon. Beg pardon. I sometimes find myself repeatin' myself. Kinda like right now," he said with a blush.

"Not to worry, Clavel. I find I repeat myself quite often these days." Clavel's smile faded as he took in Trevor's crutches.

"You hurt yo'rself." Trevor acknowledged the obvious with a short nod as he took one step ahead with his crutch. His bum leg was a bit stiff and achy from the long day of travel, but all in all, he was encouraged. Looking at the stone steps that led up to the sweeping porch, he recalled how he had to ascend the stairs at Lymas's house and hoped he would have an easier time of these.

"Did'ju take a bullet?"

"No, I...umm, it was a horse..." Trevor suddenly felt as though a fog was engulfing him. He became agitated and dizzy, no longer considering Clavel's country charms amusing. Trevor rubbed his temples in an attempt to stave off a wave of biliousness.

"Why, Trevor. Yo'r white as a ghost! Let me help you..."

"I don't need your help, Clavel." Trevor could feel his temper climb and fought to control it, so as not to cause a scene within the first ten minutes of his arrival. "I would just like to get inside where I can stretch my leg a bit." Trevor resecured the crutch under his arm and moved to ascend the first step.

"Oh, beg pardon. Beg pardon. Don't feel like talkin'. Beg pardon."

"It's quite alright, Clavel. Now, here I go." *Left leg up. Right leg will follow. Left leg up. Right leg will follow.* Now he was standing on the porch of The Esmeralda, exhausted, but once more feeling accomplished, nonetheless.

A middle-aged woman wearing a pink satin dress with burgundy trim and ribbon at the neck now loomed in the doorway. While her frame was slight, her presence seemed to permeate every inch of airspace. Her hair was pulled into a tight bun that laid atop her head and her skin glowed like alabaster.

"Trevor," Clavel motioned with a nod of his head. "This here is Mrs. Turner. Matilda Turner. She and her husband, Tom, are the innkeepers."

"Hello, Trevor! Tom and I are so happy to have you staying with us! Clavel, we can take care of The Middletons from here. I'm sure you'd like to go home to Birdie."

"Thank you, Mrs. Turner. I'll just see to Trevor here."

Trevor braced himself against the door jam, using his crutch for balance to affect a proper greeting.

Mattie placed a tender hand on Trevor's arm. "Oh, please, you mustn't trouble yourself. Like Clavel said. We are rather informal at The Esmeralda."

"Thank you, Mrs. Turner. I am not quite myself these days."

"Well then, you've come to the right place. And please. Call me Mattie. Won't you come have some tea? 'Take a load off', as we say here in The Gorge."

Mattie was neat and polished, but not overly so, much like The Esmeralda. The inn amounted to little more than a large farmhouse, but there was an air of aristocracy about it that pampered and comforted – much like a doting grandmother. Trevor followed his hostess into the lobby where he was taken before a large rock fireplace. The sight and sound of crackling hickory filled his senses.

A squatty porcelain teapot lay snuggled beneath a cozy as Clavel laid out a plate of steaming biscuits, accompanied by a smaller plate containing a pat of butter, a small cup of honey, and a shaker full of cinnamon.

Mattie stood by. "I made chamomile. It's soothing for one's nerves."

"Chamomile is perfect. I'm grateful for your hospitality, Mrs. Turner. Er, uh, Mattie." Trevor eyed the sofa, debating on which of the clumsy, awkward ways would be least embarrassing to lower himself down onto it. Exhaustion suddenly made the decision for him as he collapsed without any graceful form at all. Almost as fast as his backside hit the couch, Trevor closed his eyes and felt himself drifting to sleep.

Refusing to nap this close to bedtime, Trevor forced his eyes open to find Mattie sitting beside him, holding a plate of goodies and tea. Trevor smiled, albeit weakly, and took the plate from her, devouring a biscuit in three bites. As Trevor raised the teacup to take a sip, the base trailed a string of honey that dribbled down the front of his silk shirt. Trevor tried wiping the honey from his shirt with a napkin, but the end result was an even bigger mess.

"Here Dear, let me take care of that. Clavel, could you bring a warm cloth please?"

"Yes ma'am, right away," was heard from deep within the kitchen. Clavel reappeared with a steaming rag placed in a pottery bowl and a dry one hung over his arm. Wasn't he supposed to be leaving?

"Thank you, Clavel." Mattie took the bowl and cloth from Clavel and began to erase the sticky syrup from Trevor's shirt. "Tom will be along directly. He's gone into Asheville to retrieve some supplies. He is very excited to meet you."

"I look forward to it," Trevor acknowledged, although the thing he looked forward to the most, at present, was a restful night's sleep.

"Tom and I are most passionate about the war effort. We would be in France now if Tom hadn't made a deathbed promise to his father to take care of The Esmeralda." Mattie sighed and looked about the room with rolling eyes, almost as if The Esmeralda were somewhat of a ball and chain. "So, he does his bit to drum up local support for our volunteers in France. In fact, I believe part of his itinerary this afternoon was to meet with Anne Vanderbilt about supplying the field service with more ambulances."

Now Mattie had his full attention. "Anne Vanderbilt ... is here?" Anne and her husband, William, were well known among the troops and volunteers in France for donating copious amounts of dollars in support of the war, especially to the ambulance service and The Escadrille.

"Well, not *here*, or at least, not yet. She and her husband, William, are visiting family in Asheville. But rumor has it..." Mattie paused and leaned into Trevor's space to whisper, "...that they might just be staying at our

Esmeralda for a night on their way to Charleston." Mattie winked so as to drive home the necessity of discretion, but honestly, who would he tell?

"I'll take your secret to my grave," Trevor offered with a wink of his own. "But I look forward to personally thanking her and her husband for their generosity." This development certainly would lend itself to a more interesting stay, that was for certain. Trevor glanced down at his leg and hoped he would be able to stand at least somewhat dignified in the famous couple's presence.

Mattie reached over to the platter of biscuits and split open another one, this time sliding a slice of butter between its flaky layers. "Honey?" Trevor wasn't sure if she was using a term of endearment or if she were offering more of the sticky sweetener he'd just poured down the front of his shirt.

"Yes, I would love some ... that is if I can eat it instead of wear it." Mattie giggled as he took the refreshed plate.

Clavel meandered towards the fire, a load of hickory wood cradled high in his arms. "I'm carryin' a lazy man's load," Clavel announced with a *thud* and a *clunnnng* as his load tumbled into a copper log bucket. "I shoulda made two trips, but I need to go by Ms. Effie's before I go home. Little June, that's my daughter, she's feelin' kinda poorly with the croup. Thought I'd get some mullein to fix 'er up."

"Ms. Effie is our local medicine woman, for lack of a better term," Mattie offered.

"Some say she's a witch," Clavel added with a hint of disdain. "But I say she's a miracle worker. She makes salves and healing potions. Catches babies. Me and Birdie's all the time goin' to her for somethin'. Croup. Hives. Pleurisy."

Clavel placed one hand on the mantle and continued. "Yeah, Ol'e Lester Conner. Lives up the holler just a ways. He got her outted from the church. He's the local preacher, you see." Clavel's face exhibited something between annoyance and downright anger. "Some folks swear by 'im, but me? I swear *at* 'im."

"The Conners have a small farm just up the mountain from us," Mattie added. "They supply the inn with eggs, vegetables, and occasionally meat." Mattie shot Clavel a look, one clearly indicating he should change the subject. "His daughter comes by every few days to deliver such." Mattie cleared her throat. "Sweet girl."

"Well, it was nice to meet you, Clavel. I hope your little girl improves." Trevor stood to shake Clavel's hand when a pain unlike any he had felt in weeks shot up and down his leg, his knee the epicenter of a quake that shook his entire body and wrestled him back down onto the couch. Trevor let out a yelp.

"Oh, poor dear!" Mattie ran to his side. "What can I do?"

Trevor could barely see his hostess for the stars swirling around her head. The room was spinning and for the first time since leaving Savannah, he feared he would be sick.

"Clavel, can you get us a cool rag?" Mattie requested as Trevor leaned his head back against the leather sofa.

Lymas suddenly reappeared from wherever he and his father had taken themselves earlier, presumably to their assigned rooms. "Trevor, are you alright?" His uncle's question was tinged with renewed alarm. "I was hoping you'd feel up to eating dinner."

Dinner? The mere thought brought a renewed eddy of halos and sparkles before his eyes. Trevor heard Clavel's heavy footsteps come close then felt a wet cloth come to rest against his forehead. Soon, the constellations before his eyes began to fade as he felt his senses return.

"I ... I'm alright, Uncle. I just raised up too quickly. I suppose I should eat *something*." Trevor turned to Mattie then Clavel. "Thank you. For the cloth."

Mattie smiled. "Of course, Trevor. Anything we can do, please let us know."

What could *they* do? Hell, what could *he* do? Not much, that was for certain. Such was the harsh reality that he was faced with. And now here he was, in the middle of this godforsaken gorge, with no real medical care or resources. What did these people do when they got sick or injured? Rely on the superstitions and folksy tales from some old mountain woman? And no offense to his uncle, but there was only so much any physician could do with such limited services. He really should have stood up to his father and Doc Andrew and remained in France.

Suddenly, panic returned. What if this was as good as he would ever be? What if he never became a pilot? Even worse - what if he never walked normally again ... anywhere, ever?

Get a grip on yourself, Trevor. Don't be daft. He had miles to go, but he reminded himself of how far he had come in just a short period of time. He had defied the French doctor's prognosis many times over, and if he remained focus and determined, he would have himself back on the trajectory of airplane pilot faster than you could say *German Fokker*. It wasn't the case today, nor even tomorrow, but it would happen ... and soon.

<h1 style="text-align:center">Chapter 7</h1>

"Effie, he ain't movin'!" Effie could hear Jacob's voice shake, but there was no time for comfort. She was shuffling around the kitchen, heating water over the cook stove, going through her cupboard, pulling out jars, jugs, and bundles of herbs tied with twine. She loaded Jacob's arms up with potions and salves, doubting anything she had would help but it would at least give Jacob something to do.

"Is he dead'?"

Effie sighed and turned. "He ain't dead, Jacob, but he's bad off. Now keep yo'r wits about yo'rself. I need ..." Effie paused. "Virgil needs to know it's gonna be alright."

"But it ain't alright, Effie!" Jacob whimpered. "He's dyin'!"

Effie placed a wizened, sage hand on his arm. She never was good at sugarcoating. What color that had returned to Jacob's face drained to his feet as he limped into Virgil's room, setting down the miscellaneous burdens he held in his arms at the foot of the bed.

"Come on, Virge." Jacob began rocking his cousin's motionless body. "You know, I got us a shiny new catalog. The kind with all the girls' drawers in it? What'cha say, you and me. Up in the barn loft. You bring the flashlight." Then Jacob leaned into his cousin's ear and whispered, *"Boobies..."* waiting for the boyish giggle that never came.

Neil held up an oil lamp for Effie as she removed her mortar and pestle from the shelf and began cutting up one of the herb bundles into a bowl with a pair of scissors. The strong smell of yarrow floated through the air with each *snip-snip-snip.*

"You know you got a rat?" Jacob asked as he brought the emptied kettle back into the kitchen.

"Yeah. Damned carpetbagger." Effie dripped some oil of clove onto the yarrow, covering the concoction with hot water to steep. "If you see him again, shoot him."

"But that'll put holes in yo'r floor, Effie."

"Don't give a tinker's damn if the floor looks like Swiss cheese. Now fill that kettle and set it to boilin'. We'll need plenty'a hot water. And wood. Can you split us some wood, Jacob? I know yo'r hurt, too."

"I can split wood," Neil offered, but Effie cast a glance at him and shook her head. She wanted to keep Jacob occupied with something other than watching his cousin die. By the look on Neil's face, however, she might have to find something for him to do, too. He'd seen a lot in Mr. Lincoln's War, but to watch a young'un suffer was another thing entirely.

"Yes ma'am. I can split wood," Jacob replied. "Just my foot's stowed up is all."

"Take my gloves there on the hearth," Neil instructed. Jacob hobbled to the back porch, setting to work on the pile of logs. Effie relaxed a bit, as the *critch---critch---critch* of the maul splintering the wood created a gentle rhythm she found oddly comforting. Effie tenderly applied a yarrow and clove poultice over Virgil's ribs, the gentle kneading of her hands sending a sharp, herbal aroma into the air.

"He's in a bad way, Neil. Real bad," Effie declared. The bleeding around the bull's gouges had slowed, but Virgil's color remained grey, the only sound an eerie gurgling from the child's lungs.

Suddenly, Virgil's entire body began to convulse, his little chest heaving high into the air as his fingers and arms drew tight into his body.

"Jesus, Mary and Joseph!" Neil yelled.

"Get a wooden spoon!" Effie cried. Neil flew into the kitchen, nearly toppling Jacob with his armload of wood, before returning to the bedroom. Effie shoved the spoon handle sideways into Virgil's mouth just as another convulsion shook him like an angry evangelist. His good eye shot open then rolled back into his head.

"Leave him be! Just make sure he don't roll off the bed!" Virgil's body flipped and flopped, then as quickly as the seizure had begun, it ceased, easing Virgil back into the lifeless heap he'd been just moments before.

"Brain's swellin'," Effie surmised as she returned to dabbing the balm on Virgil's open wounds. An agitated knock on the back door startled everyone in the room. "Who'n the hell...?"

"Must be Pa," Jacob said with a worried sigh. "He's bound to be missin' us by now." Another series of knocks resounded, followed by a popping noise of the sticky door being prized open.

"Annie?" Jacob exclaimed.

"Jacob, what the devil's goin' on?" Annie queried with her hands placed squarely on her hips. Jacob looked to Effie, then to Neil, then fell against the wall of the bedroom, shaking his head.

"It's Virgil, Annie. I may have killed him. It's all my fault."

Chapter 8

Annie sat beside the wood stove, a mug of chicory in her hand, listening to Jacob relay the night's harrowing events. He'd explained that as he was falling asleep, he'd heard the clanging of their metal gate and looked outside to see a couple of boys with a dog, rounding up the cattle and herding them up the mountain.

"Why didn't you do somethin', Jacob?" She was trying not to make her brother feel worse than he already did, but something about his story just didn't make sense.

"I *tried*," he insisted. "I grabbed my Winchester and ran outside. Had my sights locked on 'em, but then I saw it was Eldridge and Ronnie Rogers."

"Eldridge and Ronnie," Annie repeated. Jacob hung his head. "So you just turned the other cheek, so to speak."

"Yeah, I guess you could say that." A swift *ssssmack* across Jacob's chapped face made him wish he hadn't said that. "Damn it, Annie! What was I s'pose to do? They're my friends!"

"Friends? *Friends?!*" Annie was incensed beyond belief. "Friends don't steal from you, Jacob! You know that's food on our table. How could you?" Annie started to backhand Jacob's other cheek when he grabbed her arm and twisted it around her back, bringing her wrist up to her shoulder blades. Annie dropped to the floor, begging for mercy; but as

Jacob released his grip, his sister wheeled around and kicked him between the legs.

"The two of you quit actin' like fools!" Effie stood in the doorway, her arms akimbo and her eyes shooting fire. "I got enough on my hands without worryin' about y'all killin' one another."

Jacob couldn't breathe, his hands grabbing his crotch as he sought to coax air back into his lungs. Annie turned back to her brother. "You wait here, and don't you move or so help me God, I'll knock yo'r teeth into yo'r eyes."

Annie stood at the foot of Virgil's bed, his body motionless and drool caked in white blotches around his cracked, swollen lips.

"He looks bad," Annie remarked, her voice soft and trembling.

Effie nodded in agreement. "Had him a fit. Must have smashed his head on a rock."

Annie sighed. "What can I do, Effie?"

"You can start by easin' up on yo'r brother. No matter if Virgil lives or dies, Jacob's gonna have a rough time. Ain't no tellin' what yo'r Pa'll do."

Annie nodded and walked back to the stove where her brother sat, head in his hands, sobbing into his torn shirt sleeve. "Jacob. I'm sorry. I had no right..."

"Damn straight you had no right. God a'mighty! Virgil's hanging on by a horse's hair and all you can think about is them damn cows!"

"Well, pardon me all t'hell for thinkin' about our next meal, Jacob!"

"Children!" Effie yelled from Virgil's room. "I ain't gonna tell you again!"

Annie huffed and rolled her eyes. Jacob winched himself to his feet, raising his fist in defiance. "I'll beat the shit outta you if you ever do that again, girl or not." Annie repeated that she was sorry and urged Jacob to finish his account of that night.

He told her the Rogers boys were making trouble out of spite for their daddy ratting out their moonshine still to the law. Jacob said he knew where they were headed and returned to the house to retrieve his jacket. But Virgil was awake and asking questions. That's when he had the bright idea to take Virgil with him. Told him they were going cow tipping. By the time they got to the top of Burnt Shirt, Eldridge and Ronnie were gone, so he decided to just have some fun with Virgil, an idea he now deeply regretted.

"With God as my witness, Annie, I tried to protect him." He pulled at his own tattered shirt, proof that he'd done all that he could. "I pushed. I pulled. I cussed and I shouted, but nothin' I did helped. Nothin'." Jacob began to cry. "That bull's possessed, I tell you. He's the Devil himself!" Jacob dabbed his running nose on his torn sleeve. "If Virgil dies, it's my fault. "All me," he emphasized by pounding the middle of his chest with his fist.

Suddenly, Annie had a thought. Maybe The Turner's might be able to take Virgil into Asheville in that fancy automobile of theirs. There were doctors there. She could see a glimmer of dawn trickling onto the horizon and with it, the tiniest bit of hope.

"Effie!" Annie shouted. "I'm going to The Esmeralda. I'll be back as soon as I can."

"The Esmeralda?" she heard Effie question from the other room. There was no time to explain. Without further response, Annie grabbed her coat and ran out the door.

Annie tried to run down the path, but last night's storm had spread a layer of ice and sleet beneath the knotty roots that were now covered in several inches of snow, making the descent to The Esmeralda most precarious. But the sun was glowing atop the canyon walls. Perhaps this would all melt and be gone by dinnertime.

Some thought the sun glowing against the canyon walls was beautiful, but to her? It was like shining a light through prison bars. She'd had sights on leaving this godforsaken place and making something of herself. She was going to run away with her friend, Birdie, and they were going to become nurses. But that plan had been thwarted when Birdie decided to up and marry Clavel Lyons and have a young'un, though not necessarily in that order.

Annie had never forgiven her. Birdie encouraged her to go on her own, but that wasn't the plan. Birdie's sister was going to pay tuition for them both, and without Birdie, it seemed more like charity than gift. She might be a lot of things, but a scrounger wasn't one of them.

Even if she could afford it, her father was a formidable obstacle. He would hogtie and horsewhip her if she even uttered the thought of getting a formal education.

"Nurses are whores!" he'd shout whenever she'd dared crack the lid on her aspirations.

Her only hope was to marry and leave this hellhole, like Birdie's sister, Lola, but that was a pie-in-the-sky plan, too. How would she ever meet anyone with the means to make her hopes a reality? Every man and boy in this gorge came from subsistence farmer stock, just like hers. And no man from the outside world would dare look twice at her sunburned face, kiss her wind-chapped lips, or hold her calloused hands. Why would they? It seemed that there were just some fences she would never see the other side of. And if Virgil ended up requiring constant care, her fate was sealed for good. She hated that she was being so selfish in her thoughts, but she seemed unable to control them.

As she neared the kitchen entrance of The Esmeralda, she saw Mr. Turner milling about and picked up her pace. A gust of wind pierced straight through her holey coat, stinging her eyes and turning the tips of her fingers purple. Her nose burned and felt as though it would fall off if she rubbed it. In her haste, Annie slipped on the icy back step, cursing as she sprawled flat before the door.

"Annie!" Tom exclaimed. "What in the blue blazes?" Tom extended his hand and pulled her to her feet. "Come in, come in. Your hand's frozen as an icicle."

Annie brushed herself off and followed Tom into the kitchen where the heat began to thaw her chilled bones.

"Are you alright, Dear? You look frightful!"

"It's Virgil, Mr. Turner," she cried. "That bull of Pa's gored him ... real bad. I was wonderin' if you could carry him to a doctor?"

"Annie, that's terrible!" Tom exclaimed as a defeated expression drifted across his face. "I wish I could help, but I don't believe a car would make it up the mountain in this weather." Annie hung her head in despair.

Then Tom had an idea. "I think I can do you one better, though. We have a physician staying with us. Got here just last night before the storm hit. His name is Dr. Middleton. Perhaps he would take a look at Virgil."

"Oh, would you ask him for me?"

"Of course, of course. I haven't met him myself yet, as I was out last evening when he and his family arrived, but Mattie says that he is a most kind man. I have no doubt he would be willing."

"Thank you, Mr. Turner. Thank you so much!" Tom asked her to sit at the kitchen while he went to wake the doctor. Mattie overheard their conversation from the front desk and fetched a cup of coffee, coming to sit beside Annie in an effort to calm her jangled nerves. Annie provided Mattie with all the harrowing details, or at least as much as she knew.

A short time later, a stout older gentleman with graying hair and a burgundy velvet robe tied loose around his waist appeared with Tom close behind him.

"Annie, I'm Dr. Middleton. Mr. Turner tells me you have a bit of a situation on your hands. Can you tell me a bit more?"

Dr. Middleton sat in a vacant chair across from Annie as she explained Virgil's condition as best she could. He mumbled a few, "I sees," and several "uh-huhs", but for the most part, he just listened. When she described the gurgling sounds coming from Virgil's lungs, Dr. Middleton winced.

"Well, it sounds as if I may be very limited in what I can do for the young child. I would normally recommend transport to one of the larger cities, such as you are suggesting." Annie nodded. "However, given the weather has made such travel practically impossible," Lymas added, looking to Tom and Mattie, "I will do what I can. Is Virgil at your place, Annie?"

"No sir. He's at our neighbor's. Effie. Effie Buchanan."

"And how far is this Effie Buchanan's?"

"It's just up the path," Annie pointed towards the window which looked out on the trail she had just traipsed down.

Tom spoke up. "It's about a mile's walk, but this snow will make walking difficult."

Annie was quick to ask, "Could we borrow a couple of horses?"

"I was just about to suggest the same thing," he replied. "Annie serves as our stable hand from time to time if we are out of town," Tom explained to Lymas with a smile. "She's quite talented with the horses." Annie blushed and turned her head. She wasn't used to compliments.

"Well, a horse it shall be then!" Lymas agreed.

Suddenly, a new voice accosted her senses from the hallway of the inn.

"Did someone say something about a horse? You'll pardon me if I don't get too excited."

Annie looked up to see a dashing young man standing just inside the doorway behind Mr. Turner. He was probably a head taller, but was leaning to one side on a crutch, making it hard to say for certain. A wary grin hung from his protruding cheekbones like a chain suspended between two fenceposts. His fiery red hair lay dutifully across his crown and forehead, save for a slight cowlick in the back that was reminiscent of a cock's comb. Despite the tense nature of her mood, she had to suppress a giggle. The gentleman nodded to her as their eyes held one another's, albeit for a brief few seconds.

"Trevor! I did not expect you up so early," Dr. Middleton announced. "Please, please. Come in and meet our neighbor. Miss Annie ... uh, Annie ... Oh dear. I fear I did not get your last name."

"Annie Conner," she offered as she stood with her hand extended.

It took Trevor a moment to cross the distance between them then balance his weight on the crutch, leaving Annie's hand dangling in the air for an awkward moment. Was she supposed to offer her hand first, or at all? Good grief. They'd only spent an hour or so on proper manners in school. She could not remember what her teacher had said about such things.

"Trevor Middleton," the gentleman said with a slight nod as he took her hand and squeezed it, just the right amount, before placing a light kiss on top of it. "I apologize for the delay. It would seem the only thing slower than my wits is my step."

Annie snickered, Trevor's hand still in her grip. "Oh, dear. I am so sorry," she said as she let his hand drop back to his side. "It appears I ain't, er uh, I am not altogether myself."

"Annie's cousin has been injured in a farm accident and she wishes for me to attend to him," the doctor explained. "Would you like to accompany me, Trevor? I could use your assistance. I must tell you, however, it will involve riding a horse."

After a momentary, internal debate, Trevor responded, "I … I think, well, if you think it's advisable, I could give it a go."

Lymas turned to Annie and explained. "Trevor drove an ambulance in France and was helping clear a road when he was severely injured … by a horse."

"Oh, I see," Annie replied, casting her eyes back to Trevor. He swayed and shifted about on his crutch, his hand clutching it a bit tighter than necessary. She could that the prospect of mounting a horse made him quite nervous.

"Yes, Uncle. I overheard the bit about the horse. But I decided last evening that I was not going to allow my situation, or my fears, to dictate my recovery, and if getting back on the horse is what is required…both literally and metaphorically, then I believe this would be a most worthy opportunity."

"Well then, it's settled," Tom acknowledged. "Annie, do you need help saddling the horses?"

"No, Mr. Turner. I'll be fine. And I'll lead Trevor's horse, on foot. That is, if yo'r agreeable," she queried, looking back into Trevor's haunting blue eyes.

"It will lessen my angst to have such an expert guide," Trevor said with a slight bow. Annie felt her cheeks flush. Then she remembered her cousin lying on his death bed and felt guilty for allowing such feelings to overtake her. Then again, it would serve Virgil no good purpose for her to rend her clothes and wear ashes. Even so, she felt conflicted and began to fidget.

"We really must hurry," Annie declared, shaking herself from her momentary daydream. "I'll meet y'all around back. Just outside," tilting her head toward the kitchen door. "You'll want a heavy jacket. It's colder than a frog's ass."

She was certain she heard Trevor snicker. God, she must try and not be such a bumpkin!

"I'll be waiting," Trevor said with a smile.

She certainly hoped so.

Chapter 9

Trevor could see Annie waiting in the gusty wind, clutching her coat tight around her. She was now wearing a hat that she must have found in the stables. She alternated between fussing and pulling at the leather straps and blowing into her hands to warm them. Did the girl not own any gloves? Perhaps she forgot them in her haste to come for help.

Tethered to a hitching post, just a few feet away, stood two horses; one a dark brown in color and looking for all the world as if it could fall asleep right where it stood. The other, a cream-colored specimen, seemed a bit more anxious, snorting and pawing at the gathering snow.

Trevor could sympathize. What sounded like a good idea now seemed rash and self-indulgent. He then reminded himself he was doing this at his uncle's behest, though Trevor doubted his uncle needed his help. Even so, it provided him with motivation to do something other than wallow in self-pity and the murky mire of "what-ifs". If he could get on the horse, and stay on, without his body or his fears careening over the edge, then he would have accomplished something – though what exactly, he couldn't be sure.

Reading his mind, Lymas stood beside him with a steady hand on his shoulder. "Are you sure you're up for this?"

"No, Uncle. I am not. But I will never be sure of myself again if I don't push past my limitations. So let's be on our way, shall we?"

Lymas nodded in agreement. "You know your father will have us strung up by our toenails."

"Well, he'll have to catch me on that gallant steed first," Trevor laughed, pointing out the window to the sleeping horse. This simple act elicited a sharp twinge in his ribcage – a reminder his leg wasn't the only part of his body that was still recovering.

"I assume you know how'ta mount a horse, Dr. Middleton?" Annie asked as they stepped outside. Lymas said he did. "Good then. I'll leave you to it. Trevor, wait here at the bottom of the steps."

With that, Annie grabbed the reins of the chocolate-colored horse and led it to the porch.

"This is Coffee," Annie said. "Stroke his nose. He likes that." Trevor did as he was told. So far so good. "He's as easy a-goin' horse as you'll ever ride."

Well, there was some good news. Even so, his head began to spin with thoughts of all the horrible things that could go wrong.

"I'm not sure how I'm going to do this," Trevor admitted. "My going along probably is a bad idea." His hands were trembling, and it wasn't from the cold. *Dammit.*

"It's not what *yo'r* gonna do," Annie said with a knowing grin. "It's what *he's* gonna do."

With that, Annie tapped Coffee's belly. Trevor stared in amazement as the steed bowed his head then knelt on his front legs. Annie then touched his hindquarters, prompting Coffee to fully lay down on top of the frosty snow. Coffee drew in a breath of air and let it out slowly, a thick fog from his nostrils lifting before Trevor's eyes.

"There you go, Trevor. Easy as flies to a pie. Now just climb aboard."

Trevor straddled the horse, using his crutch to balance himself, certain that at any moment, the horse would spook, flinging him high into the snow-laden canopy.

"Let Coffee do all the work," and with that, Annie patted the horse's belly once more, for which the horse gently rose, first on his front legs then his rear, seating Trevor neatly in the saddle.

"Well done, Trevor!" Lymas cheered from atop his horse, bringing his ride alongside Coffee. The two horses nuzzled, their affections for one another conveying a fondness that Trevor found both comforting and annoying.

"Dr. Middleton, your horse's name's Cream. She and Coffee are sweet on each other."

Coffee and Cream, Trevor thought to himself. *How quaint.* Trevor then noted that Lymas was carrying his medical bag in front of him instead of storing its contents in the saddlebag. He supposed it was too bulky.

"I'm gonna lead us up the trail for a bit, then take off onto the road. It's a bit longer, but the horses'll make better time."

"We trust your expertise, Annie. Whatever you believe is best," Lymas responded with another cautious glance towards his nephew.

"Good. I'll move ahead with Coffee here and Cream will follow. And let me take that," Annie said as she reached up to relieve Lymas of his medical bag. "You'll wanna hold on with both hands." That reminded Trevor - Annie had no gloves.

"Annie, would you like to borrow my gloves?" Trevor asked, his now bare hands outstretched. Annie turned her face upwards, considering this offer far more than Trevor deemed necessary.

"No," she said rather curtly. "I'm fine." Had he offended her? His offer was born out of gentlemanly grace, not charity, but he must remember that chivalry and good manners weren't always the same thing.

The first quarter mile or so on the trail, Trevor was a bundle of nerves. But soon, the gentle rhythm of Coffee's haunches began to relax the tension in his neck and shoulders, settling his jagged nerves. Had it not been for the ache in his knee, he believed he could have fallen asleep. When Coffee stepped into a snow-covered hole, however, it brought Trevor back to the reality that he was still in a precarious state. Coffee seemed none too thrilled about situation, either.

"Woah now, Coffee. Steady boy." Annie halted the two horses and patted Coffee's nose. "There's lotsa ruts and holes in these roads and paths," she explained. "Damned loggin' companies."

"Logging companies?" Lymas echoed.

"Yep. They've sawed half this mountain down and used our roads like they were their own. Our wagon wheels get all marred up in those ruts.

One of our horses broke its leg here awhile back. We had to put her down." Trevor believed he could have done without *that* particular piece of information. "Everybody doin' okay now?" Annie questioned. "It's not much further."

Lymas said he was just fine, and while Trevor tried to sound equally confident, the tremor in his voice suggested otherwise.

For the next bit, Trevor decided to mentally tick off things he could see, feel, and hear. He believed it a good exercise to distract his mind from its daily litany of woes. A cardinal called to his mate, *Pretty bird, Pretty bird, Pretty Bird,* as a pair of wrens chased a crow away from its nest. A nuthatch *yank-yank-yanked* up and down the side of a Hickory Nut Tree while two grey squirrels raced around its base. Above him, he could see patches of blue sky as the growing wind flung white blobs of snow from the arms of the Jack Pines. One landed on Coffee's nose, causing the horse to shake his head and scatter a cold spray across Trevor's chilled face. The forest was incredibly beautiful – a stark contrast from his six months in France seeing charred trees, bumping along bombed out roads, his hearing under the constant barrage of shellfire.

As Trevor relaxed, he decided to initiate some light conversation. "You seem to know a lot about horses."

Annie looked back towards Trevor's voice and raised her shoulders in indifference.

"I s'pose. When it's all you got..." Her pace had become more cautious since Coffee's misstep into the hole. At the very thought, his knee began to throb as though a knife were being driven into it.

"Here we are." Annie pointed her chin towards an old, dilapidated house that looked as though the slightest breeze could flatten it. The disparity between the poshness of The Esmeralda and the poverty that existed just a short mile away shook his head clear of the pain he had been feeling the past several minutes. He shuddered to think of the scene that lay just on the other side of those thin, fragile walls.

Annie led both riders up to a hitching post, where Lymas climbed off his horse and extended his hand towards Annie's. "I'll take that bag from you now, my dear," Lymas said in that tender manner Trevor always found such a comfort. He hoped his uncle would be able to provide more than comfort here today.

Placing the medical bag in his uncle's hands, Trevor noted a misty reflection in Annie's eyes.

"I hope you got a miracle stashed away in that bag, Dr. Middleton. Yo'r gonna need it."

Chapter 10

Annie paced the floor until there was a well-worn path where the hem of her skirt had pushed accumulated dirt and mud into a dusty wake. Dr. Middleton and Trevor were in the room with Effie behind a closed door, giving Virgil a thorough going over. She tried to listen in through the wall with a mason jar glued to her ear, but the doctor had said little aloud save a few muffled humms and I sees, just like he had at The Esmeralda. She heard him ask Effie if Virgil had suffered any more seizures and if so, how far apart they'd been, but he'd offered nothing more. It was maddening.

Adding to her anxiety was worry about their mother. She'd encouraged Jacob to go check on her, but he'd said that their Pa was probably still around, his circuit riding most likely being delayed by the storm. It was clear Jacob feared the worst from their father and was delaying the inevitable as long as possible.

Perhaps it was another convenient excuse, but Jacob had volunteered to take Trevor to Effie's barn to warm up the horses and give them some feed. Neil, seeing nothing he could do inside the house, had accompanied them.

Pressing her forehead against the windowpane, a deluge of tears plunged onto her apron. If Virgil lived, there was no doubt she would bear the burden of care. Since her stroke, her mother, Ida, was barely able to take care of herself, and her Pa? She could hear him now, quoting scripture from the Bible and explaining, through those holy verses, that taking care of Virgil and her mother was a woman's work. His mind must be free of such encumbrances in order to lead his flock, and that Annie should be proud God had chosen her for such duties.

If only Myrtle was here. The day after Virgil's daddy, Uncle Phipp, had died, his wife, Myrtle left. Just like that. Said she was going to the old home place in South Carolina to see family and set up somewhere for them to live. Said she'd send for Virgil when she got settled, and would the Conner's look after him 'til she got back?

Last thing anyone saw of Aunt Myrtle was her rather large backside climbing aboard that stagecoach bound for Rutherfordton. That was one year ago, and no one had seen hide nor hair of her since. Any and all letters sent asking for her whereabouts had been met with tomblike silence. Annie wondered if Myrtle knew of her son's predicament, would she come back to care for him? Isn't that what a mother did? Not Myrtle, apparently. Sometimes Annie wished she had that sort of reckless abandon. Just to leave and never look back.

Through the bubbled windowpane, the tall, straight trunks of the Jack Pines refracted into bowing forms – evil spirits concocting spells of doom. Their shadows locked arms and formed prison-like bars that continued their threat. She would be their captive … forever.

Out of the corner of her eye, Annie could see Jacob and Neil ambling back from the barn up to Effie's front porch, with Trevor tottering along on his crutch.

Once at the door, Trevor straightened himself, removed his hat and ran a hand through his red, tousled hair. He was a tall blade of grass, compared to the boys she knew at least. When he came inside and removed his coat, she could see his pink shirt was spun from silk and his trousers, though dabbed with mud, spoke of connections to a family of well-to-dos. Annie straightened her own hair and tugged at her dress, finding herself most ill at ease in an odd, giddy sort of way. Jacob cut a suspicious look at her, then turned his gaze back towards the bedroom where Virgil lay.

Just as Annie was about to make polite conversation with their guest, the door to Virgil's room opened. Doctor Middleton motioned for everyone to join him at the kitchen table, but Effie remained behind, sitting with

Virgil on his bed, mumbling words Annie could not quite make out as the old woman stroked her cousin's forehead.

Effie's farm table served as a dining, butchering, and herb chopping station – depending on the most immediate need. Annie could smell the aroma of yarrow, arnica, and comfrey that Effie had chopped the night before rising from it like a prayer. She breathed a prayer herself - that all Effie's efforts had not been in vain.

Jacob and Neil joined Annie to her right, Neil placing one calloused hand on her shoulder and the other on her brother's. Trevor stood before the stove, giving the family some space and privacy.

"Annie and Jacob, I understand you are Virgil's next of kin." They both nodded. "Now, I would prefer that your father be here, but I also understand that might, uh…" Lymas cleared his throat, "…not be possible, so I am relying on you both to convey this information to him. Are you alright with that?"

"Yes, Dr. Middleton. I am more than capable." Jacob didn't respond but that was just as well. Annie could feel her pulse quicken and a stabbing pain begin deep inside her gut. Lymas's lips curled in a polite but nervous smile.

"You are indeed most capable, Annie. And so are you, Jacob. I know you care about Virgil a great deal."

"Please," Jacob encouraged. "Tell me … tell us … Virge is gonna be okay."

"Well, here it is, the difficult truth of it. Virgil has suffered multiple, very serious injuries. He has a punctured lung, which has now caused the other to enlarge, making it work harder than it should. That in and of itself would be difficult but not impossible to overcome, but he also has a punctured kidney, broken ribs, and a head injury. I also suspect that one of his legs has been broken in multiple places. The brain injury is what is causing the seizures. With every convulsion, he loses a little more of his ability to think. To just be … Virgil."

"So…so…" Jacob stuttered. "Are you saying Virgil's gonna die?"

Lymas frowned and lifted his shoulders. "More than likely, and if I may be blunt, it would be a blessing." Dr. Middleton's eyes darted back and forth between the two siblings then to Neil. "If he lives, he will most likely be little more than what he is right now. Another seizure might take him, but then he could live in this state indefinitely." Annie glanced into Virgil's room and saw Effie stroking Virgil's hair, greasy from sweat, compresses, and the various sundry ointments she had been applying night and day. Dr. Middleton followed her eyes then carried on with his assessment.

"Ms. Buchanan has done everything one could possibly do. Effie is an amazing woman. The fact Virgil has survived this long is a testament to what great care he has been given." Annie heard a sniff and looked up to see tears spilling down Neil's cheek, catching in his peppered-gray beard.

"I ... I don't know what to say, Dr. Middleton." Annie's own tears now poured as the doctor handed her a soft, clean handkerchief. Jacob shook beside her, his knees knocking so hard she believed her brother would fold into the floor like egg yolks. She looked to see Trevor gazing at them with a look that conveyed both compassion and pity.

"I would suggest moving him to your place, Annie. When the weather allows. That's his home. He might feel more comfortable there and could make some recovery."

"Some?" Annie questioned.

"Yes, though minimal at best. It's a difficult pill to swallow, no doubt. But I have seen miracles. I have declared women dead on Saturday and seen them cooking Sunday supper. I've sworn men would never walk again one day and watched them plow fields of corn under the next week. I remember being called to a child's house in the morning, the young boy burning up with fever and screaming with a headache so loud I thought my ears would explode, only to find him playing on his mother's knee that night. It happens, but not often, and this is the worst condition I have ever had the displeasure to assess." He glanced at Trevor as though he meant to convey some lesson, some point, between them.

"If I may be blunt, Ms. Buchanan does not look well herself. I understand she has had little sleep since Virgil was brought here. She can't hold up under this strain much longer, regardless of her insistence to the contrary." Dr. Middleton leaned towards the middle of the table and whispered, *"Like me, she's no spring chicken."* Annie smiled and shook her head in agreement. "I also realize your personal situation is not ideal but perhaps once Virgil is home, everyone will pitch in to help."

Neil was next to speak. "Dr. Middleton, I could take Virgil with me..."

"And that is most gracious of you, sir, but it truly doesn't solve anything. Everyone needs to return to as much normalcy as possible. If Virgil is at your place, it still remains that one sole caretaker is bearing the vast majority of the burden, and I have seen it much too often." Dr. Middleton tapped his knuckles upon the table to emphasize. "It is usually the caretaker who gets the undertaker."

An air of defeat and shock filled the air. Annie had hoped for better news, but she wasn't surprised by any of Dr. Middleton's words. She glanced towards the woodstove once more to find that Trevor had disappeared. Something about having this handsome stranger around had distracted her, and without his presence, she felt the full weight of sorrow fall across her shoulders.

"In the meantime, I have told Ms. Buchanan I will be in the area for the next several months. I will see what connections can be made in Asheville or another nearby city – to inquire as to a doctor who could offer another opinion - but I honestly do not see what anyone else could do." Grief now gave way to panic as Annie realized her worst nightmare was coming true. If Virgil lived, she would die. She would have to remain in The Gorge ... forever.

Jacob buried his head deep inside his folded arms as Annie shot up from the table and marched over to a pot of soup that had been simmering on the stove. She lifted the cast iron lid then slammed it back down. Seeing an opened sack of flour, she grabbed a handful and flung the flour into a bowl, covering herself and most of the kitchen in a spray of snowy white. Pouring some salt out in her hand, she tossed that into the pot. She then grabbed a worn-out wooden spoon and began to stir the soup with a bit more exuberance than necessary, which snapped the utensil in two. Annie lobbed the splintered pieces across the room, sending a slurry of turnips, tomatoes, and beans against the wall.

Neil moved to comfort her but she screamed, "Leave me alone!" and raced down the porch steps and into the woods, nearly knocking Trevor off his crutch where he stood at the corner of the porch smoking a cigarette.

Just when she thought life could not be any worse, fate reared its ugly head and said, "Think again."

Annie peeked out from behind the rotting woodshed that drooped at the edge of Effie's backyard. She realized that she'd looked the fool in front of the doctor and his nephew. What they must be thinking of her right now! She dried her tears on her arm sleeve and smiled as she watched the woodhens tear a hole into an oak tree stump, preparing for their spring clutch. As her breathing slowed and her weeping subsided, she homed in on Trevor. He was leant back against the house in seeming deep thought, the glow of his dwindling cigarette pulsing in the late morning light.

Annie propped herself against a used-up whiskey barrel and contemplated what she was going to do. She supposed nothing. At least nothing different than what circumstances had placed upon her. Then again, she shouldn't be racing to conclusions about anything. Virgil *could* make a full recovery. Even the doctor had said he'd seen miracles. Effie was always telling her, *Annie, don't go bleedin' before yo'r cut!* She would have to pull herself together and act like she had the sense God gave her.

Annie looked back towards the porch, allowing her mind to wander. Trevor was quite handsome and despite his injuries, which she still must inquire about, he seemed nice. And he was funny, which to her was a sign of good smarts. She wondered what it would be like to have someone to lean on in times such as these. Someone to make her laugh – to make her feel as though she wasn't bearing these burdens all alone.

Suddenly, such innocent thoughts turned to wilder imaginings. She could see them sitting on one of those big wide porch swings, like the one at The Esmeralda, sipping mint juleps and discussing world events as reported in the papers. He would ask her thoughts about President Wilson, and she would feign boredom as she cooled herself with a lace fan. As the heat of day and their bodies rose, they would cool their lust within the shelter of their bedroom, teasing and tickling one another as they rolled and tumbled on silk sheets and rose petals.

Good Lord, what was she thinking?! Virgil was lying on his death bed just a stone's throw away, and all she could think about was a roll in the hay with this man she didn't even know. Heat flushed into her cheeks, spreading into other parts of her body. She felt a mantle of shame fall upon her, but the harder she tried to push these naughty notions out of her mind, the faster they came. She then decided there was nothing to be ashamed of. If she couldn't flee this canyon prison in a literal sense, then she could at least escape it in her mind.

From her vantage point just behind the shed, she took in a long look at this Trevor boy, allowing her fantasies to roam, untamed. She'd been waiting for someone to waltz into this gorge and take her far, far away. Maybe this was the chance she'd been waiting for – the answer to her prayers. But if she'd learned one thing about this life, it was that prayers were merely seeds, and those seeds needed tending and watering to bloom. Her Pa preached of miracles, but she'd never seen a miracle – not one without some intention behind it.

Intention. That's what she'd been lacking. She could see it all so clearly now.

Chapter 11

Neil stepped onto the porch and sidled up beside Trevor, puffing on a clay pipe that filled the air around them with the scent of cherrywood. Trevor tossed the butt of his cigarette into the melting snow, hearing it sizzle, and acknowledged the old man with a nod of his head. The two men continued their gaze out into the woods as Neil rocked back and forth from toe to heel.

"That girl," he mumbled, the pipe clenched tight between his teeth.

"Well, to be fair," Trevor began, "she's probably feeling a lot of emotions right now." Hell, *he* was feeling a lot of emotions. "Sounds like she'll be the caregiver and I'm sure that's the last thing she wants, with her whole life ahead of her.

Neil nodded. "Eeee-yep."

"She's a beautiful girl. Seems pretty smart, too. If these circumstances hadn't come about, she could probably do well for herself."

"Prob'ly," Neil concurred.

"So what's the story with her family?"

"Ah, well, that story's a long one, but the short of it is her father's a bat-shit crazy preacher man. Her mother had a stroke givin' birth to a child who was stillborn, so Annie's been the backbone of that family ever since she could reach the stove. Lester put the brakes on her schoolin' 'cause he thinks education's the Devil. You can pretty much make up what you want to fill in the gaps and it wouldn't be far from the truth."

"What about Jacob?"

Neil motioned his head inside the house towards the boy, who had not lifted his head from the kitchen table since landing there. "He's a good kid. But there'll be never-ending hell to pay for Virgil's accident. That Lester Conner is one sum'bitch."

Neil puffed on his pipe, sending wisps of smoke into the air that rose towards the frothy-white train of clouds barreling across the sky. The sun's rays were now reaching towards the ground, melting the snow at a feverish pace. Large drops of water dripped from the corners of the old house, making puddles where a robin and few intrepid bees gathered to drink.

The old man pulled his pocket watch out of his worn-out jacket and called out. "Annie Grace, where are you?"

Trevor raised up on his crutch and craned his neck. From behind the woodshed, he thought he saw the hem of her skirt – a brief flash of pinks and reds. He could understand her needing some space to breathe. Despite the circumstances that brought him here, he was grateful to be outside in the fresh mountain air.

It reminded him that Wallace was most likely stewing back at The Esmeralda and he began to dread what he and his uncle might face, although he was becoming more and more uncomfortable being here. He felt very out of place.

"I'm coming, Neil!" Annie's feet snapped twigs and acorn hulls beneath her as she made her way towards the house. Neil edged up beside Trevor and leaned in, speaking low but clear.

"May be none of my business but man to man, let me give you some advice." Trevor squinted at the graybeard, unsure of what possible guidance he could have for *him* at this precise moment. "A wildcat trapped in a cage usually comes out scratchin'."

"I'm not sure I understand," Trevor replied.

Neil looked him square in the eyes. "Yo'r a handsome young man, and she's a beautiful young woman. These canyon walls can make a soul feel like there's nothing else in this whole wide world."

Trevor began to sense an unwanted lecture coming, and though Neil's intentions were pure, Trevor was in no mood to hear it. He had received enough unsolicited advice to do him a lifetime.

Even so, the old man pressed on. "I mean, I love that girl like she's one of my own. She's had a hard life, and it's gonna get harder. But because she *ain't* mine, I can see things others cain't, or won't. You catch my meanin'?"

"Maybe, but not really," Trevor managed to reply.

"Just watch yo'rself, ya hear?"

Neil met Annie at the bottom of the porch steps, gathering her up in a wide embrace. She glanced in Trevor's direction, then buried her face deep inside Neil's jacket. Trevor could smell applewood tobacco, warmed by Annie's breath, rising from the pocket where Neil stowed his pipe. Jacob now crouched inside the house, one arm leaning against the door jam and the other, limp by his side.

"They God Almighty, Annie, you'd think yo'r the one who got gored by a bull," Jacob taunted.

Annie snapped her head up and pushed Neil to the side. "And what is that supposed to mean?" she shouted as she marched up the steps and stood nose to nose with Jacob.

"It means just what I said. All this wailin' and moanin' and groanin' ain't gonna change a thing. I say we bundle Virgil up and carry him home. Like the doctor said."

"I don't like it," she said, pointing a critical finger in his direction.

"I didn't say you had to like it. I'm sayin' we sometimes have to do things we *don't* like, and this is one of 'em." Jacob grabbed her finger and bent it backwards, causing her to yelp. "And don't ever point that finger of yours at me!"

Annie shook her hand up and down, trying to get the feeling back where Jacob's grip had cut off the blood. Trevor took in a breath to intervene, then thought better of it, taking a couple of cautious steps backwards.

"I just don't see how that's gonna work," Annie whined. "Ma cain't take care of Virgil. She can barely take care of herself, and you know Pa ain't gonna do *shit.*"

"That's the point, Annie," Jacob countered. "Ma needs our help, too, and we cain't do for 'em both with Virge bein' here. It ain't fair to ask Effie to take on anything else. This is my doin' and I intend to do right by it."

"You know Pa will never agree to you takin' care of him. He'll double yo'r chores just to make a point. He'll say, 'That's a woman's work,' and then I'll be left to do all the feedin' and butt wipin'!"

Effie suddenly appeared along with Dr. Middleton. "Enough!" she shouted, leveling her hands in front of her. "We got plenty a'trouble goin' round without the two of you spreadin' it like manure!" Annie and Jacob looked back and forth between each other, unsure of what to do or say next. It wasn't like Effie to say *manure* instead of *shit*. "Ain't gonna make no never mind anyway," Effie mumbled as she cast a slide glance towards Uncle Lymas.

"Why's that, Effie?" Jacob asked.

Effie looked Jacob square in the eye as a tear rolled down her cheek. "'Cause Virgil's dead, that's why."

Dogwood Winter

*I saw a woman sitting on a red beast
that had names insulting to God written all over it.
The woman was dressed in purple and scarlet... .*

Revelation 17:3-4 (GNT)

Chapter 12

Jacob ran inside the house like he'd been set on fire. A loud wailing rose from the bedroom that sent Neil scuttling after him. Uncertain as to what he should do, Trevor decided to stay put and out of the way. His uncle joined him, arms folded, head down.

"Oh, God. *NOOoooooo! Virgil. VIRGIL!* Wake-up. *WAKE-UP!*" Popping sounds from Jacob's hand slapping against his cousin's cooling cheeks ricocheted throughout the house. "It's me...Jacob. Hey, man! You...you...you cain't leave. Who's gonna squeeze them cows' tits, Cuz!" Jacob erupted in nervous laughter. "Come on, Virgil. *Quit fuckin' around!*"

Annie ran after her brother, pleading for him to stop. Jacob shoved her off and climbed into bed, rocking Virgil as he sobbed into his sandy, blonde curls.

"God's punishin' me!" Jacob wailed, over and over. "No, God. No. No. Please. I'll do anything. Please, Virge. Come back to me, man. Come back...'

"Jacob, stop!" Annie screamed. "He's dead!" Annie wrapped her arms around her brother, but he pushed her off, clutching Virgil tighter, swaying and howling so loud the glass globe in the oil lamp began to vibrate.

Trevor had heard the shrieks of men when their comrades died; men who were left to bury bodies when sometimes they, themselves, lacked arms or legs to do so. It was heart-wrenching – something he never got used to. He supposed no one ever did. Some of the driver's claimed they were numb to it, but he never found it possible.

That's why, when he returned to France, it would be as a pilot. In the air, he wouldn't have to hear the death rattles and the moans of the maimed and dying. And he'd stand a chance at ending the goddamned war instead of perpetuating it.

"Perhaps we should go," Lymas whispered. Trevor concurred as they made their way inside to extend their condolences and take their leave.

"Y'all leavin'?" Annie asked, a hint of panic in her voice.

"We should be on our way," Lymas said with a nod. "You need your privacy."

Effie stepped up and wrapped her arms around Annie. "I am much obliged by yo'r assistance, Dr. Middleton, but you should be gettin' on down the mountain. We'll be just fine."

Annie began tapping her disagreement on the buckled wood floor. "Effie! Who's gonna wash Virgil and lay him out? He's my *cousin!* It ain't fittin'!"

"Bah! That ain't the doctor's job. Have you lost yo'r damn mind?" Effie scolded. "Go tend to yo'r Ma if yo'r so consarned worried about what's *fittin'.* That poor woman's been left alone in that house worried sick about where her children are. And it's a two-bit wonder yo'r Pa ain't down here already, raisin' the Devil. Somebody needs to keep him outta my hair." Annie looked as though she'd been slapped. "'Sides. I got Neil here to help, if you all the sudden got some bashful burr stuck up yo'r ass."

"But Effie, I cain't.."

"*Enough!* I cain't take it anymore!" Jacob screamed from Effie's kitchen, holding his head between his hands as he ran out of the house, stopping at the bottom of the porch steps. Jacob pounded his fists into his thighs and howled, "Virgil's dead! *DEAD!* And there ain't no amount of arguin' gonna change that!"

Jacob wiped his running nose on his shirt sleeve. "They God Almighty. I'm snibblin' like a girl." The boy took a deep breath, trying to gather at least some of his wits. "I'm gonna go ring the church bell. Not that anybody cares." Jacob hobbled onto the path that led up the mountain.

Everyone froze - the awkward silence holding them to their places like nails. Finally, Annie spoke up. "Effie, did you stop the clock?"

"'Course I did." Trevor looked up at the clock on the mantel and confirmed that the pendulum was no longer swinging, the hands on the clock indicating Virgil had died at 11:30 in the morning. Neil moved over to Effie, kissing her gently on the cheek as he pulled her close to his side. Trevor saw her tense then relax. She didn't seem the type who gave, or accepted, physical emotion easily. But that didn't mean she wasn't comforted by it.

"Well, then. Shall we?" Lymas queried with a gentle nudge to Trevor's back. The two men donned their jackets and moved towards the door as Annie gathered herself up in a shawl and wrapped it loosely around her shoulders.

"Annie, where're you goin'" There was a coldness in Effie's tone that stopped all three of them.

"I gotta lead Trevor and Doctor Middleton back down the mountain," Annie answered with a bit of irritation. "To The Esmeralda. Remember, the horses?"

"I'd forgot about them horses," Effie admitted. "Alright, but after that, go straight home."

"What else would I do, Effie?" Annie scowled.

"Bah. Nothin', I don't reckon," she said with a dismissive wave of her hand. But as she turned Trevor heard her whisper under her breath.

"I just got this feelin'..."

Chapter 13

With Trevor and Lymas gone, Effie and Neil went to work preparing Virgil's body. She worried about Jacob going off by himself, but she had to admit it was a relief having the house mostly to herself.

That boy. He'd always had a hankering for the dramatic although this time, she figured, he was entitled. He would blame himself for the boy's death the rest of his life. Lester could be counted on to heap his own guilt onto his son, and whether Jacob was conscious of that fact or not, she knew it was weighing heavy on some part of his mind.

As for Annie, well, that was another story. No doubt that child was traumatized, too, but Effie knew her all too well. She could see the cogs inside that brain of hers smoking and could venture a real good guess as to where her scheming ways were taking her. She'd bet the leaky roof over her head that girl was conjuring up a storm. Effie'd told Annie a hundred times, when she would start daydreaming of a life outside The Gorge, she just had to be patient. Her day would come, but Annie couldn't see it. At sixteen she thought she was thirty-six. She always talked about running away – of meeting someone who would steal her off into the pitch-black night. Effie told her to run towards a thing, not from it, but Annie never seemed to understand.

The clanging of the church bell tore Effie away from her ponderings. It rang seven times – once for each year of little Virgil's life. Something about that deep, metal clang bore a sense of finality that made her shiver. Like up until now, Virgil might leap back to life.

She'd have to hurry. In about the time it took to throw a pie in the oven or a pot of beans on the stove, the entire community would congregate at her house for tedious hours upon end. Maybe Neil and Jacob could take Virgil's body back home. That was where he belonged, and as much as Effie loved the boy, she wanted her house back to herself. She was exhausted. She'd probably aged ten years since Neil brought Virgil to her.

Effie reached into her herb pantry and pulled down a vial of camphor along with a soft, white rag. Neil placed a bowl of warmed water from the stove and sat it alongside Virgil's head, into which Effie poured the camphor and steeped the rag. Neil wrang it out and placed it on Virgil's placid face, his young lips curling up in what appeared to be a smile – the pain of his injuries no longer dragging down the corners into a frown. The medicinal, sweet smell of rosemary and cinnamon rose through the air as it soaked into the cornhusks deep inside the pillow tick mattress below. A strange sense of peace fell over the house, the ritual of tending to Virgil's body becoming a soothing act of kindness that benefited both the living as well as the dead. Just then, Neil looked up towards the edge of the forest.

"They Lord God Almighty." Effie followed Neil's eyes and cursed.

Through the bubbled glass window, Effie saw Lester and his black horse riding down the trail, the fires of Hell burning a path before him. As quick as her twisted toes would allow, Effie shuffled back to the bedroom where she covered Virgil's body up with the last good sheet she owned and found two buffalo nickels in the drawer beside the bed to place over his eyes, just as Lester barged into her kitchen.

"I've come to take Virgil home," Lester barked.

"Funny you weren't too keen on takin' him home when he was alive," Effie fired back. Neil strode into the room, planting himself firmly by her side.

"You old crone! I was out doin' the Lord's work! Not that you would know anything about that." Lester paused and gave a derisive chuckle. "But I heard the church bell and knew God had called my young'un home and I'm here to see he gets a proper burial."

"Suit yo'rself, Lester. I just find yo'r timing to be quite self-serving. None of the guts and all the glory, so to speak."

Lester hissed as he tramped into the bedroom, scooping up Virgil's limp body; the nickels clanking against one another as they rolled along the sloped floor, coming to rest against a pile of pumpkin seed hulls.

Neil shook his head and called out. "We were just preparing his body, Lester. Won't you let us help you and Ida?"

"You think I cain't take care'a my own?"

"It ain't a matter of *can*, Lester. It's a matter of neighbor helpin' neighbor. I'd think you'd have a little more gratitude, after all Effie's done..." Lester whipped around in a whirlwind, Virgil's limp neck dangling across his arms.

"Done, you say? Done?! What you and that witch have done is killed Virgil, here. Nah. I think you've done quite enough." Neil balled up his fist as Effie grabbed him by the coattail just inches before he walloped Lester across the jaw.

Lester jeered. "Well, now. It would seem I struck a nerve there, Neil. What's that they say? Bit dog always hollers?" Effie thought about letting Neil go at him but something of her good sense held him tight.

Neil clenched his teeth. "You sorry, good for nothin' swindler. You ain't got a bit more'a God in you than a chamber pot, and yo'r certainly more full'a shit. I'd shoot you dead right now if I could."

"Bah!" Effie interrupted. "Be a waste of good bullets." Neil tugged at Effie's hand, encouraging her to let him loose. Lester stared at Neil's still balled-up fist as Virgil's body became visibly stiffer. Neil moved into Lester's face, not a quarter inch to spare between their two noses.

"You better be grateful Effie here stopped me," Neil snarled as he lightly pounded his fist into Lester's chest. "One day, you'll be out huntin'. Out in the field, thinkin' there ain't no one around for miles. Hell, you might even be layin' between the legs of that whore of yo'rs ." Lester turned white as snow.

"Yeah, I know what yo'r up to', you goddamned piece of shit. You say yo'r out there harvestin' souls, but yo'r just plowin' her fields." Lester gulped. "One day, when you think no one's around, I'll put a bullet through that spineless back of yours and not think twice about it. Now get the hell outta here and home to yo'r wife." Lester jerked away from Neil's fist and waddled to his horse fast as his shaking legs could carry him.

Effie and Neil watched from the porch as Lester dropped Virgil's body in a makeshift sled he'd tied behind his horse and began to secure the body with jute twine – the kind you'd stake a tomato plant up with. Unable to bear the sacrilege any further, Neil stomped into the yard, dodging a few of Effie's chickens, and grabbed a roll of rope from off a fence post and stuffed it into Lester's chest.

"Ain't got the sense God gave a Billy Goat," he muttered as he walked back to Effie's side. Effie leaned into Neil's ear.

"How'd you know?"

"'Bout what?"

"The other woman."

One corner of Neil's mouth curled up. "Let's just say I may or may not have followed him once or twice."

Effie let out a rueful laugh as they watched Lester hightail it up the path. "You old fool. Yo'r gonna get yo'rself killed one day."

"Nah. Yo'r more liable to shoot me than that stupid sum'bitch," Neil laughed. "Then again, you cain't do much damage with a flashlight."

Chapter 14

Where was Jacob? Annie hadn't seen him since he tore out of Effie's. She'd assumed, after escorting Trevor and Dr. Middleton back to the inn, she'd run into her brother coming back from the church, but he'd never showed. She'd sat up with Virgil's body until midnight sure that Jacob would come relieve her, but when he didn't, she went on to bed when Clavel, Birdie, and Little June came to take their turn at Virgil's side. Maybe Jacob had gone back to Effie's, but with Virgil gone that didn't make sense.

Yesterday evening, the house had been full of distant kin and curious neighbors. It made Annie's blood boil. She just wanted to be left alone. Death brought out people like worms in chestnut, and she couldn't understand it. If you didn't care to be around a soul when they were alive, what reason could you possibly have to be around 'em when they were dead? People were quar, as her grandmother used to say. Just plum quar.

And her mother. Dear Lord in heaven. Since her stroke Ida couldn't say sooey if the hogs was eatin' her, but she'd had no trouble wailing and carrying on since the first gawker had arrived. Annie believed she and her mother would've been just fine despite her father stomping about, but the mourners seemed to wring out all the heartache Ida had ever endured since the day she was born, and that was a lot. It took Annie another hour after their visitors left to calm her down.

Her father, on the other hand, immersed himself in the drama. Couldn't get enough of it, and if the truth be told, he went to great lengths to provoke it. "Poor Virgil. He's in God's hands now. Praise Jesus," he lamented with one hand raised towards the heavens and his eyes rolled back in his head. The suffocating crowd echoed. *Bless him, Lord! Come quickly, Lord, Jesus. Take us all home.* Annie wished Jesus *would* come and take these sorry hypocrites away somewhere. She'd gladly stay behind.

Annie had been sure that Jacob would be back when she woke, but he wasn't. She stomped and cursed around the house, as if her war dance would summon her brother home. When Eldridge and Ronnie Rogers arrived with the other pallbearers to take Virgil's body to the church, she'd given them wherefor for instigating this mess to begin with, then questioned them as to her brother's whereabouts. Eldridge confessed they last saw Jacob hightailing it towards the river, but those were words coming from a couple of cattle thieves. Annie didn't put much stock in it.

"We're sorry, Annie," Eldridge offered with a crack in his voice. "We were just tryin' to ..."

"Never mind what you were tryin' to do," she chastised. "What you did? You'll have to answer to God for." Eldridge hung his head with the truth of it.

"We'll go round up the cattle after the funeral," Ronnie offered. "They ain't far."

"You damn well better," she echoed. "And you'll be payin' for our bull, too."

"Pa's givin' you one of ours," Eldridge uttered between his now constant sobs.

Annie nodded, unable to control her own tears and decided she'd said enough on the subject. "Well, if you see Jacob, tell him we need him at home." Ronnie said they'd be sure to.

The rest of the mourners and well-doers met at the house to follow Virgil's coffin up the hill; some on foot - some with horses and wagons. Annie wished to protect Ida from the melodramatic crowd, however, and said they'd ride up to the church when Neil and Effie came to call, which could be any minute.

Now, she stood by her bed, trying to figure out what to wear to Virgil's funeral. She pulled out the same old tired dress she'd worn at Uncle Phipp's graveside. The corner of her lip curled in repulsion as she tossed the moth-ridden rag onto the gathering pile on the bed where her few other garbs had been discarded. One was tight through the bosom, another unraveled where her heel had caught the hem and tore at its weakest point. There was the navy blouse with the crocheted collar and matching skirt, an ensemble sewn and worn by her grandmother before rheumatism rendered her fingers too bent to thread a needle. The remaining shirts and skirts composed a monotonous medley of hand-me-downs, given to her by Birdie's sister, Lola, the one who'd married a lawyer and moved to Charlotte. The one who was going to pay her and Birdie's way through nursing school. Even on this solemn day, or perhaps because of it, she felt her ire boil.

Annie pilfered through the remaining garments inside the box before tossing it into the corner of her room. What difference did her attire make anyway? Not like anybody she cared about would be there, unless of course, Trevor and his uncle attended the services. But why would they do that? She chastened herself for such a juvenile fancy.

The thought had no sooner crossed her mind when she caught a glint of something red in the sunbeams that mingled with the gathering dust. At the bottom of the discarded heap, a burgundy laced dress peaked its hem out from beneath the otherwise yellowed, sleepy garments. She'd nearly forgotten about it, as the dress had been relegated to its hiding place at the bottom of the box so her father would not find it. If he did, he most certainly would have burned it on a pyre. Annie suppressed a squeal as she rushed to put it on.

She slipped the dress over her head and stood to admire herself in the mirror, forgetting it had been covered with a black cloth. Her mother had done so because people in these parts believed that when someone died, the next person to see their image in a mirror would be the next one to die. Annie scoffed at the thought as she ripped down the shroud, her reflection now beaming back at her through the scratches and knicks in the glass. The burgundy red capped sleeves draped gracefully over her milky white shoulders, leading the eye to a broad, pleated, black velvet ribbon which began high at the waist, then drifted to midcalf down the back. The skirt then flowed to an A-line, ending just short of her briar-scratched ankles. To match, Lola had included a pair of slightly worn, but nonetheless elegant, black Mary Janes, that were secured by a single button strap – a matching red velvet bow adorning the toe.

She should wear black, but doing what she *should* most of her life had gotten her nowhere. And what difference did the color of a frock make to Virgil? He was dead. Gone. And weren't the dead depressing enough without giving them more reason to be?

Her father would certainly have something to say about it, but he could kiss her pasty white backside. Then again, was she up to doing battle with her father on such a day?

She let out an exasperated breath as she lifted the red dress above her head and let it fall to the floor, replacing it with the Raiment of Doom. She supposed she should wear her hair up, too. Wouldn't want hair gettin' in the way of a proper mourning.

Assessing herself in the mirror once more, she cried. She looked like the Grim Reaper. All she needed was a scythe. No way could she endure this day wearing black. She wrangled the dress off and threw it to the ground, stomping and grinding it with the heel of her Mary Janes until the black wool was covered in dusty footprints. If she couldn't wear the dress she wanted, she certainly wasn't going to wear that one. She'd go naked first.

Suddenly, Annie was aware of her mother leaning against the wall with weepy eyes. She had her chalkboard with her, which is what she used to communicate, limp by her side.

"Ma, I … I … didn't see you standin' there. What's wrong?" Ida shook her head as tears flowed down onto her own moth-eaten black dress. Annie, half clothed, went over to her mother and held her close.

Ida pushed away and wrote on her chalkboard. *Jacob?*

"I don't know," Annie answered. "He left Effie's to ring the church bell, like I told you last night. Ain't seen him since." Her mother began to shake. "He'll be back, Ma. I know he will. He just needs some time to himself, that's all." Ida nodded with the hope of it, but Annie could sense her doubts. She hugged her mother again.

"Is Pa gone?" Annie asked, peeking her head around the door frame. Her mother bobbed her head up and down again.

Perfect! Her father would not see her, or what she was wearing, before the funeral. Once at the church, there was little he could do about it.

Annie kissed her mother on the cheek just as she heard footsteps on the front porch. "Ma, go let Neil and Effie in. I need to finish gettin' ready," Annie coached as she nudged her mother towards the front door. In a flash, she'd slipped the red gown back on and let down her wild, red hair from the bun perched atop of her head.

Yes. Much better.

When Annie came out of her room, her mother gasped. Neil stood stolid with his mouth agape as Effie looked on in a rare, speechless moment.

"What?" Annie asked, batting her eyelashes. "Y'all look like you just seen a ghost."

Chapter 15

Lymas slowed his car on the approach to the church, dividing the horses and wagons down the middle. Just ahead, Trevor could see a tall, lanky man shaking hands with the gathered mourners as he occasionally took out a brown handkerchief to dab his face and forehead. He surmised that must be Lester, Annie's father, and felt a wave of dread. He decided to keep an open mind, however. He and his own father were prime examples of how parents and children could have a completely different relationship from the ones they shared with the outside world. Maybe the reverend wasn't so bad.

It had been Lymas's idea to attend the child's funeral. Wallace believed it to be an idea born of pure insanity, and this time Trevor was inclined to agree. It seemed unnecessary and even a tad inappropriate.

Adding to the already tense air between them, Wallace was predictably irate that the two of them had skulked off to parts unknown the day before without so much as a how-do-you-do ... on horses no less! While Trevor didn't necessarily agree his father should be consulted about every detail of his life, he did not want their visit to continue in the tumultuous spirit in which Savannah had ended. It did not seem like a windmill worth tilting. He needed to focus on his recovery, both mentally and physically.

Still, his uncle believed that in this rural community, the bereaved family would have few attendees and if he and Trevor could be of some support, they should. Trevor first declined the invitation but then curiosity got the best of him and he decided, "What the hell?" He had little else to do, and the mere thought of being alone with his father for the better part of the day exhausted him.

Lymas had been wrong about the lack of attendees. There may not be many folks living in Hickory Nut Gorge, but it seemed every one of them had arrived for Virgil's funeral. Through the opened double doors, Trevor could see the church was nearing full capacity.

As they parked the car beside the horses and wagons, a flock of children swooshed in to run their hands over the flivver's fenders and sides, despite the admonishing calls from their parents.

"I'll tan yo'r hide!" he heard one father yell.

"You act like you ain't had no raisin'!" another distraught mother cried.

Lymas waved, explaining that he didn't mind their children's curiosity. In fact, he welcomed such enthusiasm! As the kids clambered into the car, Lymas stood by the driver's door watching over them as they crawled in and out of the seats.

Suddenly everyone's eyes were drawn toward a rise in the road where a mule's head crested the top - her head hung low. Behind the jenny sat a boy, probably no more than fourteen, and behind him a flatbed wagon with Virgil's small coffin strapped on. Even from this distance, Trevor could see the boy's eyes were red and swollen with grief. He wore his Sunday best overalls and a crisp, white linen shirt beneath.

Behind the funeral wagon came a host of mourners, ushered in by the sweet, spicy aroma of trailing arbutus; some of them singing a song as they funneled through the laurel thicket that arched just over top of their heads.

I am Jesus' little lamb.
Ever glad at heart I am.
Jesus loves me, Jesus knows me.
All things fair and good he shows me.
Even calls me by my name.
Every day he is the same.

Trevor and Lymas removed their hats as the procession neared the church entrance. Five other men of varying ages broke from the throng and loosened the rope that held Virgil to his transport, hoisting the coffin onto their shoulders. No one made a sound; not even the youngsters who, just moments before, seemed not to have a care in the world. Trevor scanned the crowd but could not locate Annie, Neil or Effie. Maybe they were already inside.

"Well, Uncle, shall we?" Trevor waved his hand towards the church door.

"After you, Nephew." Trevor proceeded to hobble towards the church door when he heard his uncle gasp, "Jesus, Mary and Joseph."

Trevor turned to see what had grabbed his uncle's attention and observed another wagon coming towards the church. Neil was driving with Effie by his side. Behind them sat another woman looking more worn than aged, and beside her was Annie wearing a garnet-colored dress that would have been more appropriate at a Christmas ball rather than a funeral.

"Why, Trevor! Dr. Middleton! I didn't expect to see you here!" Annie crooned, allowing Lymas to take her hand as she nearly leapt off the wagon. The woman beside her sat, unmoving, her face a blend of consternation and sorrow. "I'd like for you to meet my mother, Ida."

If Ida had heard her daughter, she pretended not to.

"Ma. I said I'd like for you to meet the doctor and his nephew. The one's I was tellin' you about." Ida remained motionless.

"Leave her be, Annie," Neil admonished. "I think you've upset yo'r Ma enough today."

Annie rolled her eyes and shook her head, as though she was the mother and Ida, *her* child. Effie turned to look over her shoulder, clearly disapproving of Annie's present behavior.

"Well, it is very kind of you both to come to Virgil's funeral. Ma didn't want much fuss so we got here a bit late." Neil cleared his throat. Trevor thought he saw Ida cut her eyes at her daughter, but he couldn't be sure.

Lymas helped Effie down from her seat on the wagon as Neil went to Ida's side to assist her. The stroke Neil mentioned had left the woman with total paralysis in her right arm and notable weakness on the same side, making the task of descending a wagon seat quite daunting. Trevor thought about how the simplest of tasks had become difficult for him since his accident and felt a deep sense of knowing for her. He had hope for recovery, however. Ida was as good as she would ever be.

The first verse of the hymn had already been sung and the second was halfway through when Trevor and Lymas eased into the pew as Annie and her family filed up the aisle towards their reserved bench closest to the coffin. Even on this warm spring day, Trevor could feel the air turn to frost.

Above the out of tune piano, Trevor heard gasps and whispers. Waving bonnets flapped their disapproval. Men young and old alike stared with their mouths agape; their girlfriends and wives redirecting their attention with sharp elbow jabs to their ribs. Even the pianist skipped a few beats as the last verse of the hymn began. Trevor laughed to himself as he recalled this same hymn being sung in his church back in Charleston, and though he couldn't recount the last verse well, he belted out the words he did know in the hopes of dragging the parishioners' attention away from Annie. His father always joked the Middleton men were as tuneful as a scalded cat, but that didn't dissuade him from trying:

> *When I draw this fleeting breath,*
> *When mine eyes shall close in death.*
> *When I soar to worlds unknown,*
> *See thee on thy judgment throne,*
> *Rock of Ages, cleft for me.*
> *Let me hide myself in thee.*

Annie's father, who'd been leading the singing, turned red as Annie's dress. Though Trevor could not see her face, it was clear that his daughter was meeting his searing gaze head on – both their eyes ablaze with a fiery contempt. Trevor wondered if Lester would stop the proceedings right then and there, ripping the gown from his daughter's pale, white flesh. But then calm seemed to settle upon the preacher's shoulder to persuade him otherwise.

Lymas, who had been maintaining a soft gaze forwards, turned to his nephew, his eyebrow furrowed in confusion. Trevor hoped his uncle would decide to leave, but Lymas returned his befuddled gaze forward.

Annie led the family by Virgil's now opened casket as her father glared from the pulpit. Why was he not with his family? It was as though he had elevated himself above all the pain and suffering mere mortals must endure. Ida looked up at her husband when she filed by Virgil's body, but Lester gave her no more thought than the flies now gathering on the church windows. Perhaps he blamed her for Annie's offensive attire. Perhaps he blamed her for Virgil's death. Perhaps he blamed her for all the wrong that had ever befallen him. He looked to be the type.

Pausing at Virgil's head, Ida stroked his blonde curls and bent to kiss him on the cheek, Effie and Neil providing the only support that kept her from crumpling to the splintered floor beneath her.

In stark contrast, Annie's dress shone like a blood moon from where she now rested in the family pew. Neil and Effie brought Ida to sit beside her daughter as the congregation looked on in pity – now for more reasons than Virgil's untimely death.

Two pallbearers came and nailed the casket lid shut, Annie's bared shoulders jerking with each *thud* of the hammer. At least she was somewhat aware she was at her cousin's funeral and not a dueling match with her father.

Muffled sobs began from within the mourners' crowd, their white handkerchiefs bobbing up and down – flags of surrender to the inevitability of death. Trevor suddenly realized that he could easily have been lying in a coffin, and for the first time, he began to understand how fortunate he was. One day, his time would come, but he'd been spared for now, and he vowed he would make himself worthy of this second chance. His knee throbbed with each beat of his heart, reminding him the path back would not be easy, but he was determined he would not squander this opportunity.

At once Lester stood tall, his worn, black *King James* clutched tight in his hand.

"Let us hear the words of our Lord!" Lester's voice reverberated off the worm-eaten rafters.

"If a man has a *stubborn* and rebellious son, which will not obey the voice of his father, or his mother," Lester paused, looking directly at Ida for the first time. "And that, when they have chastened him, will not hearken unto them!"

Was Lester quoting scripture from memory? He had yet to open the cracked and worn cover of the Bible he clenched.

"Then shall his father and his mother lay *HOLT* of him and bring him out unto the elders. And they shall say..." Lester halted again, waving his arm above Virgil's casket.

"This. *Thissssss...*" Lester hissed. "This son is a stubborn and rebellious one. He will not obey our voice." Lester said these last words almost in a whisper as he looked upon Virgil's casket and shook his head in a pity that bordered on disgust.

Suddenly, Lester slammed his palm upon the pulpit and shouted, "He is a glutton and a drunkard!" Everyone in the church jumped, including Lymas, whose pallor shown whiter than the dogwoods blooming outside the church doors.

What a bizarre scripture for a funeral service! What was this man trying to say? That Virgil got his just deserts? Maybe Lester was referring to Jacob but even so, Trevor deemed this topic more inappropriate than Annie's dress. No. It was beyond inappropriate. It was downright frightening. In a voice that seethed of hatred and judgment, Lester continued.

"And all the men shall stone him with *sssstones*, that he die." Trevor heard someone near the front begin to wail. "So shalt thou put evil away from among you. Hear ... and *fffffear* ... the Lord."

Trevor didn't know about fearing the Lord, but he could see why Annie, or anyone else for that matter, would be frightened of this man. But if Annie was fearful of her father, why did she provoke him? Perhaps she was tired of living in constant dread and decided to meet him, and her fears, head on.

Lester began to pace back and forth between the walls of the church, his Bible now tucked under his arm as he scratched his chin with the other.

Trevor craned his neck to see Effie's black bonnet shaking from side to side in disbelief.

The preacher returned to the pulpit, placing his crack-covered Bible in the center. Trevor hoped this was going to be the end of his theatrics but apparently Lester was just warming up. This time, as he continued quoting Bible verses, the man looked squarely at his daughter. The only thing glowing redder than her dress were his eyes.

"And there came one of the seven angels which had seven vials, saying unto me, 'Come hither, Lester. I will show you the judgment of the great *whore* that sitteth upon many waters.'"

Lymas leaned over and whispered, "Did he just call his daughter a whore?"

Trevor squirmed in his seat. "I believe he did, Uncle."

A young man in the next pew, about Trevor's age, turned with a look that admonished, *you better be quiet or you'll be next.* A couple of older women across the aisle began thumbing through their own bibles, pointing at pages, then wrinkling their noses, not readily finding the scripture being quoted.

"And I saw a woman sit upon a scarlet beast, full of blasphemy, having seven heads and ten horns. And this woman..." Lester extended his arm, again, towards his daughter. "She was arrayed in a scarlet color and decked with gold and precious stones and pearls." Ida dropped her head into her hand and began to moan.

"She was an *ABOMINATION* to her family ... and *filled* with adulterous thoughts! And I saw the woman drunken with the blood of the saints, and when I saw her, I wondered ... is this my daughter?"

"Oh my God," Lymas said aloud. Trevor elbowed him. "I think we should go," Lymas whispered, but now, it was Trevor who was held firm to his seat. Annie might need someone when this production ended, and while he hardly knew her, he wanted to be around – just in case. One of the women who had been sifting through her Bible did get up and leave. Lester then opened his own copy of The Good Book.

"The beast that thou sawest was ... and ... is not. And shall ascend out of the bottomless pit and go into perdition: and they that dwell on the earth shall wonder, whose names were not written in the book of life from the foundation of the world, when they behold the beast that was, and is not, and yet is. These shall make war with the Lamb, and the Lamb shall overcome them."

Lester frowned at his congregants and shouted, "For he is Lord of LORDS! King of *KINGS!*" His words settled over the parishioners like ash. "And they that are with him are called. And chosen ... and faithful." Lester smiled. "Faithful," he repeated.

From across the church, Trevor heard, "Bless him, Lord!" Nothing like the book of Revelation to fire up the zealots.

"And the ten horns which thou sawest upon the beast, these shall *hate* the whore and shall make her desolate. And naked." Lester's eyes flashed. "And shall *eatttttt* her flesh. And burn her ... with *FIRE!*"

Another gentleman stood up to leave, but his wife pulled him back down to his seat by the coattail. One of the pallbearers exposed a toothless grin. A couple of young girls snickered among themselves as they pointed accusing fingers at this real-life *Mary Magdalene* who sat amongst them.

Ida shot up from her seat and uttered some gut-wrenching sound that Trevor could not discern, but from the shaking of her left fist in the air, Trevor gathered it wasn't a *Hallelujah.* Neil grabbed ahold of her waist and urged her out the side door.

Effie stood up to follow, but as she reached the door she turned to Lester and cried out, "That Bible of yo'rs missin' some pages?" Lester scowled, then laughed.

"No, Sister Effie. They're all right here." Lester patted his Bible for emphasis.

"Good. Then you'll have no problem turnin' to Colossians 3:21." Lester's face blazed.

She thrust her crooked finger towards the pulpit and shouted, "Fathers, provoke not your children to *anger*, lest they be discouraged." Effie grabbed Annie's hand, jerking her towards the door, but before she left, she twisted her neck backwards.

"And I ain't yo'r goddamn sister."

Chapter 16

Annie's knees buckled beneath the weight of her father's rebukes as she slunk towards the wagon. It was a good thing Neil was there to hoist her up. She doubted she had the strength to do it on her own.

She knew she had been risking her father's ire when she chose to buck convention, but she had grown tired of kowtowing to his erratic moods. Now, her mother sat beside her, her left arm patting Annie on the knee like she used to when she was a little girl; scared of yellow jackets. Scared of thunder. Scared of her father...

"I'm taking you and yo'r Ma to my place," Neil said matter-of-factly as he turned to face them. "Ain't no use going to the graveside when yo'r Pa's got his dander up." Ida nodded her approval as Effie climbed into the wagon.

Annie knew that this solution was a temporary one. They'd have to go home sometime. Even so, it might give her father a chance to calm down. He'd always backed down from Neil, so it was probably the safest place to be.

Annie turned to see Trevor hopping on his crutch towards the wagon. Lymas was cranking his car as a few more appalled funeral-goers emerged from the church. She looked around to see if Jacob was hiding in the shadows, but the woods seemed as empty as her heart. She decided it was best he had not been there to catch his share of Lester's fire and damnation.

Birdie and Clavel were among the dissenters leaving the church, in addition to Tom and Mattie Turner. She'd not seen the owners of The Esmeralda come in and was horrified they had witnessed such a spectacle. Mattie and Tom's patronage provided them with what little income they had. She prayed they would continue to support her family, but wouldn't blame them if they never spoke to her again.

Birdie and Clavel caught up with Trevor, the trio forming a hardline between the wagon and the church. Annie watched Tom and Mattie walk swiftly to their automobile.

"Annie? Ida? Are you okay? That was just horrible!" Birdie cried.

"I…I'm okay, I s'pose." The quiver in Annie's voice wasn't too convincing, however.

"Annie, I … I am so sorry," Trevor offered. Birdie put a knowing hand on Trevor's arm, even though she'd never met the man until now. Annie felt a jealous burn rise from her chest and up through her head but told herself that was just Birdie. Nothing was meant by it. Clavel jangled Little June on his hip – the child cooing and giggling as if there weren't a care in the world. Trevor removed his hat.

"Ma'am," he said to her mother. "I am terribly sorry for what you and your daughter are going through. As you know, my uncle and I are guests at The Esmeralda, and I am sure Tom and Mattie would be delighted to have you join us for a time. You know. Until things settle down a bit."

Ida stared at Trevor like he was a chicken with four legs. Trevor pushed ahead, undaunted. "It would me my pleasure if you and your daughter would at least accompany us to dinner." Trevor bowed his head slightly.

By that time, Tom and Mattie had come alongside the wagon, the engine of their Packard humming in duet with Lymas's Model-T. "Ida. Annie. Please come stay with us. We have rooms available, and you could rest there a bit before going home," Mattie offered. Ida shook her head from side to side and raised her left hand to shush them.

Tom concurred. "If you're worried about money, we would never think of taking payment, Mrs. Conner. After all you've done for us? It's the least we could do."

Ida waved her hand again in the negative but pointed to her daughter and then back to Trevor.

"You want us to take Annie but not you?" Trevor asked. Ida nodded that was the case.

Effie spoke up. "Alright, Ida. But you'll still come with me and Neil, won't you? Lester's as liable to go after you as Annie here. Sorry sum'bitch."

It didn't surprise Annie that her mother turned down the chance to go to The Esmeralda. While she appreciated Tom and Mattie as a source of income, that's what they were to her. A business relationship. Not friends. There was too much of a fissure between them. That was the difference between her and her mother. Her mother saw expansive chasms between the classes. Annie saw bridges of opportunity.

"So, it's settled then," Mattie said. "Tom, let's go back to the inn and make sure things are in order. Annie, we'll see you and Trevor soon." Trevor nodded then eased over to where his uncle and the flivver sat idling, bringing him up to speed regarding their plans.

Annie's mood began to lift with the breeze that caressed the cherry blossoms. She thought of the possibilities of spending time with Trevor in a posh setting, with Tom and Mattie gushing over her like she was royalty.

Lymas looked from Annie, then to Trevor, then back to Annie and cast a wary glance at his nephew. *What was Dr. Middleton being all uppity about?* she wondered. Well, it didn't matter. Like Mattie said. It was settled.

Trevor ushered Annie over to Lymas's idling vehicle and opened the door, gesturing for her to sit. Trevor made his place behind Annie and slapped the flivver on its side to signal he was ready to go. Lymas looked at Annie and forced a smile before pulling out onto the rutty lane that led from the church to the main road. Annie returned his awkward gaze, then watched the church fade from her vision, the boom of her father's voice still ringing in her ears. *And shall eat her flesh and burn her with fire!*

Annie cast a brazen eye towards the backseat and smiled, steeling her eyes on this man fate had dropped into her lap.

And shall eat her flesh and burn her with fire! Perhaps there was some good to come out of this day. Indeed, her flesh was on fire. She felt herself burning in places she didn't even know she had.

Chapter 17

Lymas, who was most always comfortable around anyone, was quiet and distant on the drive to the inn. Trevor had attempted light conversation, but his uncle's only responses had been guttural, ambivalent grunts or a slight shrug of his shoulders. Except for that one look she had given him, even Annie seemed awkward and reserved; but after the public dressing down she had received at Virgil's funeral, her conversational withdrawal was understandable. Maybe Lymas was reeling from it, too. He was a true gentleman – kind, caring, always showering the ladies with his own special brand of Southern, genteel respect. Perhaps he was trying to process the afternoon's events. It was quite the show, to be certain.

Mattie and Tom formed a welcoming party as Lymas pulled up to the entrance. There were two automobiles in front of the inn - men and women shouting out orders as hired hands unloaded trunks and hat boxes. A couple of gentlemen on horseback milled around in the background; their crisp white shirts reflecting the afternoon sun back into the cerulean sky. These were dapper young men sporting ties and formal riding caps; far from the overall-clad, sun-tanned farmers and farmhands that made daily deliveries to the inn. The impatient *tap-tap-tap-tap* of his uncle's fingers on the steering wheel made Trevor's own heart flip-flop inside his chest. He was about to ask Lymas to stop when his uncle sat forward and muttered, "What in Hell's blue blazes?"

Trevor could see that the first car was in the process of being loaded, and to his great surprise, or perhaps, relief, discovered it was his father's Cadillac. Lymas backed off the throttle, engaged the parking brake and bolted from his Model-T. Wallace looked up to see his brother stomping towards him with the ferocity of a mad goose.

"What's happening, Trevor?" Annie quizzed. Trevor said he wasn't sure, but he had an idea.

Trevor and Annie watched as both men gestured at one another. Wallace punched his balled-up fist into the top of the Caddy. Lymas threw up his arms and walked away, only to pivot and turn with a loud and another thing exploding from his puffed-up lips. Trevor watched his father shy away from the fight, merely shaking his head as he lifted the last and final trunk into the car.

"Your father," Lymas huffed.

"Why? What's going on, Uncle?"

"Wallace has decided, based on your actions in recent days, that you are fine to be left alone and that he will take his leave *today* to return to Savannah. He claims he has urgent business to tend to, but I don't believe a word of it."

A smile crept across Trevor's face. He had to handle this delicately, or his good fortune might turn on him.

"Will you be staying Dr. Middleton?" Annie queried. Trevor wanted to kick the seat behind her but couldn't raise his leg to do the trick.

"It would seem not," Lymas answered. "I mean, certainly, I could if I so desired, but..." Lymas turned to look at his nephew. "...your father seems to be of the mind that my 'careless actions' will merely impede your recovery. Therefore, and I use his words, he believes you should be 'thrown into the river, ever to sink or to swim for yourself.'"

Trevor thought of the Rocky Broad that pulsed just below them across the road. He'd have a shot at catching some trout or to simply take an easy stroll without being under the thumb of his father. Maybe the Turners would even let him drive their car. It would be excellent therapy to get his knee and leg loosened up. He became excited for the first time since coming to The Gorge and prayed this opportunity would not blow up in his face.

"I'll take real good care of 'im, Dr. Middleton!" Annie exclaimed. Lymas formed a cagy scowl, seeming to imagine all the implications of such an arrangement.

"Well," Lymas paused. "For the love of Pete, Trevor. I just don't think you're ready…"

"Uncle, I will be fine. I have Tom and Mattie to look after me. Neil expressed doing some repairs at Effie's place, too. I could help him…"

"Trevor! You aren't ready to climb up on roofs and patch floors. You're going to push yourself too far, I fear." Lymas's ears were reddening at the tips, his normally low baritone voice edging towards a tinny whine.

"Really, Uncle. I am not stupid. I won't do anything that will jeopardize my recovery."

"And I'll take real good care of 'im, Dr. Middleton!"

"And yes. Annie here will take real good care of me," he parroted, rolling his eyes at her with a good-natured wink. Lymas looked at Annie with a doubtful glance, then to the Caddy where Wallace was tightening down some straps, then back to Trevor.

"Alright then," Lymas groaned in resignation. Trevor nearly shouted but caught himself. "But you have to promise me that you will not push yourself too far, and that you will write me of your progress once a week."

"I promise, Uncle."

"I mean it, Trevor," Lymas emphasized by jabbing his finger into the top of his seat. "I want detailed reports. What still hurts. What has improved. Do you have any new sensations, good or bad … anywhere. Do you understand?"

Trevor started to chime, *and if I don't?* but caught himself before tossing his own grenade into this most fortuitous development.

"I'll see to it that he does, Dr. Middleton. I'll take real good…"

"Yes, I know, Annie. You'll take real good care of him." Annie blushed. Even his uncle had a slight, comical grin upon his lips. "Well, alright then. I'll just be gathering the rest of my things and be off."

"But Uncle, won't you be staying for dinner? I assume you'll just be driving to Spartanburg tonight and catching the train tomorrow."

Lymas puckered his lips as he considered. "It depends on how hellbent your father is on leaving now, but I suppose I could persuade him to stay for one last evening," he agreed.

Lymas exited the car once more to speak with his brother. This time, the conversation was amicable - more talking and less gesturing. Trevor then watched his father as he accompanied Lymas back to the Model-T.

"Trevor, Lymas and I believe it would be best if we stayed one more night then made our way to Spartanburg tomorrow. No reason to be hasty, right Brother?" Wallace gave Lymas an uncharacteristic fist punch to the shoulder.

"I think that would be splendid, Father. Annie is going to stay at the inn as well." Wallace opened Annie's door, extending his hand to escort her.

"Hello, Annie. I'm Wallace Middleton. Trevor's father."

"I'm Annie Conner." Annie expressed with her curtsy. "Pleased to meet you."

Wallace took in her dress from shoulder to hem, his look more one of confusion than judgment. Lymas moved to Trevor's door, offering a hand as well, but Trevor refused. With a movement that proved much more difficult than he would have hoped, he forced himself upright with his crutch. Perhaps a cane would provide better leverage. This crutch was becoming a nuisance.

Trevor could see now that Tom and Mattie were sweeping the porch. Pitchers of lemonade glistened from a silver tray; the smell of fresh baked shortbread wafting over their heads.

Annie waited for Trevor to hobble towards the front of the car where Lymas stood, ready to crank his Model-T into submission with the flip of his wrist. The first attempt yielded little more than a sputter, as did the second.

"May I try, Uncle?" Lymas cast him a wary look, but then lifted a skeptical shoulder.

"You may as well. I'm leaving you the flivver for the duration of your stay." Now it was Trevor's turn to be speechless. "It would be foolish to drive both vehicles back to South Carolina," Lymas explained. "Now, you'll have your own transportation when you're feeling more recovered.

Hell, you can drive yourself back to Charleston whenever you'd like!" Lymas looked Annie up and down, as though that moment might come sooner rather than later. Annie's smile morphed into a scowl.

"Thank you, Uncle. That's most generous." Trevor hobbled back to the driver's seat and turned the ignition back on – something his uncle had forgotten to do. Trevor exploded with an incredulous laugh.

"Alright, old man. How long have you been driving this car?" Lymas rolled his eyes and wagged his head. Trevor then ensured the emergency brake was all the way back, and that the spark lever was completely down. He nudged the gas lever ever-so-slightly, then using the body of the car for support, made his way back to the crankshaft. Trevor wrapped his hand around the crank, thumb firmly on the same side as his fingers and gave the crank a twist. To his delight, the car sputtered to life. Lymas ran to move the spark lever up, bringing the automobile to a steady hum.

Trevor moved to the steps of the inn as his uncle parked the car, Annie's arm threaded through his own. He was feeling buoyed by his ability to start the Model-T. Of course, starting the automobile did not require a lot of cooperation from his leg, apart from a little strength and balance. Still, it was a win in his book – one which placed him another step closer to his recovery and a triumphant return to France.

Chapter 18

Annie stood beneath the high rafters of The Esmeralda and stared in childlike wonder. She had been inside the inn numerous times, but when making deliveries her normal field of vision rarely made it past the walls of the kitchen, and if she ever did venture into the inn itself, it was to follow Mattie or Tom to the front desk to obtain payment for the eggs, hams, or the occasional beef roast when her Pa had slaughtered a bull. For an uncomfortable moment, she wondered what had become of the bull that had killed Virgil, but just as quickly buried the thought. It seemed a waste to allow the meat to rot, but the mere thought of eating it made her stomach do somersaults. The intrusion of such an idea threatened to dampen her spirit, so she forced it from her mind.

For now? She was a guest. She should enjoy herself, but that seemed to invoke another set of emotions altogether. She shouldn't be "enjoying herself" after her cousin's funeral. Her fingers balled up into a fist, a stress reaction she'd picked up from her mother.

"You seem to be in deep thought." Annie gasped, a bit startled at the sound of Trevor's voice.

"Oh, yes. Well, I guess I am. It's been quite a day, and it ain't over." Annie reflected, tugging nervously at the shoulders of her dress. Feeling a wave of sudden exhaustion she sat down at the dining room table, taking care not to jangle the silverware that had been laid out for the evening's fare. Trevor sat down beside her but said nothing.

"I ... I am sorry you had to see all that. Back at the church."

"Well, Annie, I'm sorry, too. I know it must have been terribly embarrassing for you. You must feel ... well, there are no words for it, frankly."

Annie shrugged. "I s'pose I asked for it." Tears filled her eyes and dropped onto the tablecloth where they disappeared into the fibers, leaving inky blots that would be slow to dry in the mountain humidity. Trevor handed her his handkerchief.

"For what it's worth, you look beautiful." Her moist eyes rose to meet his, twinkling with the reflection of the diamond-cut glass in the chandelier.

"Thank you," she managed between sniffs. "I guess I just don't understand."

"From what I gather, this sort of behavior from your father is not surprising. Am I right?" Annie crumpled the handkerchief into a wad inside her fist.

"You are, but he outdid himself today. Surprised the sh...I mean, the heck outta me."

Trevor laughed just a little. "It's okay, Annie. You don't have to shield me from foul language. I've been in the war. In France. I've pretty much heard it all."

"I guess you have," Annie snickered.

"But if I may be honest, you can't go around breaking social conventions and then expect people, especially your father, not to confront you."

"Are you sayin' I deserve this?" Annie glowered.

"Deserve? No, not at all. I'm just saying that for every action, there is an equal and opposite reaction." Annie folded her hands across her chest, daring him to continue. "It's Isaac Newton's third law of motion. When you push someone or some *thing*, it pushes back." Her shoulders relaxed, but she kept her arms wrapped tight around herself. "And I am not judging. I have the same, rebellious tendencies."

"Have you ever worn a red dress to a funeral?"

"Once, but don't tell anyone." That made Annie snort, which precipitated a slight blush. "But just so you know, I *refused* to go to my mother's funeral and that had my father seeing red."

Annie smiled. "I'll bet that stirred up quite the hornet's nest."

Trevor laughed again. "My father wasn't happy, to be sure. But I had the excuse of being in France. It helped soothe some of my critics."

"Then you lost yo'r mother recently," Annie remarked. "That must be hard."

Trevor explained how his mother was an alcoholic, and mostly absent, mentally at least, during his childhood. If it hadn't been for his grandmother, he would have had no matriarchal influence. When he confessed his mother had hung herself in her bedroom closet, Annie gulped. It reinforced her mounting fears about Jacob - that he might do something if she didn't find him soon.

"Trevor, I ... I'm very sorry."

"None of us get out of this world unscathed," he reasoned. "I just couldn't face the humiliation. All the questions. The well-meaning clichés. *She's in a better place, Trevor. She loved you, Trevor. Time will heal, Trevor.* And if I am being honest, I suppose I was a little angry."

"Angry?" Annie queried.

"Yes. Angry at my mother for being the way she was. Angry at myself for not being able to save her. Angry at my father for never being home. Okay, I was *a lot* angry!" Trevor admitted with a slight guffaw. "It was just easier to hide across the big ocean and not face it. My mother was gone. There was nothing I could do about that, and the war needed me. At least that's what I told myself."

Annie took her hand and laid it on top of his. "Well, I think it's okay to be angry," she offered. "Lord knows I *stay* angry at my Pa. He's so ornery, the Devil himself wouldn't have him." Trevor gave her a sweet smile, like he understood. "I think yo'r very brave. Goin' to France and all. Speakin' of, what happened to yo'r leg? I mean, yo'r uncle said it was a horse and all but..."

Trevor hesitated, struggling with how much to tell her. "I was helping to clear an accident in the road. There were injured horses, and men, and ...

well, I will spare you the gory details. It was a horrible sight. Let's just leave it at that. I thought one of the horses was, you know, dying. Suffering." Trevor's voice caught as he remembered the ordeal. "I put a gun to its head and ... before I could fire, the thing rose up and kicked me unconscious." Annie's eyes widened. "The son-of-a-bitch then proceeded to mangle my knee as it reared up and down on it. Or at least, that's what I was told."

"Oh, Trevor, that's horrible!" Annie exclaimed. "No wonder you were nervous about ridin' Coffee up to Effie's."

"Fortunately, I don't recall anything after I was knocked out - not until I woke up in the hospital." The conversation trailed off, Trevor seeming to come to the end of all that he was willing to share. Then again, maybe that was all he could remember.

"I wish I could run off to France," she offered in the hopes of continuing their chat.

"Well, you see how well that worked out for me," Trevor joked, pointing to his leg.

Annie sighed. "I suppose a ticket anywhere but here would suit me just fine."

Trevor nodded, like he understood, but then grew quiet once more. "You know, they wanted to take my leg," he finally spoke.

Annie gulped. "Take ... yo'r leg?"

"Yes," he nodded. "I did not believe my injuries warranted such extremes, and it appears, at least on the surface of it, I was right. However, I may have quashed my dream of becoming a pilot."

"I don't understand."

"I could never drive an ambulance again. Not for the war, in my current state. It requires too much leg work, but if I had agreed to ... God. I can hardly bring myself even say the word."

"Amputation?"

"Yes. That. If I had agreed to ... amputation," Trevor gulped. "I would have probably stood a better chance of flying."

"How would losin' yo'r leg make you a better pilot?"

"That's a good question. Right now, I could not climb into the plane without assistance, if at all. With a prosthetic leg, I could probably manage quite well on my own. I might even walk more normally. But I just couldn't bear the thought of it."

Awkward silence fell over the room, Annie struggling with how to respond. While Trevor's story was difficult to hear, she felt emboldened that he would share such with the likes of someone like her.

"I believed it would make me less of a man," he blurted. "That no one, especially a woman, would want me."

"What?!" Annie stared at him with incredulity. "I ... I don't think that's possible." She felt her face flush, red as the dress that had brought her to this most unusual set of circumstances.

"And let's be honest," Trevor pushed on, seeming not to notice her embarrassment. "I was scared as hell."

"Well, of course you were," she empathized. "Who'd wanna lose their leg?"

"Well, thank you for understanding, Annie. You're very kind. But I can't help but wonder what would've happened if I'd done as the doctor recommended."

"Well, I think you did the right thing," Annie replied with a slight pat on his leg. "Although I'd give my right arm to get outta this gorge," Annie said with a flirtatious wink.

"I guess you would," Trevor acknowledged with a knowing touch to her shoulder. "But don't. Please. There has to be another way."

"I s'pose," she said with a weak grin, glancing down at her hands which were now fretting with the lace on her dress.

"Trevor. Not to bring up a sore subject, but what if Jacob hurt himself? You know, like yo'r mom did?"

Trevor straightened himself, scrunching his face with a newfound concern. "Did he ever tell you that he wanted to die, or did he talk about dying?"

"No," she answered, but he's never run away like this before. You heard him, though. He thinks Virgil dyin' is all his fault." He then asked her if she had any clue where Jacob might have gone. "I cain't say for sure, but I have me an idea."

She told him about Bat Cave and how Jacob and Eldridge would hole up there every now and then to smoke, cuss and drink whiskey. "It's the only place I can think of," she stated matter-of-factly.

Trevor asked if she had talked to any of Jacob's friends, to see if they'd heard from or seen him. Annie told Trevor about questioning his friends earlier that day, but no one had been to the cave since the snowstorm.

"If you're asking me to go with you, I fear I would not be much help. I can hardly walk across a level floor, much less up these rugged mountain trails."

"Maybe we could take Coffee and Cream again," she suggested. Annie tightened her grip on the handkerchief, watching him consider another ride and this time, up a steep mountain pass.

"Maybe we could drive to get closer to the cave?" Trevor suggested.

"That would be worse," she advised. "We could drive part way, but you'd still have to climb the bank and then hike another half mile to reach the mouth of it." She explained that the horses could take them right to the entrance.

Trevor sighed. "Alright then. But it's too late to go now."

"Oh, Trevor!" Annie cried. "If one more night passes, that cave'll be Jacob's tomb. I just know it!" Annie pressed her face into the handkerchief as Trevor patted her on the back then checked his pocket watch.

"Alright," he finally agreed. "But let's ask Mattie if she has any clothes you can change into."

"Yo'r my hero!" Annie grabbed him around the neck and hugged him tight.

"It's my pleasure to help where I can. Now dry those tears and think positive thoughts. Jacob's a tough young man. I'm sure he's fine."

While Trevor went off to find Mattie, Annie considered what Trevor had said - about being less of a man just because he injured his leg. How could he think such a thing? And yet, it was kinda sweet, even humble-like – that he'd worry a girl wouldn't find him desirable ... for any reason. And for him to help her find Jacob, despite his disposition! Now that was as manly a thing as she'd ever encountered. She'd just have to show him what kind of a man he was... .

Chapter 19

Trevor found Tom and Mattie at the front desk, sorting mail, counting cash, and ordering supplies for the inn. Trevor was certain they had overheard at least some of Annie's tearful story, but being the polite souls they were, they pretended to be hearing the tale for the first time. From his periphery, he noticed that Annie had followed him into the lobby but couldn't blame the girl for not wanting to be alone.

"Tom. Mattie. Annie is in need of a change of clothes. I was wondering if I could buy…"

"Here you are, my dear," Mattie said to Annie as she extended an armload of lace and cotton. "It's not much, but it should get you through until you're able to go back home."

"Thank you, Mrs. Turner," she replied. "I'm much obliged." Annie began sifting through the stack of clothes, her eyes widening as she rifled through the elegant garments.

"And Tom, I was wondering," Trevor continued, "if we could borrow Coffee and Cream for the evening." Tom looked confused. "Annie is very worried about Jacob. We haven't seen him since the night Virgil died. Annie believes he might be hiding out in some cave." Trevor looked to Annie for her assistance in filling in the blanks.

"I think he might be up at Bat Cave. At least, I hope that's where he's at." She looked down at her feet, as though the thought of her brother not being there was a millstone that threatened to sink her. "I'm just so worried..."

"No need to worry, Annie.," Tom consoled. "Of course. Coffee and Cream are at your service. But there's another storm brewing." As if nature wished to emphasize, there was a low rumble of thunder, though it seemed a good distance away. Annie drew in a breath to, no doubt, speak her disagreement, but Trevor jumped ahead.

"Annie, why don't you go change and I'll take care of any costs involved in securing the horses. I'll see you here in half an hour."

"Third door on your left," Mattie coached. Annie thanked her hostess then turned to find her room. Trevor waited until he heard the door latch.

"I agree it seems to be a bit of a hairbrained idea, but Annie is worried that Jacob might, well, do something." Tom and Mattie looked to one another in confusion. "To be more direct, she's afraid he might kill himself. It's not a far-fetched idea, when you consider the circumstances. She really shouldn't be alone if she does find Jacob in that cave." Mattie sighed and returned to counting out change in the cash drawer. "Even if he hasn't done the unthinkable, there are still a myriad of possibilities in between Jacob boozing it up and dying."

"I see your point," Tom spoke, "but isn't there someone else that could go with her? I mean, I could ..."

"You'll do no such thing!" Mattie snapped, causing her husband to jump. Mattie softened her tone but was steadfast in her insistence. "Tom, we have other guests here tonight. I need you *here.* I can't be expected to carry the load of polite conversation on my own, now, can I?" Tom rolled his eyes, knowing his wife was quite capable of holding up her end of any conversation.

"I really don't mind, and I will be fine, although I appreciate the concern and your kind offer, Tom." Trevor felt his knee twinge and hoped he sounded more confident than his injury made him feel. "And I will be happy to pay."

Tom insisted there would be no cost and that he would saddle up the horses and have them hitched to the porch rail just outside the kitchen. He would also ask Clavel to pack a quick sack lunch, or dinner rather.

When Trevor protested, assuring them he and Annie would be back by dinnertime, it was Tom who surprised him with his own incredulous response.

"Trevor, Bat Cave is *several* miles from here. In the best of weather, you can expect to be gone a good three hours." Trevor felt his jaw drop. "Did Annie not tell you?" Trevor stated he was led to believe it was just a mile or so. "As the crow flies," Tom laughed. "But you're not flying by crow, you're riding Coffee. That horse is a plodder on a good day."

"Well, it is what it is, I suppose. I thank you both for your generosity. I really wish you would let me pay for at least some of it. I am sure Annie appreciates it, as well." Trevor leaned against his crutch and waited.

"Nonsense," Mattie replied, closing the cash drawer and placing her palms on the oak desk. "Annie and Jacob are like family to us, and now, so are you. Just be careful. And if you find Jacob ..." Mattie paused, trying to gather herself to say the right words. "If you find the worst, well, ..."

"Don't even say such things," Tom said as he placed his own hand atop his wife's.

"Maybe you *should* go with them, Tom."

Trevor insisted Mattie's initial assertion was the best one. Trevor could manage whatever he and Annie found, if anything. After all, that's what he was trained to do – exude calm in the face of adversity. In fact, he was probably the best choice to accompany Annie to the cave, as he wasn't overly familiar with Jacob or Annie. He could detach himself and think in more pragmatic, clearheaded terms.

Like a sudden gust of wind, Trevor's father blew into the lobby, startling Trevor with a firm slap on the shoulder.

"Well, my son! It's good to see you up and about. I had my misgivings of course, but Lymas tells me you managed well over the past couple of days. I'm grateful that we get to spend a nice evening together before leaving you in the capable hands of the Turners."

Trevor winced, as he'd forgotten all about their dinner together, which, to make matters more awkward, had been his idea. His father was not going to be happy, but then, was he ever?

He had been right. His father was quite perturbed. It was as if his son had lost all good sense, traipsing up a dangerous mountain path to some dark, damp cave in the growing shadows of evening, with a storm brewing, no less. Wallace insisted that Trevor stay at The Esmeralda, spending time with "his old man" and his uncle, drinking brandy and smoking cigars. If he'd known his son was going to gad about in the wilderness, he and Lymas would have left an hour ago.

But, *oh no*, he'd whined. His typically level-headed son was, instead, casting aside all good reason and risking further injury on some misguided, chivalrous adventure, and for what? A farfetched notion that some mountain girl's prodigal brother was *possibly* hiding out in a bat-infested cave in the middle of these godforsaken mountains? Why was it up to him, and him only, to accompany her? And if they did find this boy, how was Trevor's presence going to be of any benefit? The idea was absurd. His father had looked at him as though he should be in a straitjacket and told him as much.

Lymas was equally disenchanted, but calmer in his dissent. But his reasoning had more to do with how it would appear to prying eyes rather than the potential for physical injury. After all, Trevor had already ridden a horse to Effie's and back and seemed no worse for the wear. Even so, Lymas believed that to do so without an escort was not seemly, and for once concurred with his brother. There were others, no doubt, who could assist this young girl in her predicament. In the midst of this argument, Annie appeared at the front desk, wearing a blouse of fine cotton linen with an attached scarf that hung loosely around her neck. The blouse was tucked neatly into a rust-colored, suede skirt that hit her midcalf, with tall riding boots to replace the dress shoes she had been wearing all day. Her long red hair had been brushed, left to cascade across her slender shoulders. She held a hat at her side, but Trevor hoped she wouldn't wear it. It would take away from those beautiful curls that he suddenly wanted to run his fingers through. Her green eyes reflected the dimming light that etched its way through the front windowpane. His father and Lymas seemed to be a victim of her spell – Annie appearing innocent, vulnerable, and seductive all at once.

"Well, I guess we should go," Annie encouraged as another clap of thunder rumbled through the canyon. Trevor heard a horse whinny and blow and turned to his father before following Annie to the kitchen door.

"Father, thank you for your concern, but I am an adult and you must stop trying to control my life. You seemed mostly disinterested in it these past several years, so I see no reason for your manipulation now."

Lymas sighed as he rolled his head and tossed up his hands in an "I told you so," sort of gesture.

"And Uncle," Trevor continued, "I know your heart is in the right place, but I have made a commitment to help this young lady and that is what I intend to do. I've never been one to adhere to social conventions as a general rule, and I deem the good I can do far more important than keeping up appearances." Lymas said that he understood but went on record as saying he still did not approve. Trevor said, frankly, he didn't care. If he wasn't back by the time they left for Savannah in the morning, he wished them safe travels.

On the kitchen porch, Trevor saw Clavel waiting at the edge with a tied napkin that smelled of freshly baked biscuits and something savory, like sage and onions.

"Pork chop sandwiches," Clavel explained. "In case you don't make it back."

"Thank you, Clavel. It smells delightful! I'm not sure we'll manage to save it for supper." He saw Annie's impatience reflected in a not-so-subtle roll of her eyes.

"Yes, thank you, Clavel" she offered with a disingenuous sing-song tone. "Trevor, we really must beat this storm." Trevor raised his eyes to the blackening sky above him. The wind was now whipping through the tops of the hickory trees, sending a shower of young spring blooms down around them. It was so strange, as just a few days before they were in the throes of a snowstorm. Even now, there were lingering patches beneath the shade of the laurel thickets. He was beginning to understand Neil's admonition, at least to some degree. This place really was starting to feel as though nothing else existed outside of the canyon walls. Even the clouds seemed powerless to escape. Annie patted Coffee's belly, like she had before. With an obedient flop, Coffee lay down so as to allow Trevor to slide on top.

"Sure do hope you find Jacob up there," Clavel drawled.

"We'll never find him if y'all keep jack-jawin'," Annie sniped.

"Beg pardon, Annie." Clavel tucked his head at her reproof and waved his goodbyes from the reasonable safety of the kitchen door.

With Trevor mounted, Annie saddled Cream and clucked the horse forward, leading their way up the same trail that had taken them to Effie's. That's when something occurred to Trevor.

"Annie, you led Coffee last time. On foot."

"Yeah?" she replied without turning. An implied *so...?* lingered in the air.

"Well, other than being kicked and stomped by one, I am not intimately familiar with horses. What do I do?"

Trevor braced himself for another terse response but when she turned, a gentle smile greeted him instead.

"Like I said. Coffee and Cream are lovers. Where she goes, he goes." Trevor wasn't sure that fact made him feel any more secure. Didn't horses get rather raucous during their mating rituals? What if Coffee here decided he needed some Cream? He doubted Coffee would give two shakes of a rat's ass who was riding his back if the mood struck. This thought precipitated the beginnings of a panic attack for which Trevor felt most unprepared to deal with.

Then again, Coffee didn't act as if he had much passion left in him. Maybe he was content just to follow his woman around as she led him by the nose.

"Just relax," Annie instructed.

Soon, another trail appeared, this one far more rugged and steep than the one he was familiar with – if he could consider one roundtrip enough to qualify as "familiar." He hoped they weren't taking that one.

"We're turnin' here," Annie directed as she shifted her bodyweight to the left. *So much for hope.* "It's the shortest route to the cave."

Trevor didn't care about *shortest*. He cared about *safest*. He then considered if he'd had a missing brother, he would want to take the most expedient route, too.

As they began their ascent, Trevor's heart crept into his throat. Snow still clung to the gnarled roots, obliterating the trail for long stretches at a time. The grade became so steep near the top of the ridge, Trevor struggled to stay upright.

"Lean forward. Coffee knows what to do," Annie instructed. Trevor tried, but the muscles atop his thighs were taut as a fan belt on a Model-T.

"You always wound this tight?" Annie's teased.

Trevor exhaled a nervous snort. "I'm not uptight."

"Yo'r twitchin' like a cat's tail under a rockin' chair."

"Oh, I ... well, I just don't ..."

"Don't know how to have fun," she said with a sly glance over her shoulder. "Loosen up. Sit a spell. Don't be such a tight ass."

He thought this was a rescue mission, not some joyride.

"Just close yo'r eyes. Focus on the sway of the horse, his hips rockin' back and forth, back and forth," the last of her words trailing off into a near whisper.

Indeed, the gentle clop-clop-clop of the horse proved hypnotic. Thunder and lightning bounced all around them, but Coffee didn't so much as flick his ears.

Where a deer trail dove off below them, Trevor could hear the slap of a small waterfall, but he could not see it for the thick rhododendrons and laurels. Here, the wider path began another series of switchbacks that ascended towards a flat, clear patch in the woods, revealing a round, monolithic rock that reached towards the thick canopy of hickories, oaks and hemlocks. A wide gash ran through its middle, as though someone had cracked it, like an egg.

"Here we are," Annie announced. A flash of lightening lit up the sky above them and in just a few seconds, another clap of thunder bounced off the canyon walls. "Looks like we made it just in time." Annie slipped off Cream's saddle as large drops of rain splatted across Coffee's broad, brown and white nose, causing him to whinny and stomp. It was the most energy Trevor had seen the horse exhibit, renewing his previous anxiety.

"Let's get you off that horse before we get soaked!" Annie yelled above the thundering sound of the rain. Annie led Coffee and Cream just inside the cave's entrance then tapped Coffee's underside. Again, the stallion lowered himself to the ground as Annie removed Trevor's crutch from the leather rifle scabbard.

"See? Nothin' to it. And aren't you glad I remembered this?" She waived Trevor's crutch in the air, like a prize. With that she entered the mouth of the cave, where she extracted an oil lamp from a crack in the wall and scratched a match from her pocket across the rough surface of the rock. That's when he realized he'd brought absolutely nothing in the way of supplies, save Clavel's impromptu picnic sack, and that wasn't even his idea. It seemed his accident had not just robbed him of certain physical abilities, but mental ones as well.

"Mattie gave me a few matches before we left the inn. Lucky for us they didn't get wet on the way up." Yeah. Lucky, Trevor thought.

What else hadn't he thought about? Bears? Big cats? Bats? Hostile humans? He didn't even know where his pistol was. Last he remembered; it was in the nightstand at Lymas's house in Savannah. He supposed he could beat an aggressor with his crutch. Some protector he had become. If there was any trouble, it wouldn't be him who saved them, for certain.

The oil in the lamp didn't look to be old, and Trevor deemed that a good sign. Maybe Jacob was around, just riding things out a bit until he could form a plan. A man always needed a plan.

What was *his* plan? He had a plan to be a pilot – to fly for *The Escadrille*. Come to think of it, he was to have started training this month. A wash of sadness poured over him as he realized where he should be – in France. Instead, he found himself on a remote mountain trail on some decrepit horse, in a cave, to help some girl find her lost brother. Which was ironic, considering a horse is what put him here in the first place.

To be a pilot was still paramount, to be sure. He was stubborn on that point and never once considered anything else. That had not changed. What *had* changed, however, was *how* he would get there. He needed to strengthen his leg, improve its flexibility, and bulk up his muscles. Then, perhaps the most difficult part, he must prove he was still fit for service to The Escadrille, both mentally and physically. While his father's plan to get away to the mountains might have seemed a good one at the time, Trevor now realized it wasn't enough. He needed structured therapy and expert care, and he needed it soon. Every day without it was one more day he would fall behind.

"Jacob!" Annie yelled, holding the lantern high. "Jacob! You in here? Answer me!" The flapping sound of a pair of bats alarmed by their intrusion was the only response.

"How far back does this cave go?" Trevor questioned.

Annie shrugged. "No one really knows." She then went on to explain how she and Jacob, along with some of the other children in The Gorge, used to play Cowboys and Indians. "I always wanted to be the Indian," she said with a hint of nostalgia. "'Cause they were the most beautiful. And the smartest." Trevor smiled. "Once, when Jacob and I were pretendin' to be Indians, hidin' out here in this cave, I double-dared him to go all the way to the end and come back, but he chickened out."

Trevor wondered if Jacob had found its terminus this time, never to return. If he had any thoughts of taking his own life, this would be the place. No one would discover his body for weeks or months – if at all.

"Maybe he left a note," Trevor suggested, then regretted saying such. A *note* in this instance might not be a good thing. He continued looking around for any sign that Jacob had been there. Suddenly, a tiny glow from the floor of the cave, about 20 feet in front of him, drew his eyes a little deeper. "Annie! Over here!"

Annie ran to Trevor's side to see the pulsing embers of a small campfire. The carcass of a rabbit lay just to the side. Trevor could smell the damp soot and noted drops of dried blood where someone had gutted and skinned the animal before cooking it over an improvised spit made from what appeared to be parts of a still.

"This is a good sign, Annie. Someone was here not too long ago. If it was Jacob, maybe he's gone hunting." Annie just shrugged her shoulders and sighed a *maybe.*

"Over there!" Annie exclaimed, pointing to a cream-colored jug with a brown top perched upon a rock ledge. Annie placed the oil lamp down as she grabbed the jug and extracted the cork, inhaling its aroma before passing it off to Trevor. He waved the jug under his nose, taking in one the best smelling whiskeys he'd ever had the pleasure of sniffing.

"Someone sure knows their whiskey," he remarked. "Is there a still here?"

Annie explained that there used to be, but poachers had raided the last one that Jacob and his friends had built, and ever since, they brewed in another undisclosed location. You could almost always find a jug or two hidden though, if you knew where to look. The fact that this one was left out in the open was proof that Jacob was not only alive but planning on coming back. Trevor took a swig of the jug's contents.

Woah!" (*cough, cough, cough*) "That's ... amazing! Is this your brother's recipe?" Annie walked over and took the jug from Trevor's hands, taking a long draught off the top.

"That's Effie's," she said proudly.

"How can you tell?" Trevor asked, wiping a drip from his chin. Annie explained that, while Jacob could make some fine homebrew, Effie's specialty was rye. No matter how many times Jacob had tried, he never seemed to get it right. It was either too bitter or not strong enough. He must've stolen this jug from Effie's wellhouse. Annie said she'd have a word with him about that. Trevor took the jug from Annie and slugged back another nip.

"Damn!" he announced. "I can see why Jacob wasn't in a hurry to get back home. This is fantastic!"

Annie's smile quickly evaporated into a frown. "Problem is, we cain't be sure it's Jacob, can we?" Annie walked back to the cave's opening and stared out into the mounting fog, hands on her hips, listening for any sound or movement that might indicate her brother was nearby. Trevor noticed the illuminated space between her body and blouse, her bare breasts silhouetted in the waning light. He moved to stand beside her, hearing nothing but the deafening rain as it sifted through the forest canopy.

Despite the intensity of the storm, or perhaps because of it, his attention was drawn behind him to another noise. Coffee and Cream were nuzzling one another, Coffee gently nibbling on his companion's ear, for which she seemed to not mind. In fact, if her gentle nickering was any indication, she was rather enjoying it.

"They're so sweet, aren't they, Trevor?"

"Hmm. Yeah. Sweet." He was just grateful Coffee hadn't gotten the notion while he was riding atop his saddle.

"Don't you just sometimes long for that kinda love?" Her statement caught him off balance, so instead of saying the wrong thing, he chose to remain silent. Then again, what was the right thing to say? He couldn't imagine.

"Don't look like the rain'll be lettin' up anytime soon," Annie remarked. "At least we have somethin' to eat while we wait out the storm. You must be hungry."

"Little bit," Trevor admitted. Truth was, he was starving. That was one thing the mountains had done for him: he'd seen a voracious return of his appetite.

"Okay. Let me get you that sandwich." Annie eased towards the two horses and lifted the saddlebag off Coffee's haunches and placed it beside the smoldering ashes, alongside the jug of whiskey.

As Annie unpacked the bag, Trevor could see a red and white tablecloth and a couple of matching napkins, along with a pint jar of applesauce and a couple of spoons. Annie handed him the applesauce, which was still warm. It felt good on Trevor's chilled hand. There were even a couple of carrots for the horses.

Trevor spread the tablecloth a safe distance from the flickering coals, then looked around for some small sticks to rekindle the fire. Now that his eyes had adjusted to the low light, he could see a mound of twigs, small limbs, and pinecones stacked neatly up against cave's wall. Annie saw them, too, and hurried over to grab an armful as Trevor lowered himself onto the checkered cloth, using his crutch as support. Annie sat down beside him, crossed-legged, placing a couple of pinecones and a few smaller sticks on the still-smoldering ashes, leaning in to blow a gentle breath across them. Trevor could smell the liquor on her breath and admired the way her hips filled out the borrowed skirt, like it was made just for her. The cones lit up, sending a fine spray of sparks into the damp evening air. Trevor lifted the jug to his lips and took in a drink, passing the jug off to Annie. He then unwrapped the biscuits and handed one to her.

"So," Trevor began. "You seem to know a lot about horses."

"Is that yo'r way of makin' polite conversation?"

Trevor laughed. "I suppose. But it's true. I mean, I know nothing, except that I was nearly killed by one. But I've watched soldiers tend to them over in France, and it's quite a special relationship. You have a gift."

Annie blushed. "I don't know about that, but I do love 'em. We have one of our own. Her name's Lula Bell. She's really Jacob's horse, more than mine." Annie's eyes were now set on something inside the fire, some memory that had flared.

"I had my own horse," she confided.

"You speak of it in the past tense. Did you have to sell it?"

"No," she said with a shake of her head, her eyes still gazing deep into the flames. "That's the one we had to shoot."

Suddenly, Trevor was back in France, staring over a mound of bodies, snow blowing in his eyes, his pistol trained on that horse he thought for sure was dead, and felt a tinge of panic tighten the muscles around his throat. He reached for the jug of rye and took a swig, wiping a dribble of whiskey on his shirt sleeve.

"You mean, the horse that broke it's leg in the rut caused by the logging trucks?" Annie affirmed her horse was one and the same. Trevor handed her the jug. "Annie, I am so sorry."

"Ain't yo'r fault," she said with a cynical snort.

"Well, no, but that's heartbreaking." He thought again about the horse who'd mangled his knee and pondered the irony of such a sentiment.

"That's why Mr. Turner lets me take care of his horses. When I can. I'm good at it, and he knows it helps me to, you know, get over it." Annie tilted her head towards the cave's jagged ceiling, wiping a tear that came to settle on her cheekbone. "Don't make no never-mind now."

Annie turned up the jug and took a draw then grabbed a few more small limbs to place on the fire. Silence settled between them, the warm flush of whiskey rising high into Trevor's chest. Lightning reflected off the walls of the cave as thunder rumbled through the valley below. It sounded as though someone was rolling a stone across the entrance.

This was insane. Perhaps they should leave, seeing that their worst fears had not been realized – at least, not that he could tell. But to leave the relative safety of the cave in this weather was even more insane. Even if the rains subsided, with night coming on, he wasn't about to risk another horse's life, or anyone else's, on those rutty, pitted roads.

"That biscuit ain't gonna eat itself." Annie pointed at his sandwich as she took a bite of her own. Another bat skittered into the blackening night, its twitters and squeaks becoming muffled by another rumble of thunder.

"Oh, right!" Trevor mused, admiring the sandwich he was about to enjoy. "I wouldn't want to miss this treat, especially since Clavel went to all the trouble of packing it for us." Trevor bit into the biscuit. "Wow. This is really good."

"I s'pose." Annie's brief comment was laced with a tinge of half-heartedness and derision.

"Well, I guess if you eat this sort of thing all the time, it's no big deal. But in France, I was lucky to get Bovril and crackers."

"What's Bovril?"

"It's kinda like jerky. It came in this little tin we carried with us – that is, when we could get it. You could eat it just like it was or you could mix it with water and make a tea – kinda like a broth."

Annie wrinkled her nose. "Sounds disgusting."

Trevor was enjoying sharing some of his war experiences. It had been a long time since he had been able to talk to someone without conversation descending into an argument.

"It *does* sound disgusting but believe me. You learn to adjust your expectations in war, especially where food is concerned. That being said, I know men who would kill for a sandwich like this." Trevor pointed to his biscuit as crumbs dropped from his mouth onto his jacket lapel.

Annie snickered. "Oh yeah? And here I thought men killed for love and honor." Trevor brushed his jacket clean as he watched the fog obliterate the last of the daylight.

"That, too," he laughed before taking the last bite of pork chop and biscuit with another nip off the rye.

"Give me that," Annie scolded, wresting the jug from Trevor's grip. "So did you?"

Trevor stopped in mid-swallow. "Did I what?"

"Ever kill anybody."

"Ha. No. Threatened to. Once."

"Was it for love, honor ... or a pork chop biscuit?"

"Well," Trevor related with a sly grin. "It definitely wasn't for a biscuit." Annie placed her chin in her hand, her eyes urging him to elaborate. "And it wasn't for love, not in the romantic sense at least. I had picked up this boy. A soldier who was missing an eye." Annie winced. "The surgeon wouldn't attend to him, so I threatened him."

"Why wouldn't the doctor work on 'im?" Trevor took the unburned end of a stick and began poking the fire with it.

"Because he was black." Trevor took another pull off the jug.

"So what happened?" Curiosity glinted off Annie's green eyes.

"Well, the surgeon saw the error of his ways through the hollow end of my pistol and fixed him up, but he wouldn't let the soldier stay at the hospital.

"That's terrible. I mean, it's good that he saw to 'im, but I cain't imagine carin' if someone was black before I'd help 'em."

Trevor nodded in agreement. "It's sad, but it happens. A lot."

"I wanted to be a nurse," Annie announced.

Trevor was taken aback by this sudden revelation and stared at her for a moment before responding. She certainly was smart enough, so why shouldn't she have such aspirations?

It then dawned on him. "You could be a VAD – a Voluntary Aid Detachment. Those are nurses who volunteer for the war effort but are not bound by the military's control. Kind of like airplane pilots, come to think of it."

"I s'pose there was a time … but not now." She then told him about how she and Birdie were supposed to go off to Normal School in Asheville and study nursing. Her Pa said he'd never allow it, but she and Birdie hatched a plan. They both had enrolled and were accepted to nursing school. Birdie's sister and her husband had offered to pay tuition for them both. But when Lola and Frances drove up from Charlotte to carry them to Asheville, Birdie announced she wasn't going. She had decided to marry Clavel and that was that. "I guess I kinda resent Clavel because of it," she admitted.

Once again, Trevor was baffled by her admissions. "So that just brings up all sorts of questions," Trevor remarked. "First, did you not know she and Clavel had their sights on one another?"

That was just it, Annie explained. No one had a clue. Clavel was just some nobody who worked at The Esmeralda. Never seemed interested in marrying or making anything of himself. Oh, Birdie would talk to him at church on Sundays, but Annie just thought she was being nice. Birdie was nice to everybody. Nobody saw the marriage coming. Something flitted across Annie's face at that moment, but Trevor couldn't discern what.

"So why didn't *you* go to school?" Annie looked at Trevor as though she had never considered that point.

"I dunno," she shrugged. "It didn't seem right, I guess. I couldn't ask Lola and Frances to pay for my schoolin', not bein' kin." Annie stared at the fire, seeming to sift through other various and sundry reasons as to why she didn't take charge of her own life.

"Did you ask them?" Trevor was determined to make this girl see she could control her own destiny. Annie took a big bite of her sandwich, snatched the whiskey from between Trevor's knees and took a big gulp.

"No, I just assumed, I reckon. I mean, without Birdie, I was trapped." She said this statement as though it should be obvious. Trevor wrested the whiskey back, taking another long draw off the jug before setting it down in the glow of the growing fire.

Neil's past words of warning now echoed in the chambers of his mind. Behind these canyon walls, one's vision dimmed. Kind of like living in a cave. He'd heard of people who had been trapped inside collapsed mines for weeks, even months, but when they were rescued, some begged to go back. The light was just too bright. It was easier to live in the dark – to dance with the devil you know.

"So, to be clear, you blame Clavel for *your* not going to nursing school."

Annie laughed. "Yeah, I guess I do," she admitted. Trevor lifted the jug and handed it to her, scooting a little closer to keep from having to reach so far.

"If you ask me, and you didn't," he paused with a sly grin etching across his face, "if you are going to be angry with anyone – besides yourself," he stopped again, clearing his throat for emphasis, "it would be Birdie."

Annie stared at him as if he were speaking a foreign language. Annie grimaced then said with a shrug, "She's my friend."

Trevor took another swig of whiskey. "And you feel like Clavel took your friend away from you." Annie agreed that was probably true. "You know, Birdie made her own choice, just like you."

"I don't *have* choices, Trevor! You've seen what my Pa is like!" Annie pointed as though her father were standing against the granite wall. "My Momma cain't even talk, much less stand up to the likes of Mr. Preacher Man. I've been saddled with takin' care of everyone in my family and it seems like every chance I have to get free, the warden extends my sentence!"

Trevor flinched at how angry she had become, but the whiskey was giving him courage. Maybe he could be the one to help her help herself.

"Annie, we all have challenges, and we *choose* how to surmount them." He paused for a moment, wondering what choices he would make to change *his* circumstances. "Life throws obstacles in front of us all." Trevor took another draw on the jug. "Sometimes, those hardships actually make us better people."

God, he was such a hypocrite. He'd never thought of his accident being a catalyst that could change his life for the better. Even so, Trevor continued, despite his thickening tongue and tingling lips.

"The black soldier I was telling you about? He wants to be a chef. That's all he's ever dreamed of. But he was conscripted to fight for the French. He watched his brother's head get sliced open by the Germans. That's how he lost his eye. Fighting those bastards."

"That's horrible," Annie admitted.

"Some days, it takes every ounce of strength he can muster to wake up and put one foot in front of the other. He misses his brother terribly."

"What's his name?" Annie asked.

"Ja-wah-wah." Trevor busted out laughing.

Annie emitted a nervous giggle. "What's so funny?"

"His name is Juh-juh-juh ... *whoo!* I am a bit tipsy. Wait just a second." Trevor held up his hand and took in a deep breath. "Jawara. *That's* his name," he said with a snap of his fingers. Trevor was thoroughly amusing himself ... and Annie. "And Ja-war-uh would be laughing his ass off right now if he could see me." He paused. "See us." Annie scooted a bit closer.

"So what will he do now? He cain't fight with just one eye, can he?"

Trevor shook his head. "Naw. But that's my point. He's the cook for my ambulance unit, but the shhhhills ... whoo, wait. Skills! Yes, the *sssskills* and connections he has acquired while cooking for our unit will likely give him an edge when applying to a culinary arch, er uh, arts school." God, this whiskey was strong. "Being a man of color, he's going to need more help than most."

Annie winced at that reality. She reemphasized that, despite living in an area where The Klan was a normal part of everyday life, she found the idea of racism absurd.

"My point..." Trevor trailed off, forgetting his point. "My point ..." he repeated, stabbing his finger into the air as he finally remembered what that point was. "My point is that Jawara has had to adjust his thinking." Trevor realized he liked saying *Jawara* while he was drunk. It made him feel more sober than he was.

Annie admitted she saw his *point*, but she just couldn't see how she would ever get out of Hickory Nut Gorge. Trevor pushed ahead, even as the walls of the cave began to tilt from side to side, sloshing with the remaining liquor in the jug.

"You know, Annie, you are one of the smartest girls ... women ... I've ever met." Annie blushed and turned her head, as though this was something she could never believe. "I mean it. I can tell. You would have done ... no, *will do*, very well in school."

"Yo'r just sayin' that 'cause I could leave yo'r drunk ass sittin' here in this cave," she laughed as she punched him in the arm. Trevor punched her back.

"You wouldn't dare."

"Try me," she sang, taking another long draw off the jug of rye.

"Gimme that!" Trevor shouted, snatching the jug out of her hands. "But nah, nah, nah. Seriously. You're smart. You are, oh my God. *Whew*, and I'll bet you are stubborn, too!" Trevor slurred as he jabbed a finger in her arm. "And I mean that in a good way."

"Oh, I take it as a compliment." Annie placed her elbow on her knee and rested her chin against her hand. "Sssoooo, what makes you think I'm so sah-martttt."

"I can see it in your eyes," he said with so much exuberance it sounded fake. This made her laugh.

"That's ssssooooo lame. You have to come up with somethin' better than *I can see it in yo'r eyes*," she said in a mocking, low voice.

Damn. She *was* smart, but he didn't know how to explain that, just by expressing herself that way, was an indication of higher-than-average intellect.

"Ooh, ooh! I got it. So, you handle the business for your family's farm. That takes a lot of smarts." Annie blew a derisive breath.

"It doesn't take a genius to slop pigs and hoe corn, Trevor."

"Nah, nah, nah. You hafta know math. You hafta make and remember schedules. I'll bet you have to know some husbandry, too." Annie snorted at that one.

"Husbandry? Is that the art of finding a husband?" Heaven help the man who ventured down that path with this fireball.

"Oh, it's ... it's not that," he said with an exaggerated shake of his head. "Nah, nah, nah. Husbandry is the ssssscience of how animals breed and crops grow. You know how to managgge that in order to make money for the farm."

Annie rolled her eyes and then dismissed it with a wave of her hand. "That's just what I was raised to do. What else?" Trevor sighed in exasperation. She seemed to hold her liquor better than he did. Was that a mark of intelligence?

Trevor snapped his fingers. "I got it! You aren't prejudiced. You don't regard a person's color as being any better than yuh-yuh-your own." Annie went quiet for a few seconds while she considered his point.

"I don't know, Trevor. My teacher used to say I could do anything, but my Pa…"

"Your Pa don't know *shhhhhitttt!*" he yelled with a bit too much vigor. "Sssorry. Sorry, but he … he … doesn't. I'm sssserious. You'd sail right through those nursing classes. Then you could write your ticket, Annie. Write. Your. Ticket." Trevor jabbed the air for emphasis. "Anywhere! Boston. San Francisco. London. Hell, even France! You're so … *sssssmart!*" he slurred.

"Yo'r ssssooooo … *drunk!*" Both of them doubled over with an intoxicating laughter that echoed down the dark chambers of the cave.

"Yes, yes I am. I cannot lie." Trevor placed a hand over his heart. That's when he noticed the applesauce sitting behind them. Taking the jar and opening it, he placed one of the spoons inside and took a bite.

"This applesauce is amazing! What's in it?" Trevor quizzed as he washed the fruit down with another slosh of rye.

"Umm, apples?" Annie teased as she reached for the jar. "Let me have some."

Trevor inserted the spoon into the jar once more, holding it up to Annie's lips, but his hands began to shake, and instead of hitting her mouth, the spoon's entire contents spilled onto her blouse. A rust-colored blob spread across the shirt's façade.

"Ah oh," Trevor remarked.

"Now look what you've done," Annie scolded, batting her long, red eyelashes. "Mattie is going to be sooooo mad at you!" Trevor felt genuinely frightened.

"I can clean it up." Trevor reached for the napkin that had contained the pork biscuits and began to dap it against the stain, so that it now mingled with bits of biscuit, flecks of sage and black pepper.

"Never leave a woman's job to a man," Annie sighed, as she proceeded to unbutton her blouse, sliding the linen shirt off when she loosed just enough buttons. Trevor stared at her now bare breasts, unsure of what to say or do.

"I'm going to go hang this in the rain," Annie explained, easing herself up from her place near the fire. "That should wash the stain out."

"How will you get it dry?" Trevor asked, as if that was the most pertinent question at the moment.

"We have a fire, silly." Yes. There was a fire. But wouldn't that take a while? Then again, what else did they have to do?

Trevor looked around him, not sure where to cast his eyes. He tried fixating on the fire, but the smoke floated towards his face. Annie was now walking towards him, her riding boots removed, appearing not the least bit concerned she was both barefooted and bare-breasted. Trevor averted his gaze to the flames once more, daring the heat and smoke to force his eyes elsewhere.

"What's the matter, Trevor? Ain't never seen a naked girl before?" Trevor snorted at the lunacy of such a statement. Annie eased down in front of him, her long legs extended out in front of her.

"Yes, but I just never, well, this doesn't seem like the right time..."

"The right time for what?" Annie took her foot and ran it slowly up Trevor's leg, her toes massaging him between the buttons of his fly. Trevor felt his face flush with blood and alcohol as he took her bare foot into his hand and began rubbing her ankle, slowly making his way over her calf before delving deeper toward the inside of her thigh.

"That feels so good," she whispered, leaning backwards so that the fire cast a shadow of her breasts against the cave's walls.

Trevor pushed himself forward, forgetting that this sort of motion would normally have him writhing in pain. The whiskey had not only numbed his judgment, it seemed, but his knee as well. Placing most of his weight on his good knee, Trevor hovered over top, gently kissing her forehead, the tip of her nose, her lips. She smelled of smoke. Her very breath was intoxicating. His hand gently traveled down her neck, then settled on her breast, his thumb circling one nipple as he kissed the other.

"Annie," Trevor whispered. "Have you ever been ... you know ... with a man?" There was a pause then a sigh.

"No," she whispered. "But don't stop. I'm ready." Trevor wasn't sure he was, but he really didn't think stopping was a possibility, either. For the first time since the accident, he was able to kneel as he unbuttoned his trousers, pushing them down around his knees. He then unbuttoned his shirt, casting it off into the shadows.

"It may hurt a little." When she said she didn't care, Trevor hovered over her, lifting her skirt with his teeth to expose her navel, into which he poured copious amounts of whiskey. His gentle slurps as he drank caused her to laugh and moan. He then bent her knees and gently spread them apart, exploring, searching for any sign that she might not be as ready as she claimed. When she did not resist, he slipped inside her.

Chapter 20

Next thing he knew, it was daylight. The sun, though hidden behind the granite canyon walls, was pushing a daffodil-colored light into the valley. Annie was snoring softly, her head and hand resting on his chest. Somewhere during the night, one of them had pulled the tablecloth over their naked bodies for warmth. His head throbbed with every beat of his heart, and although his vision was slow to clear, he was pretty sure he was staring down the barrel of a Winchester.

"Mornin', War Boy. How's it goin'?" Jacob towered above them, flicking the open end of the barrel against Trevor's nostrils. The smell of gunpowder stung his eyes and nose, and for a minute, Trevor believed he would throw up. He shook Annie with his left arm, but she barely stirred.

Jacob scoffed. "She's a hard one to wake up in the mornin', especially after she's been drinkin'."

Without moving the rifle from its position, Jacob lifted the whiskey jug and shook it, then tipped it back, sucking down the last small dregs of rye. "Damnnnnn! Y'all didn't leave me none much. I'm gonna have to charge you to replace that, I do believe."

Annie was now coming to her senses, slowly, rubbing her head in her hands as Trevor pulled the end of the tablecloth over her bare chest. She suddenly jumped, clutching the tablecloth around her. "Jacob! Oh my God! Put that gun away ... *NOW!*" Jacob grinned, easing the rifle back a bit but still training it in the direction of Trevor's head. "Jacob, I'm not kiddin'. I'll ..."

"You'll do what, Big Sister?"

"I'll tell Pa where yo'r at!" she squealed. Trevor's eyes were darting back and forth between the two siblings, but he dared not move any other part of his body.

"Oooh, that's a scary one," her brother laughed. "By the time you get yo'rself decent and back down the mountain, I'll be halfway to Spartan-burg." Annie looked at him with a question mark on her face. "I got a job on the railroad. Spurgeon said his uncle was a foreman down there and could set me up. Thought I'd try my hand at rail-roadin'."

Trevor's brain could not keep up with all this insanity. Annie had said that none of Jacob's friends knew where he was. Had she lied, or had they?

"So, me and Winnie here. That's what I call my Winchester," he said, looking at Trevor while patting the butt of his rifle, "We just gotta know. What happened here?" he glowered, panning the end of the barrel around the cavernous space, coming right back to Trevor's head.

"Jacob, I can explain," Annie whimpered.

"I don't need explanations, Big Sister. I got eyes. I just said I was in-terested." Jacob laughed then rotated the rifle to where Annie's shirt lay crumpled behind him and picked it up with the end of his barrel. "I found this hangin' in a tree outside. Soakin' wet. I'm just *dyin'* to know how that happened!" Jacob moved the barrel with the shirt dangling off it, stopping in front of his sister. Annie snatched it away, as though there wasn't a gun being aimed at her chest. Annie turned her back to her brother, wrestling to pull the damp shirt over her shivering, pale shoulders.

"As my sister's brother, I oughta string you toe to toe from that oak tree out there and gut you like deer," Jacob sneered.

"Yes, you probably should," Trevor replied. Jacob burst into a loud laugh.

"Well, I must say, War Boy. You do own up to yo'r sins. I hafta admire that in a man." Jacob lowered his rifle and placed it against the wall of the cave, looking far more amused than angry.

"Jacob," Annie began as she stomped her way across the cave. "I ... we ... came all the way out here 'cause I was afraid you might have hurt yourself!" she whimpered.

"Hurt myself? How do you mean?"

"Killed yo'rself, Jacob! Hung. Shot. Poisoned. I was so worried. Trevor offered to come with me so that I wouldn't be alone."

Jacob's laugh ricocheted off the thick stone walls. "He *volunteered*, did he?! Well, bless yo'r heart, Trevor. That's mighty gentlemanly of ya." Trevor said nothing, wondering if he could now move since the gun was no longer an imminent threat.

"And I'm just messin' with you, War Boy. I don't give no never mind who my sister does, or doesn't, do. If you ask me, it's about time she had some fun."

"Jacob!" Annie would have slapped him if she hadn't been holding the tablecloth around her waist, as she still had yet to find her skirt.

"Annie, yo'r gettin' me all wrong. I'm *glad* you found some comfort during yo'r time of distress. Me? I was out huntin' all night in this goddamn rain tryin' to find my next meal. Least you coulda done was saved me some likker."

"That ain't yo'r likker. It's Effie's! And she'll be none too happy to know you stole it from her!"

"Well being *stolt* sure didn't stop you from drinkin' it, did it? And I didn't steal *shit*, Annie Grace. She *gave* it to me." Annie was speechless. Trevor, though surprised at this revelation, too, took this opportunity of distraction to dress. God, his head was pounding! Coffee and Cream whinnied in a duet where they stood at the entrance to the cave, munching on something with great content.

"Effie knew where you were?"

"Hell, it ain't hard to figure. Even yo'r pea brain figured it out. I'm not stayin' here, though," Jacob continued. "Like I said, I'm headin' to Spartanburg."

"Jacob, *nooooooo!*"

"I am, Annie. I cain't take livin' here no more. Ever'where I turn, I see little Virge. Hell. I cain't even take a piss without seein' him beside me."

Jacob sniffed as his throat seemed to push back a wall of pain. "He was always tryin' to do like me, ya know? *Jacob, show me this. Jacob, how do I do that?* I gotta get away. At least … for a while."

Annie began to beg. "Jacob, please don't go! You just cain't!" Trevor came to stand between the two of them, now feeling as though he might be playing the role of referee, as opposed to the previous one of target.

"Actually, he can," Trevor heard himself say. Both siblings looked at him with shock.

"You want to leave, Annie. Why shouldn't Jacob?" A smirk stretched across Jacob's face.

"I'm likin' you more and more by the minute, War Boy." Jacob crossed his arms and began to assess him with a comradery that put Trevor's jangled nerves somewhat at ease.

"I'm just thinking about your mother," Trevor acknowledged. "For all intents and purposes, she is alone and someone needs to care for her. But I think you can both have what you want. It just might take a while."

"So what do you propose?" Jacob leaned up against the cave wall, uncomfortably close to his rifle, but he didn't reach for it. Hopefully that stage of this drama was over.

Trevor suggested that since Jacob did have the prospect of a good job with the railroad, he should take this opportunity by the horns. As luck would have it, his uncle and father were leaving for Spartanburg today and could take Jacob with them, should they get to The Esmeralda in time. When Annie whined and stomped, shrieking about the unfairness of it all, Trevor pointed out that, at the moment, she didn't have a concrete plan. It would make sense for her to give her father a few more days to cool off. Stay at The Esmeralda, as they had planned. From the inn as a safe haven, she could check on their mother and break the news of Jacob's departure so their mother wouldn't be as worried. In the meantime, Trevor would help Annie write letters and inquire about nursing schools. He said that life was like an automobile. Even the slightest, forward motion could prevent one from becoming stuck.

Damn, he needed to turn this advice on himself. Maybe this mountain therapy was working after all.

"Well, I hate to break up this sweet reunion, but we need to get moving or we will miss my father and uncle. You got your horse, Jacob?"

"Yeah, I do," Jacob said. "I snuck Lula Bell outta the pasture when everyone was bein' showered with brimstone at the church." Trevor heard another whinny and realized there were now three horses standing together, no doubt conversing in horse language about how ridiculous humans were.

Annie, now fully clothed, moved towards the horses as Jacob reached for his rifle, causing Trevor to jump. "Easy now, War Boy. I ain't gonna shoot 'cha. Not yet, anyways," he replied with a wink. Instead, he grabbed Trevor's crutch and extended it towards him. Trevor reached to accept it but Jacob held it firmly in his grip, creating a slight tug-of-war between them.

"Listen," Jacob spoke in a near whisper. "I don't know you, and I ain't one to judge. And kinda like that verse in the Bible says. *I ain't my sister's keeper.* But I just wanna be real clear. You best do right by her. Understand my meanin'?"

Trevor cast a wary eye on this young man who just minutes before had a Winchester trained on his skull. He considered ripping the crutch from Jacob's grip and walloping him below the knees, but then reconsidered. The boy had been through Hell the past few days, and if the scene at the church was any indication, there was more Hell to come. Instead, Trevor wrested his crutch away and slid it under his arm.

"I get your meaning," Trevor began. "I do. But don't you ever threaten me again. Your sister is old enough to make her own decisions. Do you get *my* meaning?"

"I do. It's just ..." Jacob paused, a noticeable catch in his throat halting his words.

"Just what?"

"She's right, you know." Trevor stared at Jacob, the morning fog and the residue of whiskey swirling through his head. "I thought about it, you know...hurtin' myself. Just like she said." Trevor's eyes widened as a tear spilled across Jacob's face. "But then my friend, Spurgeon, I saw him up at the church when I went'n rang the bell. He was puttin' flowers on his

Momma's grave. He's the one that told me about that railroad job. So I figured I'd come up here and think on it for a day or two. Went huntin' and when I came back, I heard you two a'rootin' around like two feral hogs and I hid back down yonder." Jacob pointed towards the deeper recesses of the cave. "I never heard such carryin' on," Jacob snickered. "But it did give me time to reconsider."

Trevor put a firm, assured hand on this young man's shoulder – a shoulder that had borne much and would bear a heavier load still.

"You two lollygaggers gonna get a move-on or am I gonna hafta put my foot in yo'r asses?" Annie had Coffee down on the ground, her hands planted firmly on her hips.

"Just cool yo'r tail skirt, there, missy! I'm given War Boy here wherefore!" Jacob gave a knowing look at Trevor, then leaned in close.

"You cain't ever tell her. Okay?"

"I'll take your secret to my grave, Jacob. I'm just glad you decided to stay with us. Now let's get going. You've got a brand-new life ahead of you." Jacob nodded, blowing his nose on the handkerchief Trevor extended. He hoped he could say the same for them all.

Chapter 21

Effie and Neil had decided to take Ida to Effie's place after Virgil's funeral instead of Neil's. It was a shorter distance and Effie would have more herbs and concoctions at her disposal to calm poor Ida's nerves while they figured out what to do. Neil said he could sleep over in case Lester decided to create a ruckus. Didn't know why they didn't make that their plan to begin with. She supposed everyone was a little rattled after Lester's tirade of holy terror.

Ida was beside herself, withdrawing into a stupor Effie feared she might never come out of. It would help if Jacob would show his face. She'd noticed a jug of her best rye whiskey was gone from the wellhouse and assumed Jacob had taken it, but she didn't want to give Ida any false hope and hadn't mentioned it. Her gut told her he was close though.

Effie had made a tincture of lemon balm, lavender, and a touch of poppy juice to settle Ida's nerves. She'd started to use the laudanum, but she'd known folks to become dependent, so Effie decided to wait and see if the tea would do the trick. Sure enough, Ida had slipped into a deep sleep in the early evening and hadn't stirred until this morning when Effie was making cathead biscuits and sausage gravy. She'd come out of her room with a smile on her face, clutching an old robe around her.

The faded, picked chenille robe had been her mother's, one of the few things her Pa had kept after her mother died. Her Pa told her that her mother had made it from an old bedspread when she was pregnant with Effie. When kids (and some adults) would be cruel and tease her for being, well, just different, Effie would pretend that it was her mother wrapping her arms around her. She supposed her mother's comfort was now being shared with Ida, and felt a rare tear pool up inside her eye.

Effie walked over to the kitchen sink and peered out the window. Spring was coming, and there was much to be done. How she was going to manage was beyond her. Neil would do what he could, and suggested that Trevor might be able assist, insomuch as the boy was able, but the years were showing on Neil, too. And Trevor? That was a stretch. He might be young and willing, but that boy had a lot of healing to do, inside and out, before he would ever be up to doing such work. *Don't get too far ahead of yo'rself, Effie. Things always work out.*

Suddenly she noticed a flash of white in the woods. Her eyesight was failing, like everything else about her, but she could make out three horses clomping their way at a decent clip along the path that led from her place towards Annie's. In between was The Esmeralda, and it stood to reason that Annie and Trevor might be among the three. Could the other be Jacob? Effie moved as fast as she could to the back door.

"Hey!" she hollered. "Who's that?" The horses slowed but didn't stop. "That you, Jacob? Annie? Get yo'r asses down here! Yo'r Ma's worried sick!"

At that the horses came to a halt, their noses turning towards Effie's house. Sure enough, as they emerged from the woods, she could see Trevor on that chocolate and cream-colored horse the Turners used for children's rides at the inn. Wasn't Coffee its name? The other was Jacob atop of Lula Bell. And her eyes be damned, that was Annie riding atop Cream, that other horse of the Turners.

Annie threw up her hand as Neil joined Effie on the back porch. Ida came out, too, the joy visibly bubbling up inside her at the sight of both her children, safe.

"We ain't got a lot of time," Annie explained. "We've gotta get back to The Esmeralda so that Jacob can get a ride to Spartanburg." Ida cocked her head, confused. "I'll explain later, Ma, but it's a good thing. Trust me." Ida didn't seem convinced. Jacob then eased his horse forward and spoke.

"I just wanted you to know I was alright, Ma. Sorry I worried you." Ida shook a scolding finger at him, but then eased herself into wary smile.

"How're you farin' on that horse, Trevor?" Neil asked. Trevor said he was doing alright, all things considered. They would come back later in the afternoon to check on Ida, but for now, they had to go. And with that, the three turned back on the trail. A stray tear slid down Ida's cheek as she waved her one good arm in a "goodbye".

Effie put her arm around her friend and hugged her tight. "It'll be alright, Ida. You raised good young'uns." But saying a thing didn't make it true. Effie felt a squeeze on her heart and wondered if she was doling out false comfort. Jacob would land on his feet, but it was Annie that caused her guts to tie up in a knot.

Effie watched the butt-end of Lula Bell disappear into the woods and hoped, for Ida's sake, she wasn't just blowin' smoke up her skirt. The odds were probably about fifty-fifty.

Chapter 22

"**F**ather! Lymas!" Trevor shouted at the two men as they stood on the porch of The Esmeralda, giving their farewells to their hosts. Clavel had parked The Cadillac in front of the inn, it's smooth idle sounding more like a purr than the clickity-clickity sound of the Model-T. Wallace moved to the walkway and waited for the two horses to halt in front of him. No surprise that his father's scowl preceded his words by several feet.

"Well, well, well. Nice of you to show up to see your old man off," Wallace derided.

"Father, I can explain."

Jacob laughed. "Seems everyone's tryin' to explain themselves this mornin'." Trevor shot Jacob a dagger-laden glance.

"We found Jacob, just as I'd hoped. I am grateful for your patience for it seems that our trip was, indeed … necessary." Trevor and Jacob cast a knowing glance at one another while Wallace sniffed and raised his eyebrows.

"I won't go so far as to deem it 'necessary'," Wallace began, "but I am grateful for your well-being and safety, Jacob. Now if you will excuse us, I would like to say a proper goodbye to my son. We have a long journey ahead of us."

"Father, I was hoping to ask a favor of you." Wallace stopped and glared as if even speaking such was an abomination. Jacob became uncomfortable and guided Lula Bell a short distance to a small patch where daffodils and crocuses were poking their heads above the grass. "Jacob has taken a job with the railroad in Spartanburg. Would it be too much trouble for you to take him with you?"

Wallace frowned and, for a moment, Trevor believed he would go off on another rant, but he seemed to reconsider as he watched Jacob's horse pull up grass by the roots. "Lymas, what are your thoughts on this matter?"

"Well," Lymas began, "it will be a tight squeeze, but I believe we can make the room."

"Son?" Wallace motioned Jacob over. "Do you have any belongings to take with you? We haven't a lot of room to spare."

"No sir. Only what I'm wearin'." Wallace seemed a bit surprised at that. "I'll buy me some clothes when I get paid. If you'd be so kind, I promise not to be any trouble."

"Well, it looks like we will have some company, Lymas."

"Wonderful!" Lymas chirped. "I'll have some intelligent conversation for a change." Lymas said with a wink. Even Wallace managed a weak smile.

Trevor was relieved to see his uncle back to his jovial self. Perhaps he was looking forward to seeing Ms. Dubois. He thought about how happy he would be to have someone to go home to, but he didn't know when that would be possible ... if ever.

Suddenly, memories from last night's improprieties ran through him, a shallow sword he quickly withdrew. As he had learned in dealing with his mother's death, regret was pointless. Hindsight, however, could prove most valuable. He needed to set a course – one that kept him on the straight and narrow, and with his father and uncle leaving him to himself, he'd have plenty of time to sort it all out.

Trevor saw Annie off to her room and excused himself, stating he would see her and the Turners at dinner. Her disappointment was obvious, but he was exhausted and ... he had a plan, though it wasn't much of one.

He had come a long way since arriving in Hickory Nut Gorge. He was walking somewhat better. He was getting out into society a bit – that is, if you could count one hellfire and brimstone funeral as a societal function. Hell. He'd even ridden a horse. Twice! And while he continued to wade knee-deep in the waters of regret, last evening had given him a romantic confidence boost as well.

Rifling through the amenities in his nightstand, Trevor found some yellowed stationery and began to pen another letter to Hannah, the VAD back at the *hôpital* in Paris. The task of writing took longer than he expected, but it felt good to reconnect with his life in France, the one that was torn away from him faster than you could say, *Giddy up.* Nothing might ever come of it, but if it helped take his mind off the chaos of the past month, and of what he had allowed to happen last night, then there was no harm in it. Of that one thing, he was certain.

<h1 style="text-align:center">Chapter 23</h1>

Annie heard the grandfather clock chime twice. Two in the morning. She had been in bed most of the day since seeing Jacob off, save for the hour or so at dinner where she endured the incessant chatter about the war. It was the most boring conversation she had ever had the displeasure of being a part of. It took all the muster she could dredge to not fall headfirst into her chicken gravy.

There was some woman and her husband there by the name of, what was it? Vanderbilt. Yes. That was it. Mr. and Mrs. William Vanderbilt. Apparently, they were high up the social ladder. Given the talk-talk-talk of spreading money around like it was hayseed, they certainly had several coins to spare. *How could Mrs. Vanderbilt best serve the young men and women driving ambulances at the front? Would another personal visit from her provide a morale lift for the drivers and troops? Did the AAFS need more funds? More ambulances?*

It was during this painfully dull conversation that Annie began to reflect on the past twenty-four hours. She was so happy to have found Jacob, of course, but the romantic interlude that had ensued made her skin tingle. She told herself she had not intended duplicity. She really did suspect Jacob had gone to the cave to kill himself. And, of course, she didn't want to risk finding such horrors alone. But had she planned to trick and seduce this person she hardly knew in the process? Not entirely.

She told herself that what happened was born out of all the bizarre, trau-matic events leading up to Virgil's death and funeral and subsequent grief. What red-blooded, American girl wouldn't seek comfort in the arms of a handsome young man such as Trevor Middleton? She not only suspected other girls in The Gorge had done so, but she knew it for fact. But had she set out to accomplish such a deed?

No, she had not. What had begun as a mere fantasy, designed to help her escape what seemed to be an impossible situation, simply took root and blossomed thanks to that jug of rye. She merely saw an opportunity and embraced it, and wasn't that what success was all about – embracing opportunity?

At one point in the evening, Mrs. Vanderbilt had asked Trevor about his intentions for the future. That's when Annie managed to sit up and pay attention. This nattering she needed to hear.

"Trevor, I am terribly sorry about your accident," Mrs. Vanderbilt had said. Trevor thanked her for her concerns while downplaying his injuries, but Mrs. Vanderbilt was way ahead of him. Somehow, she knew he had nearly died and expressed concern for his recovery. She even offered her assistance in that regard. Perhaps Trevor might be interested in a clerical job with her organization until he recovered enough to begin pilot training. Trevor said he would consider it, but she thought he was just being polite.

Mrs. Vanderbilt had tried to include Annie in the conversation. *Was she a guest? What was her relationship to the Turner's? To Trevor? Where did she live?* The verbal bombardment sent her already dizzy head spinning off her shoulders. Feeling awkward and out of place, Annie had excused herself to her room.

Now, in the thick of the night, in a plush bed, with extravagant bed-clothes, she tried to find comfort in it all but found herself ill at ease. Maybe it was because her Pa had always forbidden Ida to wear anything but a cotton shift to bed – that bed being a mattress filled with cornhusks tucked into one corner of a three-room shack with a tool shed attached. He said to wear fancy gowns was to invite the Devil into your bedroom. But the Devil was already in that bed, so she figured there wasn't room for another.

With the hammering in her head subsiding, Annie rose to her feet and stood in the middle of the room. It would have been dark as pitch, were it not that the room was painted in a blinding white that seemed to soak up daylight and effuse it into night. That's when she noticed the electric lamp she could have turned on. She was unaccustomed to such fineries, and felt shame rise to her cheeks. She felt so backwards and ignorant. How many times had she delivered eggs and meat to The Esmeralda and never had an inkling as to what lay behind the doors of these rooms? Certainly, she had admired the fancy furniture and draperies she could see from the kitchen, and the fine attire of the guests as they passed through the inn's lobby. She'd often dreamed of living it instead of merely catering to it, but for now, the transition felt uncomfortable. *Even a new shoe must be broken in*, she thought.

Annie returned to her bed. Just as she was about to drift off she heard a sound – a decided *kerflump* that shook her wide awake. Had her father found her? Had he come to drag her from The Esmeralda and take her back to her rightful place as a poor preacher's daughter?

Pflump. Eeeeek. Pflump, Pflump, then a cascade of trills and a longer *cheeeeep* echoed down the corridor. Annie eased into the hall to find a little brown bat flinging itself against the walls and windows of the inn. Poor thing. Annie unbolted the large oak doors, sending the bat back into the night.

The resulting breeze tossed several pieces of unsorted mail onto the floor. With only a glint of moonlight to guide her, Annie picked up the pile of mailings. Who were these letters for? Of course, it was none of her business really, but she was so curious! A return address might reveal interesting and exciting clues about who these people were - where they were from and who they consorted with.

Annie pulled the chain on the banker's light that sat atop the desk and began to sort through the correspondence. There was one letter addressed to Mrs. Vanderbilt from a Ms. Anne Morgan in New York. Another mailing appeared to be a bill of sorts, as it was addressed to "accounts payable" at The Esmeralda - no person in particular. God, these various and sundry posts were even more mundane than the dinner conversation she had endured.

Disappointed, she tossed the letters back onto the desk, sending them scattering to the floor once more. Her head pounded as she bent to gather them up and return them to the front desk. That's when she noticed a missive addressed to a Miss Hannah Gourlay, lying in a slot designated for OUTGOING MAIL, written in as elegant a handwriting as Annie had ever seen. The return address reflected the post was from Trevor.

Annie whisked the envelope inside her robe and fled down the hall to her bedroom. Maybe she could read at least some of the letter's contents without having to open it. Annie held the envelope up to the lamp - upside down and right-side up, but no matter what angle she tried, she couldn't make out any of the words except for, "Dearest Hannah." If she opened the envelope, she would have to slip it back into the stack and hope no one suspected her of such brash actions. The contents, however, had to be determined. That envelope contained poison. She was sure of it.

Annie stuck her finger under the flap and ripped it open, yelping as the sharp edge sliced her skin. She sucked on the cut until she could no longer taste the tang of blood, then removed the letter, burying the envelope between the folds of her red dress that now lay in a forlorn heap in the corner of the room.

Dearest Hannah,

I hope this letter finds you well and happy, though happiness can be difficult in the thick of this damnable war – unless, perhaps, you have single-handedly won it for us by now. I am certain any man, including the Bosche, would bow to your charms, should they come face to face with them as I had the good fortune to do.

I am recovering well here at The Esmeralda – much better than I expected. Enough feeling has returned to my leg to allow me walk unassisted, although I do still find I need my crutch. My chest is still sore, but I can at least sneeze without fearing my ribs will explode. My dizziness has abated, and overall, I cannot complain. Even my father believes that I am well

Annie re-read the letter twice before wadding it up and throwing it across the bed. She never expected this turn of events. Trevor had never mentioned this *Hannah*, not once. This discovery was most disconcerting.

It now seemed that Annie's chances of wooing Trevor with her charms, what few she had, were scarce as hen's teeth.

Then again, that little brown bat could have been a messenger – sent from out of the darkness to show her a great light. She now had information that would allow her to change the course of things, or rather, keep them on track. Providence. That's what this was, and she was not going to let such an opportunity go to waste.

Blackberry Winter

Bitterly she weeps ... tears are on her cheeks.
Among all her lovers there is no one to comfort her.
All her friends have betrayed her.
They have become her enemies.

Lamentations 1:2 (NIV)

Chapter 24

After devouring a cinnamon roll and coffee with Trevor in the garden, Annie announced that she would like to go to Birdie's for the day. Clavel expressed his concerns about this plan. He had well-grounded doubts regarding his own family's safety should Lester come looking her; but Annie plowed through his objections.

Annie persuaded Trevor to drive her to Birdie's. He didn't seem none too happy about it, but what was she to do all day around The Esmeralda? She explained that it would be to her advantage to talk to Birdie about her crazy father and forge a more long-term plan regarding her and her mother's situation. With Jacob gone, that was of utmost importance.

Annie kissed Trevor on the cheek as he opened the car door for her. It didn't even bother her (much) that Trevor had not returned her kiss. Of course, he would be guarded about such things. After all, discretion was a part of being a gentleman. And there was, potentially, another woman, but that girl was an ocean away. Trevor was here, with her, and these canyon walls could make you feel as though there was nothing else outside of them.

Birdie met Annie out on the porch with June slung across her hip, squalling like a baby bird. When Annie ascended the steps, Birdie sat the baby inside the front door and flung her arms wide - a killdeer spreading her protective wings.

The two friends sat on the front porch for a time, rocking and talking with the rhythm of idle chit-chat. Annie told her about finding Jacob and how relieved she was. Birdie said she'd been worried and was ever so grateful Jacob was safe. Birdie did not mention Annie's Pa or the events at the church, except to say she saw him and that old preacher man from down in Rutherfordton take off on horses with their black jackets, brandishing their Bibles like pistols. That meant her Pa was out circuit riding and wouldn't be back home for at least another week. Well, there was some good news.

"So, tell me. How do you like stayin' at The Esmeralda? Did you get to know that Trevor boy? He's mighty handsome, ain't he?"

Annie raised her eyes, unable to repress her smile. "He is mighty fine, Birdie. We talked…" Little June began squalling again. Lord, that child! She'd really hoped for a quiet afternoon … alone … with her friend.

"Let me go lay June down and I'll get us some lemonade." Birdie touched her friend on the shoulder. "I'm glad yo'r here, Annie. Just like old times." Birdie bussed Annie on top of her head as she made her way inside the house.

When she returned, Birdie had two glasses of lemonade on a wooden tray, along with a couple slices of poundcake. "I hope you like the cake, Annie."

"Oh, Birdie. You always did make the best pound cake. I'm sure it's just divine!" Annie chirped.

After a few minutes of quiet, listening to a mockingbird squawk and chatter atop a fence post, Annie planted her feet on the ground and stopped rocking.

"Birdie, I need some advice."

"Of course, Annie."

"Well, you know, you and I were supposed to go to Normal School, right? Before you married Clavel?" Birdie rolled her eyes. She'd been guilted over this infraction at least a thousand times by now, how she'd ruined Annie's life by marrying Clavel. "Well, I think things might be lookin' up a bit." Birdie's eyes began to flicker with the fire of Annie's infectious hope.

"What, Annie? Did you apply for school again? I always knew you would. Yo'r so much smarter than all of us here in The Gorge, put together!" Annie blushed just a bit.

"No. Nothin' like that." Annie paused for a second, then drew in a breath. "I think Trevor's sweet on me." Birdie sat back as though she'd been blown by a strong wind. "He went with me to Bat Cave."

"He...went with you?" Annie could feel a hint of judgment oozing from Birdie's pores but pretended not to notice.

"Yes, he was afraid if I found Jacob, you know ... hurt, I'd be alone. He wanted to help."

Birdie just stared.

"Then he asked me to sit with him in the garden this morning." Of course, it was the other way around, but that was straining out gnats and swallowing camels. He didn't refuse when she asked.

"As I was leavin' today, he kissed me on the cheek. He's sweet on me, Birdie. I just know it." Annie smirked with gratification at the memory of it, but Birdie simply shrugged her shoulders. "I just got one little problem."

"I already don't like the sound of this, Annie. Every time you have 'a little problem' it means yo'r feelin' guilty about somethin' you know is wrong, but you want someone to tell you it's alright."

"Birdie, yo'r supposed to be my friend. Ever since you married Clavel, yo'r just a miserable sort!"

Birdie shook her head with frustration. "I ain't changed at all, Annie. Not one bit, except for the better. Marriage suits me. And if you were my friend, you'd be happy for me. Only one who's miserable is *you*!"

"And that's what I aim to change, Birdie." Big tears began to well up in her eyes.

"Alright, Annie. What is this problem? I am yo'r friend, although friends don't have to agree."

Annie sniffed and wiped her nose on her sleeve. "There's someone else." Confusion crumpled Birdie's eyebrows into a deep furrow.

"You mean, someone else yo'r sweet on?"

"Shut yo'r mouth! Ain't no boy here in this gorge worth two seconds of my precious time!"

"Well, who then?"

Annie told Birdie how she'd found a letter addressed to some Hannah girl in France, and of course, she didn't mean to look at it, but well, she was so distraught over her daddy and all, she'd lost her ever-loving mind and opened it. Annie reached down inside her dress and pulled out the letter, perspiration now soaked into the paper's fibers. Birdie stared in disbelief.

"You didn't." Annie said, in fact, she had. What choice did she have? "Annie, you cain't just go stealin' other people's letters! If Trevor finds out, and he *will*, you'll have nothin' but shame to show for it!"

"And that's why I'm asking you what I should do?"

"*Do?* You know what you did was wrong, so just own up to it and let the chips fall where they may." Annie rolled her defiant eyes and sighed. "It's the only right thing to do."

"See, that's where you and I are different, Birdie. It's not the only right thing."

"That's not for you to decide, Annie! That's between him and...and...what's her name?"

"Hannah. Here. Read it for yourself." Birdie snatched the letter from her friend and gave it a once-over before handing it back.

"I'm gonna burn it."

"Annie, you cain't." she implored, shaking her head in disbelief that even Annie would even consider such a thing.

"I am, and I will," she announced. "I was even hopin' that Clavel would, you know, look out for any more letters." Birdie gasped.

"He will do no such thing, Annie! And why did you even bother asking my advice if you were gonna do what'chu *damn* well pleased, despite all good sense?" Annie jumped at her friend's cursing. Birdie was up on her feet, pacing the front porch. "To make matters worse, now I'm privy to this little ploy of yours and, by association, just as guilty if I don't say somethin'."

"You wouldn't!" Annie screamed.

"Yo'r not gonna burn that letter." Annie allowed she was and made her way towards the fireplace to do just that - her friend following dead on her heels. She should've just burned it at The Esmeralda.

Suddenly, Birdie reached out and snatched the letter from Annie's hand, holding it tight against her breast. Annie clenched her teeth and sneered as she held out her trembling palm.

"Give that back to me right this instant." Birdie shook her head violently, clutching the letter even tighter. "Birdie," she continued, in a suddenly much calmer voice. "I have a very good reason. Now give it to me."

"What possible good reason could you have?"

"I want my child to know it's father." Birdie stepped backwards towards the bed in the corner where Little June was lying and sat down, hard.

"What ... did you juh-juh-just say?"

"A couple of nights ago. In the cave. Trevor and I, you know..."

"What in Hell's blue blazes did you ... oh my, God." Birdie caught her breath then stood again, stabbing the letter in Annie's direction. "*Thissss!* This is low, Annie Grace! Don't even sound like the girl I grew up with. What has gotten into you? And there's no way you'd know yo'r pregnant. Not this soon!"

"I can feel it, Birdie," Annie said, all smiles. "I'm as sure of it as you standin' in front of me – judgin' me like I'm some whore..."

"You ARE a whore!" Fire flew from Annie's eyes as she attempted to snatch the letter back from Birdie but failed. "You'll get yo'r just-comeup-pances if you don't make this right. It won't stand. I couldn't sleep – bein' so devious."

"Oh, right. I forget. You are the *perfect one*. Pure as the driven snow. The white rose among the rest of us *thorns*. Well, I happen to know yo'r dirty little secret and you best be keepin' mine or I'll tell all!"

Birdie gulped, a resonance of truth filling the angry space between them.

"You ain't got nothin'," but Birdie's voice didn't sound so certain as she patted her child nervously on her back.

"You know, Birdie, yo'r right. I ain't got a thing. So, I guess when I tell Clavel that he ain't June's daddy, he'll say *that ain't nothin'*. La-tee-dah." Birdie turned white as June's hair.

"Oh, I figured it out, Birdie. Don't you deny it. You and that toe-headed, blue-eyed shoe salesman that wandered into The Gorge late one Friday night, about three years ago? Stayed at yo'r folks house all weekend? He was a looker, I'll grant you that. Ya'll made a handsome couple." Annie began stalking her prey, back and forth, the *clip-clop* of her shoe falling hard on the floor with each deliberate step. She kept her arms staunch by her side, jutting her clenched jaw and gritted teeth so close to Birdie's face she could smell the chicory on her breath, mixed with a tinge of fear. "I had my sights on 'im, too, but *YOU*, Miss Delila, sunk yo'r claws into him like a cat. You fell arsy-varsey in love the minute you laid your sweet, innocent eyes on him. I watched you work him at that taffy pullin'." Birdie began to audibly sob. "Looks like taffy wasn't the only thing you pulled that night. Am I right, Birdie?"

Birdie shook her head in disgust at Annie's sudden vulgarity. "I tell you, Annie, nothin' happened. *NOTHIN'!*" Birdie wheezed as the words caught inside her teeth.

"Well, I 'spose yo'r cryin' all the next week was nothin', too."

"I liked him, Annie, but that don't mean we..." Birdie looked as though she could explode into flames.

"It didn't work out, did it, Birdie?" Ponds of tears filled Birdie's eyes as she turned to face the window. "You thought he'd come back, take you with him, just like he promised." Annie's voice softened. "But he never came, did he?" Birdie didn't answer as she focused on some distant object outside her window, or just outside her memories.

"You hid it well, Birdie, wearin' them flour sack dresses an' all, but I could see that white swellin' just as sure as the moon rises over these cliffs. And what would yo'r Ma and Pa have said?" Birdie pretended to be watching the chickens peck the corn she'd thrown out that morning. "What was his name, Birdie? I'll bet he's forgotten yo'rs."

Birdie whipped around and shouted, "His name was *John!*"

"What was his last name?" Birdie stood there in a puddle of tears and regret. "He left you quite a bad way, didn't he? No way to find him, at least not in time. Am I right, Birdie?" Birdie remained silent. "That's where Clavel came in." Birdie made no sound to agree or disagree and returned to her focus outside the window. June was now entertaining herself by crunching on some bug that had stumbled into her path.

"Clavel's had his sights set on you since, well, forever. Didn't take a fool to figure he'd be willin' to marry you under any circumstances. So, what about you, Birdie?! Turns out, you ain't so much different than me now, are you?"

"Get outta my house." Annie stared at her friend in disbelief. "Get outta my house, Annie Grace. I won't be talked to like this in my own home."

"But Birdie, I thought friends could speak the truth about..."

"Friends? *FRIENDS?!* We ain't friends. Not anymore." Annie drew in a breath to counter, but Birdie held up her hand. "Don't you worry. You won this little battle. I won't spill yo'r beans to Trevor ... but know this. One battle don't win a war, and you *will* lose this war. You'll hang yo'r own self. Mark my words." Birdie rose to her feet, pointing to the door as though she were the angel in the Garden of Eden. "Now, get ... *OUT!*"

Annie walked to within inches of Birdie's face and snatched the letter and tossed it into the fire. The letter burst into blue flames ... and along with it, her and Birdie's friendship.

Chapter 25

Driving Annie to Birdie and Clavel's house had been quite therapeutic. Trevor was able to prove to himself he could still drive, for one thing. More than that, however, he found himself enjoying the warming sun and the sights of the freshly plowed fields as the mountain breeze blew redbud and dogwood blossoms across his windshield. Redwing Blackbirds sailed from fencepost to fencepost, flashing their red and yellow shoulders at him as they glided low above his oncoming car.

This little outing had started out as an annoyance. Annie had insisted on eating breakfast with him when all he really wanted was some time alone. The reality of their night at the cave was starting to settle upon him, and he worried if there would be long-term consequences. He wished he could say he didn't remember much of that night, but that would be a lie. He remembered all of it, even if the edges of his memories were slightly blurred. God, that was good whiskey. It had been the Devil, for sure. How could he have been so rash?

He supposed it was an accumulation of everything. His mother. The accident. The constant bickering between him and his father. The uncertainty of his future. The whiskey had merely been the wind that fanned an already smoldering fire.

Now, he guided the Model-T down the rutty path, taking care not to bounce the flivver on the deep ruts that cut across what passed for a road in these hills. For the first time in many weeks, he was able to push the negative thoughts from his mind and simply enjoy the space that was his own. He didn't even want to go back to The Esmeralda. While he'd enjoyed the enlightening conversation of the Turners and their guests, he was growing weary of the endless discussions about the war. If he was to make a full recovery, it needed to start in his head and that, he now realized, would entail stepping away from all of it – if only for a time.

Just as he rounded a curve, a familiar hand flew up from the field beside him. It was Neil, one hand on a mule-driven plow and the other motioning him to pull over. Trevor slowed the Model-T to a halt as Neil approached the car. He was feeling better about his leg, but he didn't want to push fate by walking on this uneven road, even with his crutch.

"Well, ain't you a sight for sore eyes," Neil teased. "I sure could use some help clearin' this field!" Trevor laughed.

"I fear you would be leaning on a broken stick, Neil."

The old man snickered. "I'm just pullin' yo'r leg, of course." Bad choice of words, but Trevor laughed in spite of it. That was something he hadn't done in a while, either. "Anyways, I would be much obliged if you'd do me a favor."

"What's that?" Trevor asked.

"I need to go to Harris's for some supplies. I'm fixin' to patch Effie's roof. And Ida needs some things, too. No tellin' when that sorry-sum-bitch husband of hers will show back up. Pardon my French." Trevor said no pardon was necessary. He'd heard much worse, and in French. "If you could carry me down there in that fancy auto-mo-beel of yours, it would save me a heap alotta time."

Trevor said he would be happy to help, but asked, "What are you gonna do with that mule of yours, just leave her standin' in the field?"

"Aww, Petals over there? She's fine. I'll just cut her loose and she'll make her way back. Only two places she likes to go. This field and her stall. She knows which side her bread's buttered on."

Trevor laughed. "That's a mighty fine mule then, but you'd better take care. If President Wilson gets us into the war, she's liable to get conscript-ed."

Neil heehawed. "Lord, ain't that the truth? They'd take her long before they'd take this broken bag of bones. Besides, I done paid my dues in Mr. Lincoln's war. I've seen enough killin' for one lifetime." Trevor imagined that was true. If he didn't feel it was his duty to defend France from the skies, he could forget the idea of going back to the warfront.

With that, Neil loosened the plow from Petal's shoulders and slapped her on the backside a couple of times, encouraging her back through the trees and towards what appeared to be a small stable tucked into a hill on the backside of Neil's property.

Neil opened the car door and slid in beside him, placing a calloused, strong hand on his shoulder. "You up for this? I'm guessin' this is the first time you've driven since yo'r accident."

"I'll be fine. I mean, it's not that far, is it?" Neil said it was only about two or three miles from the inn. Trevor was enjoying the idea of being of help to someone else for a change, and the prospect of a late morning drive into town, such as it was, suited him.

"I saw you takin' Annie up to Birdie's. What's that all about?" Trevor said he wasn't sure, but that Annie had insisted on going, and who was he to understand the way a woman thought? Neil laughed and said Effie had always been a source of great consternation to him, but then, that was what made this life so interesting, right?

The two men sat in silence until they got to the main road leading into Chimney Rock. Neil pointed to the large, monolithic column which was the town's namesake.

"That there's going to be a park. Man named Lucius Morse bought that entire mountain years ago. Says he's makin' trails for people to climb all the way to the top." Trevor glanced in that direction, insomuch as he dared while driving. "Supposed to be a big dedication July 4th. Barbecue. Music. Pick-a-nickin'."

Trevor said that sounded like fun, but he doubted he'd be around by that time. Neil seemed a bit saddened by the prospect but didn't pursue conversation any further. Just then, a big sign announcing they were at Harris's Mercantile came into view. Trevor pulled the car in front of the store where a horse and wagon had just left and wondered what this place would look like in another five to ten years. Automobiles would probably supplant every horse and wagon currently in operation. Then again, change came slow to these isolated mountain towns.

Neil told Trevor he wouldn't be but a few moments and asked if he wanted to wait or come inside? When he said he believed he'd like to take a look around the store, Neil reached for Trevor's crutch in the backseat and handed it to him as he stepped outside the car. Trevor eased from behind the steering wheel, wincing with the stiffness in his knee. Even so, he decided he was ready for a cane and thought he might find one inside.

Through the opened front door, the quintessential smells of a local hardware, feed, and seed store filled his senses. Corn, beans, okra, and hollyhock seeds spilled over wooden bins with brass tags. Above the seed bins lay rows of jarred pickled beets, applesauce, cabbage, and bright red tomatoes. Beyond that Trevor could smell the leather of new bridles, saddles, and horse blankets.

A sudden sneeze caught Trevor by surprise and reminded him of his still mending ribs. As healing as this morning had been, he still had miles to go.

To his right, the glint of sun on the top of a barrel filled with canes caught his eye. Trevor followed the shiny knobs and began to sort through the variety of walking sticks that stood corralled inside the staves, trying a few on to determine if he was, indeed, ready to graduate.

Some were just simple curved pieces of wood that probably served one best when hiking up the steep mountain trails. Others touted shiny brass handles in the likenesses of rams, foxes and elephants. One bore the semblance of an aged Indian chief sitting upon it, while another sported the eerie ivory-colored head of a greyhound carved into bovine bone. Ultimately, he decided upon one with a simple, brass globe perched atop a rosewood shaft. It spoke of a gentleman's air without drawing too much attention to oneself. Perhaps he would continue to carry it, even after he had outgrown the need for it.

Mr. Harris was manning the cash register, giving Trevor a knowing raise of his furry eyebrow. "That'll be $10.00," Mr. Harris said as Trevor reached for his wallet. Trevor now looked at his crutch, unsure of what to do with it. "Unless you wanna trade me that crutch." Trevor returned his gaze to

Mr. Harris, a question mark now forming across his forehead. "My son fell from a ladder stockin' shelves. Stowed up his leg real bad. That crutch would do him a world'a good. That is, if you'll not be needin' it any longer."

By this time, Neil had made his way to the register with an armload of seeds, a small sack of flour, and a bag of nails. There were also some packages of what appeared to be dried herbs, no doubt fulfilling Effie's part of Neil's "to-do" list.

"Sure, Mr. Harris. I'd be happy to give you my crutch ... *and* pay for the cane. I was just wondering what I would do with it."

"Nonsense. We'll call it an even trade. And call me John, son. Funny how things work out."

"Much obliged, Mr. Harris. I hope your son mends well."

Mr. Harris tipped his hat and smiled. "Good day, to you sir. Come again, ya hear?"

Neil paid for his wares and handed Trevor the bag of nails to carry back to the car.

"Doesn't look like you got much in the way of building supplies," Trevor acknowledged. Neil said Mr. Harris had to order most of what he needed, and it would be a few weeks.

By the time Trevor turned the car towards Neil's the two men had settled back into polite silence. Trevor wasn't sure if the car could make it to Neil's house, but the road there proved to be in better shape than most.

Neil invited Trevor in for a cup of coffee, but he declined. He probably should check on Annie. Neil thanked him for his ride and declared he would see him around.

Once back at Birdie and Clavel's house, Trevor ratcheted back the parking brake, intending to leave the car idling as he didn't want to crank it again. He was getting tired, and his leg was starting to ache from toe to hip, but Birdie met him before he could open his door.

"She ain't here," Birdie snapped. He could see her eyes were swollen and red. June sat under the apple tree on a quilt, dipping crumbs of cornbread into a saucer of buttermilk before putting them into her mouth.

"Birdie, what happened?" Trevor pushed himself out of the car and placed a gentle arm on her hand that trembled against the hood where she'd rested it.

"We had a fight." Birdie offered as she averted her eyes from Trevor's.

"About what?" Trevor wasn't sure he wanted to know, but he hated seeing someone as nice as Birdie so upset.

"Maybe you should ask her."

Chapter 26

Effie could smell the trouble coming before she saw it. Her senses were all in a dither, but she couldn't decide what she was gonna do about it. There was a reason why she chose not to have children. Women thought it couldn't be helped, but Effie was living proof that it could. You just had to know all the right signs, a few of the right herbs, and the gumption to tell a man no when your passions might suggest otherwise.

Annie came stomping through the tall grass, wiping her nose and blubbering something about friends and how she was better off without them. Lord help if she got Ida upset again. Ida's eyes had begun to clear, and the color was returning to her face. Seeing Jacob had done her a world of good. Now, Annie threatened to undo it all.

Effie met her at the edge where the grasses mingled with the sunflowers she'd planted years ago. Most of these had sprouted where seeds fell from the dying blooms, or where goldfinches shat 'em out. They weren't in bloom now, of course, but she could see where their stalks were climbing towards the light, soon to be weighed down by the thick, bright clusters of yellow that made her soul smile.

"What on earth is the matter with you, child?" Effie asked, bringing her body to block Annie's further advance. Annie flung herself into Effie's arms, forcing consolation.

"Oh, Effie, it's Birdie. She's so mean!" Effie rolled her eyes towards the gathering clouds as she patted Annie's back.

"Annie, what on earth are you talkin' about? Birdie's got more to tend to than your every whim. I don't want you carryin' on and gettin' your Ma all upset. Now tell me, what happened." Annie pulled back slightly.

"I just went to her for some advice ... you know. To talk like we used to. And she told me to leave and never come back!" Annie burst into sobs and thrust her head against Effie's slumping shoulder. If this was true, their argument had to have been bad. Birdie didn't usually create a to-do for no reason, unlike somebody else she knew.

"Advice ... about what?" Effie queried.

"Effie, you have to promise not to tell anyone. Not even Ma. Okay?" That was a promise she would have no trouble keeping, and she said as much. "I think I'm pregnant."

Effie stepped back and lifted Annie's chin, forcing their eyes to meet.

"What? How? I mean, who?" Effie wasn't often flummoxed, but she couldn't seem to find her footing. "You don't give two shits about the boys in this gorge! All this bawlin' and wailin' just don't make sense." Then, it began to dawn on her. "What did you do?"

"I didn't do nothin' Effie, except what love told me to." This child was so twisted up inside. But how could she not be, considering who her father was?

"Love? *LOVE?!* You don't know the first thing about love, Annie. And *when* is what I want to know? Did this happen when the two of you went to Bat Cave, looking for Jacob?" Annie wiped her nose on her sleeve and nodded. Effie began to chuckle under her breath.

"Child, you know better than that. It's too soon! What are you tryin' to do?"

"I'm not trying to do anything but have somebody love me!" Now that point, Effie couldn't argue. The old woman pulled her friend close and kissed her on top of the head.

"Annie, my Sweet One, you cain't force love. But if in a few weeks you think you are with child, we can take care of it. You just come see me, ya hear?"

Annie pulled away and looked at Effie as though she had grown horns. "What do you mean, *take care of it?*"

"You know what I mean. You and I've done this together, for other girls, many times."

"I'm not slippin' this baby, Effie! I won't!"

"Alright, alright. Just calm yo'rself. You don't even know that there *is* baby. All I'm sayin' is, before you do anything, come here first." Annie quietened as she wiped her nose again. "Promise me."

"I promise." Annie said with a smile that made Effie's old, wrinkled skin crawl. She could see, if the child was pregnant, that she was happy about it. Not distraught, as Effie had first thought.

"Child, you are feeling all kinds of things right now, with losing Virgil and yo'r daddy goin' on a hellbender an' all." Effie hesitated before pushing ahead. She still had questions. "Now why did Birdie throw you outtta her house? That don't sound like her."

Annie shrugged her shoulders and sniffled. "She called me a whore."

"Then shame on her," Effie empathized.

"Can I see Ma?"

"I'd rather you not. Mothers know when somethin' ain't right, and you know your Ma's fragile state." Annie seemed to consider barging through Effie's implied barrier anyway, but then thought better of it.

"Well, I guess I'll be walkin' back down to The Esmeralda."

"I hear your Pa's out ridin'. Maybe Neil could go back to your place with you, to see if it's safe. You gotta go back sometime," Effie said with some hesitation. She hated the thought of Ida and Annie returning to that hellhole, but she couldn't keep Ida, much less the two of them, at her place indefinitely. It was barely suitable for one. If Annie moved in, that'd make three. Four – if she really was pregnant. And what about Trevor … ?

Stop! she told herself. What was it her Pa used to say? "Don't worry about nothin' until there's somethin'."

"So that's it, then. Yo'r just castin' us off, like lepers." Annie was looking for a fight, and she'd be damned if she was gonna give it to her.

"I'll not argue when yo'r determined to twist things up. I'm just sayin' you need to think about what you and yo'r Ma are gonna do. This ain't the best answer," she said, pointing back towards her house, "for any of us."

Chapter 27

Trevor left Birdie standing in her yard in a stupor, looking for all the world like she'd lost her best friend. He supposed she had. She'd said she had no idea where Annie had gone, and frankly, didn't care. Hopefully time would mend the rift between them but for now, should he try to find Annie or just go back to the inn? Maybe she was there already.

If Annie wasn't at The Esmeralda, considering the severity of her and Birdie's argument, he wouldn't feel right leaving her whereabouts in question. Maybe she had stopped by Effie's to see her mother. He couldn't make the hike from the road up the path to Effie's house, but maybe he'd get lucky and see Annie along the way. At the very least, he could sit at the bottom of the trail and blow his horn. If Annie was around, surely, she would understand that he was looking for her and come meet him. Then he wondered why he cared, but he figured he was being guided by a guilty conscience.

And speaking of his conscience, why *did* he feel compelled to insert himself into this bizarre situation? He wasn't any kin – not even close. If it were chivalry that was at stake, he had to remember that Annie had walked these mountain paths and roads by herself all her life. She didn't need him.

Despite this epiphany, Trevor kept his eyes peeled along the road, scanning the woods for any sign of the hurricane that was Annie Conner. He was just about to make the turn towards Effie's when he saw a flash of white, just beyond the fence line. Trevor squeezed the rubber bulb on his horn.

"Trevor!" Annie shouted with a wave. In a few short seconds, she was at the car and had plopped herself into the passenger seat. "I'm so glad yo'r here."

Trevor made no comment for a time as he nudged the car forward towards the main road.

"I just saw Birdie," he finally spoke.

Annie dropped her head back to her chest. "What'd she have to say for herself?"

Trevor waited a time before answering. He really didn't want to get into an argument with this girl. He'd had done enough arguing for one lifetime.

"Not much. Just that the two of you had quarreled." Annie seemed to want more information but was afraid to ask. "She's your best friend and a nice girl, Annie. What would the two of you have to fuss over?"

"We just don't see eye to eye on some things, that's all." Trevor knew he should let this go, but for some reason, he could not.

"Good friends don't always agree. This seems to be more than that." Annie lifted then lowered her shoulders.

"Maybe it is. Maybe it ain't."

The remainder of the drive was made in silence save for a few sniffles Trevor heard as Annie struggled to stave the flood of tears that threatened to pour. It was clear she was in a lot of pain, but maybe that was a good thing. As Trevor pulled the car into its space, Annie spoke.

"Listen. I appreciate yo'r tryin' to help, but as Effie says, *what's done ... is.*"

"Annie, there's nothing you can't undo. My best friend died the same night that horse mangled my leg. His name was Owen. I'll never see him again. You never know when it will be the last time you see someone. Disagreements are temporary, death isn't."

"That's mighty big talk from a man who just sent his father packin' to the coast."

"Touché."

"And speakin' them fancy French words ain't gonna help. Look. I appreciate what yo'r tryin' to do. It's really sweet, but some things just ain't that easy."

"But I just don't see …"

"It's done, Trevor. And I cain't undo it. What happened between me and Birdie was more than just a quibble." She paused, seeming to measure her next words. "Someone once told me, *for every action, there is an equal and opposite reaction.*"

"You have me again, Annie. But that doesn't mean…"

"What's done … is, Trevor. Now let's go eat. I'm starvin'."

After escorting Annie to her room, Trevor flopped across his bed, burying his face in a feather pillow. *God, what a day.* He'd hoped to escape all this ruminating with a nap, but those same nattering voices refused to let him sleep. Maybe if he removed his clothes, he could drift off.

Taking another inventory of himself in the mirror, he still remained a skeleton. His razor-sharp cheekbones pushed through his skin, causing his eyes to sink deep into blue-grey sockets. He unbuttoned his trousers, letting them fall to the floor, and lifted his shirt, noting his protruding ribs and bulging tailbone.

Suddenly, there was a knock on the door. Trevor re-dressed and opened it, thinking it might be Clavel with some fresh towels or linens, but it was Annie.

"Trevor, I hope I'm not disturbin'," Annie said. "I was hopin' you could come and have some tea with me. And Clavel has made these wonderful cookies. Cain't you smell 'em?" The scent of anise and lavender filled the hallway, sending his stomach rumbling with the thought. He hadn't eaten lunch today, and the cinnamon roll they'd shared this morning had long since faded. But his head throbbed like a drum, and he wasn't sure sweets were the answer.

"Umm, isn't dinner almost ready?" he asked, rubbing his forehead. "I'm not feeling all that well, to be frank."

"Oh, I asked Clavel. He said dinner wouldn't be until eight this evening." There was an awkward pause. "And it's only seven."

"But cookies, before dinner? It seems we shouldn't spoil our appetite..."

"Do you always play by the rules, Trevor?" He thought about their illicit evening at the cave and decided no, he did not always play by the rules. He wasn't even sure what those rules were.

"Well, when it comes to Clavel's cooking, I have learned it is prudent to leave a lot of room. He lays out quite the spread." He could smell something like a roast duck, with onions and rosemary drifting behind the wake of cookie aroma.

"Then come walk with me. I've been thinkin' about what you said." This woman was a strange one, and not one to give up easily. And with his stamina worn down, he was much too malleable.

"Alright. Let me get my jacket." Trevor turned to retrieve his topcoat, then spying his cap, reached for that, too, but decided to leave it lying there on the corner of his bed where he'd tossed it. He would show her unconventional.

Once outside, Annie threaded her arm through his as they walked towards the bench where they had sat earlier in the day. Silence passed between them as Trevor listened to the cardinals call to one another low in the crabapple tree. He watched the male bring over a berry to his mate. Granny Molly had said cardinals mated for life. Would that ideal ever appeal to him? He couldn't fathom it now. Not with him going back into the thick of war.

"I just wanted to say that I was sorry if I seemed, you know, short. Me and Birdie's been friends for a long time, and I'm upset about our quarrel." Trevor said he understood and that with some time, they could mend their fences.

"I hope yo'r right," Annie said. "But a fence is one thing, and a bridge is somethin' different. I think I may have ... well, never mind. Let's talk about something else."

"I think that is a wonderful idea," Trevor agreed.

"So, did you have someone back in France?" The question zinged across his nose.

"Have ... someone?"

"Yeah. You know. Like a girlfriend."

"Well, no. I mean, not really."

"I find it hard to believe a handsome fella like you was alone." Annie's eyes evaded him. Of course she was curious about his romantic interests. For him, their tryst in the cave had been a misguided distraction. But for her? He understood how she might see things a bit differently. Even so, he couldn't think of an adequate response that wouldn't involve a passel of untruths, so he said nothing.

Annie touched his knee with her long fingers. Trevor flinched, but decided it felt pretty good. "I'm sorry. Is this yo'r injured leg?" Trevor nodded. "I'll be more careful, then," she said, patting his knee gently.

"It's alright. I'm just protective, it seems."

"I could make you forget all yo'r pain...again," she said, letting her hand linger and her voice trail off. Trevor felt his shoulders tense and the calf of his bad leg start to tremble. He adjusted his foot and removed her hand, hoping that she would get the message.

"Annie, I consider myself a gentleman – a standard I intend to uphold." Trevor thought about his behavior several nights ago and decided he had much to reconcile with himself. No better time than now, however, to begin making amends. "And if that makes me a slave to convention..."

"It makes you a bore," Annie countered. Trevor laughed out loud. "And maybe you think otherwise, but I *am* a lady." He didn't know how to respond to that statement honestly, so once again, he chose silence.

"Dinner is served!" Clavel sang from the doors to the inn. Annie raised up and gazed into Trevor's eyes. For a moment, he thought she was going to kiss him. He felt off balance and leaned hard on his cane. Suddenly, he found himself wanting Annie to touch him, and regretted his mixed signals. Drunk as he was that night, he still remembered every second they lay there by the fire in each other's arms. Now, as her hand touched his side, her thumb gently massaging the sore spot that remained in between his ribs, he wanted to experience it again. All of it.

"Lord have mercy, yo'r thin as a scarecrow! I can count every one of yo'r ribs. Let's go eat … and fatten you up a little bit."

Inside, Annie waited for him at the dining table. As he pulled the chair out for her, Trevor took notice of how different she looked in the dress Mattie had let her borrow. This was a simple, ankle-length design in solid black crepe – obviously to show that she was in mourning. If tradition prevailed here in the mountains, Annie would only have to wear such for four weeks, as Virgil was a first cousin. This was in stark comparison to widows who were forced to wear black for two horrid years. It was a silly tradition, and needlessly unfair. Life was hard enough. Why did people want to make it even more difficult by constructing rules and rituals that, ultimately, served no purpose? No amount of black attire would bring the dead back.

But as a pilot, he could do something to change the direction of the war and prevent lives from being taken in the first place.

He felt a resurgence in his determination to become a pilot. His countenance must have changed with the thought, for he caught Annie returning his slight smile and was reminded of how disparate their lives were. They could never be anything beyond friends. And it wasn't fair - leaving her to hopeful imaginations. He would have to talk to her … and soon.

Chapter 28

Annie felt awkward in the dress Mattie had let her borrow, but she didn't feel she had much choice in the matter. What good did it do to wear black? Would it bring Virgil back to life? Would it soothe the wounds her father had inflicted at the church? The answer was a resounding, "No!" The only purpose it served was to check off some box that society demanded of her because someone had the audacity to die. That was one thing the mountain folk and those of high society had in common – stupid rules about death.

Even so, she didn't want to offend Mattie. Besides, once she had it on, she realized that this sort of black looked nice on her – nothing like that horrible woolen, motheaten garb her father had insisted she wear. It might not be comfortable, like her gingham cotton dresses, but if it helped Trevor understand she could manage the demands of a socialite's wife, she could endure it.

For the time at hand, she was relieved to discover that Mrs. Vanderbilt and her husband would not be dining with them. They were visiting family in Asheville. Maybe the conversation this evening wouldn't be as boring.

As for the food, she was famished, and if there was one thing she could say about Clavel - he could cook. Tonight's feast centered around roast duck with carrots, turnips, garlic, and onions suspended in a creamy, rosemary scented gravy. Steaming wedges of cornbread were served along with a deep bowl filled with wilted, fresh spring lettuce and green onions. Annie breathed in the aroma of the milk and vinegar gravy – a recipe she had given Mattie and Tom and, by default, Clavel. Most people just wilted their greens in some grease, but her grandmother had a way of making a cream sauce (that's what Mattie had called it) from melted grease, flour, some salt and pepper, cow's milk and a dash of vinegar. She couldn't wait to sink that silver spoon deep into the bowl and ladle those greens and gravy over the cornbread. Everyone else could have that fancy duck. She could make herself a meal on cornbread and creamed lettuce alone.

With the Vanderbilts gone, Tom and Mattie readied themselves to sit at the table with their guests, an opportunity Tom confessed they rarely took advantage of.

"We are going to dispense with formalities this evening," Tom announced. "Everyone, just grab a dish and dive in!" Trevor was the first to take up the plate of sliced duck.

"Thank you, Tom. I am starving!" he announced, then turned to face to Annie. "Apparently, I am looking the worse for wear and Annie has determined to put meat on my ribs!" Everyone chuckled as Mattie poured everyone a glass of pinot noir. Annie sniffed it before taking a tiny sip, trying not to wrinkle her nose.

"So, Annie," Tom began. "How's your mother?"

Annie lowered her head. "Ma's still strugglin'."

Tom bowed his own with the burden of understanding how difficult this situation was. "To be sure, Annie, Virgil's accident and death was tragic. You must all be in a state of shock."

Annie agreed that was true but quantified it by saying that Virgil's death was actually a blessing. "He'd have been a vegetable, just like these wilted greens."

Trevor choked on his wine. Tom and Mattie looked to one another, lost for an appropriate response.

"I'm just callin' it like it is. He wouldn't have had a life, so he's better off."

"Annie is considering going to school to be a nurse!" Trevor declared, in an obvious attempt to change the subject, but that statement seemed even more random than *her* ill-stated remark. Annie fidgeted in her chair.

"Is that so?" Tom asked. "I haven't heard you mention that before." Annie was pretty sure Mattie kicked Tom in the shin. "That's fantastic!" he added.

"Yes, Mr. Turner. I almost went to nursing school a couple of years ago." About that time, Clavel walked into the room with a bottle of wine tucked beneath his arm.

"Birdie and I were going to go but ..." Trevor cocked his head and raised an eyebrow. "My mother took sick, and I thought it best to wait." Trevor's shoulders visibly relaxed. Clavel was either unaware he bore some of the blame for this ill-fated turn in Annie's life or pretended not to care. "Thanks to Trevor's encouragement, I'm thinkin' I might try again."

"Perhaps you can volunteer for the war effort in France, just like Trevor!" Mattie suggested. Annie's heart began to beat so hard she believed it showed through her dress.

"She can do anything she wants," Trevor exclaimed. "There are even women ambulance drivers in France. I can see that suiting you to a T." Trevor paused. "A Model-T!"

Annie snorted as the entire table erupted at Trevor's joke.

Trevor continued. "I know it gave me immense comfort to have a pretty nurse fussing over me in the hospital." Trevor fed himself another slice of duck and smiled.

Annie cast an impudent look his way, half flattered that he thought her *pretty* and the other half seeing green with the reminder that was there was someone else who held Trevor's interest.

Annie began to eat to distract herself. She tried some of the duck with another sip or two of wine. Ahh. That was much better! Something about the duck seemed to soften the burn of the wine. Trevor commented it was a very good wine, and he did enjoy a good glass of Pinot Noir! She could learn to like it, too, couldn't she? Could? No, she *would*.

But she had some work to do.

<h1 style="text-align:center">Chapter 29</h1>

Just before retiring, Tom exclaimed, "Trevor! I almost forgot. A letter arrived for you this afternoon." Trevor thought he saw Annie stiffen at this announcement, then decided it was just his imagination. He'd hoped it was a response from Hannah, but she'd not had time to even receive his first missive, much less send one in return. Instead, it was a letter was from Victor Chapman, the gentleman who had recruited him for The Escadrille. That was almost as good, he surmised. He didn't even wait to get to his room, ripping open the envelope with the exuberance of a child unwrapping a Christmas package.

Dear Trevor,

I trust this inquiry finds you well and healing. Your father gave me your address before you left the hospital, so I thought I would share some good news with you about The Escadrille and see how you are doing.

Are you enjoying your mountain retreat? I hear that mountain air suits whatever ails a man, so here's hoping you'll be back to France soon and ready to begin your training. We have quite the crew, one of which I know you will be proud of - and likewise.

You will be pleased to know that we can claim our first kill as a unit. On May 18th, Kiffin

Rockwell, who is from Asheville, shot down a German plane over Alsace. It was quite the night for celebration! Kiffin sends his regards and wanted me to express how excited he is to have you join us. Kiffin believes it is not mere coincidence that you find yourself recovering in the shadows of those same mountains he calls home, and wishes you a swift recovery, as we all do.

And for what it's worth, we have acquired a couple of mascots for our force – two lion cubs we have affectionately named Whiskey and Soda. They have provided much companionship and entertainment for us when we return from our sorties.

Please update me as to your status as soon as possible, and when we might expect the pleasure of your company.

With warmest regards,
Victor Chapman

This could not have been coincidence, considering his earlier thoughts. Trevor excused himself to his room and penned a response:

Dear Victor,

What a delight to have received your letter! North Carolina is indeed conducive to my recovery. This remote section, however, is quite different than what you might expect at some of the more populated towns and resorts.

Despite these unique demographics, or perhaps, because of it, The Esmeralda Inn is a draw for the rich and famous, including our lady of the AAFS, Mrs. Vanderbilt. I was privileged to have dinner with her when she and her husband, William, were guests at The Esmeralda. She sends her regards and assures us of her and William's continued support for the AAFS and The Escadrille.

To that end, please accept my humble gratitude for saving me a place with The Escadrille Américaine. I plan to live up to your high expectations and to those of my comrades. I hope to return to France by the middle of July.

Yours most sincerely,
Trevor Middleton

Chapter 30

Annie bolted upright from a deep sleep, gasping for air. Someone, or something, had her by the throat. She gagged and shrieked for help, but her voice was muffled by a dark, thick muck. She could see people standing outside this strange, thin veil: her Ma, Jacob, Effie, Neil, … and Trevor – his sweet, dark eyes looking upon her with pity, her hands reaching out to him in vain.

Thank God it was just a dream. Annie grasped her chest and drank several gulps of water from the glass she kept by her bed. The coolness flowing down her unobstructed throat soothed her. She sat on her bed for a few more moments, panting.

She dressed quickly when she heard Trevor's voice, hoping to catch him before he set out for the day. She could tell he was feeling better and expected him to start exploring his surroundings now that he proved he could drive.

Annie left her room, running headlong into Trevor exiting his own.

"Trevor!" she squeaked, her voice raspy from the previous evening's wine and salty duck. She opened her arms to hug him, which he reciprocated, but this gesture seemed more forced than genuine.

"Annie," he said, gently pushing her to arm's length. "Good morning. I'm glad you're up. I was hoping we could talk."

Trevor had arranged for them to have their breakfast in the garden. Clavel brought out a basket filled with blueberry muffins and coffee. A mated pair of Catbirds called and mewed to one another – a sure sign that Catbird Winter was on the way. It gave her shivers just to think about it.

Folks always had names for the cold spells that settled into The Gorge, each one distinguished by a particular flower or fruit blooming around the time the chill settled in. Redbud Winter. Dogwood Winter. Blackberry Winter. Catbird Winter was the only one she knew of that was named for a bird, and it was the worst, because it came just before the heat of summer overtook The Gorge. One minute you were enjoying the spring sunshine. The next, you were rubbing your arms before a fire, hoping you might not freeze to death then *wham!* The summer heat was upon you and had you sweatin' bullets. It was the extremes that got to her she guessed, but then, extremes had been her life.

Trevor pulled out an iron chair for Annie to sit as she took a still-warm muffin from the basket. Clavel had placed a half-dollar sized pat of butter inside and a knife, for which she quickly split the two muffins and stuffed them full – the butter starting to melt from the steam even as she plunged the knife into their middle. She extended a muffin to Trevor, taking a large bite of her own.

"So, to what do I owe this pleasure?" She was already starting to sound more sophisticated.

"I was hoping we could talk about the other night." Annie stopped chewing, surprised by this line of conversation. Did one actually talk about such things? She just assumed they happened, you (maybe) got pregnant, you got married, and that was that. Maybe not traditionally in that order, but things happened. Birdie was a testament.

"The other night?" she repeated. Trevor nodded. "Umm, okay." He became fidgety and nervous.

"I want you to know that I think you are beautiful." Annie beamed. "Inside and out."

"Yeah?"

"Yeah. But..."

"There's a but?" Trevor said there was. Annie put down the muffin half and wiped her mouth with a napkin. Some of the muffin stuck in her throat, or was that a chunk of disappointment?

"All those things I said that night are true. You *are* smart. Hardworking. You can do anything you want. You should get that education you've always dreamed of. Become a nurse, then move to Boston. San Francisco. Hell, go to France!"

"I don't know how you think I can do those things, Trevor. My family. We have no money. I'm just a farmgirl."

Trevor shook his head in disagreement. "No, that's not true. I know it will be hard. You just need a little boost, that's all. The rest you can do on your own. I know it."

The only thing Annie knew was … she was about to throw up. "So, are you breaking up with me?"

"Annie, we were never together. What you and I did was, well, to be frank, wrong."

"Wrong?! How could you say such a thing! It's the rightest thing I've ever done!" She was yelling through sobs.

"It was wonderful, Annie, don't misunderstand me. But it was just, well, *wrong*. If we try to make it something else, we will both end up miserable."

"No! I could never be miserable with you!" Trevor placed his index finger to her lips and asked that she lower her voice. "And I won't be quiet! How can you violate me in such a way and then toss me aside like some, some … *rag?* I guess my father was right!"

"No, Annie. Your father couldn't have been more wrong."

"I thought it was fate you had come here. Into my life, but now I see…"

"It was fate, Annie. That part I agree with, and I'm leaving you a little something to help."

"Help… me?" she said, now unable to talk above a whisper for the tears.

"Yes. I'm leaving you an education fund. Tom and Mattie will be the managers of it. You can only use it for school tuition and expenses, but it's all yours. No interest. You need not ever pay it back." Annie's fingers balled into a fist, crying so hard the table shook, sloshing coffee across its top. Trevor continued his speech, undaunted.

"I know this must feel horrible right now, but just give it a few days and you'll see. This is the best thing."

"I'm not some charity case, Trevor!"

"Of course, you aren't, Annie. This isn't about charity."

"Then wha...wha... what *is* this about?"

Annie slowly lifted her face, dabbing her tears with the napkin she could barely grasp. "You talk like yo'r goin' somewhere. Are you?"

"I never intended on staying here. I thought you understood that."

Annie looked away, watching the Catbirds flit about amongst the Hickories. A shiver racked her body as she watched the sun bake the dew off the trees.

"That letter I received last night was from Victor Chapman. He is my mentor in France. The one who asked me to join *The Escadrille* and become a pilot. They'll still take me, Annie. Can you believe that? Crippled ol'e me. It's what I've always wanted, more than anything. To fly. I thought that chance had been taken from me, but it hasn't. I want you to have that same chance."

"Oh, God..." she wailed.

"Come here, come here," he whispered, standing to take her in his arms. Annie sobbed as she pushed her face deep inside his shirt. "I'm not leaving just yet. I still have much to do, but I didn't want you getting the wrong idea. I am your friend, Annie, and always will be. Will you let me be a friend to you?" She raised her head and nodded yes.

"Good. Now, let's finish those muffins before those Catbirds take them," he said, spotting the blue-grey pair as they eyed the sparkling berries from inside the crumbly bread.

Well, Annie thought, *Catbird Winter is already here.* And it was the coldest one she'd ever felt.

Catbird Winter

He spreads the snow like wool
and scatters the frost like ashes.
He hurls down his hail like pebbles.
Who can withstand his icy blast?
He sends his word and melts them.
He stirs up his breezes, and the waters flow.

Psalm 147:16-18 (NIV)

Chapter 31

It had been nearly six weeks since Trevor had announced he wanted nothing more to do with her, at least not in that way. That afternoon, she had gone by Effie's to fetch her mother. Neil escorted them both back home, and that's where she'd mostly stayed.

Annie closed her eyes against the soft light that poured through the opened window. Tears spilled onto her pillow as her father yelled for her to begin her chores. Waves of heat began at the tips of her toes and forced their way up through her belly, filling up her face and burning red in her ears.

Though the sun itself would not rise above the walls of The Gorge until close to the noonday hour, its imminence could be sensed, like the birth of her child.

In the not-so-distant past, she'd scoffed at the young women who swooned and gagged at Effie's doorstep, seeking relief from what, at the time, Annie believed to be self-induced misery. She no longer derided them. She'd not been able to eat a bite in days, save for some corn pone that Effie fried up for her each morning after she had done her chores. As sick as she was when she woke, she found the late morning walks, and corn pone, helped ease her mind as well as her churning insides.

Lester had returned from one of his circuit rides in a particularly foul mood. Jacob's leaving had him all in a dither for which the passage of time only seemed to worsen. He had berated Annie for allowing the chickweed and crabgrass to overtake the gardens, even though Annie couldn't bend over without the world going black and gray around her. Of course, he didn't know why she was sick, but he was clear on the matter: he didn't care. She now had to do her chores *and* Jacob's, and he would not tolerate excuses.

Annie found she could do some things inside the house, away from the heat of gardening and slopping pigs, but even those lighter chores were made onerous by her ever-changing moods and unpredictable queasiness. The simple motion of sweeping floors could leave her heaving over the side of the porch.

As for her mother, all the good that Effie had done for her unraveled when Lester returned. Ida forced herself out of bed just long enough to pee and perhaps eat a bite of ham and redeye gravy. Annie had encouraged her to wash herself a couple of times, but for the most part, her mother remained disinterested in life and the world that was floating by around her. Annie found herself oddly envious, even angry at her mother's ability to disconnect, wishing she could do the same.

But there was no time to dwell on such nonsense. There was a child billowing inside of her, and in a couple of days, Trevor was leaving The Gorge – heading for his new life in France, or returning to his old one, however one chose to look at it; leaving her an ocean away to bear their child without a father.

She had to tell him. But her sickness had only come on in recent days. If she had told him any sooner, she had no proof to back it up, although she was late with her courses. That happened to many girls, so that wasn't proof in and of itself, but she could always count on the timing of her monthly visitor, and she hadn't shown her face.

At Effie's urging, she had done the old wheat and barley test when Effie herself began to suspect she was pregnant. If a woman peed on barley seeds and they sprouted, it was a boy. If she peed on wheat seeds and they sprouted, it was a girl. If none of the seeds grew, there was no pregnancy. The first two times, nothing happened, but on the third try, the tiny green sprouts from the wheat seeds pushed their faces towards the sun, and soon, the sickness came to affirm the wheat's announcement.

Effie had said little on the subject. "What's done, is," was all, then proceeded to make her a warm tea of lemon balm and ginger. She was relieved that Effie had said nothing more about an abortifacient. She didn't want to argue about it.

As for telling Trevor, Annie decided that today was the day. Lester was taking off on some pious mission and said he'd be gone for at least three days - a week, more than likely, and told her the stables better be mucked when he got back. She raised her head up from her pillow and let her feet dangle above the floor, testing herself to see if she could stand without retching. Annie reached for the dress and hat she'd laid out last night. It wasn't the prettiest outfit ever, but it would do.

She told herself she wasn't going to make a big ceremony of it – telling Trevor. They had seen each other numerous times since he'd told her he just wanted to be friends, and each time, she thought she'd done a good job of pretending she didn't give a tinker's dam about him, but now that she was having morning sickness, that charade became more and more difficult. Despite her best efforts to hide her state, he'd noticed. Trevor had asked her several times if she was okay, and each time she'd given him a smile and said she was. Just tired from all the extra chores Lester had put on her. That was all.

He had also been asking her about school. Had she applied? If not, when? Annie used her father as an excuse then, too. He would never allow it, and she needed to make plans without his knowledge. It would help if Jacob was home (another great excuse), but she would never ask him to quit his job. That wouldn't be fair. He'd already sent some money home, so at least there was that.

When Annie went to The Esmeralda, she would sometimes see Trevor working his leg on the kitchen porch, using buckets of water around his ankles as resistance as he lifted his leg up and down, up and down, to strengthen it. Effie had given him salves of arnica and comfrey and told him to warm them up and apply them to his entire leg twice a day, wrapping his knee in a soft rag for half an hour each time. She'd given him comfrey tea to drink – but only one cup at a time, per day. He'd done everything she had asked of him, and sure enough, in just a few weeks, his limp became less pronounced. He was always smiling now, and said he was sure going to miss her and Effie when he was gone. He had no idea.

She put on her dress and stood before the mirror that was still draped in black. She pushed back the ragtag piece of cloth and looked at her reflection, her hand lingering on her abdomen. What would Trevor do once she told him? Every possibility she played out in her mind terrified her – regret threating to become a vice around her previously hopeful heart.

But Effie was right. *What's done … is.* There was nothing more to be done now but tell the truth.

Chapter 32

Trevor had slept his best since, well, he couldn't remember. His knee was still swelling, but he believed that was from the hours of exercise. Effie advised his knee would probably swell for a time – at least a year. Maybe always.

As he dressed himself for breakfast, he found he could place full weight upon his leg without bringing on the cycle of pain he'd come to expect. Effie's concoction of arnica and comfrey had brought him, not just relief, but hope that his dreams of becoming a pilot would soon be a reality. In just a few short days he would drive to Spartanburg to catch the train to Savannah, where he would meet Lymas to return his car. His father agreed to rendezvous with him there, and in just a week or so after that, he would sail back to France aboard one of his father's ships.

Two weeks prior, he'd gone into Asheville with Tom and sent a telegram to Victor.

RECOVERY IS GOING WELL.
SAILING TO FRANCE IN THREE WEEKS.
WILL ADVISE UPON ARRIVAL.
TREVOR MIDDLETON

A rap on the door alerted him that breakfast was being served. Through the closed door, Clavel had announced he'd created Trevor's favorite breakfast, a running joke between them, because every breakfast had become his favorite. The only thing Trevor couldn't take in large quantities was Clavel's coffee. As Tom was fond of saying, it would put hair on a young man's chest.

"I'm up Clavel. I'll be straight on, soon as I wash my hands." The smell of cinnamon rolls seeped under the door, causing Trevor's stomach to moan with anticipation.

He'd come to appreciate breakfasts at The Esmeralda for other reasons, too. The conversations and hints of gossip served up by his hosts were delicious. Compared to the tension-laden exchanges that had passed between him and his father, these seemingly mundane banters were as refreshing as the cold mountain air.

What flowers were budding in the garden?

Did you see that towhee tossing leaves and twigs under the hydrangea?

Who of reputable fame might be coming to stay at The Esmeralda this summer?

The latter question was a topic laced with a tinge of strain between Tom and Mattie. Several film stars had graced the threshold of The Esmeralda over the past year or so. Gloria Swanson had paid a visit, and it was quite the buzz that the actress, Mary Pickford, had reserved a room at The Esmeralda in the coming weeks, conveniently arranged to coincide with the reservation of the actor, Douglas Fairbank. According to Mattie, that meant something wonderfully sordid was taking place ... right under their roof. Nearly every morning this past week, some variety of the same conversation had been heard overtop the gentle clanking of forks against china.

"Now, Mattie," Tom would admonish. "You shouldn't be such a scandalmonger. It's not becoming a lady of your grace and status."

Mattie, who was typically the epitome of social propriety, would discard all decorum and launch into a recital of the latest movie star gossip. Why, everyone knew that Mrs. Pickford was married to that Irishman, Owen Moore, and well, he wasn't exactly prime husband material now was he? And if you knew *that*, then you also knew that she and Mr. Fairbanks got on very well, and that there was talk of them making films (and other things) together, and if you considered *that*, then it could not be coincidence that Mrs. Pickford and Mr. Fairbanks were using the remote location of The Esmeralda as a hideaway for the two of them to, well, you know, get their ashes hauled and...

"Mattie! How about a little discretion, *please?!*" Tom would feign irritation, but Trevor felt he rather enjoyed the titillating prospects, too.

Mattie would then roll her eyes at herself and apologize to everyone, declaring she had no idea what had gotten into her. She would then say, "Let me just state this for the record, and then I intend not to speak on this subject further. I don't approve of any sort of extramarital consorting." She would then glance at her husband as if seeking some assurance that he didn't approve of extramarital consorting either. "I just think it would be nice if Mary kicked that sorry-good-for-nothing husband of hers to the curb and embarked upon a new journey of sorts. One that began right here." To emphasize, Mattie would pat her husband on the shoulder. "Right here at our little Esmeralda."

"So, we're on a first name basis with Mrs. Pickford, now are we?" Tom would tease. Mattie would then clear her throat and proceed to help Clavel clear some of the dishes, rubbing her perfectly tapered chin with her thumb and index finger, contemplating the implicit scandals to be had at The Esmeralda.

A bustle at the back door and a peppering of voices from the kitchen snatched Trevor back to his current reality. There was no doubt whose energy had assaulted Clavel's sacred space. Though he was defending his position as kitchen guardian with bravado and defiance, he was no match for the razor-sharp tongue of Annie Conner.

"I must see him now, Clavel. And it's really none of yo'r business why!" she all but shouted at him. Trevor followed the sound of hostilities and found the two of them squaring off where a slight breeze blew the scent of cow manure in from local pastures.

"Trevor! I was just about to come find you when this, this ..."

"Clavel, it's quite alright if Annie wants to come in." Why Clavel had been so protective over him in recent weeks he could not understand. This odd behavior began after Annie and Birdie had their argument, but he couldn't see what that had to do with him in the slightest.

"Well, alright, but do you want a chaperone?" Clavel asked. Now *he* was getting annoyed with Clavel.

"No, Clavel. I am perfectly capable of taking care of myself. I am sure Annie is harmless. She has been so far," he said with a wink.

Clavel snarled as he moved away. "Harmless as a sow bear with a cub," Trevor heard him mutter. Annie glared at him as though willing him to burst into flames.

"Come out to the garden, Annie, where we can have some privacy."

Annie walked ahead of him, and by the time he caught up with her, she had placed her arms against the exterior wall that provided the backdrop for Mattie's prized rose bush and buried herself inside her slightly bent elbow. As Trevor touched the small of her back, Annie turned slightly then crumpled into a ball at his feet.

"Annie!" He winced as he knelt beside her, his knee pounding out a warning that he best take care, or he might never get up again.

"I…I'm alright," she wheezed.

Trevor managed to right himself into a sitting position on the garden's rock wall, giving him just enough leverage to pull Annie beside him.

"I'll be fine. I just haven't eaten anything, that's all."

"I could ask Clavel to…"

"No!" she spat. "I'll maybe take a little coffee or something before I go, but … oh, Trevor!" Annie pushed her face inside the crook of Trevor's neck; raw emotion spilling down atop the freshly starched collar of his shirt. Trevor cupped the back of her head with his hand, waiting in stunned silence for some sort of explanation. Annie raised her chin.

"Trevor. I don't know how to say this easy, so I'm just gonna say it."

Annie paused, taking in several short breaths. "I'm pregnant." More sobbing ensued but this time, Trevor was too astonished to provide any comfort, his hands falling towards the ground as though they were filled with sand.

"You're … wha … wha … what?"

"I'm pregnant, Trevor. With child." Trevor was now feeling lightheaded.

"And I'm the…"

"Father? If I had the strength, I would slap the taste outta y'or mouth! How *dare* you think there's been anyone else."

"I don't. It's just that..."

"Just what, Trevor? How could you possibly believe I'd been with anybody since that time? You really are incorrigible." Trevor continued to stare at her with a blankness he believed would become a permanent feature of his face. "What?" she snapped. "You seem more surprised I know the word 'incorrigible' than the fact I'm pregnant. Wow. Well, I can spell it, too. It's i-n-c-o-r-r..."

"Okay, okay. I'm sorry. I'm just. Oh my, God." Trevor rubbed his forehead with a ferocity that threatened to strip his eyebrows. "You're sure?"

"Yes!" she shouted. "Look at me! I cain't hardly stand up without faintin'. I haven't been able to eat for almost two weeks. If you don't believe me, ask Effie!"

"I believe you! I believe you! Okay? Let's not fight and think this through. Calmly, like adults."

"What's there to think about?"

"Have you told your mother and father?"

"How stupid do you think I am, Trevor?" she chided. "We're both still alive ain't we? My father woulda killed you first, then me."

"You're not stupid. I'm just ... in shock." Trevor's head dropped into his hands. He wished he could disappear. This could not be happening. Not now. "Annie, I'm leaving for France in two days. Even if we marry, I can't, no ... I won't ... leave you and a newborn child here."

"*If* we marry, Trevor? *IF?!*" I cain't believe this!"

"I'm not saying I won't marry you, Annie. I'm just saying it isn't that simple."

"Yes, it is that simple. Yo'r the one making it complicated. You selfish, self-centered bastard! You act as though I went and got knocked up all by myself. It takes two, you know!"

Trevor held his hands up in surrender and simply sat there for a few moments, trying to process all that was happening. "What would you have us do, Annie?" He watched her release a heavy breath from her lips and shrug her shoulders.

"I just figured I'd go to France with you." Trevor couldn't help but shake his head at the audacity of such a plan.

"Even if that were possible, Annie, it's too dangerous. I won't have it."

"Well, then, I'll stay with your family in Charleston. Or we can go to your uncle's. Your servants can help me with the baby. We'll hire a nanny. When you come home from the war, we'll get our own place and raise our children." Annie beamed at her ingenuity.

"Servants? Nannies?! Jesus, Annie. How long have you known about this? You seem to have had a lot of time to plot and scheme..."

Her palm hit him solidly across his cheekbone. Trevor shifted his stinging jaw from left to right as he rubbed the stubble on his chin.

"Maybe I deserved that. It's just you don't seem to have a realistic grasp of how I live...or anything else for that matter!"

"You want reality? Here it is, Trevor. I. Am. Pregnant. That's as real as it gets."

"Annie, we can't just show up on someone's doorstep, family or not, and say, 'Hello! We're moving in...all three of us!' People have their own lives. My uncle has a medical practice, and for all intents and purposes, a live-in lover that everyone pretends isn't living there. My father is rarely home, and here's some news. *We...don't...have...servants!*" Annie seemed stupefied. "We don't. My mother was very difficult to deal with so we could never keep help. Since she died, my father hasn't bothered to hire anyone, save for an occasional maid, because he's hardly ever in town." Annie began to sob. Trevor thought a moment, then continued.

"I believe it might be best for you to stay here." Trevor watched a look of horror sweep across her face, as if he'd just delivered her death sentence. "I can send money through Tom and Mattie and ..."

Through gritted teeth and razor-sharp lips, she seethed. *"Go to Hell, Trevor Middleton!* And you'd be in good company, 'cause Hell's what it would be for me if I stayed. My God! Apparently, *YOU* don't have a grasp on how *I* live! In case you missed the show at Virgil's funeral, my father will *kill me AND you* when he finds out I'm pregnant!"* Trevor shook his head at how stupid he was being. He really couldn't think straight. "You think you can just throw money at this, and that me and the baby will just slither back into that cave?"

"No, no, no. Of course not. Listen. This is a lot to take in. Give me some space to breathe – alright?" Annie looked towards the serviceberry bush. "I will do right by you, Annie Conner. I swear it. I just need time to sort this out."

Annie inhaled for what appeared to be another biting retort, but she gathered her wits and said, "Okay, but we don't have a lot of time. I was slow in telling you because I wasn't sure, but now I am."

"I won't. I promise," he replied as he kissed the top of her shaking hand. "I'll have a plan by tomorrow, but you must promise me you'll respond with that smart brain of yours, not just your feelings, alright?"

"That wasn't insulting at all...but alright. I get yo'r meanin'. Tomorrow then."

Trevor escorted Annie back to the path from whence she came. He was a few steps away when he felt Annie's eyes burning through his back like a dagger.

"Yo'r still incorrigible, you know, but I love you all the same."

Trevor felt his entire body grow weak. This was going to be a long, long day.

Chapter 33

Relieved and revived by unloading the burden of knowledge, Annie paused behind a tulip poplar to see Trevor wander in a zigzag pattern back towards the inn. He was leaning on his cane again, something he had not done in weeks. Once they were married and raising their child together, all would be forgiven ... perhaps even forgotten. Then again, what was there to be forgiven? It wasn't like she'd planned this.

Then again, maybe she had.

Of course, he could turn tail and run, but she doubted he would do such a thing. Weren't ambulance drivers called Gentleman Volunteers? He had a reputation to protect, as well as his new family.

Annie began to make her way back up the mountain path, her newfound relief now morphing into fatigue. But at least she wasn't feeling sick. She could see Effie's crooked front porch and decided she could make it there, taking a short break on the steps before making the final ascent towards home. Maybe Effie would have something more substantial to eat. The corn pone she'd nibbled before gathering eggs for Mattie and Tom had long been depleted. Without her rebellious stomach boiling, she felt she could eat an entire chicken.

When Annie arrived at the edge of Effie's yard, she could see the old woman swaying back and forth in her rocker, breaking green beans into a bucket. As she got closer, she heard the crisp, rhythmic *snip-snap* of the shells mingling with the *pretty-bird-pretty-bird-pretty-bird* call of the cardinal sitting high atop the crabapple tree. A bit winded, Annie climbed the steps to see that Effie was setting aside the plumper ones for stringing leather britches, which were Greasy Cut-Short beans threaded with a string through the middle and then hung up on nails. People called them leather britches because that's how they looked once they dried out; all tan, browned and wrinkled up, just like a pair of cowpoke britches. Annie loved the way leather britches tasted, especially when they were doused with vinegar and a layer of sweet, yellow onions. It was one of the few things she'd miss about this place, but memories would have to do.

"Well, lookie here! Come on up and sit a spell. Grab you a lap full'a beans and get to shellin'."

"Yo'r in rare form this mornin', Effie!"

"Guess I am. It's a beautiful day. Beans are in. Ain't no blight. Tomatoes'll be ripe for pickin' soon."

"I told him, Effie. Just a little bit ago." Effie dropped her hands to the green-stained newspaper and stopped her rocking.

"What'd he say?"

"He said he wanted to think about it."

"Think about ... what? Thinkin' won't make you less pregnant."

"I know that, Effie. He just said we'd talk tomorrow." Effie let that go with a *hmpfff* and returned to her bean shelling, minus the smile she'd been smitten with just moments earlier. "Said he wants to do the right thing." A barn cat, followed by her three kittens, crept up the drunken porch stairs.

Effie took one of Annie's hands in her own. "I am yo'r friend, Annie Grace, but friends don't always say what you wanna hear. So, I'm gonna just ask you this question. What do *you* want." Annie locked eyes with the old woman and smiled.

"I want to get married. I want to have this baby and live in Charleston. Or France, or wherever."

"I don't think you do."

"I know what I want!" Annie snapped back.

"I think you want *out*, and you'll do whatever it takes, takin' out whoever you have to, to see that it happens. And Annie, that sort of conniving never brings a soul to any good end."

"What's wrong with wanting out, Effie? Livin' here sure ain't served you so well!"

"This ain't about me, Annie. This is about you." Effie emphasized by needling her long, knobby finger towards her. "There ain't a thing wrong with wantin' outta here, not when you've got dreams and ideas that are bigger'n these canyon walls, but the way yo'r goin' about it? It ain't right."

Annie threw up her hands and began pacing. "The way I'm goin' about it," she repeated. "You talk like I planned this."

Effie huffed and sat back in her rocker, *snip-snap-snip-snapping* the remaining beans on her newspaper. "I think you intended this ... at some level at least."

Annie continued to move back and forth across the porch. "Okay. Well, I wanted to go to nursing school, but Birdie up and married that Clavel Lyons and ruined both our lives!"

"And there's yo'r trouble. You keep waitin' for salvation to come, but you gotta make yo'r own. Ain't no one, nowhere - not Trevor, not me, not Birdie, not Jesus Christ hisself can do it for you."

Annie sat in the rocking chair beside Effie and stared out into the yard. "Trevor said he'd pay my way through nursing school."

Effie stopped snapping her beans and stared as though Annie had just grown another head. "He what?"

"Before he found out I was pregnant. A few weeks ago. Said he wanted to help me better myself." Annie laughed, as though that was the craziest thing she'd ever heard.

"Annie, Child. You never told me that. That's wonderful. See? You got a chance to fix all this. You can start fresh, but you gotta do as I say."

"Do what, Effie?"

"You know exactly what I'm talkin' about. It won't be easy, but we can do this. Together."

"I ain't slippin' this baby, Effie! I cain't believe yo'r still harpin' on that. Besides. It's too late."

"It ain't too late, Annie. Not if you stay here with me. It won't be a cakewalk, but we can do it slow and easy like. Then everyone can get back to their lives, or on to a new one. You can go to school…"

"*NOOOOooooooooo!* I won't do it! My daddy was right. You *ARE* a witch!" Annie stood up to leave as the sternness in Effie's voice returned.

"Call me what you will, but I'll take that over bein' a liar and a deceiver. I'm tellin' you, sure as I sit here, you and that child will come to no good end if you stay on this crooked path. We'll all suffer for it. Mark my words."

"Well, you can mark my words, Effie Buchanan. You are no longer a friend of mine." Annie turned to march down the stairs.

"That list of friends is growin' shorter by the day, Annie Grace. You might wanna go easy with that parin' knife of yours," Effie hollered after her.

She'd make new friends once she was gone. To Hell with the lot of 'em.

<h1 style="text-align:center">Chapter 34</h1>

Sweat dampened the crown of Trevor's head as he hobbled back inside The Esmeralda, the pain in his leg returning with a marked vengeance. Just when he believed he was getting his life back, another explosion erupted; this one far more threatening and destructive to his dreams than any German Bosche.

How could he have been so naïve? His father had "the talk" with him on his sixteenth birthday, which amounted to a brief description of copulation and the gift of a little brown box containing a stretchy sheath made from sheep's gut with patriarchal instructions to, "...choose your poison wisely." That box with its contents remained somewhere in his bedroom back in Charleston.

In France, however, condoms were as common as croissants. French brothels were not only accepted but mandated. The average lifespan of a *poilu* was a mere six weeks, most soldiers coming to war having never been with a woman. A young soldier had a lot of living to do in a very short span of time. Thus, trips to the whorehouses were encouraged during *en repos*. Married men were no exception. In fact, even more pity was garnered upon those with wives left behind to tend the home fires; the logic being that they were so used to being sexually gratified that their desires and needs would be even harder to quell. Couple a man's sex drive with the perils and stress of never knowing if he would make it back to camp, much less home, alive, and well, a man had to have a lacy, perfumed distraction to keep his sanity.

As a customer, you were thoroughly inspected for diseases before dipping your spoon into the buffet of ecstasy offered at a *bordel de France.* Furthermore, any *fille de rue* discovered to be carrying the scourges of syphilis or gonorrhea (for the whores were given regular, physical exams) was immediately taken off the menu. And pregnancy? That was never a worry. It was always assumed that such matters were either prevented from the outset or handled discreetly in the aftermath.

But Annie was no prostitute. That night at the cave had been born out of pain, boredom, and confusion...and alcohol. Lots and lots of alcohol. Had Annie engineered the whole thing? He'd probably never know and didn't want to. He could see now, plain as Clavel was staring at him from the bowed front window, that he'd just been damned stupid.

"Everything alright?" Clavel maintained a skeptical look of guardianship about him.

"No, Clavel. It's all quite a mess. But thanks for your concern."

"Just a word of advice from an ol'e country boy?" Trevor paused and stared, unsure of just how he was going to make it to his room before he collapsed.

"What is it, Clavel? I am really quite exhausted, and it's not even lunchtime."

"Bed pardon, beg pardon," he drawled out. "It's just that, I've known that girl all my life. I seen what her old man's done. I'd just as soon spit at the sum'bitch as to look at 'im. Every breath of air he takes is a waste, far as I'm concerned."

The walls of The Esmeralda began to flank him on all sides. Worms seemed to be oozing from the pores of his skin, and he felt as though every organ in his body would explode. He swallowed hard and tried to focus on the swinging pendulum of the clock that sat on the mantel, its silhouette now resembling the form of a crouching, black cat.

"What's your point, Clavel."

"Oh. Beg pardon. I'm just sayin'. Don't let that girl play you for the fool. Friend or enemy, she'll chew you up, pinch her nose, and blow you out 'er ears. Girl don't know what love is, 'cause she ain't never had none, except her Momma, and for what that's worth, Annie's been more of a momma than a daughter, if you catch my meanin'."

Trevor leaned hard on his cane. "Clavel, I appreciate your concern, but I fear I have not just been played for a fool. It appears that I have been proven one. Now if you'll excuse me, I think I'm going to pass out."

Chapter 35

Annie's lungs felt as though they were bulging inside her throat as she crested the top of the trail. There, the thickness of the laurels and rhododendron surrendered to the open fields of beans, red beets, mustard greens, and potatoes. Beyond these, the faint orange of ripening tomatoes glistened with the last of the morning's dew. The violet and white morning glory vines clung to stretching cornstalks. Young corn silk tassels glistened in the late morning sun. Squash and cucumbers clambered with one another for space along the outer edge of the gardens. Annie stood there at the edge of it all, catching her breath, and for a moment, believed she might one day miss this place. But a sudden movement from within the center of the rising corn brought her back from her delusions.

"Where you been, girl? Been lookin' all over for you." Lester was wearing his wide brimmed garden hat that flopped lower on one side, covering his right eye. His visible eye was a glassy, milky white, and a lip snarled from below exposing yellowed, pointed teeth that snapped and chattered together between each reproach. *This is what demons must look like,* Annie thought. She moved towards the cornrows to meet him there and hopefully settle his raised dander.

"I thought you were out ridin'. Witnessin'."

"Don't amount to a hill'a beans where I go or what I do. You been gone the entire mornin'. Now I'll ask you one more time.

Where...have...you...been?!" Lester's voice rang inside her ears so loud her teeth hurt.

"I went to take eggs and tomatoes to The Esmeralda. Like I do every morning."

"Ain't that far'a walk. Did'ju get paid?" Spittle flew from Lester's mouth as he held out his hand for the money she could not produce.

"Tom and Mattie pay us on Fridays. Today is Wednesday."

"I know what day it is, Smart Mouth. I oughta scrub yo'r disrespectin' tongue raw with lye. I swear to God above you ain't worth shootin' these days. What's gotten into you?" Lester threw up his hands and began to pace circles around her. "*See?!* You even got me takin' the Lord's name in vain. Jesus forgive yo'r soul! The Bible says..." Annie rolled her eyes and tried to focus on a caterpillar that was making its way across a waxy shuck of corn. "Look at me!" Lester grabbed her by the chin and jerked her face towards him, her eyes forced to level themselves at the cave of the Devil's mouth.

"Proverbs 19:15. *Slothfulness casteth into a deep sleep; and an idle soul shall suffer hunger.* Do you understand what that means, Annie?" Annie tried to nod that she did, but Lester's hand gripped her head like a vice. "Reckon we'd all be beggin' for scraps like stray dogs if we depended on you. I raised you to have more sense than to go whorin' around after that sorry n'er-do-well. From now on?" Lester jabbed his thumb into his chest. "*I'll* take the orders down to The Esmeralda."

Annie's eyes widened. How did her father know about her and Trevor?

"I don't know what yo'r talkin' about." Annie tried to pull away from her father's grasp, but he held tight, laughing.

"I ain't no fool. I seen how you looked at him at Virgil's funeral. In a church! I swear, sometimes I think yo'r someone else's spawn." Lester shoved her onto the clods of dirt that threatened to become her grave before day's end, knocking the wind out of her lungs.

Lester removed a hoe he'd been toting underneath the pit of his arm and tossed it on his daughter's heaving belly. "Now git yo'rself up from there and get to hoein' this corn or we'll be eatin' chickweeds this winter. And if these rows ain't cleared by nightfall, and I mean there better not be a weed pokin' it's head up through that sod, don't even bother comin' home! I'm tired of you makin' a fool of yo'r damned self and this family!" he shouted, kicking her deep in the gut with the toe of his leather boot.

Annie's chest heaved up and down – every breath a struggle. Her stomach screamed in pain each time she bent upwards. She managed to raise her arm, hoping for a hand-up, but was met instead with a wad of spit that landed firmly in her eye. Annie rolled over on her side and vomited what little was left in her stomach into the groundhog hole beside her. Bile trickled down her windpipe, causing her to choke and gasp - her world going black as she prepared to die.

"Annie. *Annie!* Talk to me. Please say somethin'." Annie rolled over, but the glare of the afternoon sun blinded her from attaching a face to the voice that was calling. A dragon fly dipped and flitted behind the silhouette, and she wondered if an angel had come to take her home.

"Annie, it's me. Birdie. What happened? Please. Yo'r scarin' me."

Annie wiped the yellow, gummed up spit from around her eyes and lips, feeling surprisingly peaceful and a bit disappointed to be back from wherever she had been.

"I, I'm not sure."

"The Hell you ain't. It was Lester, wasn't it?" Annie didn't answer. "You need to get away from here." Annie eased up to a sitting position, wrapping her arms around her legs and placing her head between her knees.

"I gotta hoe this corn, Birdie. Daddy'll see me dead sure as the mornin' if I don't."

"The Hell he will. He'll see *me* dead first!"

Annie looked around her, trying to clear the vision of a world that was solid yellow.

"Where's June?"

"June's with Clavel. He left work early today. Said he felt somethin' wasn't right and wanted me to check on you. Yo'r comin' with me. Can you walk?"

Annie felt no strength to argue. With Birdie's hand she stood, wobbling in the summer breeze until some internal ballast steadied her in the uneven field. Birdie wiped the sweat off her clammy forehead with a soft rag she pulled from her cleavage.

"I can walk," Annie offered, not so convincingly.

"Here, take hold of my arm." Birdie extended her elbow and wrapped Annie's arm through it as though she were threading a needle. "Let's go," she insisted, pulling Annie along with a fervor that nearly toppled her.

Under normal circumstances, the hike wasn't that far, but today it felt as though they had walked all the way to Asheville before they reached Birdie's house. Clavel and June were in the floor, playing with a whizzer. Each time Clavel made the propeller on the end whirr, June laughed so hard she fell headfirst into her daddy's lap.

"Auntie!" June shouted, running towards her with arms outstretched. Had the child resorted to calling her "aunt" or was that June's way of saying, "Annie?" Her foggy brain couldn't work it out.

"Not now, June. Aunt Annie is feelin' a bit poorly."

"I'm fine, Sugar," Annie said, rubbing the crown of June's hoary white hair. Birdie was hovering by her side with a glass of lemonade. June reached for it, her little fingers wiggling in and out of a fist.

"No baby, this is Annie's. I'll get you some in just a sec. Now go on with yo'r Daddy. Momma'll be along soon."

Birdie now turned to Annie. "Sit. Drink," she commanded as she nudged her friend onto the ladder-back chair. "Yo'r red as a beet. How long were you laid out like that?"

"I don't know." Annie sipped on the lemonade. Birdie looked to see if Clavel was around.

"Stand up," she commanded. "Slow." Annie stared up at her friend like she was crazy. "I mean it, Annie."

"Sit down. Stand up. Sit down. Stand up. Lord have mercy, Birdie. Make up yo'r cottonpickin' mind!"

Birdie ignored her friend's commentary as she lifted her dress, taking in the deep purple bruising between her ribs and stomach.

"Goddamn son of a bitch," Birdie whispered. Annie followed her friend's eyes and gasped when she saw the deep blue mark her father had left. "There's not a Hell hot enough for the likes of that piece of shit." Birdie dropped the hem of Annie's dress just as Clavel returned with more lemonade and a fresh rag for Annie's forehead.

"Birdie," she said as she grabbed her friend's hand. "If Pa did this to me, just for seein' Trevor, he'll kill me when he finds out I'm pregnant."

"Yo'r pregnant," Birdie said, more as a statement than a question. Annie nodded. "Dear God in heaven."

Birdie fixed her hands on her hips and began pacing. Annie sat back down, accepting the second pint of lemonade from Clavel, feeling oddly grateful for his presence.

"Does Trevor know?" Annie nodded that he did. "Clavel, did you know?" Clavel just shrugged his shoulders. Trevor must have told him. But neither she nor Birdie could be angry at Clavel right now. By following his hunches, Clavel had probably saved Annie's life.

"I wanted to tell you, Birdie, but things were so bad between us. I wasn't sure I could trust you." Birdie bent down to the floor in front of Annie, placing both hands on her knees.

"Oh, sweet girl. You can always trust me."

"Can I?" Annie stared at her, willing her to remember their last fight.

"Of course. We say things when we're upset, but when the sun goes down, we always got each other's backs. You hear me? I'll take every secret you ever tell me ... every single one ... to my grave." Birdie dabbed the caked clods of mud from Annie's legs and face, then stood as she looked to her husband and asked, "Could you leave us for a minute, Dear?"

"Sure," Clavel replied with a kiss to her cheek. "I'll just take June out back to see the calf." Birdie said she thought that a sweet idea.

"You cain't go home, Annie. Not for a second." Annie shook her head in agreement. "But you gotta go somewhere, and even if you and Trevor marry, you'll have to set up housekeepin'. And what about yo'r Ma? It ain't safe for her to stay with the likes of that, that son-of-a-bitch, either."

"If ... we marry, as you say," Annie cleared her throat and responded, "and we will, Ma can come live with us. In Charleston."

"Did Trevor suggest such an arrangement?"

"Well, not yet, but he will. I just told him about the baby this morning. I cain't throw everything at him all at once." Annie cast an unsettling glance at Birdie. "You could look in on Momma from time to time until we send for her, cain't you?" Birdie shrugged her shoulders and moved to the back window, where she watched Clavel push June in the rope swing he'd made.

"You can come live with us," she said without turning.

"Birdie, that's most kind of you, but there's no room." Annie counted on her fingers for emphasis. "There's me, Trevor, Mom and the baby. Four more people. You cain't take that on! Maybe Jacob can be persuaded to come back."

"Maybe, but I just got a bad feelin' about this, Annie. A bad feelin'. You talked to Effie about slippin' this baby?" Annie turned sharply.

"You little hypocrite!"

Birdie glared at her and placed a finger to her lips. "Shhh, now! We don't have to argue." Birdie's voice came to a forced whisper. "I'm just askin'. It's always an option, you know."

"I *ain't* arguin'. I just cain't believe you'd encourage me to do somethin' you never thought twice about when *you* were in the same way."

"This ain't the same thing, Annie, and you know it!"

"How's it different? At least Trevor's got prospects and a future." Birdie took two aggressive steps towards her friend.

"You hush yo'r mouth, Annie Grace. Clavel might not have an education or the privilege some folks do, but he's every bit a gentleman, and despite what you may think, he's smart. Smart as a whip." Tears welled up in her eyes as she glanced back out the window at her family. "He's a good man. I love him, and I won't have you talkin' down to him."

For the first time, Annie didn't know what to say on the subject. She wrapped her arms around herself and slowly walked across the floor to watch Clavel and June play hide and seek around the ungainly boxwood limbs that separated their small yard from the watering trough and tiny barn. That was where they kept a couple of cows and a bull. Any offspring, they sold to Mr. Harris for butchering in return for flour, sugar and other supplies for the winter. Harris was a kind man, giving them a few cuts from the meat for free.

"Birdie, I'm sorry. I never thought you really loved him. I just thought..."

"I know what you thought, but things ain't always black and white. I ain't sayin' I'm innocent, but I did what I thought was right. For me and Little June."

"I still wished you'd told me."

"Would it have made a difference?" Annie said nothing but conceded to herself it probably wouldn't have.

Annie paced before the back window, noticing how the sunlight and shadows played out across the fields and the barn. She leaned her now cooled head against the warm pane, watching Clavel lift June up to see a nest the wrens had built deep in the heart of their scarecrow. Mother wren flew out and landed on a rafter in the barn, screeching and fussing at the intrusion. Clavel then carried his daughter towards the barn to meet the little brown and white calf that couldn't have been more than two days old. June squealed with delight.

This is what she wanted, more than anything. A life with no fighting. No fearing her father's backhand. She wanted to laugh, and to be loved, but the thought of carving out such a life in The Gorge was inconceivable. It might have worked out for Birdie, but as the memories of the morning began to reform and converge on the present, she knew the life she wanted could never be found here. Not ever.

Chapter 36

I t only took Trevor a half hour lying on his bed, his eyes cast upwards in despondency and regret, for him to realize what he had to do. He would ask Annie for her hand in marriage - the right way, even though the mere thought of getting down on bended knee made his entire body ache. But he had made a horrible mistake, and he was determined to make it right, insomuch as possible. If that meant taking her to Charleston, then so be it. His father would not be pleased at first, but in the end, Wallace would agree this was the "best right thing" as he was known for saying. The war would be over soon and then he'd figure out the rest of their lives.

Trevor forced himself up and walked to the front desk, where he found Tom sitting under the light of a banker's lamp, the end of his pencil tapping out a rhythm of consternation. Trevor cleared his throat, causing Tom to swivel a squeaky one hundred and eighty degrees in the big oak chair.

"Can't get these blasted columns to balance," he rumbled. "Never did understand accounting. A credit's not always good, and a debit's not always bad, depending on which side of the books you're on."

"Why don't you hire a bookkeeper, Tom?"

"Nah. Mattie wouldn't hear of it. Says this war could slow business down overnight, and she's right. We're just too small of an operation to add that sort of overhead – unless you're volunteering." Tom winked at his guest.

"Sorry, but I fear you would be bankrupt faster than the war could take your business." Tom laughed at his self-effacement. "But my father said it changed his life when he hired a bookkeeper. It's something to consider." Tom said he would think about it.

"What can I do for you on this fine afternoon?

"I was wondering if you were going into Asheville again?" Tom said he wasn't anytime soon.

"That's too bad," Trevor frowned. "I was hoping to send another telegram."

"I got a pigeon that can coo 'Kitty the Telephone Girl' if you talk to 'er real nice." Trevor said that, while the entertainment merits alone might be worthy of a coin or two, he doubted that would solve his dilemma.

"If it's really important, I do have a radio back behind the mailboxes. Just got it a few days ago." Trevor looked puzzled. "I intend to keep it hidden and only plan to use it in emergencies. Is this an emergency?" Trevor wasn't sure how to respond.

"Well, in a way. I sent a letter to Victor Chapman several weeks ago, but I've ..." Trevor hesitated, "...had a slight change in plans."

"Is everything alright?"

"Yes. Well, it will be. The plans themselves haven't changed. Just a few of the details. I wanted to keep Victor abreast of my situation, as well as give my father and uncle notice." Tom nodded. "And I need to do it rather quickly."

"Well, not sure if what I have will help you. Either way, please don't let on to folks that I have this radio. President Wilson is trying to censor communications. Lots of hullabaloo about it. Obviously, I have no secrets to intercept, but I do want to keep my radio in case we ever need help from the outside. That incident with Virgil proved that if we had a better means of reaching medical services, it could save lives. Maybe if I could have radioed for help..."

"Tom, Virgil was so far gone I doubt anything you or anyone else could've done would have made a difference."

"Maybe so, but folks around these parts don't get much of a break. I figured if I could give something back, I should." Tom was a good man, someone he would miss when he returned to France.

"Well, your secret's safe with me. Could we possibly radio in a telegram message then?" Trevor asked, his eyes pleading.

"Absolutely. Let's give it a whirl, shall we?"

Chapter 37

Despite Birdie's insistence that she stay, Annie had gone home to check on her mother. To her surprise, she found Ida sitting outside on the front porch, a crocheted blanket stretched across her shoulders as she sorted through a bowl of blackberries; their inky juice staining the tips her fingers. The air was thick with water and clouds, a billowing thunderhead threatening to unleash its fury to the south. The storm was pushing a suffocating heat up the valley, but Ida clutched the blanket tight around her chest as though it was blowing up a blizzard.

"You alright, Momma?" Annie asked. Ida's eyes focused hard on the blackberries. "It's good to see you outta that bed and doin' somethin'." Ida made no effort to acknowledge her daughter's voice. "How 'bout I make a crust for a pie, or maybe some dumplin's. Would you like that, Momma? Some blackberry dumplin's?"

Annie had two reasons for suggesting such: her mother loved blackberry dumplings and blackberries, especially their juice, were good to quell a queasy stomach. Ida smiled a lopsided grin at the suggestion.

"Alright. Dumplin's it is. Where's Pa?" Ida's demeanor darkened as she shrugged her shoulders. "I gotta get down to the field and hoe out those chickweeds, but I'll be back, and then I'll fix us some supper ... and dumplin's." Her mother continued to cap the berries, sorting the green tops and the less ripe berries into a pile that would become an evening snack for the chickens. Their old rooster and his biddies had already begun to strut around the perimeter of the house, sensing the windfall of fruit and greens.

Annie peeked outside on the back porch to find Lester with his head buried deep in his cracked, leather Bible. His lips were mouthing the words of some scripture he was no doubt considering for his hell-raising sermon on Sunday. This Sunday was the one before the Fourth of July, and her father never failed to seize upon the season's heat and oppressiveness to render his most knee-bending, *Come to Jesus* sermons of the year. It was as though nature herself were flinging all her props and energies to assist him in leading the lost sheep of The Gorge to eternal salvation. *See? You think this is bad? Just imagine eternity, seven times hotter!*

Annie began to dig the weeds out from around the corn, the rhythmic *crich-crich-crich* of the hoe lulling her into a trance that, oddly, seemed to settle her ragged nerves, though it didn't do much for her aching ribs. She raised the hem of her skirt and winced at the purple and yellow bruise that now covered her entire left side.

Finishing that chore much quicker than expected, she had begun picking the earworms off the corn silks, smashing them in between her swelling fingers as she made her way in and around the leafy rows. She had no sooner finished the first row when a clap of thunder jolted her from her daydreams. By her count, the storm was less than a mile away.

Splats of raindrops pelted against her sunburned scalp, so despite her father's warning, she stopped. Hoeing wet ground only produced hard, nearly impenetrable clods that would make for more difficult work later. Besides, she was hungry. And tired. Oh my God, was she tired. By the time Annie made it back to the house, the top of Burnt Shirt Mountain had disappeared into the blue-gray clouds of the storm. To her dismay, Lester was standing outside the house, his wide brimmed hat channeling cupfuls of rain onto the shoulders of his starched-white shirt and overalls.

"Yep. That's what the top of Mt. Sinai looked like when God gave Moses the Ten Commandments. Smoke billowin'. Lightnin' flashin'. Never question God's authority. His wrath is swift and sure!" Annie ignored his posturing, the hunger in her stomach urging her to feed it soon or *its* wrath would also be swift and sure.

"Dinner'll be ready soon," Annie offered without any emotion. "Ma wanted some blackberry dumplings."

"Sounds mighty fine, Daughter. Mighty fine. There's a bowl of beans and a few new taters layin' there, if you'd fix 'em up. I wrung and plucked a chicken, too, for you to fry."

"Who picked the beans?" Annie asked.

"Well, I dug up the taters but yo'r Ma picked those few beans. 'Bout dang near took her last breath to do it, but since you weren't around, guess she decided she'd have to pick 'er own or starve. You see the trouble you caused?"

Well, there it was. Not a chance that Lester had any lightning bolt moment for himself as to the error of *his* ways. Annie walked into the kitchen and began mixing flour, salt and pepper to bread the chicken. The beans were broken and strung, but the potatoes still needed washing. She threw those into a bowl of water to soften the clinging dirt. She'd hoped her father would return to his studying on the porch, but instead, he lingered.

"It was good to see your Ma up and about. She's just wastin' away in that bed. Shows she's still got some spunk." Annie ignored his jibber-jabber. She liked it much better when they didn't speak to one another. "Maybe she can start pullin' her weight around here. First Timothy, chapter five verse eight says ..."

"I know what it says." Annie kept her gaze from meeting her father's, but she could feel his eyes stabbing her from behind.

"Then repeat it to me, so I know you know."

Annie sighed and without turning her eyes to meet him, she repeated the scripture. "But if any provide not for his own, and especially for those of his own house, he hath denied the faith, and is worse than an infidel." Tears stung her eyes. She'd rather her father beat her than to endure this humiliation.

"That's right. So, now you tell me. Yo'r Ma's seen the light. What are we to do with you?"

Annie inhaled deeply. "You don't need to do nothin' with me. I won't be yo'r problem anymore." She felt her father pause, sensing him trying to work out her meaning.

"Glad to hear it. Glad to hear it. Now get that supper on the table. I gotta meetin' with the elders tonight. Hard to hear the Lord's voice over a growlin' stomach."

The next morning, the first thought on her mind was meeting Trevor back at The Esmeralda. Lester mentioned his plans to travel to Old Man Howington's place to pay a visit. Hadn't seen him in church lately, and word was he was suffering from the gout. Maybe the Lord had a miracle to dispense today. The miracle for her was that, once her Pa was gone, he'd be absent most of the day. He and Mr. Howington would talk for hours.

Annie picked some tomatoes and pulled some onions from the ground and washed them in the sink. She'd take these down to The Esmeralda – a convenient excuse to possibly see Trevor and get a read on him. As she ambled down the path, she could hear the voices of the loggers on the ridge, the sharp sounds of *Timmmmmberrrrrrrr!* preceding the inevitable snapping and cracking of giant oaks, poplars and pines as they fell and hit the ground, sending up plumes of decaying leaves, insects and sawdust. The felled trees would be cut into manageable pieces before being loaded onto a horse drawn wagon. From there, the wagons would tow the timber to the local sawmill, where it would be planed, milled and most of it sent to bigger towns like Charlotte and Asheville. The local folk couldn't usually afford the prices of the harvested wood, but the logging companies did provide some jobs. *Always dancin' with the Devil,* Annie thought to herself.

She'd not gone a mile, however, until she felt the unsettling in her stomach return and leaned up against a fence post, struggling to keep the small biscuit she'd eaten down.

The remaining three miles between her house proved even worse. Four times she'd stopped. Just before making the final quarter mile to The Esmeralda, she paused at the creek to splash water on her face. As she bent to the water, her ribs ached from the blow of her father's boot. Catching her reflection, she gasped. Shadowy blotches collected beneath her eyes. She had even developed a rash and wondered why so many women remarked favorably about the "glow of pregnancy."

Stopping a few yards from the kitchen door, where she usually entered, Annie decided to go in through the main entrance. She felt it spoke of change – that she was now *someone*. A force to be reckoned with, and respected. Not just some farmgirl come to sell her wares.

"Annie!" Trevor threw up his hand as he met her at the top of the stone steps. "I was reading the paper just now, wondering when you might be here. It's good to see you."

It was? That was encouraging.

"How are you feeling?"

She really didn't know how to answer that. She was feeling so many things. "I'm okay, I guess."

"I know what happened yesterday ... with your father. Clavel told me. I was so worried when you didn't come to the inn." Annie hung her head. She really didn't want her father to be a part of this conversation, but she supposed there was no avoiding it. It was sweet that Trevor was concerned, though.

"He was in rare form, for sure," she snickered nervously as she looked about the inn.

"He hurt you." She thought about the spreading bruise that flowed from her ribcage and across the left side of her belly. It was a struggle just to breathe. "Are you alright? You didn't lose ... the baby did you?"

"You wished I had?" she snipped.

"God, no! I would never want to see you ... or our child, come to any harm." Well, that was nice to hear, at least. "Let's go out to the garden. There's a cottage on the terrace that Mattie says I can have for the next week or so. It's the honeymoon cottage. I want you to see it!"

"Honeymoon cottage? For the next ... week?" Annie questioned. "I thought you were going to France."

"Oh, I am so daft. I forgot to tell you. I've delayed my trip for another month. Victor says that will work better for him and *The Escadrille*, too. My father was surprisingly agreeable to delay his sail, as well." Annie cast a look towards him that danced between caution and hope.

"I have something to share with you, but maybe this isn't a good time. You seem a bit out of sorts. Which is understandable but..."

"Just tell me."

"Alright. I was hoping to do this at the cottage, but here goes." Trevor looked around him as though he were lost, patting down his pockets, picking up his cane then leaning it against the rocker. Finally, with a sigh of exasperation, he grabbed the flowers from a nearby vase and extended them towards her, the water dripping onto the ground in tiny puddles around Annie's feet.

"I don't have a ring or anything to give you, but I just picked these flowers, and I was wondering if you would do me the pleasure of marrying me?"

She'd waited for months, a lifetime, to hear those words. She'd rehearsed her response in the old, pitted mirror on the dresser, but she found herself taken aback all the same. The flowers in her hand began trembling as though all of time were concentrated in that one place.

"Oh, my. Well, I..." Annie blushed. "Yes. Yes! I will marry you!" Trevor produced a smile, albeit a bit forced. "You've made me the happiest woman in the world!"

"Then it seems I have done my job well." Trevor kissed her gently on the lips. "Now, let's go see that cottage."

Chapter 38

Less than a week later, on his wedding day, Trevor awoke to the aroma of bacon sizzling in a cast iron skillet. Wasn't there some saying about what you eat on your wedding day you'll be eating for the rest of your life? No, that was New Year's Day. Never mind.

He rubbed the sleep out of his eyes, then swung his feet over the bed, one at a time, sitting there until the blood settled into his legs. He reached for his cane but decided he would try and do without it, at least today.

Trevor eased into a standing position and walked towards the bathroom, stopping to assess his body in the tall dressing mirror, as he'd formed a habit of doing. His limp was hardly noticeable anymore, and a healthy pink had replaced the ghostliness of his face. His stomach muscles were taut and robust – a product of his fifty daily sit-ups, and his biceps were nicely bulged. It was a good thing he was leaving The Esmeralda soon, though. A few more servings of Clavel's buttermilk biscuits and sausage gravy and he'd be wider than a Renault tank.

Trevor walked to the armoire and removed his best suit from the hanger, tossing it on the unmade bed several feet away. He reached for his white shirt, but then remembered he'd given it to Mattie late Friday evening to be washed and pressed for the big day. As if on cue, Clavel knocked.

"Trevor, yo'r shirt's hangin' outside on this here doorknob." Trevor donned his bathrobe and shouted a polite thank you to the one who was going to be the best man at his wedding in just a few hours. "Annie's here, too." Trevor felt his stomach cinch into a knot.

This whole situation seemed to be fantastical, almost silly – like neighborhood children playing house. This time last week, he was setting his sights on France. Today? He was marrying a girl he barely knew and in a few short months, he would be the father to a child: another total stranger that he would be responsible for. He hoped he could equip their child to navigate this world better than he had.

When he did return to The States after the war, what then? Where would they live? Certainly, his engineering degree, along with his experience as a driver and pilot would land him a great job in just about any city. Boston came to mind. He had read some of Robert Goddard's papers on spaceflight and like Goddard, believed that it was possible to land rockets on the moon. He could apply to Clark University and obtain his PhD in physics. Living in Worcester would provide them a sense of country life alongside the convenience of a large city. He could expose Annie and their child to ballet, symphony, and fine cuisine. Maybe they would have more children. He envisioned a long line of stair-stepped siblings, padding behind their mother and father. The idea seemed both palatable and far-fetched.

He wondered if Annie would ever appreciate such things like theater and opera. Maybe she would not just appreciate the finer parts of culture but embrace them. *Don't expect too much too fast,* he warned himself.

He was reminded that the romantic notions of this marriage were few. This was a pragmatic solution to a very unromantic problem – at least as far as he was concerned. In time, he hoped he would fall in love with Annie, or at least learn to love her, but for now he had to be realistic about his feelings, or lack thereof.

Trevor put on his suit, all but his jacket, and proceeded to the breakfast table where he found Annie, Birdie and Clavel sitting together, their plates heaping with scrambled eggs, fried potatoes, and a couple of pieces of bacon draped over the sides.

"Good morning, Trevor," Mattie pronounced. "Nice of you to join us." His hostess's tone was just short of disciplinary. Trevor pulled his pocket watch from his trousers and realized he was late to the table. Mattie winked, so she must not be that upset.

As for what they would do in the days after their nuptials, Mattie and Tom, in a most generous act of kindness, had offered them the honeymoon cottage which was nestled upon a terrace on the backside of the gardens. It was impossibly romantic, Mattie had said. While Trevor had offered to pay for the upgrade, the Turners had been adamant. Annie, and now Trevor, were family. This was their gift. So be it.

At first, Mattie became obsessed with making the wedding day as celebratory as possible. But Trevor insisted they needed no pomp and circumstance. It was going to be a quiet, simple ceremony after church services. What he, no, *they*, really wanted was just a quiet day to themselves.

Trevor suddenly noticed that Clavel was at the table as a guest, not as a server. While he was pleased, he felt confused and off balance by the departure in what had become familiar to him – Clavel taking care of his every need. As if sensing his thoughts, Birdie spoke up.

"Tom and Mattie gave Clavel the whole day off. Wasn't that sweet?" She leaned into her husband and kissed him on the cheek. Clavel beamed at his wife.

Tom put his hand on Clavel's shoulder. "Least we could do for the best man. Consequently, I cooked most of what you see here, so if something's off, don't blame Clavel. I'd about forgotten my way around the kitchen!"

"As if you ever knew it," Mattie quipped, providing much-needed levity. "And Annie, you look beautiful."

"Next to my Birdie, yo'r the prettiest bride ever!" Clavel added, as Annie's face glowed beet red.

"Well, Trevor. Have you nothing to say about this splendid, beautiful woman you're about to marry?" Tom asked.

He had to admit, Annie was radiant. Light from the chandelier bounced off her bright red curls. Even her smile was strong, her morning sickness abating for at least this moment. Her dress, another gift from Mattie, was exquisite. A grayish blue linen skirt was draped to the knee in an elegant swath of champagne lace, neatly embroidered with the same gray colored thread as the skirt. Likewise, the skirt was complemented with embroidery the same color as the linen drape, so that the two pieces sung like a duet. At the bodice, fine, gray trim crisscrossed the front where her growing breasts stood, accentuating her curvy figure.

A string of champagne-colored pearls completed the ensemble. *Nothing changes the look of a dress like a nice string of pearls,* Mattie had said as she admired Annie, much as an artist would a newly finished portrait.

Annie began to fidget with all the attention. "I have a hat, a sort of veil, I mean." She sighed and rolled her eyes at herself. "For the weddin'. It just didn't seem appropriate to wear at the breakfast table, so I left it..."

"Stop," Trevor said as he moved towards her. "Don't apologize for yourself. You are stunning. I'm the ragamuffin here, and I am proud for you to be my wife." Annie folded her arms across her chest.

"Well, I think you may be right, Trevor Middleton. I've seen scarecrows dressed better'n you. Weddin's off." Annie waved her hand to dismiss her fiancé without so much as a smirk and returned to the table. "Now, would someone please pass me the applesauce?" The table erupted in laughter. "Now sit yo'rself down and eat. We've got a big day ahead and I don't want you faintin' on me like some silly girl."

Trevor laughed then did as he was told, taking a couple of steaming biscuits from the basket, splitting them down the middle and spreading them thick with pats of butter. Annie offered him the bowl of applesauce, which he immediately heaped onto the bread in copious spoonfuls. "It's gonna be fun, Trevor. Just you wait and see."

As crazy as the thought was, he was starting to believe it just might be true.

Chapter 39

After breakfast, the wedding party left in Tom and Mattie's Packard for the Methodist church, with Trevor commanding the steering wheel. It was a typical summer morning in The Gorge: cotton-ball clouds dallied high above the canyon walls. Further to the east, Annie could see thunderheads building, though their fury would not be felt for several hours.

In the churchyard, a hummingbird worked the blooms of the honey-suckle that sprawled along the edge of the cemetery. It made a dive towards Annie, hovering just inches away from her flower-laden hat.

"It thinks yo'r a flower," Birdie laughed. Annie supposed in a way, she was. A bloom of a girl, finally awakening to the bright sunshine of this world. She hadn't even been sick this morning. It was a good sign.

As the worship hour neared, folks began drifting into the churchyard. She knew most of them, but only casually, as she was never allowed to attend any other church but Middlefork Pentecostal Holiness. Church was always the focal point in these small communities, but the fact there were two less than three miles from one another was rare. Simply, folks had tired of Lester's brand of religion and set out to find their own truth. Hence, the Bat Cave Methodist Church was formed. And a portal to Hell along with it, according to her father. How appropriate that this was where she was getting married.

Annie's attentions were soon drawn towards a boy making quite a racket, all because he wanted to ring the church bell. The child was much too small, but his daddy held him up towards the frayed rope so that he could give it a tug, despite his mother's protests that it wasn't appropriate. *Let the boy have some fun,* Annie thought. The bell clanged just enough to make the little boy giggle. Trevor saw it too, each of them giving the other a knowing smile, as if that would be them one day.

"Are you ready?" Trevor said, extending a chivalrous hand to his bride. Annie took it and allowed herself to be guided into the church. She felt as if she were a cloud floating on a mountain breeze.

Once inside, Trevor suggested they sit in the back, but for all their attempts to not draw attention to themselves, everyone turned to gaze at the visitors in their midst. Annie thought she heard some of the young girls snicker, but mostly, folks just smiled and nodded – an affirming gesture that said, for whatever reason these folks had found themselves in their church today, they were welcome.

Just then, six people, two men and four women emerged from a side door and filed into the choir loft as the pastor made his way to the pulpit. With the emergence of the choir, the organist played a few bars of a hymn. The air was filled with the familiar words, sung particularly loud and slightly off key by a decrepit old woman sitting several spaces down on their pew:

> *Sowing in the morning, sowing seeds of kindness*
> *Sowing in the noontide and the dewy eve.*
> *Waiting for the harvest, and the time of reaping,*
> *We shall come rejoicing, bringing in the sheaves.*
>
> *Going forth with weeping, sowing for the Master,*
> *Though the loss sustained our spirit often grieves.*
> *When our weeping's over, He will bid us welcome,*
> *We shall come rejoicing, bringing in the sheaves.*

After the hymn, the Reverend Wilcox announced that there were visitors among them today, and to please be sure and make them feel at home. The organist pounded out another tune Annie wasn't familiar with while everyone turned to shake hands and said something like, "The Peace of Christ." At least they weren't dancin' in the aisles, like in her father's church.

Reverend Wilcox's sermon was short but thoughtful, taking his scripture from the book of Corinthians.

Though I speak in tongues, and have not charity,
I am become as sounding brass, or a tinkling cymbal.

The Reverend stopped and said, "Here, the word charity means love." He smiled sweetly to his flock before he continued.

I might prophesy, and understand all mysteries, and all knowledge,
and though I have all faith of a tee-tiny mustard seed,
so that I could climb any mountain,
and have not love ... I am nothing.

Some of the folks sounded an Amen to that, but that's all. No whoopin' and a'flailin'.

Maybe I give all I have to feed the poor. Maybe I give my body to be burned,
but if I don't have love, it doesn't amount to a hill of beans.

Everyone laughed at that, Annie getting so tickled she snorted. Trevor laughed, too. Who would've thought you could have fun in church!

Love suffers long. Love is kind.
Love isn't jealous.
If we love someone, we don't want to embarrass them.

Annie thought of Virgil's funeral - how her daddy had embarrassed her, and a tear fell onto the bodice of her wedding dress.

Love never thinks evil about the other.
Love loves the TRUTH!

Birdie cleared her throat at that part, but Annie pretended to ignore her. Besides, she'd told Trevor the truth, save for that stupid letter she'd burned.

Love believes the best in each of us.
Love wants what is best for the other – even when it hurts.
Prophesies and words will fail us.
Our minds may go and our bodies may grow weak.
But Love will always be there – even when death comes to take us home.
There is Faith. There is Hope, and there is Love.
But the greatest of these is Love.

It pleased her that Reverend Wilcox had this way of reading the Bible. And his sermon was more like he was teaching *to*, rather than preaching *at*. He used his own words to explain things, to bring God's word down to a place where you could listen, not just with your ears, but with your heart. And of all the verses in the Bible! Annie had never heard these before, but considering the topic, she wasn't surprised. What did her father know about love?

By the time the final hymn was sung, half the church was in tears. Annie was, and so was Birdie. There was no screamin' or shoutin'. No turnin' cartwheels in the aisles or mutterin' nonsense. She was convinced, now more than ever, that if you had to yell and stomp to get your point across, then you never had a point worth making in the first place.

With the closing prayer spoken, the organ rang out another tune for people to march out on, except they didn't. It seemed everyone wanted to watch this young couple get hitched.

A cross breeze from the now opened doors rustled the pages of the organist's hymnal as the little boy began running towards the church bell once more.

"Jake! Don't you touch that bell!" his mother admonished.

"But Mom, Dad said I could ring it after church was over…"

"I know, but church ain't over." The young mother snagged her son by his yellowed shirt collar and pulled him gently towards the center of the church.

"Is too! Preacher said so!" Jake's father, who Annie just realized was also the organist, left his post with a sigh and knelt beside his son.

"See these fine folk here? They're gettin' married. Daddy needs to stay and help with the service. Can you be a real good boy and sit in that pew and watch?" The little boy crinkled up his nose. "I'll take you fishin' tomorrow, if yo'r good."

"I don't wanna fish," Jake whined. "I wanna ring the bell."

"Well, you cain't just yet." Annie thought Jake was going to bust into an all-out crying fit, but then Trevor moved and knelt beside him. She could tell it pained him in his knee.

"I have an idea, Jake." Trevor put a strong hand on the young boy's shoulder. "It's not the same kind of ring, but we could use a good ring bearer for our wedding, and you look like just the man for the job. Would you do that for us?" The only eyes wider than Jake's were Annie's.

"Why, did you hear that, son? This gentleman wants you to be in their weddin'! Whaddaya say? You'll be the most special man in this church, except for the groom of course."

"Oh, yes. Yes! I'll be the ring bearer! I'll be the best ring bearer you ever did see!" Jake bounced with each word. "When do I start, Daddy? Can we do it now?" Jake's father ignored his son for a moment and extended his hand to Trevor.

"Matthew Smart," he said. "Thanks for savin' the day."

"Trevor Middleton, and I believe you and Little Jake just saved ours." Annie was observing all this activity with wide-eyed amazement.

"Umm, Trevor, could I speak to you for a moment?" Trevor rose from his place beside Jake, albeit slowly, and went to his bride's side.

"Yes, ma'am?"

"I hate to throw a shoe in yo'r gears, but ..." Annie lowered her voice to a whisper, "...we don't *have* a ring!" Trevor's gaze was incredulous as he continued in a hushed tone.

"What?! I thought *you* had rings."

"Me? How...why...whatever... why would I have rings? Seriously, Trevor. I'm beginnin' to wonder if yo'r smart enough to be flyin' an airplane!" Little Jake stood in the middle of the church, hands to his side and his lower lip quivering.

"Well, shoot. Clavel? You wouldn't happen to have any rings on you, would'ja?" The corner of Clavel's mouth curled up in a grin as he reached deep in his vest pocket, pulling out nothing but a couple of pieces of lint.

"Nope. Cain't say that I do." Trevor looked anxiously around the sanctuary, patting his own pockets and coming up nil. He prepared to stall a bit more when Annie heard a familiar voice outside on the church's front steps.

"Jacob!" Annie shouted as she ran to hug her brother.

"Woah there, Big Sister. Don't knock me down!" Jacob went up to Trevor with his hand extended. "Sorry I'm late. My ride up from Spartanburg had a bit of car trouble."

"But yo'r here now!" Annie sang. "Just look at you, all grown up," she teased as she ruffled the short beard he'd grown since she last saw him. "How'd you know, Jacob?" She still couldn't believe her eyes.

"Well, yo'r husband-to-be here got a message to me by means I am not allowed to discuss," he said with a wink towards his future brother-in-law, "and it just happened to be my day off so ... here I am." Jacob bussed his sister on the cheek.

"Umm, you have something for us, Jacob?" Trevor's tone seemed to be laced with a tinge of anxiety. Jacob peeled Annie loose from his neck and reached into his pants pocket, extracting two modest rings.

"Annie, this here's a little somethin' I had made. Now, it ain't much, and I know I can be a real pain in the ass sometimes..."

"I'll have you mind your language in the church here, son!" The preacher was now free of his hand shaking and was making his way back towards the altar. His stern tone belied the chuckle he was trying to suppress.

"Oh, sorry, Reverend. No offense. I'm just a little bit excitable, my sister gettin' married and all."

"That's alright, son," the reverend offered. He then leaned into Jacob's ear and whispered, "I've said a lot worse, right here." Reverend Wilcox winked then began replacing scattered hymnals into their respective holders behind each pew.

"Anyways," Jacob continued. "I've been savin' my wages for somethin' special, and well, it don't get more special than this. I had these weddin' bands made. They ain't much, but it's somethin'."

The bands were, indeed, simple: just two dull-silver bands, one slightly larger than the other, but Annie understood the sacrifice Jacob had made. She felt her throat tighten as she choked back tears.

"Well, now all that's settled, what do you say we move on with the reason we're all gathered here?" Everyone turned towards the voice of Reverend Wilcox, who looked a bit in need of his Sunday lunch.

The ceremony was simple and efficient. About a dozen or so people settled in the center pews to watch them exchange vows – Annie and Trevor pledging they would honor and cherish one another until death carried one or the other away. Clavel and Birdie stood beside Trevor and Annie, respectively, tossing knowing glances at one another, no doubt recalling their own wedding day. Little Jake took a place beside Reverend Wilcox - a crisp, white linen handkerchief becoming a makeshift pillow in the absence of the real thing.

When Reverend Wilcox pronounced them husband and wife, Jake hightailed it to the front of the church and began pulling on the church bell rope with all his might as his father pounded out a foot tapping rendition of "Shall We Gather at the River" for a postlude. Annie thought it an odd choice for a wedding, but then they'd not planned on any music, so it could've been "Old MacDonald" for all she cared. For all the fantasies she had stored up about her wedding day from the time she was a child, it suddenly didn't seem to matter whether there was music, a formal dress, or a ring bearer. She was glad for it, but it wasn't what was important. She may have been a bit off in her methods, but she was now living proof that the circumstances that you are born into, the shackles of the past, need not dictate your future.

A clap of thunder rattled the church windows, shaking Annie awake from her reveries. That storm was moving in quicker than she'd thought it would. If they were going to make to Effie's before the rain began, they'd better hurry.

Chapter 40

Miraculously, the storm clouds that had threatened them at the church took an unexpected turn back to the southeast, providing the newlyweds with a dry jaunt up the mountain road to Effie's place. Effie and Neil had not attended the wedding ceremony, but instead had prepared a celebratory meal. It seemed the fitting end to a perfect day.

When the wedding party arrived, Effie was standing in the yard, shading the afternoon sun from her eyes with one hand and clenching her apron into a knot with the other. Birdie's parents were pulling up in their wagon. From her grandmother's lap, Little June stretched her chubby arms towards Annie, but was intercepted by Trevor.

"Come to Uncle Trevor, you sweet little munchkin!" he teased, tossing her high into the air. His strong arms caught her as the child's melodious laughter filled the air around them.

When Jacob saw Effie, he leaped from the Packard's backdoor and embraced her in a bearhug. Trevor watched the old woman wipe a tear with her apron.

Effie's lunch spread was fit for royalty. A beef roast took center stage, surrounded by chunks of carrots, turnips, and onions. A Dutch oven boasted what Effie called a "mess of beans" and whole, new potatoes. Two cakes of cornbread steamed in cast iron skillets on top of the wood stove. Slices of sweet green peppers, tomatoes and onions crowned another plate in one corner of the table, and boiled ears of corn were stacked like cordwood on an old, cracked platter at the opposite end. Cucumber slices sprinkled with black pepper glistened in a shallow bowl of vinegar alongside another plate mounded with pickled beets. Finally, a jar of chow-chow was passed around for folks to garnish their victuals if they so desired.

Trevor ate at least two helpings of everything, and with some encouragement from his new brother-in-law, went back for thirds before Effie and Neil brought out the buttermilk pies.

"Buttermilk pie's always been Annie's favorite," Effie beamed as her knife made a smooth slice through the custard filling.

"My sister loves pie so much, she'd eat one made'a cow turds," Jacob mused, sending up a roar of laughter. Annie kicked him from under the table.

"Jacob, it sure is good to have you home," Birdie's father, July, remarked. He seemed to be a man of few words, so when he spoke, Trevor believed him to be sincere. "Mountain ain't been the same since you left."

"Yes, Jacob. I know yo'r mother's missed you somethin' fierce," Birdie's mother echoed. Unlike her husband, Birdie's mother could talk up a storm. She'd buzzed like a beehive ever since arriving at Effie's asking Annie and Trevor all sorts of questions: *Where were they going? When were they leaving? Did they need to spend the night at their place? Wasn't Annie's dress just the prettiest thing?!*

Annie feigned enjoyment, but ever since leaving the church, Trevor could see she was a fading flower. At least she had eaten and seemed to be keeping it down.

"I think my wife could use a nap." Trevor wasn't sure how much Birdie's parents knew of their situation.

Annie had, indeed, gone to lie down. Hearing nothing from her after about a half hour, Trevor peeked his head in to find his wife sound asleep, her light snores and twitching eyelids proof she was out cold. When Jacob invited him outside for a smoke, he obliged.

"So, War Boy. Welcome to the family!" Jacob gripped Trevor's hand with a hold that felt like a woodworker's clamp.

"Welcome home!" Trevor responded in kind. "I know Annie is over the moon to have you here." Trevor paused, gauging Jacob's reaction. "I assume you are not going back to your house." He continued to watch Jacob, ready to advise him against it if Jacob had any crazy notions. "At least, not alone."

Jacob winced, as though something had dug deep into his side, and turned his head, lighting his Camel with a match. Jacob handed Trevor a cigarette, avoiding eye contact.

"I gotta go back, Trevor. I have to take care of Ma."

"Of course, you do, and I want to help you with that."

"Help me? You and Annie are leaving." he said, trying to hide some resentment.

"I mean, help you leave. With Ida. You can't stay there. He's crazy, Jacob."

"Crazy as a cat with a corncob stuck up its ass." The two men leaned up against the apple tree, inhaling their cigarettes as they each pondered the options, and consequences.

"Have you seen Annie's bruises?" Annie had shown Trevor her side just before they left for the church. It took all of his resolve not to abandon the wedding and track Lester down. He'd settle for that son-of-a-bitch's funeral over a wedding. If he ever saw him, he would beat the ever-loving shit out of him.

"Bruises. Pa hit her?"

"Kicked her. Hard." Jacob flushed with anger and shook his head.

"Goddamned asshole," he cursed, throwing down his cigarette and stomping it into a rotted apple. If the two of them set out to hunt Lester down, they could take him. Trevor was sure of it. He stopped just short of broaching the subject, however. He hardly knew this boy. Or his sister, for that matter.

"Well, I get what yo'r sayin'," Jacob continued, "but I cain't just pack Momma up and take her away from the only place she's ever known. I've quit my job at the railroad, so I got some time to figure it out."

"You quit? Jacob!"

"What the hell was I s'pose to do, Trevor? No offense, but yo'r takin' Annie to parts unknown and somebody's gotta look out for Ma." Jacob extracted another cigarette but didn't light it – just chewed on it a bit.

"I was thinking you could take her to Spartanburg with you," Trevor suggested. Jacob half laughed.

"Well, that's still a possibility. I say I quit, but I was told I had a job anytime I wanted to come back." Jacob's chest swelled with pride. "They like my work. Bossman says he'd make me a supervisor if I came back before fall."

"That's great, Jacob. I'm really proud of you."

"Ain't no reason to be proud. I'm just doin' what a man oughta. More than my sorry ass father ever did, that's for sure."

Trevor sighed, squashing the stub of his cigarette into the dirt. "Listen. We're here for a few more weeks, so if I can do anything..."

"Likewise, Brother. And thanks, you know, for doin' right by my sister." Trevor nodded. "We may fight like feral cats, but she's all I got."

Chapter 41

Trevor slipped into the bed beside his bride, the events of the past days and weeks catching up to them both. But though Annie was lost in a deep sleep, he could not find the same relief. He'd counted one-hundred-and-fifty sheep, but rest had evaded him. There was simply too much to sort through.

He was now a husband, soon to be a father. Mother and child were equal strangers to him. He wondered what his father would say when he told him, how he would have reacted had he been here in the mountains. Though he had wished in some sentimental way his father could have witnessed his nuptials he was, ultimately, grateful for his absence.

He was married. Somehow that had not sunk in and felt as though it never would. He'd never given much thought to marriage. That was something he was going to do after the war was over and he'd had some time to travel, untethered. He thought about the nurse, Hannah, and felt guilty for wishing he'd spent some more time with her.

The reality was that he and Annie were from completely different worlds, and while storybooks were filled with fairytales of two very dissimilar people falling in love - blending their incongruent lives - those were, indeed, fairytales. Writers could make life turn out however they wanted for their characters; but Trevor was a realist. Someone else seemed to be writing a script, and he, the author's unwitting *dramatis personae*.

As he lay on his back listening to Annie's breaths deepen, he knew they were facing the impossible. He'd faced the impossible before and frankly, he didn't feel too good about his record.

While Annie slept, and since Trevor could not, he and Jacob borrowed Neil's wagon and made their way up the red clay path to Lester's house. It was nearly five in the evening, and as the wagon rounded the last curve, Trevor could see Lester sitting in a ladder-back chair just outside the wood-shed. He was leant back against a stack of oaks and poplars a good three rows higher than his head. Trevor imagined himself grabbing a log and bashing Lester's skull in.

Trevor asked Jacob to stay behind in the wagon with his cane, so as not to look weak. He prayed he wouldn't fall as he slowly lowered himself to the earth below him. It felt like he dropped ten feet. Lester raised his rutty face and squinted his eyes.

"Good Afternoon, Mr. Conner. I'm Trevor ..."

"I know who you are. Where's my daughter?"

"Well, sir, that's why I'm here. Annie and I..."

"She's s'posed to have been in church today..."

"Mr. Conner!" Trevor shouted. "Do not interrupt me when I am speaking." Lester scowled, willing the fires of Hell to swallow him whole. "Annie and I married today. I am here to inform you that she will be living with me now."

"Livin' with *you*?!" Lester bawled, casting a suspicious eye towards his son. "Now that's the funniest thing I've heard all day."

"Yessir. We will be leaving for South Carolina in a few weeks and until then, I expect you to leave us in peace. I don't wish any trouble between us, but I will protect my wife and myself at all costs. So for everyone's sake, I trust you will respect our wishes."

"*RESPECT*?! You come here askin' for *respect*? You got some nerve, boy! You ain't nothin' but a sorry ne'er-do-well who don't know the first *thing* about respect. Now bring my daughter home and..."

"That ain't gonna happen, Pa." Jacob was now off the wagon, standing shoulder to shoulder beside his brother-in-law.

"And *YOU!*" Lester shouted. "It's about high time you showed back up! You out carousin' around, makin' a fool of yo'rself, too?"

"Pa, I don't wanna fight, I just wanna..."

"Damn you BOTH!" Lester screamed as he slammed his fist into the stack of wood behind him – logs splaying on the ground like splinters. A trickle of blood ran down Lester's arm. "Guess I'll hafta go and get her myself." Trevor moved into his path as Jacob squared up behind him.

"Guess you won't." Trevor grabbed Lester by the collar and pulled him within a paper's breadth of his own face. "Annie is my wife, and I will stand between you, the Devil and anyone else who wishes her and our child harm." Lester's eyes blinked, one eye opening and closing slower than the other, his breathing little more than a rasp. Trevor felt as if he could choke the man until he turned blue and died. He wondered if Jacob would intervene, but he didn't. Trevor then tightened his grip.

"Now if I see your shadow, if you so much as even *think* about kicking my wife and child again, I'll rip off your leg off and shove it up your hypocritical ass. Do I make myself abundantly clear?" Lester choked and coughed, his eyes bulging. *"Do I?!"*

Jacob inserted himself and pried Trevor's blue fingers loose, one by one, from his father's throat. "I don't think he can breathe." Trevor placed his hand flat on Lester's chest and pushed him, sending the preacher stumbling backwards, choking and spewing.

The two men stormed towards the wagon, but when they looked back, Lester was on his feet, stumbling towards them as he rubbed his Adam's apple. He had the snarl of a rabid dog on his lips, and his laughter filled the valley.

"I knew it." Lester sneered. He coughed and cleared his throat. "I knew that little whore would come to this." The old man let out a snort. "You think yo'r so *sssssmart!*" Lester stabbed his thumb into his own chest. "We mountain folk, why, we're the fools. *SLAVES* to our own ignorance, but *YOU*... you are *MOSES*." Lester lifted his arms into the air. "Sent to save us from ourselves." He then let out a cackle that made chills run up Trevor's spine. Jacob grabbed his brother-in-law by the shoulder, willing him to hold his ground as Lester barreled through his tirade.

"You done pissed yo'rself, though. You think yo'r so big..." Lester exaggerated puffing out his own chest, ... "standin' up to this poor ol'e country preacher." Lester stepped into Trevor's face and jabbed his blood-covered fingers into his chest, leaving a crimson set of fingerprints and sawdust in the center of his blue silk shirt. "Jesus said, *'Inasmuch as ye have done it unto one of the LEAST of these my brethren, ye have done it unto me'.* Know what that means?" Trevor steeled himself, feeling the veins in his neck bulge from under his collar. "Course you don't, 'cause you ain't nothin' but a Phillistine. It means, you mess with me? Yo'r messin' with God Himself! The whole lot'a you's gonna rot in Hell...and that bastard child with you!"

Trevor balled up his fist and moved to throw a head smashing punch, but Jacob grabbed his arm.

"He ain't worth it, Brother," although something on Jacob's breath told Trevor he believed otherwise. "Leave him be. You done what you came here for."

Trevor stayed his eyes on Lester as he backed towards the wagon, his fist remaining clenched until he had to unfurl his fingers to climb in.

Jacob remained behind until Trevor hoisted himself into the seat. Lula Bell blew and pawed, anxious to get away from the tension-filled air around her. Suddenly, Trevor saw him spin like a top and storm back towards the woodpile, fist balled. Lester took his son's fist square across the jaw, knocking him against the wood stack.

"Don't you *ever* disgrace my sister or my niece again. You hear me?" Lester wiped the streaming blood from the corner of his mouth, mingling it with the sawdust and splinters still sticking out of his knuckles. "And if you so much as *look* at Ma the wrong way, I'll kill you. Don't think I won't. I'm comin' back tonight, and you better not be here."

Chapter 42

Effie stepped out on her porch, one hand rubbing her hungry belly and the other, fanning herself with a folded newspaper left by Mr. Harris who'd brought her some green beans. It was humid, even for mid-July. Perspiration beaded atop her shoulders, then spilled south along her spine, forming tiny puddles at her heels. A trail of black ants carrying cornbread crumbs, left out for the barn cats, detoured around the brackish little ponds, diving through a nearby crack between the decaying porch boards. She could smell the rain moving in from the south, and despite the wetness on her skin, the hair on her arms rose like thistle prickles.

She returned inside to find a large sewing needle and heavy thread to string the beans for drying. She'd have to find a spot safe from the summer rains to ensure these beans didn't get the rot. She supposed a soul could live without beans for a season, but the thought made her anxious and even more determined to protect them from any sort of moldy demise.

With her arm threaded through a bucket of beans and a newspaper tucked under her arm, Effie returned to her rocker on the porch and phlulmped into its seat, her arthritic knees too painful to make a more graceful descent. Her ever-failing eyesight made threading the needle an even more arduous task. After numerous pokes and stabs, she was able to guide the thread through the needle's eye without splicing it. She then spread the sheet of newspaper across her lap – something she'd always done to catch the strings before they landed on the floor. As she smoothed the paper out before her, a headline caught her eye.

First American Aviator Dies
Saving Lives of Comrades

From deep inside the black and white print, staring back at her, was a strapping young pilot standing tall beside seven others, his left hand holding a pipe. He exuded an air few men his age could. His countenance was serious. Some might call it arrogance. He was handsome, erect, and virile, reminding Effie of Neil in his Confederate uniform when he was about the same age. She felt a knowing twinge in her gut and hoped it was wrong.

Decorated war hero, Victor Emmanuel Chapman, was killed on June 24, 1916, over Teuton Lines at Verdun by German Flying Ace Kurt Wittgenstein. Chapman, still recovering from head wounds sustained just days earlier, was enroute to visit his friend and fellow pilot, Clyde Balsley, who was recovering in the hospital from injuries received from an early incident. Chapman dashed to aid fellow pilots of the Escadrille Américaine who were being attacked by five German flyers. Chapman and his aircraft were riddled with bullets, his plane torn to shreds. Sergeant Chapman will be buried at the Meuse-Argonne American Cemetery in France after a memorial service, to be held on July 4, 1916. A monument to his bravery and service will be erected at St. Matthew's Episcopal Church in Bedford, New York.

Wasn't Victor Chapman the pilot and friend who had recruited Trevor to fly with The Escadrille? Trevor and Annie were coming by her house this morning for a visit. Would Effie have to be the harbinger of bad news? She shuddered at the thought as she stabbed the needle through the center of a bean, gouging herself in the process. "Dammit all to hell!" she cursed, licking a bead of blood from her finger.

Barely a minute later she heard the sputter of Trevor's Model-T pulling up at the bottom of the path. It wouldn't be long. He was able to make the climb on foot now that his leg was nearly healed. Annie seemed to be faring better with her morning sickness, too. The climb would do them both good. It was the descent that had her worried. Trevor was going to be carrying a heavy load.

Effie traded the headlined news page for one with advertisements of women's petticoats. That made her chuckle. She always had possessed a "thrill for the frills", as Neil used to tease. Back in the day, when she went to church, she'd been brought up on charges of being "worldly minded" because she dared let her frilly lace petticoat show - "worldly minded" being a polite way of calling her a witch. She never could figure out why wearing pretty lace on your petticoat made you a witch. People were such hypocrites.

The problem was, folks depended on her for medicine and doctoring, so the charge was dismissed for fear she'd stop dispensing her potions and commence with casting spells. But for Effie, it was too little too late. She vowed never to set foot inside the door of a church again. She never refused to help anyone though, even that old codger, Ed Fowler, who brought up the charge in the first place. Besides, she knew a thing or two about Ed and his penchant for frilly petticoats.

Just as she heard Annie and Trevor's voices at the crest of the path, big splats of raindrops began to pelt the tin roof. They sounded big as walnuts. Thank goodness Neil and Jacob had patched the roof a few days earlier. It was good to have the boy back, although she worried Lester would punish his son for helping a "worldly minded" old woman.

Within minutes, thick fog formed, filling in the crevices of the canyon, seeping in between the layers of rock. This wasn't going to be a passing shower. It was set in for at least the day, maybe more.

"Mornin', Effie," Trevor said with the tip of his hat. "I can see you dredged up a rainstorm for the day." Effie looked up then returned her anxious gaze to her lap.

"You got anything inside the house I can do?" Annie asked. Effie put down the handful of beans she'd gathered from the pail beside her.

"Nah. Just the two of you, come and sit a spell. We need to talk." Trevor shook the rain from his jacket as he pulled up a chair for him and his wife.

"So what's on your mind, Ms. Effie?" Trevor picked up a kitten that was spilling around his legs, but Effie said nothing, trying to gather the right words. "What's the matter? Cat got your tongue?" Trevor wiggled the little cat back and forth, mimicking a playful *meeeowwww* for effect. Annie giggled at her husband's mindless humor.

"Trevor, what was your friend's name?" Trevor released the kitten back to the wilds of Effie's porch and looked at her with puzzlement.

"My friend? I have lots of friends." Of course, he did. That wasn't the best way to start this difficult conversation.

"That pilot friend of yours."

"Oh, you mean Victor. Victor Chapman! That sorry son-of-a-gun hasn't sent me any words as to how I am to meet up with him. I'm a bit put out. Why do you ask?" Effie winced and looked out across the yard, the heavy rains pushing their way up through the valley. A crack of lightning and thunder made her jerk so hard the beans scattered across the porch's floor.

"Trevor, this mornin'... just a minute ago..." She could not control the shaking in her voice. Effie reached for the paper at her feet, took a deep breath and tried again. "I believe yo'r friend has ... died."

Trevor took the newspaper and snapped it open. Like Victor's plane, Effie watched Trevor's smile turn upside down and crash to the earth below.

Trevor looked to Effie for the punchline – affirmation that this was some cruel joke or misprint. The new, healthy pink of his face faded to a ghostly white. Annie placed her hand on her husband's shoulder.

Trevor pulled the paper to a reading position once more, this time taking in the news in its awful, deathly fullness. The boy paced, stomped, and cursed under his breath. At the end of the porch, Trevor wadded up the newspaper into a tight ball and tossed the headline towards the oak tree, hitting a roosting hen squarely on its side. The hen flew up in an explosion of surprise, rising up into the lowest tree limb to settle and wait out the rain.

"Oh, my God. I can't … I can't believe this."

"Trevor, I am so sorry," Annie offered.

"I, I don't know what to say. I don't know what to do." With that Trevor walked into Effie's house, his emotions swaying with the to-and-fro of the trees.

"What can I do?" Annie whispered into Effie's ear.

"Ain't nothin' you can do. You better just leave 'im be. He'll come to you soon enough." Annie leaned up against the rail and watched the newspaper soak up the pouring rain, the print running in black rivers to the ground.

"What do you think he'll do?"

"Ain't no way to tell, but I'm guessin' he'll have some sorta score to settle with them Germans." Effie gathered the beans from around her feet and returned to stabbing them with the needle. So much had happened to that boy in the past several months. She wasn't sure how much more he could stand. At least he had Annie to lean on now.

Chapter 43

Annie found Trevor at the kitchen table and pulled his head to her breast. "It'll be alright," Annie consoled.

"This ... this is just such a shock. I don't know what to do."

"*You* aren't gonna do a thing by yo'rself. *We're* gonna get through this. Together." Annie lifted his chin with her hand and kissed him, evoking a weak smile from somewhere inside of him.

As the minutes passed, a calm descended. Maybe it was detachment. Whatever it was, he composed himself somewhat and took his wife's hand. A stray tear slid down his face that Annie wiped away with the tip of her thumb.

"I'm sorry, Annie." Trevor turned towards the door to find Effie standing there. "Sorry, Effie. I seem to have no control over my thoughts and actions. Not today anyway."

"A dammed river'll bust. Best to let the floods roll," she said, hobbling her way to the stove to fetch Trevor and Annie a mug of coffee.

Standing on Effie's back porch, taking in the aroma of his coffee more than drinking it, shock dissolved into confusion. This damnable weather mirrored his mood. But then, maybe a walk in the rain would help clear his head – make some sense of the insensible. He pulled his jacket over top of his head and excused himself, leaving Annie standing in the doorway.

As he wandered through the dripping hemlocks, so did his thoughts. He should be angry, determined; his resolve to shoot down the Germans reinforced. Instead, he found himself afloat and without any mooring. He reminded himself that he had just received devastating news that could turn his entire future on its head. It would take some time before clear-headedness overruled his turbulent emotions.

He began to rationalize that someone would step into Victor's position and, consequently, his pilot training, but somehow, that thought was not reassuring and seemed grossly selfish.

What if *he* were shot down by the Germans? A pilot could count on no more than two and a half days of flying before he was taken out – a week if he was lucky. Victor had beaten the odds by months, making the statistics seem farcical. But now, faced with the harsh reality of Victor's death, he wasn't laughing.

If he were killed, Annie would be a widow and their child, fatherless. She had no dependable family to speak of except Jacob, and that boy shouldn't be expected to bear the burden of Trevor's misguided choices, both past and future. Similarly, it was not plausible to thrust his new bride and child on his father. And here was a wonderfully unnerving thought: he wanted to live to see his child. To see his or her silly smile and to feel their tiny hand squeeze tight around his finger.

Less than an hour ago, much of his future revolved around becoming a pilot. But in the time it had taken for him and Annie to shake the rain from their coats, that future was no longer a foregone conclusion. He considered young Virgil, and how one minute he'd been making mischief with his cousin in a pasture and the next, he lay dying on a bed of cornhusks – his young body succumbing to the whimsy of a mad bull.

The same could be said for him. One second he was an ambulance driver and the next, he was a passenger, teetering between life and death. Here, as he stood amidst the drizzle and smell of loam, he was reminded that, like Virgil ... like Victor ... life had zero assurances and infinite variables.

But unlike Virgil, Trevor was alive. And that was due in large part to the fact that he had been transported in an ambulance to a military hospital and provided the highest quality of medical care. In the thick of an ugly war, inclement weather, and chaos, his opportunities for survival and re-covery had still exceeded any Virgil had been given.

A woodhen jumped from behind a decaying stump, scattering his thoughts as it left a spray of wood chips in its wake; its glowing red crown shining in the dark gloom of the storm. The bird's forlorn *cack-cack-cack-cackcack* rang through the forest, accentuating the desolation of these mountains, and at present, his soul. His knee throbbed with a renewed fervency, and while the rain and damp could be somewhat to blame, Trevor wondered if these were all signs urging him to reconsider his life choices before it was too late.

Chapter 44

"There you are! I've been so worried. Are you alright?" Annie smiled as she wrapped her arms around her husband's wet jacket. "Oh, my stars! Yo'r soaked to the bone. Let's get you into some dry things before you catch yo'r death."

Trevor held a faint smile upon his face, like he wanted to say something to her but was afraid to. "I've just had a wonderful idea, Annie. I think this may all work out. I mean, I know Victor's death is horrible, but maybe something good can come out of it."

"Of course things will work out. They always do." Her sudden optimism surprised even her. She then saw her husband gulp and felt more confused than reassured. "What exactly do you mean?" she prodded with a nervous laugh.

Trevor kissed the top of her hand as beads of water rolled off his cap and between her trembling fingers. Annie tittered at her husband's affections, but something in her gut went weak, as if moths had been set loose inside her.

"Can we talk, just me and you?" Annie assumed he meant without Effie's presence, but this was her house. They couldn't exactly ask her to leave. Then she heard the *snap-snap-snap* of breaking beans through the still opened front door and believed they'd have some privacy before they all sat down for lunch – which had been the reason for their visit in the first place.

"Sure," she responded. Annie took Trevor's hand and led him towards the stove, removing his hat and jacket before hanging them on the back of a kitchen chair to dry. "Y'or cold as a corpse," she remarked, then winced at her poor choice of words. Annie picked up one of Effie's quilts and spread it across his shoulders. "Now let me fix you some coffee..."

"I don't want coffee. I want to talk," he insisted, with an urgency that added to her uneasiness. Annie sat beside him at the kitchen table and took his hands into her own, blowing a warm breath between her thumbs to take the chill from his white, pasty knuckles.

"So, tell me. What's on yo'r mind, Trevor Middleton." She watched him go somewhere deep inside himself, to places she could only hope to reach one day. He was a complicated one, but they had a lifetime to get to know one another.

"I know that I just received the news about ..." his breath caught and, for a second, she thought he might cry. But in the next second, he had found his voice again and soldiered on. "I know I just found out about Victor's death..."

"Honey, I am so sorry." She leant over to take him into her arms, but Trevor gently pushed her back down into her chair.

"I know you're trying to help, but I need you to listen, okay? I think things maybe aren't as bad as they seem." Annie nodded for him to continue, but her insides pitched - her emotions tangled in a knot of confusion and uncertainty.

"Victor Chapman being shot down was not an isolated incident. This happens – all the time. And my friend I told you about earlier. Owen. Can't you see, I've outlived two of my comrades. There has to be a reason."

She wasn't sure what she was supposed to say to that. She understood at some level that flying a plane, in a war no less, involved risk. And that among those risks was death. But she was so unsophisticated about such matters. She had just assumed the odds were in Trevor's (and her) favor and that he would return to her without a scratch. She realized, now, that had been foolhardy.

"So, what yo'r sayin' is..."

"What I'm saying is, I can't risk being killed, leaving you and our child without a husband and a father."

"Oh, well, of course. I guess I hadn't thought about it that way." Annie swallowed the bulge that was forming in her throat. "So, are you going to be an ambulance driver again?"

Trevor shook his head. "No, well, at least not in the way you might think. Not in France." Annie was baffled. If not France, then where?

"It occurred to me, standing in the rain like the village idiot..." Trevor dabbed the damp rain from his face with a kitchen rag. "...if Virgil had access to the same care I did, he might still be alive."

"What's Virgil got to do with yo'r flyin' a plane?" The ominous sensation that began in the pit of her stomach a few moments ago was now forming a taproot. There were forces at work far beyond her control, and she didn't like it. Not one little bit.

"Everything, Annie. Don't you see? I am alive because an ambulance driver carried me to a hospital. I am alive because doctors and nurses gave me the care I needed." For a fleeting moment Annie recalled the letter she'd burned. Wasn't that *Hannah* a nurse? She fought to suppress the flare of jealousy she could feel growing deep inside her. "I've been feeling sorry for myself ever since my accident. But I'm *alive,* and I shouldn't be. *I'm alive, Annie!* And I must ask myself, *why?* And the answer is as plain as the nose on my face. I'm supposed to help others who aren't as fortunate."

"Trevor, yo'r talkin' craziness," Annie half-laughed. "Wha...wha...what are you sayin'?"

"*Crazy* was ever considering going back to France and that war. I've never been more lucid or clear-headed. My accident was *pure gift!* It brought me here, to this gorge. To you..." he whispered, his voice trailing off as a tear rolled down his face.

"So ... so ... yo'r sayin' you ... you ... wanna stay here?" Annie jabbed her index finger into Effie's kitchen table for emphasis, pushing a splinter deep into her flesh, but she felt no pain, save for the dagger splitting her heart wide open.

"Yes. I believe I do."

"Oh ... my ... God ..."

"Annie, I'm not certain yet, but let's think about it, okay?"

"Think about it?" Annie snapped. "*Think about it?!* Here's something to think about! My father almost killed me and our baby! *I ... CAIN'T ... STAY ... HERE!*"

"Of course, Annie. There are other things to consider but..."

"You ain't considered *nothin'!*" she shouted. "If you had, you wouldn't even *think* of doin' such."

"I'm not saying I'm set on it, but I am saying we can't ignore the implications."

"What about what *I'm* set on, Trevor? Even if I wanted to stay here, which I dee-double-damn-gar-uhn-TEE you I don't, I cain't! *My GOD!* Cain't you hear yo'rself?

Effie moved into the door with her bowl of beans tucked under her arm. "Ever'thing alright?" she said with a look that indicated she knew better.

"Oh, it's all just *hunky-dory,* Effie! Trevor has seen a great light!" she wailed, pushing her palms into the air and casting her eyes up towards the heavens in Pentecostal fashion. "He wants to stay here and save all the little people. *HERE!* And do ... do what exactly, Mr. Middleton?" She towered over him, arms crossed, tapping her foot on the hardwood floor. She realized she'd never even allowed him to finish his thoughts. But if they were as insane as the ones he'd just uttered, she didn't want to hear any of them.

"I was just telling Annie that I believe it is irresponsible of me to return to France. What with our child and all," Trevor explained. "Victor's unfortunate demise not only *could* happen to me, it most certainly would. It's not right."

"I understand that, Trevor," Annie interrupted. "I just don't understand why we have to stay *here!*"

As Annie paced and stomped around the kitchen table, Trevor explained that he could use his knowledge regarding automobiles and medical services to organize an emergency transport system in The Gorge. Perhaps it could grow into something even more, like a clinic. Annie huffed with the insanity of such. He reiterated Virgil's life might have been saved if he'd been provided with proper medical care instead of relying on antiquated folk medicine.

"So now this is Effie's fault?" Annie bawled.

"No! Of course not, but you can't honestly stand there and tell me I'm wrong!"

"Yes, I can and I *WILL!*" Annie shouted.

"Both of you *STOP!*" Effie bellowed with a slam of the door. "You sound like two cats yowlin' and a'howlin'. I invited you here for a nice lunch but from where I stand, it looks like I started another war." Annie moved to the stove and stirred up the stew with a bit more vigor than was necessary. "Now take that pot off the stove for a minute and calm yo'r asses down!"

Annie did as she was told but threw the spoon into the sink, sending a spray of gravy and herbs onto the front of her dress. Annie folded her arms against herself, wincing as she felt the sting of the bruised rib her father gifted her, which served as reinforcement to her point.

"Now I ain't one to crawl up into the ass-crack of another couple's argument, but since yo'r in my house, I figger I have a right."

"Please, Effie. I would love to hear your take," Trevor persuaded. Annie rolled her eyes so far back into her head, it made them hurt.

"First, let me say that Trevor is right."

"*What?*" Annie began.

"Listen to me 'fore you go and get yo'r pantaloons all in a knot!" Effie demanded with a raised hand as she sat her beans down on the kitchen table with a thud, ejecting several pods over the top. "First things first. Trevor? I think it right smart for you to reconsider yo'r plans."

Trevor gave an affirming nod.

"Now, I'm just an old woman, in case you both missed that about me," Effie cackled to herself. "I know a few things, but there's a lot I don't know. And that makes me just smart enough to be dangerous. I ain't tryin' to put no guilt trip on myself nor anybody else, but Virgil might have lived if he could have seen a doctor or surgeon early on. That point, I cain't argue."

"But Effie, he..."

"*Shut yo'r piehole!*" Effie barked. Annie's hand clasped her throat at the reprimand. She couldn't remember her friend ever rebuking her in such fashion.

"As I was sayin'…" Effie cleared her throat. "I see yo'r side, too, Child. I been seein' it all yo'r life." Effie pointed a buckled finger in Annie's direction. "Yo'r daddy's one mean sum'bitch. So, here's what I'm gonna suggest." The two of them stared, waiting for her to impart words of wisdom that would serve to prove each of their points.

"Ain't no good decision ever come on the heels of bad news. Give it a rest. Let the creek roll over the lizard's back a few days, so to speak." Effie walked over and put her hand on Trevor's shoulder. "See how're you feelin' about all this ambulance drivin' and clinic buildin'. I don't think it's the worst idea I ever heard, but I ain't sayin' it's the best idea, either."

"That's all I was asking, Annie," Trevor said as he turned to his wife. "Just think about it."

Annie didn't like the way he sounded all victorious. This fight wasn't over.

"And Annie, you need to consider there's more than one way to skin a cat, that cat bein' yo'r daddy. But neither of you can figure out nothin' in the state yo'r in. Now set yo'r asses down and eat some lunch. I'm hungry as a bitch wolf in heat."

Chapter 45

The meal they'd had at Effie's was eaten mostly in awkward silence. Well, that wasn't entirely true. She had been silent. But as for Trevor, he couldn't stop yammering on. All he could talk about was how he was going to procure Model-Ts and convert them into ambulances, and how he should start looking for a building to construct a clinic, and how silly he had been to think he could continue his ambitions as a pilot with a child on the way and blah, blah, blah.

To Effie's credit, she'd tried to change the subject, but whether it was a case of nerves or just plain disregard for her feelings on the subject, Trevor was like a cawing young crow. That's when she'd insisted that Trevor take her to Birdie's. If she was to get a handle on this situation, she needed some space and some time to think.

She'd slept all afternoon on Birdie's sofa. The nap had settled the renewed roiling in her stomach, but the rain continued in torrents, the clouds caught in the arms of the looming cliffs and mountains.

The sound of Trevor's Model-T sputtering up the road prompted her to move from the couch to the window, watching the automobile swish and slide in the deepening mud. Should she go back with Trevor or stay? Birdie said she could stay as long as she wanted, but her back was sore and, mad as she was, the posh mattress at the cottage sounded heavenly.

"Be nice," Birdie said as she, too, looked out the window. "Oh, and he's brought Clavel home. Ain't that nice!" Birdie opened the door and stepped onto the porch. Little June toddled behind, holding her mother's hand. Clavel kissed his wife on the lips then Little June on the forehead.

"Let's give these two some privacy," Birdie said to her family as Trevor climbed the front porch steps. Birdie shut the door behind them, leaving the two newlyweds to shuffle and shift on the porch as a hummingbird sipped from the Sweet Bubby Bush below them, its fiery red throat glowing against the dark fog that gathered in the valley below.

"I want to apologize, Annie. I was most inconsiderate this morning."

"You were an ass."

Trevor bowed his head. "Yes. Yes, I was. You would be within your rights to put me in a stockade and beat me about the neck and shoulders." Trevor held out his arms in mock surrender. "Will you forgive me?"

"Maybe. What do you offer in the way of gifts to your spurned bride?"

Trevor smiled. "How about a honeymoon in Charleston with a lovely dinner at The Gilded Radish?" Annie's hand rose to her mouth to suppress a yelp. "It's my favorite restaurant. I know you'll love it, too!"

"What? You mean ... we're really going to Charleston? Oh! I have so much to do. I need to pack! I need to say goodbye to Birdie! I ... I ... oh, Trevor! Wait! I don't have any clothes fittin' for a fancy restaurant." He held his wife and laughed.

"We'll find you a magnificent dress when we're in Charleston." Trevor paused for a moment to let that sink in. "Shopping will be fun! At least, that's what I've heard." Annie laughed. "I have a cousin who can take you to the finest shops. You'll absolutely love her – and she, you. I'm so glad you approve!"

"Approve? I ... I mean. It's what I want more than anything! I knew you'd change your mind!" she squealed as she reached up and hugged his neck. Trevor gently pushed her away.

"Annie, I haven't necessarily changed my mind. I still think we should consider my idea." Annie felt the blood rush from her head to her feet.

"Why would I, I mean, *we ...* do that?"

"I believe that building this ambulance service and clinic is still a viable concept. People here need help, and I believe I have the skills and resources to do just that. But I want us to go away for a while, to get to know one another. See how we feel about it once we've put some time and distance between us and all the bad that's happened."

"Are you sayin' that marryin' me was bad?"

"No ... *no!*" Trevor cried. "Please. Don't twist my words when I'm trying so hard to clear a path for us to follow."

"Well, it just sounds like me and this baby are nothin' but a millstone 'round yo'r neck! You were all fine and dandy about going back to France until this child came into the picture."

"No, Annie. You are *not* a millstone. But you and this baby are what grounds me. Had it not been for you I would be heading towards a most certain death. I have no reason to go back to France."

Suddenly, Annie had a thought. It was just a little voice in the back of her head, really. Something that niggled at her, like a splinter stuck under a fingernail.

"So, can I ask you a question?"

"Ask me anything," Trevor encouraged.

"If I weren't carryin' this baby, would you still be hellbent on building this, this ambulance thing yo'r talkin' about?"

Trevor hesitated for a second before replying. "Annie, that's not fair."

"Why ain't it? You said me and this baby grounded you, and I ain't so sure that's a good thing."

"Annie, be realistic. If you and I had never ... you know, gotten together at the cave that night, who knows what would or would not have happened. But neither of us can change that, whether we wish to or not. And now we plan accordingly. We can make something good come of all of this, and to ask *what-ifs* and second guess reality is completely useless!"

Annie paced to the other end of the porch and watched the rain run off the corners of the roof, forming red puddles that were now inches deep around the foundation. After a few moments, she turned on her heel to face her husband.

"But you cain't deny that if I weren't pregnant, you'd not even thought twice about marryin' me. Much less stayin' here in The Gorge."

Trevor sighed in resignation. "No. I probably would not have. But that's also kind of my point. Does that make you feel better?"

"No!"

"See? This is all so futile! It's crazy talk and hurtful to us both. Please! It's wasted energy. We did meet. You are pregnant, and now? We deal with the consequences."

"I'm not some consequence to just be dealt with, Trevor!" Annie wailed. "I want to be something ... *somebody you LOVE!*"

Annie buried her head deep inside her hands, tears sliding between the gaps in her fingers.

"Annie. Shhh, now," Trevor consoled, folding his arms around her. "Don't cry. That was a poor choice of words." Trevor raised her chin to meet her eyes with his own. "I'm so sorry."

"But you don't love me, Trevor. You don't! I mean, how could you?"

Trevor blew an exasperated breath. "Love is complicated, Annie."

"No, no it ain't, Trevor." Annie wiped her eyes with the back of her hand and pulled to walk away but Trevor held her to him.

"It is for me. But that's why I think Charleston is a grand idea. Please. I'm beggin you. Let's just get away from here. Have some *fun*. Something neither of us has done ... ever!" He smiled, producing a sliver of a grin on his wife's face. "I'll show you where I grew up and we can start our life together ... all over. Let's allow time to dictate what our next steps will be."

Annie shrugged her shoulders, more in resignation than full agreement. "Maybe ... I, I might just like that."

"Good," he said. "I would, too."

"But I want to be clear," Annie continued, waving her hands back and forth in front of her. "I cain't see that I'd *ever* wanna come back here to The Gorge."

"I know you don't see that now, Annie, but you might. Things change. Your father won't live forever."

"There's not enough dirt to cover him and all the bad memories!"

"Okay, okay. I get that. But don't you want to see your mother again?"

"Jacob can bring her to Charleston," she countered.

"Okay, maybe, but your mother doesn't seem able to travel and … no. Stop it. See? We're doing it again. I don't want to fight anymore. I think when we're out of this place and breathing in fresh air, we'll both have a new perspective and can make sounder decisions. I'm sure of it."

"I suppose," she agreed with another hint of reluctance.

"By the way, I dreamed about our little girl last night. She has your eyes. And those dimples in your cheeks."

"A girl?" Trevor nodded. "Well, that's what Effie's barley seeds said, too. Did this girl in yo'r dreams have a name?"

"Elizabeth," he answered with a renewed spark in his eye.

"Elizabeth," Annie repeated with an approving nod of her head. "Well, I'd want to discuss it more," she laughed, "…but I like the sound of it. We can call her *Lizzy*."

"I love that," Trevor replied as he gently squeezed his wife between his arms.

"Trevor, if we do stay in Charleston, do you think … well, maybe…oh, never mind. It's silly."

"What, Annie? You can tell me anything. Nothing is silly."

"Do you think I could still go to nursing school, you know, like we'd thought before I knew I was … well, pregnant?"

Trevor's smile turned upside down. "Oh. Well, I don't know Annie. I mean, it's hard for a woman with a child to go to school and …"

"Never mind," she deflected with a nervous laugh. "It was stupid of me."

"No, no, no! Not stupid. I love that you are still thinking about that. Like I said. Let's just give it some time. Okay?"

Annie nodded, but she was beginning to see that the odds of her becoming anything else but a farmgirl who'd snagged a rich boy in her net were next to nil.

"I have an idea," Trevor said. "Let's go back to The Esmeralda. We can have our dinner brought to the cottage." A mischievous glint shimmered in his eyes. "I'd like to have you all to myself." Annie shivered as his hand cupped her breast, her lips melting into his. "Things are going to be alright. You'll see."

She wanted to believe that, but that voice in her head, the one that now rolled across the valley overtop the lightning and thunder, spewing hellfire from his pulpit, stabbing his accusing finger towards her, bellowed:

And the ten horns which thou sawest upon the beast, these shall hate the whore and shall make her desolate. And naked. And shall eatttttt her flesh. And burn her ... with FIRE!

Maybe she *was* just a whore. Certainly, Trevor didn't love her, not yet anyways. They were from two very different worlds. Even worse, he would probably come to hate her – resent her and their baby for trapping him, crushing his dreams of becoming a war hero.

This child she had believed was her ticket out of The Gorge had become a millstone around her neck, and Trevor's. Maybe it wasn't too late to stop this insanity. She had to see Effie. And soon.

Chapter 46

The sun pushed aside the clouds, a harsh glint reflecting off the car door handle as Trevor opened it for Annie. He noted a red slurry of mud covering the floorboards which he would have to clean before returning his uncle's car. Lymas would have a fit if he could see his flivver in its current state. It took three tries to get the car cranked this time, perhaps because of the dampness, but now the car rumbled down the road that, for all intents and purposes, had become a small creek. As they neared Effie's drive, Annie jumped.

"Stop!" she ordered.

"What on earth for?"

"I need tea," she offered as her hand reached to turn the door handle. Her face flared red when the handle jammed, triggering a flustered sigh.

"Tea? There's tea at The Esmeralda."

Another sigh and a roll of her eyes told Trevor she was not going to tolerate a lot of questions around the subject. "For my mornin' sickness."

"Oh, well of course." Then another thought occurred to him. "Wait. You said you were over your morning sickness. Are you alright, Annie? Do you need to see a physician?"

"NO!" she shouted with an exuberance that seemed to startle herself as much as Trevor. Tears pooled inside her sage green eyes, turning the tip of her nose red as her hands began to fidget with the skirt of her dress.

"Okay, okay. It's alright. Please don't cry." Trevor pulled his wife deep inside his arms as one hand stroked her long, red hair. "Have you eaten? Maybe you're just hungry."

Trevor felt a tear or two soak into his shirt before she pulled away. "I'm fine. I just need tea."

"Okay, then let's get you some tea."

"As in, yo'r coming, too?"

What was it with this woman? "Yes, Annie. I'm going with you."

"Trevor, you cain't!" she nearly screamed.

Was it the pregnancy that had her so riled, or was something else amiss? "I most certainly can and I am!"

"But yo'r knee! You'll never make it up that trail without hurtin' yo'rself!"

"Annie, I've been walking all over this mountainside for weeks. I'm fine, mostly...", he quantified, "...and I'm not letting you go up that hill alone!"

"Trevor, what if you fall?!"

"I can be just as stubborn as you, Annie Grace Middleton!"

"Oh, I doubt that!" she screeched.

"Annie, please, I don't want to argue."

"Then *don't!* I'm pregnant, *not lame!*" Neither was he, but he decided not to pile fuel on the fire. Big tears tumbled down his wife's face once more as her fingers balled into a fist, then unfurled. *Were all pregnant women this weepy?* He had no point of reference and wasn't sure he had the wherewithal to endure such a seesaw of emotions for the next several months. Then again, what choice did he have?

Trevor took Annie's calloused hands in his own and kissed the tops of her knuckles which were as red as the tip of her nose. "Of course you aren't lame. Now, please. How about a compromise?" Annie withdrew from Trevor's grasp and wrapped her arms around herself, her jaw set and her eyes daring him to speak. "I'll start out with you, and if my leg bothers me, I'll wait by that old hickory nut tree, about halfway up."

Annie threw up her hands in surrender. "Fine."

"Good."

"Fine," she added once more as she stomped up the path, her actions clearly denoting she was anything but.

Trevor grabbed his cane and began following his wife up the path towards Effie's. Despite his calls for her to slow down, Annie stayed focused on her mission, climbing the hill with a ferocity that contradicted any sickness she may have been feeling. The first fifty feet or so weren't so bad, but Trevor soon began to struggle against the orange sludge that gushed down the hill. Wet weather springs bubbled up everywhere, creating full-flowing streams where just days before there had been a forest floor. His knee began to ache and his calf muscles seized with spasms. Maybe this wasn't such a good decision after all.

About halfway up, Trevor acknowledged, amidst much wheezing, that he'd been daft and shouted to his wife that he would just wait for her to return. Annie never acknowledged she'd heard him, though he was most certain she had. *Women,* Trevor pondered. *What are you gonna do?*

Chapter 47

Annie raced up the steps towards Effie's door, tripping over an old, warped step. Shit fire! She listened for Trevor to call after her but heard nothing, save for a pair of Catbirds mewing deep inside the laurel thicket. Righting herself, she plucked a jagged gray splinter from her hand and cursed once more at her clumsiness. The sun was settling in the valley below, the sky glowing a pale pink against her sweat-tinged cheeks. Time was slipping. She must be quick about things.

Annie knocked and waited a few seconds. No answer. She knocked louder. Nothing.

Annie turned the knob on the door and poked her nose inside. "Effie!" Annie shouted. "You here?" On the kitchen counter sat a pile of fresh corn and next to that, a bucket of shiny ripe tomatoes.

From inside the bedroom, she heard a rustling and scratching, like someone's nails grinding on the floor. Fearing her friend might have fallen, she ran. "Effie, you alright?"

Much to her initial relief and then dismay, there sat Otis, the rat, pretty as you please on top of the bed, shucking an ear of fresh corn, his chest puffed out in miscreant pride.

"Shooo!" she shouted, waving her arms and hands. Otis sulked away, looking over his furry shoulder as if to assure her, he would return. Annie gathered the remaining corn, placing the ears in a paper sack and storing

them and the bucket of tomatoes in the icebox on the back porch. Effie never liked for her tomatoes to be cold, but Annie figured she would like it even less if Otis ate them.

"Effie?" she called out once more. Still no answer. She must've gone to stay with Neil for the night. While she would have loved Effie's advice on the subject, she was ultimately relieved to be alone. The fewer questions, the better.

Annie walked over to Effie's herb cabinet and scanned the shelves. What was it Effie had used? Annie began to leaf through the old woman's notebook for the herbs she would require. *Remedies for the Croup. Piles Therapies and Prevention. Rheumatism. Uses for Adder's Tongue. Vitriol. Stinging Nettle.* The clock ticked out a warning – Trevor would come for her soon. *Where in the blue blazes is … ahh!*

Abortifacients.

If a woman is expecting, and she comes to you, asking to restore her to her previous state, it shall be in the best interest of both midwife and mother to counsel her regarding such a request, for it is not to be taken lightly. If it is determined, after adequate counseling, that the girl truly does not wish to carry her child to term, and she is no more than ten weeks from her last catamenia, then shall the midwife administer the following tea, which may also be made into a tincture:

~ 1 teaspoon dried pennyroyal (do not use oil)
~ 1 teaspoon tansy, parsley, or Queen Anne's Lace

Steep into a tea for twenty minutes and consume every four hours, even throughout the night, to induce bleeding. When bleeding begins, the tea should be discontinued. It is advisable that the woman not be alone during this waiting period, as

Annie pilfered through the jars. She needed an empty one to take her concoction in and found a small half pint in the back corner of the cabinet. *Tick-tock-tick-tock.*

She located the pennyroyal but couldn't find the tansy. She oscillated between the parsley and Queen Anne's Lace, then decided upon the latter. Effie would never miss a meager teaspoon of Queen Anne's. She then recalled Effie's caution against using ginger early in her pregnancy and decided to spoon some of that into her jar as well. If the concoction upset her stomach, maybe the ginger would not only move the process along but ease her stomach pains as well.

Was the tea to be made into a larger batch and then divided up into equal doses throughout the treatment period, or was it a teaspoon of dry herbs for each dose? She'd better quadruple the batch, just to be sure.

As she reached into the cabinet, she noticed a larger jar tucked away in the far back corner labeled *Abortifacient.* The proper herbs were already blended. Perfect! She dumped about half of its ingredients into her own, then hurried out of the house and back down the hill, reaching the hickory nut tree where Trevor had insisted upon meeting her.

"Just in time. I was on my way to fetch you. Is Effie alright?"

"Effie's fine," she acknowledged as she marched past Trevor in stubborn defiance. She was still a bit miffed at her husband's meddling and wasn't going to let him off easily.

"Did you get your tea?" he queried from behind. Annie held up the herb-filled jar above her head, keeping her countenance straight ahead and providing no commentary.

Beating Trevor to the car, she opened the door and plunked into the seat, wrapping her arms about herself as she pouted in mulish pride. Out of the corner of her eye, she saw him shake his head and throw up his free hand as he made his way towards the car.

"You know, you really are the most stubborn girl I've ever met," Trevor half-shouted as he leaned in to crank the Model-T. Nothing. He tried again, cursing as his second attempt rendered no result. "More stubborn than this flivver!" Trevor remarked, stabbing his finger into the hood of the car so hard he jammed up his index finger. That made her laugh. God, he was handsome. She really couldn't stay mad at him.

She watched him draw in a hefty breath and wince as he placed his left hand on the crank for another go. "Third time's a charm!" he yelled over the now rumbling engine, and in just a few moments, they were back on the main road heading towards the inn.

"I'm sorry, Annie," Trevor offered as they pulled in front of The Esmeralda. His apology caught her off guard. She wasn't used to men acknowledging they were in the wrong.

"I don't get yo'r meanin'." The car lurched before groaning to a stop. Trevor turned and took her hand in his own and held it to his chest.

"Annie, if we're going to be married, we're going to have to trust each other."

Trust? There was another concept she had little reference for. She felt a response was required, but for the life of her, couldn't think of one, so Trevor pushed on.

"As much as I loathe my own father for being so controlling, it seems as though the proverbial apple has not fallen far from the tree." Trevor made a fist and tapped his as though he were knocking on a door. "Hard-headed as that hemlock standing over there." Annie smiled. "I disregarded the fact that you...", Trevor paused and brought his hand to touch her face, his thumb gently stroking her quaking lips, "...have a good head on your shoulders and would never do *anything* to hurt yourself or our child. From now on, I will trust you to do the right thing. Okay?"

Guilt and indecision rose inside of her like bile. *Was she doing the right thing?*

She wanted their marriage to be perfect, and if it couldn't be perfect, she would die trying to make it so. Certainly, its beginnings had been as rocky as the river that raged below them, swollen and tumultuous from the deluge of the recent rains. But Trevor was a good man, and despite Lester's voice telling her otherwise, she was a good woman. Trust *was* important.

But Trevor said he trusted her to *do* the right thing. He never said they had to *confess* as to what that right thing was. And besides, Trevor had a secret or two that he'd never shared, like his relationship to that Hannah girl back in France. Perhaps Trevor was doing his own right thing by keeping his secret close, too. She wouldn't begrudge him that.

Suddenly, he burst out laughing.

"What's so funny?"

"I just had this scary thought," he continued, turning her downcast eyes up to meet his own. "If our child is twice as obstinate as we are, the world won't survive it."

"God forbid," Annie tittered with a roll of her eyes, but the weight of the herb jar now felt heavy in her lap. She didn't feel like laughing anymore. If she didn't get on with this, she might not do it at all. "Trevor, I ... I'm very tired. Let's go inside."

Mattie met them at the door of The Esmeralda, her hands worn red with fret and worry. "Trevor! Annie! Oh, thank heavens you're here!" There had been landslides upriver, she said. Trevor accused her of being a worrywart. Tom, however, said he had also been concerned, believing his wife's fussing was justified.

"We're sorry to have caused you to worry," Trevor offered. "Right, Annie?" but she had already rushed inside, fussing around the kitchen. The aroma of tarragon wafted through the opened door, making Trevor's nose twitch and his stomach grumble. He'd not eaten anything since breakfast.

"Annie, you seem flustered," Mattie observed. "Are you looking for something?"

"Yes, what are you doing, Annie?" her husband asked, looking a bit confused.

"I told you, I need to make some tea! I cain't find the kettle."

Mattie laughed. "There's hot water in that silver carafe over there," she instructed, pointing to the tea set just inside the dining room doors. "There are jars of black tea and chamomile. Please help yourself."

Annie reappeared from inside the kitchen. "Oh, no. Effie gave me some of hers. It'll do just fine." Annie scurried over to the tea service but seemed unsure what to do next.

"Now be sure to eat some soup. Clavel made chicken and rice tonight before Trevor gave him a ride home." Mattie smiled and patted him on the shoulder. "Which was very kind of you. I'm sure he appreciated it." Trevor said it was no bother at all.

"I think I'd just like to go to bed," Annie said. "I ... I don't want to be rude, but I'm very tired."

Trevor gave her a worried glance. "Mattie, maybe I could impose upon you or Tom to bring us dinner at the cottage. As you can see, Annie is exhausted, and I would like to stay with her. Would that be acceptable?"

Before Mattie could respond, Annie piped up. "But I would like some hot water *now*," she stated.

"I'll get that for you," her husband offered. Trevor held his hand out for the jar that Annie was hugging close to her chest. "Please. It's the least I can do. I've been quite the ... *ass,*" he whispered. Annie relinquished her grip and extended the jar towards him, dropping it to the floor.

"Annie, you're shaking like a baby deer! Are you sure you're alright?" Annie assured him that she was. She just needed to lie down. "I told you that hike up to Effie's wasn't wise." She said that perhaps it wasn't, but there was no help for it now except some rest. "Go lie down. I'll be right behind you."

Chapter 48

"Poor dear," Mattie breathed as Annie left towards the garden and up the stone stairs. "She's been through so much." Trevor, realizing Annie had forgotten to tell him how much of the herbs to use, dumped a heaping teaspoon into a teacup and poured steaming water over top.

"Whew!" he exclaimed, wrinkling his nose. "What is this stuff?"

Mattie took a whiff and waved her hand in front of her face. "I don't know. What's it for?"

"Annie says it's to soothe her stomach. Now, I can't speak from personal experience, but I do believe that if I had morning sickness, this would have the exact opposite effect on me," he said with a light-hearted smile.

"Ah, well, Effie knows what she's doing, so who are we to argue with the likes of her?" Trevor agreed he certainly would not be one to dispute Effie's wisdom.

From the dining room, the Turner's Victrola began to croon, *Let Me Call You Sweetheart* as Tom suddenly appeared before his wife with an outstretched hand. "Madeline, my love. Care to dance?"

Mattie blushed as candlelight danced in her misty eyes. "It would be my greatest pleasure," she beamed.

Trevor wagered that they'd been gazing at each other that way for all their married life. Would he and Annie find that sort of affection for one another? He certainly hoped so.

"Well," Trevor began with a clearing of his throat. "They say *three's a crowd,* so I should be getting back to Annie. You two lovebirds have a wonderful evening."

"Thank you, Trevor. We'll bring the soup to the cottage in just a bit."

"No rush at all," he smiled as the Victrola continued to scratch out the tune.

Keep the love light glowing.
In your eyes so true.
Let me call you sweetheart.
I'm in love with you.

Trevor walked slowly so as not to spill the cupful of tea, thinking how grateful he was for a break in the rains. Hopefully, the clouds and all they carried were gone for a while. He was starting to think he needed gills. As he opened the cottage door, he found Annie wrapped up in a comforter, still in her day clothes, two pillows propped behind her head.

"Here's your tea," he said, extending his hand towards her. "I must warn you. It doesn't smell very comforting." Annie took a whiff and sat it down on the table beside her.

"I never carried you over the threshold," Trevor remarked, glancing from the door to his wife. "Would you allow me to do that?"

"You mean I have to get up? I just now got settled."

Trevor laughed. "You make a valid point." He saw Annie look at the tea then back to him. "You look beautiful today," he continued as he laid down beside her, his warm hand coming to rest over her belly. He could feel it grumble and roll beneath his touch. "Pregnancy suits you." Annie's eyes averted his, but perhaps it was just fatigue.

Within seconds she was asleep. Trevor strained out the tea into the cup, then left Annie to rest. She could sip Effie's concoction when she woke up, which he hoped was soon. They were married now. There were things he would like to do.

Chapter 49

Her eyes flashed open when she heard Trevor leave. She looked to the teacup then to the door, questioning her resolve. She decided one cup of tea couldn't hurt, or help, and gulped it in three swallows.

In no time, Trevor returned with the jar of herbs and a teapot full of hot water, this one porcelain, on a silver tray with a couple of teacups.

"Thought I would have a cup myself," Trevor mused.

"No!" Annie snapped. "I mean, that's a special blend. Just for expectin' women. Men shouldn't drink it."

Trevor laughed. "What will happen? Will my voice get high in pitch?" he mockingly squeaked. "Will I get a big belly and start craving pickles and ice cream?" Trevor placed his hand way out in front of his stomach, pretending to be cradling a child inside. Annie laughed, snatching the jar from the tray and placing it under her pillows.

"I'm just teasing," he continued. "I couldn't drink that stuff if my life depended on it. I brought some chamomile for myself. What's in that stuff Effie gave you, eye of newt ... tongue of frog?"

"That's *toe of frog*," she corrected. Trevor flushed red beneath his collar. "We read *Macbeth* in school," Annie offered with a wistfulness that fell somewhere between nostalgia and melancholy.

Trevor pointed to the jar of herbs. "Okay, but my point is, that's a witch's brew."

"Effie is not a witch."

"Well, she may not be, but that tea is pure evil," Trevor surmised as he reached to take his wife's hand in his own. Instead of reciprocating, however, Annie pulled away, clenching the skirt of her dress deep inside her fists as though readying herself for a fight.

"Effie says she's a witch with a capital *B*," Annie snickered.

"Well, I give her an *F* for Friend!" Trevor mused. That made his wife laugh. "You're lucky to have her."

"Yes, I am. I just hope she's with Neil."

"Wait, what? I thought you saw her."

Annie flushed. "Oh, well, yes! I *did* see her. I just mean, I hope, well ... I don't want her spendin' the night there alone."

"She spends most nights alone, doesn't she? Why would tonight be any different?" Annie slightly shrugged and began biting her lower lip. "Are you sure you're alright, Annie? You seem to be ill at ease."

"I'm *fine,* Trevor. Now please. Let's talk about something else. Or nothin'. I'm very tired." Annie leaned back against her pillows once more, leaving Trevor confused and a bit stunned. She began to fuss with the cuff of her husband's shirt sleeve. "Trevor," she began.

Trevor stopped pouring the water into the teacups. "Yes?"

"Do you think that, well, if we'd met somewhere else. Another time, another place, as they say. Do you think you would ever love me?"

Trevor set the pot down and stared into her moss-green eyes. "We've been through this before, Annie. Seriously. What kind of a question is that?"

"I just feel like some ... some ... circus freak!" Annie exclaimed as huge tears fell from onto her dress. "Everyone hates me. Yo'r friends'll hate me, I just know it. If you don't have another reason to be with me, other than the baby, then..."

"Stop right there. I don't know of a soul who hates you. And you most certainly are not a freak. You are my wife. Beautiful. Strong. Intelligent... ." He kissed the top of her head as he pulled her towards him, drying her tears with the top of the bed sheet. "I promised I would cherish you, for better or for worse, and I intend to do just that." Annie stared at him with a vacancy that came from somewhere so deep, he wasn't sure he could ever find the bottom.

"My father hates me."

Trevor sighed and looked out the window as the last smidge of twilight faded outside their cottage.

"Annie, your father is a very confused and sick man. He doesn't love himself, so he is incapable of showing love to anyone else. But that doesn't mean he hates you. Now let's talk about other things. *Nice* things. Okay?"

"Okay," she agreed.

Annie eyed the cup of tea Trevor now extended to her. She raised the porcelain to her lips and sipped, still pondering which direction she should go. One cup wasn't enough to cause a miscarriage, but she'd also not been sure about the proportions. And how much had Trevor put into the cup before she drank the first dose? Moreover, she knew from the instructions that she was supposed to wait four hours in between doses, and it had barely been thirty minutes.

Annie sat the cup and saucer on the nightstand, closed her eyes and sat back once more against the pillows, knees bent. Her back was aching. She must've wrenched a muscle thrashing around in all that mud. Trevor sat his teacup down, lifting her dress to expose her bare belly that had begun to swell with just the slightest hint of a child. He pressed his ear against her, his hand drifting ever so low between her navel and hairline. She felt a tingling sensation down there as Trevor coaxed her knees apart, his hand gently probing and exploring the tiny bits of her anatomy she didn't even know the names of. Annie surprised herself with a soft moan that seemed to please her husband.

Trevor lifted the dress over her head, exposing her naked body in the soft evening light that struggled to find its way between the clouds, leaves, and cottage.

"You are so beautiful," he smiled.

"I'm gonna be fat," she laughed.

"You're beautiful." Trevor stood to remove his shirt and trousers. Annie slid down to a flatter position on the bed. To be exposed like this was something previously unimaginable. It was both naughty and wonderful.

Suddenly Trevor's lips covered her own, his large hands cupping her face, like he was holding a china doll. He moved on top, his knees straddling her on each side as he held her breasts and kissed first one, then the other. It took every ounce of resolve to suppress a scream.

"Does that feel good?" he asked. She whispered a breathy yes. "You want more?" Annie lay there in rapturous silence: his lips making their way towards her belly, caressing her breast with one hand and her buttocks with the other. Her breasts were so sore, but his touch made them feel as though they were on fire.

Just when she thought she could not take anymore, Trevor eased his head between her legs and placed his mouth ... there! Weren't there laws against this sort of thing? She didn't care. She would die in a prison cell before she would ask him to stop. His day-old beard tickled the inside of her thighs as his fingers searched deep inside of her, all the while his tongue performing a dance of ecstasy she had never imagined in her wildest fantasies.

Trevor then made a gentle push inside her, careful, but sure. She gripped the bedspread between her fingers and raised herself to bring him closer, deeper. She wanted to absorb his body into hers. Every beautiful inch of it. She could feel his heartbeat against her bare chest as she lowered her legs to wrap them around his waist, now moving her hips in a tight circle. It was as if her body and mind had been created for this very moment. Her fingers slipped through his soft, auburn hair. Between the two of them, there was no way this child wasn't going to have red hair, she laughed to herself.

Still clinging to the bedspread in one hand, she dug her nails into his back with the other. One more drive deep inside and she felt herself explode with a ferocity that made her scream out loud. She watched Trevor's face contort into something like pain, a beautiful death. The spasms in her privates came like ripples upon the Rocky Broad, for which she hoped there would be no end. Trevor collapsed on top of her, his face buried in the soft space inside of her neck.

"I love you," she whispered. But there was only the sound of his gentle snores in return.

Chapter 50

It was three in the morning, and though Trevor had fallen asleep immediately after he and Annie had made love, he was now fully awake. Random thoughts raced inside his mind, making him wide-eyed and restless.

Annie, on the other hand, slept soundly beside him, her naked body bathed in the light of a half-moon, her long arm draped lazily across his chest.

When morning came, if the rains held off, he wanted to inspect a building he'd heard Mr. Harris had for sale. He'd promised Annie he wouldn't officially pursue his idea immediately, but he wanted to know what his options were so they could have a conversation based on as many facts as possible, not just conjecture.

If the building was suitable, he would have to withdraw funds from the bank as soon as he returned to Charleston. Moreover, he wanted to confer with his father and uncle on the matter, and they would have questions. He wanted to show them he was up to the task, even if he decided against pursuing it. He would even invite Annie to go with him to inspect the building, giving the transaction full transparency.

He had this romantic notion that the ambulance service and clinic could be ready by the time Elizabeth came into this world, and that she would be the first to be born there. It would be like giving birth to two children –

one his own flesh and blood and the other, his brainchild. It would also give the community of Hickory Nut Gorge confidence to see that even the owner and developer thought enough of it to deliver their own child there.

But he had to be realistic. There was no way he could procure the funds and investors and set up shop, at least in the proper way, by that time. Even so, the idea had invigorated him. His entire outlook on life had changed. He was no longer worrying about his leg or how he was going to fly a plane. The craziest thing, though, was how he felt towards Annie. He wasn't sure it was love, but it was certainly the beginnings of it. Life had a funny way of turning on a proverbial dime.

As he lay in the faint moonlight, watching his wife sleep, a smile supplanted the scowl he thought had become permanent. He stroked Annie's long red curls where they fell across her arm and his chest, the warmth of her every breath assuring him he was in the right place – for once.

She might be a fiery redhead, but so was he. Between the two of them, they would make this work. He was determined.

Chapter 51

On July 11th, the rains that had battered The Gorge for six straight days began to subside in earnest, but the saturated ground pushed back against the runoff that plummeted from high on the mountain tops. Hickory Nut Falls was a raging cataract, its long gentle plume now a runaway train of water that arched over the canyon walls, threatening to bury the town below it. People stopped and gawked, whispering prayers of gratitude and a certain disbelief that they had fared as well as they had. But it was still bad. Crops had been beaten to the ground. Horses and cattle stumbled through the knee-high mud, some becoming lodged in hidden holes, trapped with broken legs, many dying of shock and fear before they could be rescued.

The stormy waters between Annie and Trevor were also in recession. When Trevor had asked her to meet with him and Mr. Harris, her smile was bright and her excitement, seemingly genuine. He said they'd be partners, and that, she'd said, had a nice ring to it.

Still, there was something unsettled – in the weather, and in his wife. For three straight days the sun peaked through waves of clouds, even as the swollen creeks and wet springs raged. Large puddles stood deep enough for small fish to survive in.

Like the storm, Annie's weepy moods seemed to have abated, but if he caught her at the right moment – brushing her hair, holding a fork, or drinking cup after cup of that tea, he could not help but notice the tremors in her hands. He felt she should see a physician, and suggested they drive into Asheville, but she wouldn't hear of it. He did take this opportunity to point out that if they had a hospital here in The Gorge, they, and other expectant mothers, would have a sense of comfort. She said she took his meaning and left it at that. It was like he was living in the eye of a hurricane.

She had agreed to see Effie though, and that's what had brought them to Effie's front porch. Trevor stood alongside his wife as they knocked on the old woman's door.

"Trevor, Annie. Come in, come in!" she beckoned. They both moved to step over the threshold, but Annie halted Trevor with a firm hand.

"I want to talk to Effie ... alone," she'd said. Not surprising, considering the nature of the conversation that needed to be had. Trevor nodded in compliance and said he'd just wander the property. Annie could shout at him when she was ready to go. He saw Neil throw up his hand just beyond the fence line and went to meet him where he was replacing strands of barbed wire and posts. Clouds were boiling up again from the south, and the rumble of thunder warned of more rain. Not a good sign, as the ground had absorbed all that it could.

Annie folded into Effie's arms, huge sobs heaving her shoulders up and down like bellows.

"Child, child! Whatever's the matter? Talk to me! You look white as a ghost!"

"Effie, I ... I ... I've been spottin'."

"Alright, alright," she whispered, placing a calm hand on her shoulder. "Don't cry. It prob'ly ain't nothin'. Yo'r young with your child. Sometimes, nature just forgets and tries to get your courses flowin' again. Is it bad?" Annie shook her head that it wasn't. "Does Trevor know?" Annie again acknowledged in the negative. Effie rolled her eyes.

"He cain't know, Effie. He just cain't."

"Why on earth not? He's yo'r husband and this is his child, too. Besides, it's kind of hard to hide."

"I know, but things have been different lately. We don't fight anymore. And we're going to Charleston, at least for a little while." Effie's eyes encouraged her to continue. "And if we come back, well ... maybe, I might just be alright with that."

"Of course you'd be alright with that. It ain't so bad here, not once you get out and see some of this crazy ol'e world."

"Oh, Effie!" Annie wailed, throwing herself onto the couch, sobbing. Effie stood in the dimming afternoon light, hearing the thunderclap in the distance, unsure of what to do. Something was wrong, but she couldn't divine what exactly. "I... I've done something horrible." A shiver ran up Effie's spine. As prone as this child was to drama, she felt certain that in this instance, the crisis was genuine. Effie sat beside her, stroking her long, red curls, rocking her back and forth.

"What, Child? What have you done that's so terrible you cain't even speak it?"

"Oh, God. I ... I ... I thought I was doin' the right thing."

This was like pulling splinters. "Well, I cain't help you if you won't tell me. There's little one can do that cain't be fixed. Talk to me." Annie took in a deep breath and pointed to the herb cabinet. "You want some tea?"

"God, no!" Annie nearly shouted. "I ... I ... I took some of yo'r herbs." Effie looked at her, puzzled.

"So what, child? You know that whatever I have is yo'rs."

"No, you ... you ... you don't understand," she gasped. "I t-t-t-took some puh-puh-penny..."

"You took pennyroyal?!" Effie questioned with more alarm than she intended. Annie affirmed such with a violent shake of her head.

"How much?" Annie said she didn't know, but she'd taken Queen Anne's Lace, too. Trevor made the first cup of tea, then she'd made the subsequent dosages. Of course, Trevor had no idea what he had helped facilitate.

"How many cups have you had?" Effie gathered her shawl around her shoulders, trying to stave off the chills that were coming upon her faster than that storm moving in. Thunder clapped over top of them.

"I ... I don't know. I've drunk a cup every four hours or so for the past several days. Just like yo'r instructions said."

"Dear Lord in heaven," Effie sighed to herself. "I also told you to never do something like this by yo'rself," she admonished, although she realized it was too late for that sort of talk.

"I wasn't alone, Effie. I had Trevor..."

"Who knows nothing about what yo'r trying to do!" Effie thought for a minute and said, "And just what *is it* yo'r trying to do?!" Annie continued to gasp for air in between words.

"I thought that ... that if we dih...dih...didn't have this baby, Trevor muh...muh...might not feel so trapped. That he might wanna fly again!"

"Trapped?" Annie bounced her head in agreement. "Has he ever said he felt trapped?"

"No," she managed to say without hyperventilating. "But he feels trapped Effie. I know it. If this baby wasn't comin', he'd be flyin' planes. He nearly told me as much!"

"Sweet Jesus," Effie muttered. "He said those exact words to you, and you in this condition?"

"No, not exactly, but I'm not stupid, Effie. This is *ALL* my fault! The dress, the cave, and now I'm pregnant and ohhhh...*Effie!* How could he *not* feel trapped! But now things are...are... better with us. I think he might really love me, at least one day. And he seems excited about the baby. I don't want to hurt him. How can I stop this?"

Effie had never been asked to stop someone from slipping their baby once it started. She'd been asked to stop a natural miscarriage, though. Maybe the same method would apply.

"Are you hurtin', runnin' a fever?" Effie put the back of her hand on Annie's forehead, but she was cool as a cucumber.

"I just had a little sting in my side, this mornin'."

"Alright, now first thing is, calm down. Losin' yo'r wits'll only make it worse." Effie stood up and shambled to her herb cabinet, retrieving a couple of jars along with her mortar and pestle, setting them on the counter. "Get yo'rself a kettle full of water, about two quarts, and start it to boilin'." Annie followed instructions as Effie began to grind down the contents of one jar to a fine powder. The other jar was already in powder form.

"What is that?" Annie asked, her breathing a little less jerky.

"It's Lobelia and Unicorn Root." Effie combined the powder in the jar with the content in her mortar and stirred. Effie hurried over to the kettle and dropped the contents inside. "Let this boil for twenty minutes. Then I want you to take a tablespoon with water four times a day until the bleedin' stops, then for five days after." Annie's eyes wandered off to where Neil and Trevor were mending Effie's fence.

"Now, repeat what I just said." Annie repeated Effie's instructions word for word as the herbs began to roll inside the kettle. Effie noted the time on the clock and told Annie to sit.

"Next thing you gotta do is tell Trevor."

"Oh, God, Effie. I cain't. He'll hate me for sure."

"The way I see it, if yo'r honest you stand a chance. If you ain't? He's gone." Annie buried her head in her hands. "Just like a baby, dead or alive, the truth always comes."

"Cain't we just tell him I started to miscarry? He doesn't need to know I did it on purpose."

Effie sighed. "I ain't gonna lie for you, child," she responded. "But if he don't ask, I won't tell." Annie reached out and hugged her friend as the water in the tea kettle continued to simmer.

"Thank you," she whispered.

"No need to thank me. Now in another fifteen minutes, take yo'r medicine. I'll put the rest in a jar that you can take with you. And don't be doin' anything that strains you or the baby, understand?"

Twenty minutes after she'd started the boil, Effie saw lightning flash across the top of Burnt Shirt and counted. Three seconds later, another loud crack of thunder echoed between the canyon walls. A minute later Trevor and Neil stomped up on the porch, their feet covered in red mud and grass.

"Shew-weeee!" Neil exclaimed. "Got that fence patched up just in time. Now what's for lunch?"

Nothin' but trouble, Effie thought.

Chapter 52

Annie told Trevor that she might be losing the baby. He took it calmly enough, but maybe he was shoring up his own emotions. Men were like that.

The stinging that had awakened her in the middle of the night had subsided with just the first few sips of the Unicorn Root. While it was too soon for the infusion to have worked, perhaps the relief she felt was, for now, a blissful trick of the mind. Once back inside the cottage Annie stripped down to her shift and crawled under the covers. The trip to Effie's had drained what little bit of energy she'd had, but tired as she was, she felt much easier about things.

A few moments later, Trevor brought in the quart jar of Effie's brown, muddy concoction, and another teapot full of clean water. "I believe you said a tablespoon of this stuff in water, right?" Without waiting for an answer, Trevor made her a cup and handed it to her. Annie drank it as though her very life depended on it. It was one o'clock in the afternoon. She made a mental note to have another at five.

The tea had a sedating effect – calming her without making her feel drugged up like other herbs sometimes did. It helped, too, in an odd way, that the skies had darkened once more from the swelling storm clouds. Hopefully, this one wouldn't wear out its welcome the way the other storm had.

Annie awoke to the sound of rain pelting against the windows. What time was it? She squinted to see the clock, but her head ached with the effort of it. Thunder rolled and bounced between the canyon walls, causing the teacup beside her to vibrate atop its matching saucer. Pulling the cover overtop her head, Annie fell back to sleep, only to be awakened by an insistent pounding on the cottage door.

Annie grabbed her robe and moved slowly towards the noise in the hopes of silencing it sooner rather than later. It was Mattie.

"Hello, darling. I hope I didn't disturb you," Mattie chimed. "But that's silly. I can see that I have."

"Oh no, Mrs. Tur – I mean, Mattie. What time is it?"

"It's about six in the evening, dear." Annie panicked. She was supposed to drink another dose of Effie's antidote an hour earlier.

"Where is Trevor?"

"He's been reading in the parlor all afternoon. Will you be joining us for dinner?"

"Yeah. I mean, yes. What time? Are there other guests?"

"Seven p.m. and it will be just us chickens tonight. We have one more evening before Mary Pickard and her friend, Douglas Fairbanks, arrive." She smiled a deviant smile. "I'm so excited!" Annie managed a weak laugh.

"Seven o'clock then. I'll be there."

Just before seven, Trevor came to escort her to dinner. He chattered on and on about a book he had found in the Turner's library by some author named Lord Dunsany. Apparently, Trevor had met him briefly in a tavern somewhere in Paris and was all in a dither about getting to read *Fifty-One Tales*. Normally, she would be able to feign interest, but tonight it was taking every ounce of energy she had to stand upright. Maybe after she ate a bite she would feel better.

The meal was simple: a beef roast with gravy and mashed potatoes, spinach, fried okra, and for dessert, homemade vanilla ice cream.

The meal had gone down easily enough, but by the time she'd finished her ice cream, she felt her insides were going to fall out of her. Once inside the cottage, Annie collapsed into the porcelain bowl of the water closet, the fiery contents of her stomach emptied in just a few short heaves. Trevor followed close behind, holding her hair and rubbing her back, begging her to let him take her into Asheville or even Rutherfordton. In this horrid weather? No. She would be fine.

She'd told him that this was no different than the sickness she'd been having and that this was just part of being pregnant, even though Trevor tried to argue he'd not seen her this sick. She had him fix another cup of Effie's tea and, setting the cup and saucer back on the nightstand, she undressed, taking care to notice if there was any more blood. She breathed a sigh of relief when she saw none then drank the remaining potion before slipping into bed.

<h1 style="text-align:center">Chapter 53</h1>

Effie tossed in her bed as though she was wheat being flailed on a threshing floor. This was the second time in as many hours she had been shaken from her sleep. There was this hard needling that began in her gut and poked, like the steely end of a knife on a fish's underbelly.

Neil had insisted on staying the night, and that was just fine. She'd never admit it, but she didn't want to be alone. They'd stayed up late, listening to the rain and talking about all the work that would need to be done to save as much of the garden as possible from rot and blight. Effie had cracked open a jar of homemade wine she'd brewed from the last bunch of grapes that had produced anything worth messing with. The vines hadn't been pruned in a donkey's years, so anything more than a handful of flesh and hulls was just that – a meager allotment of grace she could share with her lover.

Shortly after midnight they'd gone to bed, the buzz from the wine pulling her down into a deep sleep into the crook of Neil's shoulder. She loved the way the gray hair of his chest glistened in the lamplight. His arms were still well defined from lifting piglets, hauling fence posts, and generally working his fool ass off. For an old man, he was still quite the looker. She wondered if he felt the same about her old and worn-out body.

Around two in the morning Effie found herself pacing the floor of her kitchen, unable to shake the heavy blanket of dread from her shoulders.

It was just like the time Virgil had been brought to her. Surely there was something she was missing. Something she could do to prevent the demons who danced around her from working their spells. Damn these premonitions! What good were they if you couldn't do a goddamned thing about them? She turned up the last bit of wine dregs inside the crock, savoring a generous gulp in the hope it would lull her back to sleep.

Chapter 54

A deep shiver shook Annie awake; this despite the warm, humid air that seemed set upon smothering her. What had been a mere annoying pain in her side was now a hammer beating on her hipbone from the inside. And her shoulder! It was aching as though a tree had fallen on it. To make matters worse, her belly was swollen – much more so than the tiny bud of a child could make it, and an orange-sized spot of blood was spreading under her on the white sheet and through to the mattress.

Trevor slept beside her, oblivious. She knew she should awaken him but by doing so, she would be admitting things were going from bad to worse. What could she do? The pain could be what Effie called a healing crisis, when things for the ailment you were treating got worse before they got better. It was a healthy sign the herbs were working. But the blood. That was most unsettling. Maybe if she got up and peed, she would see things weren't so bad.

She pushed herself up from the bed but the room around her swirled and churned as another searing stab sent her to the floor with a yelp. Within seconds, Trevor was kneeling beside her.

"Annie! Can you hear me? Talk to me." Annie tried to pry her eyes open, but it was near impossible. She could feel the pull of sleep, and she wanted that now - more than anything. "Annie!" Suddenly a caustic, burning sensation filled her nostrils and forced her to lift her eyelids. Trevor was holding an enameled vial with pretty Victorians painted on it. Whatever was in that vial had aroused her from blissful sleep, and she wanted to slap him for it. The only thing she managed, however, was a tiny moan.

Trevor moved behind her, placing his hands under her arms and lifting her to the bed. She fell back onto his bare chest as another whiff of the smelling salts passed under her nose.

"Trevor, stop!" she yelled at a level that surprised even her.

"Oh, thank God! I thought I'd lost you. Are you hurting? Talk to me. Please." Annie wiped her lips, noting they were hot and dry. She remembered Effie saying if a dog's nose was cold and wet, she was healthy. If it was hot and dry, not so good. She was definitely in the not so good camp.

"I just fainted a little, that's all."

"You more than fainted, my dear. We really must get you to a doctor."

"Eff..." she whispered. "Eff..."

"Effie. You want Effie?"

"Yes." It was feeble but at least she managed that much. Trevor tripled the pillows behind her and propped her up against them.

Trevor felt Annie's forehead to find it hot as the eye of a stove against his clammy, cold hand. A quick visual assessment and the palpitation of her abdomen proved there was internal bleeding, as if the growing stain on the sheet weren't enough. He quickly put on his trousers, running out the door barefooted to summon Mattie and Tom. He needed someone to drive so that he could sit in the back of the car with his wife. They had to get to Asheville ... to a hospital. This was far beyond anything he, or even Effie, could handle. He entered the inn, crying for help.

Mattie came to the lobby, a silk robe drawn tightly around her waist and a look of horror to accompany it. Tom soon followed. "Whatever is the matter, Trevor? Is it Annie?"

"Yes, I'm afraid so," Trevor panted. "Tom, can you drive? Annie needs to go a hospital. Immediately!" Tom moved forward, his red and white pinstriped pajamas giving him the appearance of a candy cane.

"Certainly, just let me get dressed."

"She needs a doctor," Trevor repeated. Maybe if he said it three times, like a genie, one would appear. God, he wished Uncle Lymas were still here.

"Oh, the poor dear," Mattie said to Tom as her husband returned to their room to dress.

"I'll go get the car and meet you out front," Tom shouted from the bedroom. "Do you need help carrying her down?" Trevor believed he could manage, but Mattie followed him to the cottage, just in case.

Trevor found Annie to be in slightly better shape than when he'd left her. She even smiled a little. Trevor scooped her up, pushing through the downpour, carefully navigating the garden rock steps one shaky foot at a time. He prayed his knee wouldn't give out on him. Mattie did her part by opening and closing doors as Tom pulled the Packard to the front.

Trevor placed Annie into the back seat, his shirt and trousers now soaked with blood. He'd seen worse, hadn't he? As much as he cared about the men he transported in the ambulance, they were detached by culture, geography, and the duty of doing one's job. This was different in a most sobering and frightening way. While it seemed certain they were losing their child, hopefully, Annie would survive.

"I know we should drive to Asheville," Tom said. "Just not sure the roads are passable."

"Go that direction and pray for the best," Trevor coached. With that, Tom lurched the car forward, spinning wet mud and gravel behind him.

They hadn't gotten two miles up the road when their worst fear was realized. Across the highway lay an oak tree, at least ten feet around and five times as long.

"Fuck!" Trevor shouted. Tom beat his hands on the steering wheel in frustration.

"I'll turn around, but I'm guessing the road into Rutherfordton isn't any better." It was raining so hard now Tom was having to yell to be heard over the torrents.

"Go to Effie's," Trevor shouted.

"What? This car'll never make it up that pitted road."

"Just go as far as you can! I'll carry her if I have to." Tom made a three-point turn and headed back the way they'd come. Once at the turnoff for Effie's, Tom asked Trevor if he was sure about his decision. No, he most certainly was not, but what choice did they have?

The Packard sputtered and spewed as it lurched up the mountain road where torrents of water obliterated the once visible path. Trevor worried the jostling would make Annie's bleeding worse but then, would it make any difference in the end? Probably not.

Tom braked hard when another tree crashed just inches in front of them. Two seconds later it would have flattened the car and them along with it. There was no way around, but Trevor could see a dim light glowing in Effie's house and believed he could carry Annie from there. Tom disagreed but Trevor was fueled by months of feeling inadequate and helpless. He was determined to see his wife safe. He bundled Annie in his arms and headed towards the light just as the Packard began to slide down the mountain.

"She won't hold! I gotta get her down off this hill or she'll roll!"

"Go on! I've got her!" Trevor yelled.

Tom kept his foot on the brake with the dim headlights of his Packard pointed on the path. Trevor struggled in the mud and muck across the gaping expanse that lay between the car and Effie's front porch. Halfway across, Trevor's leg gave and sent him down to the ground on one knee, the rain and mud seeping into his trousers. Annie emitted a delirious giggle as Trevor cursed. Even with the cooling rain, he could feel her fever, hot and pulsing through his shirt sleeves. As Trevor pushed himself up and forward, he slipped again. Looking straight on, he saw Neil running down Effie's steps. Neil rushed over and took Annie in his own arms. With his load lighter, Trevor ran on Neil's heels as Effie stood at the opened door with nothing but a sliver of candle burning in her hand.

"Put 'er in the spare," he heard her instruct Neil. Effie kept the door open for Trevor. "Been expectin' ya. Come on in."

Annie looked bad. She was hot as a matchstick and just as thin. Hadn't it been just a few hours since Effie'd seen her?

Neil brought in a pan full of cold water and a rag, along with a stack of soft cloths, which he laid on the bedside table. Effie wringed one out and placed it across Annie's forehead. Effie saw her lips move and leaned in closer.

"Save ... my ... baby," she whispered.

"I cain't save yo'r baby, sweet child, but I'm gonna save you," Effie whispered as she reached under Annie's wet shift and palpated her abdomen, causing Annie to yell out. "Help me raise her up." Trevor did as he was told. She then placed a stack of rags under Annie's hips and breathed a sigh of some relief when she saw the bleeding had slowed.

"Is she going to die? Is our baby lost?" Trevor leaned up against the windowsill at the head of the bed, his arms folded in a protective stance – a shield to fend off the sting of the news he must already know.

"She's lost a lot of blood. Girl didn't have any meat on her bones to begin with." Trevor's eyes pleaded for some better news. "But her bleedin' has slowed. If I can get her fever down, she might come outta this on the other side." But the baby, she was certain, was gone.

Trevor told her about trying to get to Asheville and said that, come morning, he was going to try again.

"Well, this rain ain't gonna let up. Not anytime soon." As if on cue there was a loud crack of a tree, and another, then a thunderous cacophony that sounded as if the entire forest was uprooted and rolling towards them. The sound grew closer, closer, then stopped.

"Whole mountain's lettin' go," Effie warned. "Goddamn loggers," she added. Suddenly Annie shifted under her quilt and released a tiny groan, her green eyes glowing through narrow slits. She reached out and touched Effie's wrinkled hand.

"Why, look who's back with us," Effie chuckled. Trevor appeared at Annie's side, taking her other hand in his and raising it to his lips.

"Hello, Love," he whispered. Annie gave a weak smile. "I thought I'd lost you."

"Cain't…" Annie licked her dry and chapped lips. "Cain't get rid'a me…" her voice trailed off before she could finish.

"Shhh, don't talk." Trevor kissed her again on her burning scalp.

"Neil!" Effie hollered.

"Yes ma'am," Neil answered.

"Fix this child some bone broth. I think there's some on the cannin' shelf in the wellhouse." Neil obeyed, turning to face the elements outside. "You need to eat somethin', Child. Yo'r weak as cat water." Annie seemed to have slipped back into her dreams, her hand now a limp rag in Trevor's own.

"Law, this girl is burnin' up. Trevor, make yo'rself useful and get me that vinegar that's sittin' in the herb cabinet … and the whiskey." Trevor gave her a quizzical look but knew better than to argue. Effie poured out a goodly amount from the vinegar jug into the basin of water. She freshened up the rag and returned it to Annie's head.

"What's the whiskey for, Effie? Are you going to cut on her?" Trevor's eyes were wide with fear.

"Naw, you fool. The whiskey's for us. She reached below the bed and pulled out two stone mugs. "Drink," she admonished.

"I don't think…"

"Don't be such a tight ass. You ain't gonna do yo'r wife any good, bein' all worked up in a dither." He took the cup but did nothing. "Drink, goddammit!" Effie tossed back her dose in one big gulp. She now took the last four rags Neil had brought in and dumped them into the water and vinegar mix.

"Here. Take these and wrap 'em tight around her feet." Trevor pulled back the quilt and did as he was told just as Neil came back into the house carrying a couple of jars of broth, one dark as blood and another a light shade of gold.

"Brought some chicken broth, too, Effie," Neil said as he raised the jars into the air.

"Good, good. Now get it good'n warm on the stove, but not boilin'." Neil shuffled towards the stove, looking as helpless as they all felt. Trevor wrapped Annie's feet in the vinegar-soaked rags and inquired if there was anything else he should be doing.

"Pray," Effie uttered. Trevor looked at her with a mix of surprise and fear. "It's pretty much all we got."

For the next twelve hours Annie faded in and out of consciousness. Her fever would break, only to return with a fiery vengeance. During those hours when things seemed to be normal, she would sip on teaspoons of cold water and warm broth but would throw that up just before the heat within her body surged back. Neil tried to distract Trevor by talking of Mr. Lincoln's War or hunting stories, but if Annie was lucid enough to realize he was gone, she would call out, wanting him by her side.

"Boy's exhausted," Neil told Effie.

"Bet he ain't eaten either."

"Nope. I made us a pot of stew. Says he thinks he'll just throw up if he eats."

"Well, no sense in wastin' food. He'll eat when he's ready." Effie flopped down in the kitchen chair. Neil brought her a bowl of the stew that steamed with the smell of carrots, turnips, and tender chunks of rabbit." Effie nodded in gratitude.

It had been nearly fourteen hours since Neil had carried Annie up those steps. Annie had bled a bit more, but for the most part, the crimson flood that had threatened to take her had eased, thanks to Effie's care. The flood outside Effie's house, however, had not. Effie could hear the sound of snapping trees being drug by the mud flows all around her. If they survived this night, that would, indeed, be a miracle.

The rain became a hypnotic distraction that Trevor found he missed during those rare intermissions when the downpour relented. The mud flowing around them, however, was something he could do without. The popping and cracking of the trees reminded him of shellfire, and like those bullets, you never knew where they might lodge. He briefly wondered if someone should go check on Ida and Jacob but decided to let that be. His first priority was here, by his wife.

It seemed if he left her side for more than five minutes, she would sense his absence and cry out. He desperately wanted to get her out of this gorge and to proper medical care, but in the meantime, if she could gain some strength, it would help.

Effie brought him a bowl of stew and cornbread, which he had refused earlier, but now felt he might be able to swallow. He took the spoon and brought up a heaping chunk of rabbit and carrots to his mouth, savoring the saltiness and the comfort of the broth more than the meat itself. Deciding it couldn't hurt, he withdrew a small amount of broth and placed it to Annie's crinkled lips, letting the spoon rest there, allowing the aroma to drift up to her nose. When she stirred, Trevor jumped out of his skin, spilling the broth on her shift.

He noticed her fever had broken again. She was moving more now, and when Trevor placed the back of his hand against her forehead, she felt cool. Almost normal.

"Effie!" Trevor shouted. Neil and Effie ran to the bedroom door, their looks giving away the fact they feared the worst. "Annie's fever broke. I think she may be through the worst of it!"

Effie trundled over, most certainly believing it was nothing different than what they had seen before, but after feeling Annie's head and arms and noting the drenched bedding, she agreed. "Well, I'll be a suck-egg mule."

As if these words had been the summoner of her spirit, Annie's eyes blinked open, a weak smile supplanting the deathly grimace that had painted her face earlier. She kicked at the mummy-like wrappings on her feet.

"Hey there, stranger," Trevor said with a smile as he leaned into Annie's pale face.

"Huh..." Annie coughed and then winced with the soreness still evident in her belly. "Hi," she said back with a weak grin. "Do I know you?" Effie and Neil laughed in the background.

"Well, some guy around here claims to be your husband," Effie teased, "but I sent him packin'." Annie laughed. She then took her hand and moved it to her belly, feeling around as though she knew something was missing. "Muh ... muh ... my baby. Is it ..." Effie made a move to intervene, but Trevor held up his hand.

"Don't you worry about that right now, Sweetheart. Save your strength."

But Annie was having none of it. Even in her weakened state, she was aware that something was very wrong and bolted up.

"Our baby ... she's gone?" Annie looked to her husband, for him to tell her that everything was okay. That her worst fears weren't the harsh reality. Trevor tipped his head in despair then returned his eyes to face hers.

"Yes, Annie. She's gone."

"Noooooo," she cried. Effie and Neil turned to leave, giving the two the privacy and space to process the events of the past thirty-six hours. "No, no, no, no, no..." she sobbed. Trevor sat beside her and held her, his own tears mingling with hers.

"Listen," he soothed as he brought her face to look at his. "I know it's hard, but we'll get through this." Annie cried harder. "We will, Annie. We'll try again, when it's right. I know it seems horrible right now, but it will be much better. You'll see." Her sobs turned into something inaudible as she let go of Trevor's hand and pulled her knees up to her chest, rocking back and forth.

"What have I done? What have I done? What have I done ..." she kept repeating.

"No darling, no! This isn't your fault. How could any of this be your fault?" His reassurances only made her more hysterical. "That's like saying the rain is your fault. It's irrational. Things happen and we have ..."

"*NOOOOO!*" She shouted so loudly it made Trevor jump off the bed. "I ... I ... I ... oh my God!"

"What, Annie?"

"I ... I ..." This was just too much. There was nothing that warranted this much self-flagellation.

"Annie, please. Calm down. You aren't well and ..."

"I killed our baby!" she cried. Trevor stood aghast, unsure of whether or not these were the ravings of another fever, or perhaps worse - the truth. Out of the periphery of his eye, Trevor could see Effie standing close.

"Annie, you aren't making any sense," he forced a laugh as he coaxed his wife to lie back down. "Is she, Effie?" He could hear the doubt in his own voice. Effie said nothing. Trevor retrieved the soup bowl and lifted a spoonful of meat and broth up to her lips. "Here you go. Eat some ..."

Annie slapped the bowl and spoon across the room, the porcelain breaking into quarters against the wall as its contents spilled across the floor.

"Tell her it's not true, Effie," Trevor begged. "Tell her. Tell me ... it's not true." Trevor thought he saw a tear fall from the corner of Effie's eye. He turned back to his wife, who continued her morbid mantra. *I killed our baby. I killed our baby. I killed our baby...*

"Huh ... huh ... how did you...?" A clap of thunder and another *crack-crack-crack* of trees being uprooted echoed from the valley floor.

"She snuck into my cabinet and took some pennyroyal and Queen Anne's Lace." Trevor's hand went slack to his side as he began to pace.

"I don't understand. What does that do? What does any of this mean?" Trevor's voice was shaking.

"It means, she tried slip the baby," Effie pronounced.

"Slip ... the baby?" Trevor was confused.

"Miscarry," Effie clarified, as she left the room.

Trevor looked back to his wife, his face pleading for better answers. "Annie, why?" Annie continued her rocking and sobbing. "Why would you do such a thing?"

When she did not respond, he stormed over to her and grabbed her wrists, prying her hands away from her tear-stained face. *"ANSWER ME!"* he screamed, his hands maintaining their strong grip.

"Let go of me," she demanded. Trevor did so, but again asked, *"Why?"*

"I ... I ... don't ... I thought, that if you ... didn't have a baby to worry with, you'd want to fly again. I know ... how ... much it means ... to you."

"What? No. No. That ... this ... makes no sense," he mumbled, pacing the floor and wagging his finger into the air. "You aren't going to pin this one on me. I told you I didn't want to fly anymore. It was a childish, romantic notion that I had ... *have* ... put out of my mind. I was very clear about that."

Annie continued to openly weep. "I know ... I know ... I know ..." was all she could manage.

"You know? Then I will ask you again. *WHY DID YOU DO IT?*"

"I tried," Annie whispered. "I tried ..."

"Well, it looks like you *succeeded!*"

"No. I tried to ... to ... stop ... it."

"The other tea," he said, recalling Effie and Annie talking among themselves.

"Effie ... wanted ... me to ... tell you," she wheezed. "Don't be angry..."

"*Angry* doesn't come *CLOSE* to describing how I feel!"

"Trevor," Effie cautioned, now back in the doorway. "Not now. She's weak."

"Oh, I think she's strong as an OX!" he screamed. "Sure as hell seems to be working the rest of us to suit her schemes! How *stupid* of me to ever think that it could work between us! I should've left this gorge the very second you told me you were having a baby. For all I know, it wasn't even mine!"

"Trevor Middleton!" Effie yelled. "This ain't the time nor the place!"

"Trevor," Annie whispered. "Please. You know..."

"I don't know a goddamned *THING* anymore!" Trevor yelled. "You really are a piece of work..."

"Effie, Trevor! Come quick!" Neil shouted from just inside the back door. Trevor moved towards the sound of Neil's voice, then back to Annie's side, unsure of where to go.

"We're not through, Annie," Trevor warned with a wag of his finger as he made his way to see what had Neil worried so.

Through the fog, Neil's flashlight showed on the well, or at least, what was left of it. A significant amount of the packed ground around it had been carried away into the river below. The stone walls remained steady, for the time, but by morning, the whole thing could burst wide open. If that was the case with the well, what greater danger could the house, and everyone in it, be in? They had to move to higher ground. Now.

Annie could feel something working beneath her, against her. It wasn't just Trevor's harsh words, though they cut her deeper than the knifing pain that had returned in her side. It was as though the ground under her was writhing, like a giant pile of snakes. She had been feeling it, the twisting and the churning, but in her fevered state she had taken it to be part of her dreams. And what lovely dreams they were! Uncle Phipp had come to visit, his gentle smile soothing her pain and assuring her that soon, everything would all be right. Then Virgil had appeared, taking his father's hand, leading him deep into the swirling fog.

"Not yet, Pa," she'd heard her cousin say. How she wanted to follow them into whatever peaceful oblivion they had come from, but then she had seen a little girl – a beautiful child, about five years of age, with strawberry blonde ringlets that tumbled across her small shoulders. She wore white lace stockings underneath a matching dress that fell in cascades to her little knees. White gloves and shoes completed her angelic ensemble. Her face shone with a soft light, and Annie wanted nothing more than to take her in her arms and hold her, never to let go.

Hi! My name is Lizzy, she'd said, taking Annie's deathly cold hand in her own. It felt so warm! *You must be Mommy. Is Daddy coming?* Annie shook her head that he was not. *It's okay. We'll be together ... soon. You've got a secret. Don't bring it with you.* And with that she had vanished into the rain and fog. Annie reached into the mist, wanting desperately to take Lizzy's hand, to follow her into the swirling void from which she had emerged, but she was gone.

The strong smell of game and sage had sent her careening back to this hell she now occupied. She had hoped in those delirious, waking moments that her dream had been only that, but when Trevor confirmed their child was dead, leaving no hope of ever seeing her or holding her little hand again, the heart she no longer believed existed within her shattered into a million pieces.

Trevor and Effie came rushing into the room. Her husband's face no longer bore the hard lines of anger but instead, those of sheer terror. She could hear Petals bay from her stable and realized Neil must be doing something inside the barn.

"Annie, can you walk?" Trevor asked.

"I, I don't know. I can try. What's wrong?"

"There's no time to explain." Trevor collected his wife in his arms, forcing her upright, but her knees were jelly. She could bear no weight on them. None whatsoever.

"Dammit!" Trevor shouted.

"I'm sorry, Trevor, I'm trying," Annie whimpered.

"It's not you. The foundation is washing from under the house. We have to leave. Now!" He tried to wrest her once more, but there was no way she could walk.

"Put your arms around me." She tried, but it was like lifting two limp ropes. There was a roaring inside her head, but whether it was from the rain or remnants from her broken fever, she could not tell. "Hold on, Sweetheart. Here we go." Trevor gathered her close, the heat of his body soaking into her still wet shift. She could smell fear seeping through his pores and felt both their hearts throb as felled logs from the mountainside collided into the foundation of Effie's house.

"I'm sorry for those horrible things I said," Trevor whispered as he struggled to keep his balance, navigating the heaving floor beneath them. She wanted to absolve him, to tell him he was forgiven, but she didn't have the strength.

Slogging through molasses would have been easier. Trevor was unable to make any sort of speed across the uneven wood floors, his locked-up knee forbidding anything more than one painful step at a time. The floors beneath her creaked and moaned. The *pop-pop-pop* of uprooted trees being thrust against the foundation were battering rams. She felt another stabbing pain in her side, burying her face in Trevor's shoulder to suppress her scream.

"Hold on! We're going back to Tom and Mattie's..." Another knife bore into her hip and down into her groin.

"I won't make it, Trevor." She was in full voice now, a strength fueled by equal parts fear and resignation. Trevor moved another step forward.

"Yes, you will make it! You have to!" One more step forward. They were only halfway across the room. Mere feet may as well have been miles. She heard Neil open the front door and ask if Trevor needed help.

"Yes," Trevor shouted. "The wagon ready?"

"Yep, Petals is rarin' to go," Neil assured him. Just then Trevor went down. Hard. Annie sat in a stunned puddle, watching the wooden planks of the floor around them swell and pitch. She could hear the raging water *whoosh* and boil beneath them, and felt every thud of the hemlocks, birches, and oaks as they knocked the spindly timbers of the foundation out from under them. The look of terror on Trevor's face drained any strength she had managed to acquire in the past several minutes.

Trevor tried to stand, but the floorboards rose in an angry surge. Each time he pushed himself up, a plank shifted, bringing him down with a pronounced *thud*.

Annie screamed. "Crawl, Trevor! Crawl!"

The roar around them was deafening. She watched with horror as Neil attempted to cross the threshold but was pushed backwards by a tree thrusting itself through the floor and into the ceiling. Trevor shoved himself upright, placing his feet wide apart to spread out his center of gravity. With his balance steadier, he reached down to take his wife's hand, pulling her to his side, but no sooner had he collected her back into his arms when the floor beneath them opened. Trevor pitched forward, stumbled, tried to regain his balance. Annie clung to his neck, but her weight pulled them both into the gaping mouth of the watery beast, its wooden teeth gnawing and chewing on tender flesh. She could feel Trevor's tenuous grasp on her hand as the world around her went black. The force of the flowing mud pulled her deeper into the earth. Her ears and nose filled with black sludge as large stumps and trees slammed hard against her body, the crack of her bones mingling with the snapping of the house's supports. At times, she was lifted as though she were riding a wave, but each time she thought she would surface, the cold mud and churning water pulled her down again. She felt Trevor's hand slip from hers, only to grasp her wrist, then lose it. She opened her mouth to scream, but her throat was full of viscous silt and debris. The mud lifted her up and up, this time towards a glimmer of light. She pushed her hand up through the muck, reaching for the hand she could now see stretching out for hers. Was it Trevor? Neil? It didn't matter. She would shake hands with the Devil right now if it meant she could breathe.

Hello, Mommy! Lizzy said. I've been waiting.

Trevor clung to one of the few trees left standing in the wake of the mudslide, blood from his nose and ears mingling with the black ooze in his throat and lungs. He gagged and gasped for air. His eyes searched the dark around him. He must find his wife.

He'd held on to Annie until the force of the mud separated them - dragging her through a grove of apple trees two-hundred feet or more down the mountainside. His gut-wrenching screams were met with silence, but he clung to the hope that she'd done as he had – grabbed the first vertical object she could find and held on. She had lost so much strength over the past several days, but her will was strong. He could not, would not, give up.

Climbing to the top of the sapling that had saved his life, he lowered himself onto a bank that had escaped the path of the mudslide. He could hear Neil calling as he clawed his way over boulders, barbed wire, fenceposts, cooking pots, pig shit, and a church pew, his leg raging with a new pain.

Neil heard his shouts from the other side of the bank and met him halfway with the flashlight Effie had managed to save. The two men shouted, scouring the scarred mountainside for any sign of Annie. Their calls mingled with the mournful cries of Effie's ewe, all of them searching for their lost ones. Neil searched the opposite side of the gulley, venturing as close into the waist deep mud as he dared. The threat of more mudslides was ever-looming, and he had warned Trevor it would do no one any good if they got stuck, or worse, killed.

As the sun rose over The Gorge, there was no sign of Annie. Jacob came as soon as he could to join the search. *Annnnnnniiiieeeeeeee!* he cried, his screams reverberating against the canyon walls. Neighbors who had fared some better heard of the missing girl and came to offer their assistance in the hunt. Trevor took charge of the search parties and instructed them to confine their resources to the apple orchard where he was certain he lost his grip on her hand.

One day passed, then two. Finally, on the evening of July 18th, a cry rang out through the canyon. Jacob had found his sister, her neck nested in the fork of an apple tree, the hoof of a young lamb still held firmly in her grip.

Chapter 55

The clearing of the clouds revealed a tragedy unlike anything The Gorge had ever witnessed. Roiling mud, logs, and boulders the size of railroad cars had swept entire houses, with families inside, into the river. The mountainous, rocky slopes had been stripped of all vegetation. Oaks, poplars, and hemlocks were chewed into mere splinters. Hickory Nut trees, once the stately guardians of The Gorge, were worn bare of their bark. Sharp pointed stones were ground smooth – the storm accomplishing in hours what normally took thousands of years. Not one business along the river survived.

Neil and Effie's hog pen had been lifted and carried down the mountain, the squeals and screams of the sows and hogs indiscernible above the somersaulting rocks and trees. The next day, while searching for his sister, Jacob heard grunts and snuffles. Turning towards the noise in hopes it was Annie, he saw the snout of a pig, rooting up from beneath the knee-deep sludge. Soon, eight other swine pushed their way to the surface, no worse the wear for their tumble down the mountain, save for some superficial cuts and gashes. Trevor was grateful Neil and Effie's passel had survived, but he thought it a cruel irony.

Over the next week, the rivers would recede, only to swell over their banks once more. For every inch gained, a mile seemed to be lost.

Chimney Rock Park lay in ruins. Lucius Morse, the visionary developer who'd celebrated its opening not two weeks prior, walked eighteen hours into Hendersonville, bedraggled and heartbroken, to bring word of the devastation in The Gorge and ask for help. Nearly all of the road leading to Asheville was wiped away by the floods. Governor Locke Craig ensured his resources were at the ready. What money could not heal, perhaps time would.

A few days after finding Annie, rescuers heard the screams of a woman coming from a ramshackle cabin as they sifted through the storm debris. A tall oak had fallen on the house, and upon entering, they discovered the pale, bare-assed body of Lester Conner laying atop a woman of similar pallor – her gangly legs wrapped tight around his neck. The pointed end of a tree snag was plunged deep into his back, the woman pinned beneath.

Jacob refused to give his father a decent burial, stating such would be as hypocritical as his father was. Instead, Jacob had him tossed into the ground by the stump of the tree that had killed him. His strumpet could visit him as she pleased. The woman cursed and screamed at the gravediggers until she was hoarse, but her protests only gave them fuel to shovel faster.

Birdie said she wanted Annie's funeral to be a celebration, but Trevor found such a sentiment difficult to fathom. He had never been good at pretending, and for the life of him, he was unable to conceive what there was to celebrate. Weighing heavier on him was the fact that he hardly knew this woman who had been his wife for just a few short weeks. And the things he had said to her. Forgiveness would be a long time coming, if it ever came at all.

And their child? That was even more difficult to wrap his head around. How could you grieve the loss of something, of someone, you never had? He supposed that was a thing to mourn in and of itself. His obsessive rumination precipitated panic attacks for which Effie's concoctions of lemon balm and chamomile could not stave off. She did have that whiskey though, which dulled some of the sharper edges.

Trevor buried Annie in her wedding gown. Mattie insisted that the pearls go with her. *Nothing changes the look of a dress like a nice string of pearls* she'd said.

When Mathias Carmine, owner of the logging company, received word of Annie's death, he offered to donate the lumber for her coffin. Hell, he'd have his own men craft it from the finest of oak, he'd declared! Effie cursed the very idea and said if he'd given two shits about Annie, or anyone else on that goddamned mountain, he'd not've stripped it bald. As far as she was concerned, Annie's blood was on his hands. Carmine skulked away, with a renewed hex or two mingled in the spit Effie fired onto his black patent-leather oxfords.

With all the trees and timber washed down the mountain, Trevor, Jacob, and Neil constructed a crude pine box from the few sheets Mr. Harris could salvage from behind his store. Jacob found some rusty old door hinges in their barn, and with a little planing to smooth the edges, Trevor figured it would do.

There were no flowers to place on Annie's grave. All greenery and vegetation had either been waterlogged or swallowed whole by the mudflow that stained the Rocky Broad red. Neil had found one solitary sunflower blooming in the shelter of his barn, which he placed inside the pine box. When Jacob nailed the coffin shut, Trevor's body shook with each pounding of the hammer. It seemed so final and confining – the last thing Annie would have wanted.

Reverend Wilcox presided over the service. It was such a mental whiplash, considering just a few short weeks ago he had married them. He was a man of slight stature, but his voice boomed throughout the valley as he read from the Song of Solomon:

I am the rose of Sharon, and the lily of the valleys.
As the lily among thorns, so is my love among the daughters.
Stay me with flagons, comfort me with apples: for I am sick of love.
I charge you, O ye daughters of Jerusalem, by the roes,
and by the hinds of the field, that ye stir not up, nor awake my love, till he
please.

Neil and Effie bound Trevor up in their arms and held him tight as Ida rocked to and fro, garbled words forming on her withering lips. Jacob supported her as best he could, but he was showing his own signs of wear.

The rain might be over and gone, but the floods would continue for quite some time.

Chapter 56

After Annie's funeral, Trevor threw himself into helping Effie, Jacob, and Ida sift through the rubble and debris, though there wasn't much to be salvaged. Neil had jerked Effie away from the churning hole that had swallowed Annie, dislocating her shoulder in the process. That was healing well enough, but Effie's house was a total loss.

Jacob and Ida's home had survived, but their barn had not. What few possessions any of them could call their own had been stirred into the churning mudslide with complete disregard for the destitution and horror left in its wake.

Ida plunged headlong into a hellish abyss. The most communication she could manage on her chalkboard were the words, "The girl. The girl. Where's the girl?" She followed Jacob around the house, banging the chalkboard on his shoulder, demanding her son provide an answer – one that she could get her head around. Trevor heard Jacob tell her, more times than he could count, that Annie was dead. She was never coming back.

Exasperated, Jacob took the chalkboard and broke it across his knee, tossing the pieces onto the bonfire that served to consume the fragments of stalls, feed troughs, and eventually, Lula Bell, found buried in a drying mound of mud and rock about twenty feet from where the old barn had stood. Trevor looked with pity upon his brother-in-law as the realization of all that had been lost brought Jacob to his knees. He wasn't sure how much more that boy, or any of them, could take.

Ida then resorted to pacing the floors, wringing her hands, looking in cabinets, drawers, and under mounds of quilts that could not be rid of the mildew. Trevor supposed she would be looking for "the girl" as long as she had breath in her, which turned out to not be that long. Ida died in her sleep on August 16th, one month to the day after the flood.

The Esmeralda survived the storm with minimal damage, save for some holes where copious amounts of water had poured into the kitchen. With the renewed pain and inflexibility in his leg, climbing up on a roof would be foolhardy, so Trevor lifted boards and cans of nails to Tom, Clavel and Jacob as they hammered and patched.

Mattie and Tom opened the inn to folks who had nowhere else to go and with the help of Tom's radio, assisted the residents of The Gorge in communicating with concerned families and friends on the outside, as travel and mail service were impossible.

Trevor had hoped that by training his sights on helping others he could heal, or at least forestall, his pain. He had moved in with Jacob, but this only served to worsen his dark moods. Jacob was grateful for the help and the companionship, but Trevor had his own grieving to do and as long as he was in The Gorge, he saw no way out of the black forest of dismay and confusion.

The irony was not lost on him: he had been so adamant about staying in the gorge but now that Annie was gone, he couldn't wait to leave.

As soon as travel became possible Trevor returned to Charleston, believing that, once in familiar territory, he could cobble together the fragments and shards of his life and start over, but his frustration only mounted. He felt nothing. No sadness. No anger. No ambition. He couldn't even muster the energy to get out of bed most mornings, and on the rare occasion he did put one foot before the other, he stared out the large bay windows in his father's library, regarding the passersby. He wondered how they could go on living a normal happy-go-lucky life, when in a flash of lightning, their fragile little world could be thrashed upon the shoals and washed out to sea. It seemed wrong that they should enjoy such naïveté while he grappled with opposing realities.

He considered returning to France but with his reinjured leg, driving an ambulance was not realistic, and while he no longer had to consider a wife and child, flying no longer appealed to him either.

What about a clerical position within the AAFS? His father assured him that Doc Andrew would be thrilled to have him back in any capacity. But Trevor had no desire to push paper into neat little piles on a desk, enduring the looks of pity from passersby. *It wouldn't be like that,* his father insisted. *No one believed him to be pitiful,* but to this Trevor simply said, *no thanks.*

His father then offered him a partnership in the shipping business, but Trevor said the mere thought made him seasick. Lymas offered to send him to medical school and set up a joint practice. Trevor said he would think about it and provide his uncle with an answer in a few weeks. Those weeks had come and gone, and still he remained paralyzed - powerless to shake the malaise that consumed him.

That was the worst thing, he'd decided. Numbness. He felt nothing. Then again, how was someone in his situation supposed to feel?

He kept reminding himself that, had Annie not become pregnant, he would never have considered any formal relationship with her. Certainly, she was beautiful, sometimes funny, and possessed an aptitude to make something more of her life – far from the horrible existence she had known. It was, indeed, a tragic loss that she would never have the chance to realize all her potential. But even had such potential been realized, it would never have made the two of them compatible. He doubted, even with sheer willpower, that their marriage would have ever survived.

Guilt. That, he now realized, was his problem. Had he listened to his father's and uncle's admonitions that night he went with Annie to the cave, things might have turned out differently. No. There was no *might* about it. He couldn't have prevented the flood, but he could have prevented his role in her pregnancy, and consequently, her death. Regret was becoming an albatross around his neck.

One November evening, after a particularly dreadful day with a cold, chilling rain, Trevor went for a walk along the Ashley River. Standing on the shore, gazing out into the vast, murky waters that seemed to mimic his sullen mood, he felt a hand come to rest on his shoulder, giving him a start. Trevor turned to see Lymas, staring into his eyes with that gentleness that always was in stark contrast to his father's stalwart demeanor.

"Uncle! You nearly caused my heart to stop. What are you doing here?"

"Oh, I just wanted to see what my favorite nephew was up to these days."

Trevor laughed. "Your compliment is lost in the obvious, Uncle. You have no other nephew."

"This is true. But if I had one thousand nephews, you would still be my favorite." Trevor smiled and returned the sentiment with a slight pat on his uncle's arm, reverting his stare towards the river.

"Well, I fear I am not up to much of anything, Uncle," Trevor sighed. "But let's not kid ourselves. You knew this. I'm sure father has kept you apprised of my *nothingness*."

Lymas nodded. "Yes, he has. I will not pretend my presence here is pure folly. Can we sit for a moment?" Lymas motioned to the park bench poised just behind them.

Trevor ambled over and plopped himself down, sending a grey squirrel scrambling up the nearest oak tree with a scavenged scone in her mouth.

"If you are wondering why I haven't accepted your offer to attend medical school, I haven't exactly..."

"Good grief, Trevor! I am not offended by that. I want you to be happy! If I can help, then I am at your service. I just believe you should set your sights on something. *Anything!* It keeps your eyes on the shore when you are drowning in a sea of self-loathing and guilt."

Several minutes of silence passed before Trevor spoke.

"I suppose that's the trouble, Uncle. I *am* drowning, and the more I flail, the deeper I sink. It's as though I was set down in another world, and just by my presence there, I upended the status quo and turned everyone's lives upside down. But I can't change the past, so I'm stuck."

"So, you caused the storm and the flood."

"Though your point is rhetorical, don't be silly. I see what you're trying to do ... so don't." Trevor retorted. "I did act irresponsibly, therefore I can't just pretend I had no role in what transpired. If Annie had not been pregnant, she would not have been at Effie's, and then ..."

"And then ... what? Trevor, ultimately, you *did* act responsibly. And I must remind you, you did not act alone. It takes two to become pregnant, you know." Trevor shrugged his shoulders. "Certainly, yours and Annie's actions created a child under less-than-ideal circumstances, but how many of us can say we haven't been rash and impulsive? Certainly, you do not have the market cornered on the consequences of spontaneity."

"But I don't understand why..."

"No. You don't understand, Trevor, and you never will. As a physician, I see things every single day of my life I cannot rationalize. Things I second guess myself over. *If I had done this, then that ... or not.* But in the end, we are not to be condemned for what we did, but only for all the good we did *not* do."

"Voltaire?" His uncle nodded in the affirmative. Trevor leaned back and fixated on a chain of Spanish moss that swayed in the oak above them. "But where do I even begin to do the good?"

"When you don't know where to start, start with what you do know."

Trevor laughed. "I prefer Voltaire."

"*Hmmpf.* Your insult is noted."

"No offense intended, Uncle."

Lymas smiled, producing two cigars from his coat pocket. Passing the other to his nephew, the two men gazed across the river while a pair of blue herons squawked and skimmed the water in the darkening shadows of the evening.

In the days after Lymas returned to Savannah, Trevor thought hard upon his uncle's advice. *When you don't know where to start, start with what you do know.*

What did he know? He knew how to drive an ambulance and knew how to keep one running. He was quite certain he could organize and motivate, thanks to the tutelage of Doc Andrew and the AAFS. He knew his leg would never be solid enough to drive the grueling hours required of an ambulance driver in France, but he could do short stints here in the states, and he could train others in the skills he had acquired. And most importantly, he had the financial means and resources to bring it all together. It wasn't so much a start as it was the continuance of the idea. It was time to stop flailing, and swim to shore.

Epilogue

In the fall, just over a year since the Great Flood in The Gorge, Trevor found himself sweeping sawdust and shavings from the floor of Bat Cave Clinic, putting the final touches on the space before the formal ribbon cutting ceremony in a few short days. Butterflies tickled him inside, but things were coming together nicely.

The funding had poured in, not only from family and friends, but from Mrs. Vanderbilt and Doc Andrew, too. Mattie and Tom donated what they could and opened The Esmeralda to prospective investors and other guests related to the building project.

Having been given a faded tintype of Annie by Jacob, Trevor had taken it to a local artist in Asheville, who had produced a portrait that now hung in the waiting room with a plaque of dedication. Trevor's fingers traced the raised lettering:

> Bat Cave Clinic is hereby dedicated
> to the indelible memory of
> Annie Grace Middleton
> whose high spirit of hope and determination
> will forever inspire us all.

The construction crew, which consisted of craftsmen from the community, bid him a good night, promising to attend the ribbon cutting ceremony in a few short days. Trevor retreated to his office, pouring himself a glass of brandy before returning to the small, one-bedroom house he had built on the hill just above the clinic. A confirmed bachelor required little space.

While the clinic was being built, Trevor taught Jacob everything he knew about ambulances and cars. Jacob had proved gifted in the field of math and mechanics. Consequently, he had been accepted to The North Carolina College of Agriculture and Mechanic Arts. He had even earned a scholarship, his benefactor wishing to remain anonymous. Only Trevor knew it was his father.

Jacob vowed to return to The Gorge upon graduation, but Trevor knew better than anyone – life could take that boy in a thousand different directions. Selfishly, Trevor wished Jacob would stay. He needed a good mechanic and ambulance driver. But with his entire family gone, there was nothing to hold Jacob in The Gorge.

Trevor wasn't even sure he himself would still be here in four years. He was committed to starting the clinic and supporting ambulance service; but once those projects were running smoothly, he had a mind to go to Boston – to medical school – just as Uncle Lymas had once suggested.

He suddenly recalled Hannah, his nurse back in France – and wondered what might have become of her and how different his life might have been if they'd had the opportunity to get to know one another more. Just as quickly as the thought came to him, however, he pushed it aside. No sense in dwelling on what might have been.

Trevor rubbed his knee, a renewed stiffness settling deep within the joint. *Cold weather must be moving in,* he mused. He should get some arnica and comfrey from Effie, which reminded him, he needed to retrieve the salves and ointments he'd ordered from her. The clinic's shelves needed to be stocked before opening day next week.

He looked forward to his visits there, which had become fairly regular since Trevor's return to The Gorge. Effie and Neil had opened their home and heart to him, making him one of their own. He'd missed much of her story when he was in Charleston, but one evening while he and Neil were sharing a pipe on the back porch, Neil had divulged a good bit.

Though Effie had professed she didn't "...give two shits about that infernal sinkhole," the loss of her home, and Annie, took a toll. Neil said Effie had lost all sense of purpose. Grief pressed her shoulders low. She slept until noon every day, rousing just long enough to fix something to eat. She'd do a few chores – like taking some feed to their new flock of sheep or seeing that the chickens had water and grain. With her energy drained, she'd spend the rest of the daylight, rocking back and forth, back and forth, in the new rocker Neil had bought her, staring into the valley. She spoke no more than a handful of words a day.

Neil picked her bouquets of coneflowers. He bought a small sack of Greasy Cut-Short seeds in the hopes she'd find purpose in planting and tending the vines, but she never opened the bag.

On one particularly cool evening this past spring, cool enough to force Neil to don on his duster coat to slop the pigs, he heard a commotion in the house. Pots and pans crashing. Glass breaking. Squawking and screeching. He dropped his slop buckets and hightailed it to the house to find a Catbird thrashing itself up against the windows and walls.

And there stood Effie, right in the middle of it all, her eyes following its erratic flight as it bounced from one wall to the other. Neil swatted at the bird, encouraging it towards the door, but his gestures only served to frighten it more.

Effie hollered. "Dammit, you old fool. Leave her be!"

"What?" he shouted back, deflecting the bird with his arm as it dove towards his head. "Leave who be?"

"Annie! She's gotta find her own way!"

"Annie? Have you gone and lost yo'r cotton pickin' mind?" The Catbird, panting, clung to the tattered lace curtain. Neil moved to take the bird in his weathered, calloused hand, but it darted before he could form his fingers around it, resuming its *thuds* and *kerflops* against the pine-knotted wallboards.

"Leave her be!" Effie screamed.

"I'll do more than that, you crazy old bat! You and that goddamned bird can *have* this place. I'm done!"

"Good riddance!" she hollered back.

Neil said he threw up his hands and stomped back to the pigsty. He'd been afraid Effie was losing her good senses. Now, he was sure of it.

Neil spent the night in the hayloft underneath Petal's blanket. He couldn't sleep and wondered if it was the chill in the air or the iciness that had settled between him and Effie. They might bicker from time to time, poking and jabbing at one another just for fun, but they rarely fought. Not since his mother had died, anyways.

It *was* Catbird Winter, he allowed. They always did get feisty and noisy during this spring cold snap, but he'd never seen one get inside a house before. To say that the bird was Annie come back from the dead, though, was just too much.

The next morning, having slept no more than maybe an hour or two total, he awoke with the first light over the canyon walls and slunk back to the house. First thing he'd do was make their favorite breakfast of corned beef hash and gravy, then if she hadn't thrown it back at him, he'd apologize – proper. Mr. Harris had set aside a can of corned beef for him since it was a bit of a commodity these days. Neil had been saving it for a special celebration, and he figured this was as good as any.

When he got to the house, he found the door shut. He twisted the knob and poked his head inside, bracing himself for another assault. Instead, he found Effie asleep in their bed and no sign of the Catbird anywhere.

Neil was stirring up the gravy when Effie slipped her arms around his waist. Scared him so bad he flung the wooden spoon against the kitchen cabinet, hurling bits of corned beef onto the ceiling above them. Neil grabbed his chest.

"Sweet Jesus! You tryin' to give me a heart attack, woman?" Effie swiped a spot of gravy from his cheek with her fingertip, then stuck it in her mouth.

"Needs salt," she said.

Neil and Effie busted out laughing. All the grief and worry since the flood came gushing out of them, like pus from an infected wound. They'd held each other so tight, they forgot about the gravy, which scorched inside the cast iron skillet.

"You damned old fool. You never could make gravy," she teased as she scraped the blackened goop from the pan. "Now get outta my way."

After breakfast, Effie put on her sweater and took to the barn, just like she used to. Neil wanted to ask about the Catbird, but was afraid of ruining this unexpected, good day. As Neil milked the cow, Effie tended the ewe and her lambs - the first interest she'd taken in the farm in a month of Sundays. She cooed and cuddled and then laughed as they skittered across the hillside. It wasn't until late morning, nearly lunch, when Neil noticed the Catbird's return. Everywhere Effie went, it followed, resting on a tree limb where she sat or landing on the beanpoles as Effie hoed between the rows. *Mewwww! Mewww!* it sang throughout the barn rafters as they dove into chores that had been neglected for months.

That night, Neil said they'd loved on each other like they were teenagers. He didn't normally kiss and tell, but he was just so happy to have her back, he couldn't help himself. Trevor never thought about old people doing that sort of thing, but the idea made him smile. *Maybe one day I'll be silly over someone.* But right now, that was the furthest thing from his mind.

And speaking of gravy, Effie had promised him supper. His stomach growled with the prospect, but no sooner had he slipped his arms into his jacket than he heard the door to the clinic open and close. *Damn your eyes,* he mumbled under his breath. He really wasn't in the mood for curiosity seekers, which was starting to become an everyday occurrence since the clinic was nearly operational.

"Who is it?" Trevor asked, hearing his uninvited guest wander through the halls and vacant rooms. "May I help you?" he called out, half-limping towards the lobby.

"Trevor," Birdie said softly. "I hope I'm not disturbing."

"Birdie, of course not! What a pleasant surprise!" He had seen Birdie and Clavel numerous times since returning to The Gorge, and while Clavel had been his usual, jovial self, Birdie had been distant. Any conversation they had attempted only proved forced and terce.

He had written it off to, perhaps, a bit of understandable awkwardness. Their only connection had been Annie and perhaps, with the passage of time, she had come to blame him for her death. He had to admit, he still fought to silence those demons himself, but of late had managed to at least muffle their incessant murmurings.

Birdie cast her eyes down, then around the clinic, shuffling and fidgeting, clutching something yellowy-white in her hand. "This looks real nice," she offered. "Real nice. I know you must be proud."

Trevor said that he was, but then that difficult space between them opened back up, rendering them both uneasy and mute.

"So, what can I do for you this evening, Birdie. Would you like a tour? Some tea?"

"Oh, no. No. I ... I'm fine." Trevor saw Birdie catch her first glimpse of Annie's portrait and watched her wipe a tear away with the back of her hand. "Clavel and I will be at the ribbon cuttin' ceremony on Sunday. We'll take a good look then."

Trevor said that pleased him, and that he hoped Little June would be there, too. There would be plenty of games and some fresh squeezed apple juice for the kids. Birdie smiled, then turned towards the window once more, taking in the chartreuse, yellow and red fringes of the early autumn leaves. Suddenly, she spun on her heel and faced him, her hand now trembling around the object in her hand.

"Trevor, there is something I want to show you." Birdie extended her arm and handed him the paper – a tattered envelope that had been ripped open, yellowed with the passage of time.

Trevor took it from Birdie and turned it over. It was his handwriting, and at once he realized it was the correspondence he thought had been sent to Hannah in France well over a year ago – minus the letter itself. Trevor's face contorted with all the puzzlement and confusion he felt.

"I'm afraid I don't understand."

"Of course not. How could you? This is hard for me to ...well, never mind. But Annie..." Birdie cleared her throat. "Annie found the letter you intended to send to this Hannah person. She ... she destroyed it."

"Destroyed it?"

"Burned it. Right there in my own house."

"Your house?" Trevor was annoyed that he was merely repeating Birdie's words, but nothing else came to mind in his ever-growing state of confusion.

"Yes. I guess she wanted me to tell her it was alright, but I didn't. We got into a big fight."

"I remember that day," Trevor remarked.

"Yes, well, I have felt horrible about it ever since. I shoulda told you about it, but I felt it wasn't my business, except it was…"

"Birdie, no!" Trevor cried, easing up to give her a gentle hug. "You aren't responsible for Annie's actions!" Even as he tried to console Birdie, however, a thousand other emotions and questions were now bubbling up inside of him – none of which would ever see a proper resolution.

"Well, I do feel responsible. But it cain't be helped now. Or at least I didn't think so, until a few days ago."

"I don't understand."

"Trevor, remember that red dress?"

"How could I forget," Trevor admitted.

"Well, I was going through some of Annie's things. Jacob, you know, he's been cleaning up his house, fixin' to leave for school. He brought me a box of her things, thinkin' I'd like them. For the memories."

Trevor said that was nice of Jacob but couldn't imagine how this pertained to the envelope that was now absorbing sweat from his palms.

"I pulled out that red dress and went to hang it up, and that envelope dropped out of the folds. When I realized what it was, I felt like it was a sign."

"A sign?" Trevor questioned.

"Yes. I believe it's a sign that I can make things right, between us."

"Birdie, I really appreciate what you're trying to say, but as far as I am concerned, then - and especially now, you have nothing to make reparations for. It's really okay."

Birdie smiled, fresh tears now flowing down her face. "I appreciate that, but I thought you might wanna try writin' this Hannah girl again. You know. Make a fresh start."

Ahh. There it was.

"Birdie, that is most kind of you. But believe me, I am not ready for any sort of romantic involvement. I'm not sure I will ever…"

"Shut yo'r mouth, Trevor Middleton! Yo'r handsome. Smart. Hard-workin'. Any girl would be lucky to have you for a husband!"

"Well, thank you, Birdie, but I just don't think …"

"Clavel talks about it all the time. Yo'r up early every mornin'. You work y'or poor self to death, even on Sundays. You stay late every evenin', pourin' yo'rself into this place." Birdie waved her arms about the lobby. "But bricks and mortar make for a cold bed, if you catch my meanin'."

Trevor said nothing, hoping this sermon was finished, but apparently, Birdie was just getting warmed up.

"What are you gonna do when this is done, Trevor?"

"Done? This clinic will never be *done.* There will always be something to …"

"To distract you?"

Trevor snorted and looked down at his feet, his head heavy with the weight of Birdie's brutal honestly. "Maybe," he admitted. "But what else have I got to do?" He regretted his words the moment they slipped out of his mouth.

"And that's my point. Trevor, this is a wonderful thing yo'r doin' here, but it won't fix what happened."

"I know that but…"

"You cain't keep punishin' yo'rself. You tried to do all the right things, but sometimes, it just ain't in the cards. Annie was a runaway train bound for destruction, and there was nothin' any of us could do to stop it. We have to forgive her, but mostly, we have to forgive ourselves for what we couldn't do and move on."

"Maybe you're right, Birdie. But.."

"Damn straight, I'm right!" she nearly shouted. "Write her!"

"Hannah? She's probably long gone from her post in France. I doubt I could ever find her."

"Well, Hells bells, Trevor! You don't know a thing until you try it. And if she *is* gone, at least it's a start."

When you don't know where to start, start with what you do know.

"Alright, Birdie. I concede your point."

"Good," she replied. "I'll leave you to it then." Birdie placed her hand on the doorknob. "Promise?"

"I'll think about it, okay? It's a big step."

"Shit, Trevor! It ain't no *big step*," she mocked. "It's a teency, weency letter. Trevor sighed.

"Can I give you a ride home?" Birdie thanked him but said that a walk in the cool fall air would do her good.

"Well, let me at least walk you out," Trevor insisted, grabbing his jacket off the coatrack. Birdie threaded her arm inside Trevor's as he escorted her to the path that led back to her and Clavel's house. "See you Sunday," he concluded, kissing her on the forehead. "And thank you, Birdie. You've given me a lot to think about."

That night, at home, his belly full of Effie's fried chicken, mustard greens and buttermilk chess pie, Trevor sat down in front of the crackling fire – his mind drifting back to his and Birdie's conversation. He pulled the envelope from out of his pocket and stared, recalling that fateful night in the cave: the warmth of the sizzling fire as Annie's body melted beneath him, the touch of her hands across his bare back, the scent of her hair that smelled like woodsmoke... and that whiskey. Even though Effie kept him supplied with a jug, it never seemed to taste quite as sweet as it had that night.

Was it wrong – to remember that ill-fated evening in a good light? He used to think so, but he was starting to think not. While his and Annie's short relationship might have been fraught with strain and, ultimately, tragedy, there were some good memories, too. It was okay to hold those close, to hold Annie close, and to smile. Anything less would be a dishonor to her spirit and memory. Perhaps that's where healing started... with what he knew, the good and beautiful things he could remember.

Trevor laid the envelope on the table beside him and extracted a piece of stationery from the drawer. He picked up a pen to write but he still had no idea what to say – after all this time. And so, so much water over the dam – quite literally. *When you don't know where to start, start with what you do know.*

Dearest Hannah,

I hope this letter finds you in good spirits...or even finds you at all. I realize my correspondence might catch you by surprise, as so much time has passed, but I think of you often and was hoping you did the same. You would not believe the changes in my life. I have opened a clinic, and am seeking qualified nurses to staff it...

Historical Notes

Several decades ago, at the behest of a family member (I cannot recall who), my paternal grandfather, Arthur Hill, recorded an oral history of his life on cassette tape. At some point after his death, I transcribed these stories into a written document, which allowed me to dive deep into his words and stories.

It was his recounting of The Great Flood of 1916 that inspired the climax to this otherwise fictional narrative. Arthur, along with a brother and a sister, Stacy, were swept up in a mudslide that rolled through their small home and carried it down the mountain. Arthur was injured, but Stacy lost her life on that terrifying day in July. She was fourteen.

Please note, however, that Annie Conner is a fictional character based solely upon my imagination. No similarities to the real-life Stacy Hill are implied or explicit in any way.

The cause of The Great Flood is multifaceted. In early July of 1916, a Category 3 hurricane made landfall in the Gulf of Mexico and tracked over the Appalachians, wringing out the rain it carried over Hickory Nut Gorge and all of Western North Carolina.

Just as the waters were receding, a Category 2 hurricane landed in Charleston, SC on July 14th, and continued its march northwest – an unusual precedent for Atlantic storms that more typically arc towards the northeast and out to sea. On July 16th, nearly two feet of rain fell into The

Gorge. Exacerbated by overlogging of the area during the early part of the twentieth century, the already saturated ground could hold no more water, and quite literally ... burst.

As fascinating as the story of the flood was, I knew that it wasn't the story I wanted to write. I had a good start on Annie's character when an acquaintance suggested incorporating a WW1 *La Fayette Escadrille* pilot to the plot. This tickled my historical fancy, but as I began my research, I hit a snag. *The Lafayette Escadrille* would not exist until December of 1916, well after the flood. The Escadrille Américaine, however, would be sanctioned in March of 1916 and deployed that April. (Note that the name was changed from *Escadrille Américaine* to the *Lafayette Escadrille* when the Germans objected to the use of *Américaine*, as The United States was claiming neutrality at the time.)

Even so, working backwards from the flood date, I still had a problem with making Trevor a pilot without manipulating significant historical dates. Through further research, I discovered the significant role that ambulance drivers played in the Western Front, and that many of the *Escadrille's* pilots were plucked from their ranks. Thus began my journey into the fascinating history of the American Ambulance Field Service, or the AAFS.

If you want to know more, I highly encourage you to read *Gentlemen Volunteers* by Arlen J. Hansen. It not only provides a detailed, entertaining account of the AAFS, but gives the reader a strong sense of what it was like to be in the thick of war. I have enjoyed this aspect of the research so much that I have considered writing a prequel, or perhaps a separate story altogether, about the young men and women who served.

Though not exclusively, ambulance drivers were typically well-educated and affluent. Prior to the war, they spent weeks, months, and sometimes years, in France. The French culture and people became a part of their fabric. Thus, thousands of young Americans felt obliged to support The French Cause and volunteered their services long before the United States was officially drawn into the war.

How would a wealthy, young, WW1 ambulance driver find himself in the rural mountains of Hickory Nut Gorge? As The Gorge was a burgeoning retreat for the affluent, silent film stars of the day, and for those seeking relief from tuberculosis (the founder of Chimney Rock Park, Dr. Lucius Morse, being one such person) it stood to reason that someone with Trevor's background and social status would travel there to convalesce from an injury.

Once that concept was solidified, the next question became: what would happen when two young people from wildly disparate backgrounds were thrust together in a remote part of the world, where it seemed as though no one else existed outside of it? The rest of the story, as they say, is history. Or in this case, historical fiction.

Inspiration for Effie Buchanan's character was derived from another real-life resident of The Gorge, Nancy "Ann" Ashworth, though her life and death predates Effie's by many years. Ann was hard-working, strong-willed, intelligent, and a knowledgeable physician who had taught herself the art of herbal medicines from a very young age. (Some considered her a witch, unless of course, they needed her services.) The more I learned about Ann, the more I adored her. It seemed only fitting that her spirit have a place in the telling of *Catbird Winter*.

The incorporation of Leather Britches into this story is based upon a wonderful part of my childhood and, in my biased opinion, a necessary component to any story set in Appalachia. My great-grandmother, Verna Smart Hudgins, used this method of preserving green beans as a means of necessity, but oh what the process does to the flavor or a bean! The best Leather Britches start with good quality bean pods – usually of the Greasy Cut-Shorts or Half Runners variety. Once nice and full on the vine, they are picked and strung on a long piece of strong thread, then hung to dry in an attic or room until they become shriveled and "leathery." I can still see dozens of Leather Britches strings adorning the walls inside Mom Hudgins' washroom, which received a lot of southerly sunlight.

Whenever the Leather Britches were cooked, it was a family holiday. My cousins and I were allowed to miss school for the feast, which included other various and assorted dishes. However, I do not recall eating anything else besides the beans and a side of homemade cornbread. I preferred my Leather Britches covered with a layer of sweet onions, then doused in copious amounts of apple cider vinegar. I would literally eat them until my mother throttled me for fear I would get sick.

Bat Cave is a real cave!

The Little People referenced in Jacob's teasing with Virgil are also "real" – at least in regional folklore. Their existence can be traced back to the stories of The Cherokee (known to them as *Yunwi Tsunsdi*), along with The Catawba, who frequented The Gorge in search of tobacco, game, and to perform sacred rituals on this hallowed ground.

Nearly all accounts of *The Little People* speak to their insatiable affinity for tobacco and their vehemence to protect the sacred plant at all costs – including inflicting bodily harm, or even death, to the would-be thieves. Others, however, claim that they are kind and benevolent creatures who have been known to lead lost children back to their parents.

To my knowledge, there was not an actual store called "Harris's", but there was an inn located in the Chimney Rock area that also predates this story by several decades known as Harris Inn. That is where any similarity ends, however. (Ah, the benefits of being a writer of fiction.)

The fictional cameo appearances made by Anne Harriman Vanderbilt and her husband, William Kissam Vanderbilt, have a fascinating historical precedence. William was born into the wealthy Vanderbilt family of Biltmore House fame in Asheville, North Carolina, making his own fortunes in railroad investments. Anne was his second wife, whom he married in 1903. Together, they built Château Vanderbilt and several horseracing tracks just outside of Paris, and therefore had a significant, personal stake in the outcome of the war.

Anne brought her own wealth into the marriage, and together, Anne and William were a powerhouse for The French Cause. Anne, in particular, was a staunch devotee to the AAFS, providing not only financial and emotional support, but administrative direction as well. She even went so far as to visit the front lines in Verdun to see for herself how the men of the AAFS worked and lived, disguised as a nurse in the event she and her party were captured by the Germans. The ambulance drivers adored her, and she, them. Thus, it seemed a fitting and logical leap that she and Trevor would cross paths.

If you would care to know more about this amazing woman, as well as others, I suggest reading *Ladies and Not So Gentle Women*, by Alfred Allan Lewis. And once more, *Gentleman Volunteers* by Arlen J. Hansen is quite detailed and exhaustive regarding Anne Vanderbilt's role in the AAFS.

The Esmeralda Inn was in existence in 1916 and is still in operation as of this writing. Note, however, that as a result of several fires and multiple renovations over the past century-plus, the floor layouts and mentions of specific rooms, buildings, etc. described in *Catbird Winter* are purely representations of the author's imagination. For information about dining and overnight accommodations, please contact:

The Esmeralda Inn
910 Main Street
Chimney Rock, NC 28720
Phone: (828) 625-2999
Website: https://theesmeralda.com/

Acknowledgements

When I began this project, I had no concept as to the breadth of its undertaking. Writing has always been a passion, although I tabled it for a career in music for a time.

As a writer, a few of my short stories and essays had been published in some nerdy publications. I also volunteered as a regular columnist for my community newspaper back in the day. I believed I could apply those skills to writing a novel, and while I didn't believe it would be a cakewalk, I wasn't prepared for the commitment level and discipline writing a book entails. Inexperience said, "Psst, you can write a novel. It can't be that hard!" Experience split its sides laughing.

After finishing what I believed was my final rewrite, I still felt something was off. I knew the story needed more work but the thought of pushing myself another proverbial mile literally made me sick to my stomach. I reached out to my developmental editor, Duncan Murrell, who, like me, is a runner. I had hoped he would "there-there" me and tell me it was all okay, but he didn't.

In the midst of my whining, offering up a myriad of excuses as to why I couldn't do the things he believed I should, he coached, "Monté, this is an ultra, not a marathon!" So I dusted myself off and re-wrote my manuscript, and here I am, over the finish line.

Consequently, any writer (or athlete) is only as good as the people who support them, but there are a multitude of friends and professionals to thank and a 100% chance I will forget someone, so I beg your forgiveness in advance.

Even though I sent much of what I wrote to the cutting room floor due to practical word count limitations, I wish to thank Arlen J. Hansen, posthumously, for his book *Gentlemen Volunteers*. This book provided invaluable information that allowed me to get my head around Trevor Middleton. I knew little about WW1 and absolutely nothing about WW1 ambulance drivers. This book provided a wealth of information in an easy to read, interesting, well-researched format – one that I referred to again and again.

My mother, Melva Hill, first encouraged me to write this story. Sadly, she isn't here, physically at least, to see its completion, but she was my biggest fan. Despite her own physical limitations (or perhaps because of them) she taught me to never ever give up or to accept perceived boundaries. There's not a day that goes by that I don't ache to share all of my successes and challenges with her. I love and miss her in ways I didn't know were possible.

And as if it weren't obvious … a tremendous amount of gratitude is due to my developmental editor, Duncan Murrell, of CraftBook Editorial. Thank you for taking on this project, and for doing so with such enthusiasm and competence. After living with this story for so long, I didn't think I was married to any of it, but you proved me wrong. *Catbird Winter* and I are the better for it.

To my friend, Angie Baker, what an honor that you agreed to take on the artistic portion of this novel! Your vision for the *Catbird Winter* cover completely blew me away, and the enthusiasm you brought with it was inspiring and edifying. You have invested so much love and soul into this project. It is everything and more than I could have ever imagined. The only thing that outshines your talent is your heart.

To my beta readers: Angela Powers, Joanne Wilcox, Lori Rasmussen, DeAnn Grayson and Vicki Crutcher … you put your shoulder to the plow and provided invaluable insight that brought this story into its own. I owe you a proverbial debt I can never repay. Not ever.

Kelly Arthur, thank you for your sweet friendship and encouragement, and for being my "French consultant". You make my heart smile.

Thank you, Christy Tucker-Polly and Erin Fletcher, for helping me sort out all things equine. I hope I have assimilated your knowledge with my research in a manner that doesn't have you shaking your head in incredulity.

When I began researching radio communications in rural WNC during WW1, there was little information to be found, and what I did find was murky and ambiguous. By a token of sweet luck, I found Stuart Smolkin, the curator of the Asheville Radio Museum, who provided some solid facts I was able to use to make this story interesting and accurate. (Any inaccuracies are totally on me.) Stuart, you are a fount of information, and what a beautiful coincidence that you are in Asheville! Funny how The Universe works sometimes.

Scott Williams, thanks for helping me with the Vanderbilt lineage. You definitely know your stuff.

A very special token of gratitude goes out to The Esmeralda Inn for their permission to use this historical lodge as the backdrop for *Catbird Winter*. To sit and dine on its sweeping, covered porch while listening to The Rocky Broad (as you read your copy of the book!) is an experience worth the journey. Please see the historical notes for more information on this beautiful inn.

I am particularly grateful to my writing colleague, Donna Frelick. The day of our chance meeting at a local brewery was most auspicious. Publishing this book has been a wonderful but sometimes daunting process, but your willingness to share your knowledge made the impossible seem probable. You are an amazing soul, writer, and businesswoman, and I am most fortunate to have met you. Beer is good.

And speaking of breweries...an Extra Special Bravo (aka ESB) goes to Hi-Wire Brewing, Chimney Rock Brewing and Riverbend Malt House for jumping on this train to brew a special beer in celebration of Catbird's release. I feel like I've just been invited to share the stage with rock stars!

Your support and enthusiasm is humbling – I hope I can live up to your generosity and talents.

To everyone who has asked me throughout this process how the book writing was going – and especially to Kenn Haring who was the first person to ever introduce me to another as a writer. Even the most subtle forms of encouragement can make the difference.

To you, the reader, thank you for taking this risk. To purchase a book at any price is a leap of faith, for it isn't just about the dollars but the sense – the investment of heart a reader makes of their time and soul. I trust *Catbird Winter* has been worthy of your undertaking.

And finally, to my Partner, Editor in Chief, Tech Guru, and Beta Reader Extraordinaire, Kevin Dobo – if I could find the words to adequately express all that I wish to and should, I would win a Pulitzer. Without you, this project would still be flailing in the muck and mud of uncertainty and indecision. I wanted to toss *Catbird Winter* in the trash bin, and when I finally let you read my first chapter (which is no longer the first chapter) I had hoped you would toss it yourself, but you didn't. You are the Tabitha to my Stephen King.

Your brutally honest but ferocious love continues to astound and inspire me. You push me to do things that, left to my own devices, I would not - publishing this book and hiking Angel's Landing being among them; both prospects equal in their ability to induce fear and insomnia. This life we share together is pure gift. So here's to hiking amongst the red rocks, biking The Loop, drinking craft beer, reading in bed until late on Sunday afternoon ... and to writing first chapters that you absolutely hate. I love you...

About The Author

Monté Hill is a native of Western North Carolina where she lived before moving to Denver, Colorado with her partner in 2019. Two years later, they became digital nomads, traversing the Lower Forty-Eight with a side trip to Belgium and France, where they indulged their passion for Belgian ales, chocolate, and frites.

She does her best writing in brewpubs.

When she's not conjuring her next story, you will find her and her partner exploring craft breweries, hiking red rocks, gravel grinding on their pedal bikes, photographing Saguaros, or squeezing through slot canyons in waist deep water. If you look close, you might even glimpse her crossing the finish line of the occasional half-marathon.

Monté currently makes her home amongst the saguaros of Arizona and the Vermilion Cliffs of southern Utah, but the Appalachians will always occupy that singular place of heart.

Forthcoming

"Taz", a Pre-Civil War Novel

When a small southern town seeks vigilante justice for a crime committed in self-defense, Anastasia "Taz" Hudgins, and her slaves, Emi and Hector, are forced from their plantation home in the foothills of South Carolina. They flee north, where Taz intends to entrust her bondservants to the care of her abolitionist relatives in Grey Eagle, North Carolina. But more tragedy follows, leaving the two women to make their way alone in the wilderness of the Hickory Nut Gorge.

When they encounter a solitary Cherokee named Inola, their circumstances change for the better. Inola teaches them not only how to survive, but how to embrace the rugged, remote land that threatens to be their undoing ... and even a little about love. Through Inola's teaching, the dizzying beauty of the gorge begins to create a sense of safety and freedom that, for Taz and Emi, was previously unthinkable. But for every inch that is gained, another is inevitably lost, and all that Taz and Emi held as truth is brought into question, including their friendship...

...but when someone with an old score to settle suddenly appears, he threatens to annihilate this unlikely union and the idyllic life they have made together.

For updates on a release date for *Taz*, please follow the author's social media platforms.